The Puppets' Tale

Manik Bandyopadhyay (1908–1956), born Prabodh Kumar Bandyopadhyay in Dumka, Bihar, into a family from Dhaka, is considered a founding father of modern Bengali fiction and one of the most influential and original writers of Bengali literature. A prolific writer, in his brief and struggling life of forty-eight years plagued by sickness, death and poverty, he produced an astonishing thirty-nine novels, over two hundred and sixty short stories, poems, a play, diary fragments, essays, and also works for children; several of his writings have been published posthumously. His important novels include *Dibaratrir Kabya* (1935), *Padma Nadir Majhi* (1936), *Putulnacher Itikatha* (1936) and *Chatushkone* (1942). *Padma Nadir Majhi* was made into an acclaimed and award-winning film of the same title by Goutam Ghose in 1993. His works have been translated into both Indian and foreign languages—including Hindi, Assamese, English, Chinese, Russian, French, German and Italian—and are widely read even today.

Ratan Kumar Chattopadhyay, a translator from Bengali to English, is a graduate from the University of Calcutta. His published translations include *Selections from Galpagucchha*, an anthology of short stories by Rabindranath Tagore in three volumes (2010), and *The Boatman of the Padma* by Manik Bandyopadhyay (2012).

Samantak Das is Professor, Department of Comparative Literature, Jadavpur University, Kolkata.

THE PUPPETS' TALE

Manik Bandyopadhyay

Translated from the original Bengali by

RATAN KUMAR CHATTOPADHYAY

Orient BlackSwan

THE PUPPETS' TALE: MANIK BANDYOPADHYAY

ORIENT BLACKSWAN PRIVATE LIMITED

Registered Office
3-6-752 Himayatnagar, Hyderabad 500 029, Telangana, India
e-mail: centraloffice@orientblackswan.com

Other Offices
Bengaluru, Chennai, Guwahati, Hyderabad, Kolkata, Mumbai, New Delhi, Noida, Patna

First published by Orient Blackswan Private Limited 2022

ISBN 978-93-5442-025-2

040928

Typeset in
Dante MT Std 11/13.5
by Le Studio Graphique, Gurgaon

Printed in India at
Avantika Printers Private Limited, New Delhi 110 020

Published by
Orient Blackswan Private Limited
3-6-752 Himayatnagar, Hyderabad 500 029, Telangana, India
e-mail: info@orientblackswan.com

Contents

Manik Bandyopadhyay and *Putulnacher Itikatha*

Manik Bandyopadhyay (1908–56) blazed across the firmament of Bengali literature like a comet, reshaping forever the shape and nature of the Bangla novel, and, also, the short story, in his relatively short career as a writer. Brief his earthly span may have been, as a patient of epilepsy, his life being tragically cut short at the age of forty-eight, but in this period he produced no less than thirty-nine novels (several of which were published posthumously), and some two hundred and sixty short stories. Plagued by ill-health, poverty, and alcoholism, it is somewhat ironic that he is now one of the recognised masters of Bangla fiction, a path-breaker whose works appear on school and college syllabi, a man whose writings have spawned a mini industry of literary exegesis and scholarly research.

Yet, somewhat surprisingly, the celebrated novelist did not set out to be a writer of fiction, or not at least until he had mastered the art of writing. Born in Dumka in the erstwhile Santhal Parganas, the fifth child of Harihar and Niroda, he was named Prabodh Kumar and attended a dozen schools and junior colleges, as his father's job as a sub-registrar led to frequent postings and transfers. A voracious reader from childhood, by the time he was in his early teens Prabodh had read the works of Bankimchandra Chattopadhyay, Rabindranath Tagore (the 1913 Nobel Prize winner for Literature), and Saratchandra Chattopadhyay, among others—including works then deemed unsuitable for young minds. The would-be author did not just read, but read with complete absorption. As he wrote in his essay 'Golpo Lekhar Golpo' (The Story of Story-writing):

> I don't remember when the thought of learning how to write and then setting out to be a writer first took hold of me—perhaps in childhood when I would secretly read forbidden books, probably then. By the time I was twelve or thirteen I had finished reading [the novels] *Bishbriksha* [Bankim], *Gora* [Rabindranath], and *Charitraheen* [Saratchandra]. And what reading it was! Once I'd read a book like these, it would take me three-four days to absorb its shock. I would wander about through fields and riverbanks, climb trees, go on boats, to markets and fairs, in hustle and bustle, fighting and creating chaos, before I regained my balance. I envied those who wrote books. Maybe the desire to try and become a writer myself was hidden in that envy.[1]

Here we find a reference not only to the young Prabodh's intense engagement with books, but also to his wild and wayward ways as a boy—the mention of wandering, hustle-bustle and fighting is an acknowledgement of his impetuous nature—something that frequently brought him into conflict with his respectable, and rather staid, bourgeois family.

As a student of Mathematics honours in Presidency College (now Presidency University) in Calcutta (now Kolkata), Prabodh was wholly absorbed in his chosen subject of study. The ability of mathematics to pose questions and attempt to answer them through the use of logic and reason fascinated him. As he wrote in the essay quoted above:

> I've suffered from the psychological illness called 'Why?' from childhood, whose chief symptom is the desire to penetrate to the truth of an idea, whether large or small. The need to know in minute detail. The subject-matter might be trivial, the knowledge gained might be of little value and well-known even to children—but until such time as I had sifted through it like shredding cotton and made it my own just like the body absorbs food and turns it into blood and flesh, I knew no peace.[2]

This same desire to know in the minutest of detail, to get to the very heart of things, the need to know life before attempting to write about it also made the budding mathematician resolve not to put pen to paper until he was at least thirty years old—until then, he felt, one lacked the experience and the knowledge necessary to become an author. But things changed when a discussion in the Presidency College canteen about the relative merits and demerits of literary journals turned into a full-blown argument about what it took to get one's work published in them. Prabodh's friends were of the opinion that what was necessary in order to be published in these journals was less a matter of merit and had more to do with whom one knew, whether one belonged to a certain circle, held the same political views, and so on. Prabodh disagreed, asserting that the editors of these journals surely had discernment enough to recognise quality even in an unknown author's writing, and would thus publish a good piece even if it was by a completely new name. In a sudden burst of enthusiasm and bravado, he wagered that he could get a short story published in a reputed journal in three months' time. His friends accepted the bet, and young Prabodh was left with the task of figuring out what to write and how to go about writing it. First, he thought it would be best to play it safe by writing a love story. But of what kind? Surely not the usual girl-meets-boy—they fall in love, parental opposition to the match blights the path of true love, but finally love wins through—sort of short story? Thinking furiously, Prabodh was reminded of an allegedly true tale he had heard when quite young. This was the story of a couple where the husband was a renowned but somewhat moody clarinet player, one who had to be coaxed and cajoled into playing at various private and public occasions. The man would play, but only if the mood took him. In a further twist, the more beautifully he played the more affected his vocal cords would become, until he would end up coughing blood—his art was both the source of his fame, and a potentially fatal gift. This would become the basis of Prabodh's first published short story, 'Atasi Mami' (Aunt Atasi), which was accepted within a month's time of being submitted to one of the best-known literary journals of the time, *Bichitra*—a rare honour indeed for an unknown college student. When submitting the work to the journal, Prabodh, feeling diffident about using his own name and no doubt fearing rejection and failure, substituted his given name of Prabodh Kumar with his nickname, 'Manik'. And thus began the luminous career of one of Bengali literature's giants.

Although not considered to be among his best works, many of the themes that would recur in his later fiction are present in this first short story. Jatin, the musician who bleeds every time he plays his flute, lives a simple, secluded life, mired in poverty, with his beloved wife Atasi. The story makes it clear that what keeps Jatin going, despite his illness (probably tuberculosis), is his love for his music and his wife. Desperate to keep her husband healthy, Atasi asks Satish, the narrator of the story (the nephew of a friend of Jatin's, hence the title of the tale[3]) to stop Jatin from playing his musical instrument. Satish uses a ploy to buy the flute from Jatin shortly before the family leaves Kolkata for their home in Jatin's ancestral village. Years pass; Satish finishes college, gets a job, marries, becomes a father, and reads of Jatin's death in a train accident. Four years after the accident, Satish unexpectedly meets his Aunt Atasi on a train, and discovers that she is on her way to the spot where her beloved Jatin had died. What transpires next may be found out by the curious reader, but it is not necessary for making an assessment of Manik's oeuvre. What is interesting, however, is the way in which the themes of the story penned by the twenty-year-old not only recur in his later fiction but also eerily prefigure the contours of the author's own life. Like Jatin, Manik's art was both his salvation and his doom; like the flautist he was prone to bouts of alcohol abuse; like the musician Manik's life was marred by illness and poverty; and, in what is probably the strangest twist of all, like Jatin, Manik too died tragically young.

That initial success led to Manik's abandoning his studies at Presidency College to pursue a full-time career as a writer—a decision that caused shock and consternation to his family, who had hoped that by joining the most prestigious educational establishment of the state, and among the best in the country, he had left his wayward ways behind. This decision to end his college education is something which Manik would refer to in his later writings, but always with the proviso that he really did not have any choice in the matter. Yet, although he gave up his formal studies, Manik always retained respect for the rational analysis and logical deduction that form the bedrock of reasoned enquiry, and which he felt were vital for anyone who wished to be a writer of any worth. He also laid great store by the experimental method; as he put it in several of his essays and letters, for the novelist the world was a laboratory, and human activity the primary focus of a writer's attention. Mere book learning was not enough for one needed to experience life in all its bewildering variety in order to create fiction of value. For him the creative writer of fiction and the rational person of science both had to keep going back to lived reality; to do otherwise would be irresponsible. In later life, Manik became a committed Marxist, but this did not mean that his works were infused with the kind of dogmatism that one associates with certain kinds of ideological writing typically labelled—somewhat pejoratively—'socialist realism'. For him, the litmus test of a work of fiction was how true it was to life and how accurately the responses of the women and men who lived in society were depicted in it. 'I write in order to reveal those aspects that cannot be made known through any other means,' is how he put it in the opening sentence of his essay, 'Kyano Likhi' (Why I Write).[4]

These qualities are amply evident in his third published novel, *Putulnacher Itikatha* (literally, 'tale or chronicle of the puppet dance', usually rendered as 'The Puppets' Tale'), written when the author was twenty-eight years of age. In its bare bones the story goes like this: Shashi is a Calcutta-trained doctor who returns to his ancestral village of Gaodiya, only to be confronted by poverty, feudal exploitation, superstition, casteism, and an apparent unwillingness on the part of the villagers to fight against these evils. Undeterred, he continues his medical practice, and as the seasons roll by, more and more of the invisible strings that make the villagers dance to the tunes of backwardness and misery become visible to him. But Shashi, the trained man of science, is not a mere mirror in which the wretched condition of the impoverished rural masses is reflected; rather, he is a fully fleshed-out young man with his own contradictions, a mixture of selfless service and selfish desires. As Manik describes him in the second chapter of his novel,

> There were two distinct sides to Shashi's character. While he had no dearth of imagination, emotion, and a sense of humour, he had considerable practical wisdom and attachment for wealth and property as well. The imaginative aspect was covert and mute. Unless one mixed with him intimately, one would never know that he also had a deeply sympathetic discernment of the aesthetic sense of life. It was his intelligent, self-restrained, and frugal nature that generally came to the fore. For these qualities, which are essential for survival in the world, everyone treated him with awe and respect. (p. 11 of this volume)

Shashi is the son of the notorious Gopal Das (in Manik's words, 'Gopal Das's profession … was to hold a knife to people's throats', p. 11 of this volume)—usurer, moneylender, exploiter of the poor and helpless, the consummate middleman who is not averse to trading even in human lives, marrying off young girls to old men for the sake of lining his own pockets. One such young woman is Shashi's 'Sen-didi', married off to the much older Jamini Kabiraj, and the subject of much village gossip because of her alleged illicit relationship with Gopal. Despite this bloodline, Shashi becomes something akin to a paradigm of the modern, rational person of science, and yet one—as Manik is always at some pains to point out—in whom vestiges of his progenitor's selfish lust for power still resides. Calcutta changes him, not least because of his friend, Kumud, whose influence transforms Shashi from little more than a rustic lad whose 'mind was narrow, his imagination blunt and his sense of humour coarse' (p. 13 of this volume) into someone who is able to recognise and appreciate how, 'with the intermingling of science and poetry' (p. 14 of this volume), life becomes complex and worthy of both learning and enjoyment.

This is not the place to provide brief sketches of the large cast of characters who populate the novel, but one other unforgettable character needs to be mentioned before drawing this discussion to a close. Kusum is the daughter-in-law of the farmer Haru Ghosh. An unconventionally beautiful young woman of considerable physical strength, unafraid to challenge the hidebound and reactionary mores of Gaodiya, Kusum, perhaps inevitably, finds herself attracted to the young doctor recently returned to his native village, whose looks and intellectual appeal exceed those of her rather simple husband, Haru's son Paran. Shashi's initial indifference, slowly turning into something akin to love, commingled with his growing physical desire for Kusum, is one of the most acutely delineated man–woman relationships in Bangla literature. Its depiction brings out Manik's ability for subtle psychological exploration, with the strong-willed rustic woman and the sophisticated city-returned doctor providing insights into the nature of human lust and desire—forbidden or otherwise. The conflict in Shashi's heart is perceptively portrayed in the scene where he calls Kusum to him but cannot find the words to express his feelings—feelings he knows are not considered legitimate by society. As they speak, Shashi realises both Kusum's long-unexpressed love for him and his own attraction towards her.

> Not just for a day or two but for a great many long years, Kusum had been crazy about him. Then, little by little, day by day, that frenzied love of hers had wilted, perhaps even withered away. Who could tell? However disastrous this might seem to Shashi today, this was but the only natural consequence. Kusum was a country girl, a housewife: how irresistible the longing of her heart must have grown so that day after day she had held herself out to Shashi like an offering. Only now Shashi could begin to realise: the fact that this fierce, starved love of Kusum's had survived so vibrantly all these years was in itself miraculous. (p. 222 of this volume)

What one finds here is not just Shashi's realisation of Kusum's devotion, but also his inability to understand, examine, and analyse his own emotions—the peculiar blindness to one's own feelings that is engendered in men by patriarchal society. By not adopting the point of view of his doctor-hero, Manik shows us that, like the other villagers, the modern, educated Shashi too is akin to a puppet manipulated by strings held by the forces of tradition, feudal relations, and gender conditioning. Yet, to see Shashi as a mere puppet would be doing him, and his creator, an injustice, even though this interpretation found fairly wide currency, especially in the years immediately following the novel's publication. The second edition of the work, published in 1947, carried a blurb that baldly stated that the book showed how 'Man is like a mere puppet in this great theatre of life. Human beings dance, cry, and speak at the push and pull of strings manipulated by invisible hands.'[5] Manik himself found such analyses immature, the result of a misreading of the book's title. In an essay fragment entitled '*Atmasamalochana*' (Self-criticism), unpublished in his lifetime, he had this to say about this particular interpretation of his novel:

> Not the book—but the book's name has confused critics as well as the writer of the advertisement printed on its back cover intended to increase the book's sales. The puppet's tale? There's nothing more to be said. Manik-*babu* has turned human beings into puppets, into the slaves of fate. Such is the verdict of the judges. But those who do not judge, those who have kept the book alive these last twenty years, they understand that this book is a heartfelt protest against those who make human beings dance like puppets. Not a great revolt, but a continuous heartfelt protest.[6]

It is this dialectic between being manipulated and trying to overcome such manipulation that provides much of the novel's narrative drive.

Unlike his contemporary, Bibhutibhushan Bandyopadhyay (1894–1950), whose career ran in parallel with Manik's (their first stories were published the same year, 1928, in the same journal, *Bichitra*), there is no essentialising of the rural poor as somehow purer, simpler, less tainted by the modern world in Manik—something one can discern in the works of the older, and arguably better-known, novelist. Although no less a lover and artist of nature and natural processes, Manik consciously avoided the transcendental romanticism that is a feature of Bibhutibhushan's oeuvre; and by so doing he placed himself firmly on the side of those who thought of art as a means for interpreting, and thus finally transforming, society. Which is not to say that his works offer answers to complex social questions; rather they offer nuanced readings of, and raise subtle questions about, the material conditions of existence of different kinds of human beings, widely separated in time and space, and their emotional and psychological responses to such existence. Throughout, Manik's characters remain quintessentially human—in their acts of generosity and selfishness, in their follies and foibles, in their strangely divided and often contradictory selves—and this is probably one of the most important reasons for his enduring popularity. Another significant reason is the apparently natural ease with which his stories unfold, almost as if one is listening to an older relative or friend telling a simple unvarnished tale, much in the way of the oral narratives that formed such an important part of young Manik's life in the villages and small towns he had lived in with his family. It takes a bit of an effort to discern the conscious aesthetic design in Manik's method, in the way in which elements—that will subsequently mesh, literally or metaphorically, to form a larger, subtler, richer picture—are arranged in the grand tapestry of his storytelling. Examples abound in *The Puppets' Tale* when an apparently extraneous detail or a superfluous character is brought in, only to have its significance made evident later, or even right at the end of the novel.

Ninety-three years after its first appearance in print, the world that Manik Bandyopadhyay portrayed is, tragically, still with us. The division between rural and urban, the exploitation of the commons by the rapacious greed of human beings, and the dominance of one individual over another, usually for ultimately trivial and often unnecessary reasons, are features of our own present state of being. Perhaps even more poignantly, we are still unable to understand ourselves, leave alone others, and our attempts to change—whether it be the world, or our own modes of being and doing—are so often doomed to fail. As a chronicler of the human condition, this impecunious, passionate, indefatigably inquisitive author still has much to offer his readers, if only they take the pains to read, reflect and act on the things he told us of so long ago. The pity is, in a global village dominated by the ten-second sound bite and the thoughtless

WhatsApp forward, the space for a Manik Bandyopadhyay and his comprehensively imagined, finely-wrought world seems to have markedly shrunk. But as long as there exist readers for this strange, fiery, unrepentantly human writer and his luminous creations, there is still hope. Or so one would like to believe.

Samantak Das
Professor of Comparative Literature
Jadavpur University, Kolkata

Notes

1. Manik Bandyopadhyay, 'Golpo Lekhar Golpo', in *Lekhaker Katha* (Kolkata: New Age Publishers, 1957); my translation.
2. Ibid.
3. *Mami* is the wife of a maternal uncle; also a polite or affectionate address for an older woman, as in this story.
4. Bandyopadhyay, 'Kyano Likhi', in *Lekhaker Katha* op. cit.; my translation.
5. Publisher's note to the second edition of *Putulnacher Itikatha* (Kolkata: Bookman, 1947); quoted in *Manik Bandyopadhyay Rachanasamagra* (Kolkata: Paschimbanga Bangla Academy, 1998; second ed. 2001), Vol. I, p. 515; my translation.
6. *Manik Bandyopadhyay Rachanasamagra*, Vol. I, p. 515; my translation.

Translator's Preface

Sharing his surname with Bibhutibhushan and Tarashankar (no relatives), Manik Bandyopadhyay was one of the Bandyopadhyay triumvirate of modern classic Bengali literature in the great tradition of Bankimchandra, Rabindranath and Saratchandra. He shot into prominence with his debut short story 'Atasi Mami' [Aunt Atasi] which was written to fulfil a challenge thrown in the college canteen to get himself published in a reputed magazine in three months' time. Little did he know that it was eventually to launch him on a successful literary career.

As the passion for literature grew, his studies began to suffer and he failed to clear the final examination for the Bachelor's degree in Science from Presidency College, Calcutta. But when his novels *Dibaratrir Kabya* [Poetry of Day and Night], *Padmanadir Majhi* [The Boatman of the Padma], and *Putulnacher Itikatha* were published in quick succession seven years later, he was catapulted to fame.

However, he had to live under financial hardship because of his uncompromising idealism to remain true to his calling and stay away from the lure of cheap, commercial writing. He began to suffer from epilepsy at an early age. The scourge of poverty and this incurable disease blighted his life. He tried to fight back by toiling harder and taking to drink, but he died at the age of forty-eight on 3 December 1956. Despite all odds, Manik left behind thirty-nine novels, over two hundred and sixty stories, a hundred or so poems, one short play and several diaries, besides thirty-two stories and a novel for children, in a dedicated writing career of nearly twenty-five years.

Born Prabodh Kumar Bandyopadhyay on 19 May 1908 at Dumka into a middle-class family hailing from Dhaka in present-day Bangladesh, Manik's (Manik being his nickname which stuck as his pen-name) childhood and boyhood years were spent in far-flung parts of undivided Bengal, Odisha and Bihar because of his father's transferable government service. Since very early in life he had mixed intimately with the so-called low-born and marginal people. This exposure to life in its various strata is reflected in the realism of his literature. Manik was free from all kinds of prejudice and he was not hamstrung by a bourgeois mentality and outlook. He vowed to pierce the facade of the hypocrisy and sentimentalism that had long been the staple of segments of Bengali literature. To explore the caverns of the human mind he had studied the Freudian theory of the subconscious. He held that sexual passion was an unrelieved, dark and primitive biological instinct which may have undergone cosmetic changes with the advance of civilisation through the ages but its basic character remained intact. This appears in almost brutal form in some of his stories, such as 'Pragoitihasik' [Prehistoric] and 'Kushthorogir Bou' [The Leper's Wife]. Later in life while seeking the cause of human depravity he was convinced that it lay less in the Freudian libido than in the social economy. And that led to his initiation into Marxism, which was to remain his credo till his last days. He was largely disabused of his Freudian persuasions, convinced that Marxism could show the right path of human progress, for in it lay the deliverance of man. It was impossible, he held, without the keenness of observation offered by Marxism to analyse and comprehend life in its entirety.

The topics Manik dealt with are remarkably varied: from the pre-Independence famine to communal riots, from moral degradation and peasant uprising to post-Independence inflation, and from refugee rehabilitation to social ills. Any political or contemporary issue was grist to his literary mill. His indoctrination into Marxism infused a new vigour into his intellectual pursuits and left its imprint on his subsequent work. He seemed to rediscover the myriad facets of life, delineated city and country life with unmatched skill, and explored the human mind with rare acumen. He was disturbed by the narrowness and artificiality of civil society, by its meanness, both open and covert, and by its hypocrisy and chicanery. He wanted from the beginning to bring the bleak reality of life to the fore by stripping the veneer of pseudo-sentimentalism and melodramatic nature-worship; he wanted to be a realist and he did lend a sharp touch of reality, as he saw it, to Bengali literature. He had very well caught the zeitgeist of rural Bengal in the pre-Independence period. The backdrop of nearly a third of his stories is village life. The starkness of his writings mercilessly exposes the squalor of life to the blinding light of truth. His aim was to hold a mirror to the pockmarked face of society in order to startle it at the sight of its own effeteness, and to galvanise it to reform itself. Time and again he lambasted the bankruptcy of a middle-class mentality.

The name of the present novel seems to allude to a familiar metaphor about existence: that on the centrestage of the world is being played out the drama of human life, the protagonists going about their roles assigned by an invisible dramatist just as marionettes dance to the pulls of a puppeteer. The symbolism of dolls or puppets that comes up at a number of places and the reference to an invisible power indicates the author's intention of conveying his central idea through a rather random set of events.

We have Kusum's father Ananta speaking from his heart to Shashi:

> In this world man proposes, and God disposes; this is what I've seen all my life, Doctor-babu. We are but puppets; an Invisible One is pulling the strings. [p. 211]

Shashi felt his own conviction:

> Whatever he entrusted himself with fizzled out. An irresistible, invisible power seemed to be constantly at work against him. [p. 113]

Or the author bemoaning man's helplessness in the epilogue:

> Can man's life-stream flow like a river along the course charted by its own free will? It proceeds along a canal of man's own making at the inexorable signal of an unknown force, which, like gravitation, is eternal and immutable. [p. 249]

But on this count a section of critics, especially his peers in the Communist Party, labelled the novel as fatalistic. They thought an individual's surrender to fate had sacrificed the novel at the altar of an eternal Indian idealism, subjugating to providence man's individual and collective power of struggle, resistance and rebellion, with the people as mere puppets.

We are of the opinion that far from glorifying idealism or endorsing fatalism or any idle metaphysical speculation, Manik, as a man of scientific temper and a consummate artist of realism, has captured a close-up of the minds of the characters and masterfully portrayed human thoughts and emotions at work. The treatment underscores that it is the intricate workings of the human mind that propel man in his speech and actions and thus shape his destiny. Man is forever tied to various bonds in this mortal life, veritably enslaved by his ego and pulled by the strings of his own desires and infatuations.

With all his cherished desires and large imagination for an enjoyable and meaningful life in an educated, cultured and aristocratic ambience, the protagonist Shashi's plans to move out of the stagnation of the pond-jungle-mosquito-infested village life were foiled every time. Certainly, he was a doctor who valued his professional duties and personal obligations to his family and village relationships, but the factor that forever fettered him to the village was his strong yet for long unexpressed attraction for the enigmatic Kusum. When Kusum left the village he developed an attachment towards the hospital he had so assiduously built and got involved in, and which came to be known as Shashi Doctor's Hospital.

> Yet, inwardly, Shashi began to feel a resentment without any apparent reason. It seemed as if someone had come to dispossess him of a kingdom all his own: what care, what effort it had taken Shashi to build up this hospital of his—people knew it as Shashi Doctor's hospital!...Once he was gone, Amulya would be the one in command....
>
> Well, what was his grievance about going anyway? Had he not in so many ways for so many years nurtured a desire to leave? What had happened to his vow of not wavering,

> of not being lax when the time came to prepare for leaving? Was he upset just because he visualised his successor in Amulya? One who used to spend his days dreaming of the vast and all-pervading expanse of life was not supposed to want to be bound by a fascination for this small hospital in this nondescript village called Gaodiya! [p. 241]

Then we have the episode of Jadab Pandit, the putative holy man of the village who found himself caught in a trap of his own words and had to sacrifice his and his wife's lives at the altar of his craving to win over the sceptical Shashi and to perpetuate the venerated image of a seer in the minds of the villagers. Manik has skilfully crafted the story bringing out Jadab's predicament in having to choose between death and infamy, as also Shashi's momentary straying from his rational disbelief.

All his life the shrewd moneylender Gopal amassed property by whatever means he could under the eternal urge of a householder, but he continued to suffer the anxiety of how to bequeath it to his son Shashi who often talked of his ambitious dreams of settling elsewhere. Gopal could not quite gauge the mind of his educated son, and despite all his worldly-wise endeavours failed to command his respect and obedience to the extent that he wished. Finally, torn between parental affection for the grown-up Shashi and for the seemingly posthumous son (possibly his own?) of Sen-didi, who died at childbirth, and the anxiety of preserving the property, Gopal resolved his crisis by tactfully leaving for Kashi, taking the newborn infant along, never to return, abruptly devolving the custody of his home and homestead upon Shashi.

> His long and eventful life studded with extraordinary happenings seemed to him today to have had no meaning: it had come to absolutely no use. Right from the day Shashi was born, focusing his eyes on him alone, Gopal had dreamed his covey of dreams that soared into the sky and bloomed...Garden, house, land, wealth, kith and kin—Gopal had accumulated so much: were all these for his own sake? How many more days were left to him? If, rejecting

> all this, Shashi were to go away, would not Gopal's entire life be rendered futile? [p. 247–248]

Kusum's intimations of love over the years Shashi did not really comprehend and misconstrued them as her erratic behaviour, with which he was nevertheless infatuated. When Shashi finally woke up to them and was eager to run away with her, it was too late, and he was met with a stern rebuff:

> Even a red-hot iron left to itself cools off steadily, does it not?...All my feelings and emotions have been blunted, Chhoto-babu. I used to hear people speak of heartbreak—now at last I know what it means. Whom are you calling, Chhoto-babu? Who will go with you? Is Kusum alive? She is dead. [p. 221]

The language of the novel is simple, free-flowing, devoid of superfluous embellishment or verbosity yet deeply engaging. Unlike his famous contemporaries, Manik does not follow the idyllic prototype of rural Bengal but with an economy of words and appropriate dialogue brings out as acutely the unpleasant aspects of village life, its backwardness and meanness, its ignorance and superstition. An interesting variation is the frequent use of a kind of indirect narration juxtaposed with normal conversation, which adds to the literary effect. He employs it to express the thoughts of the characters instead of commenting from the author's perspective.

> 'You would never have got such a girl, Kumud. Not that you hadn't seen her. Tell me, you tell me honestly, is a girl like her easy to find? But you never took a fancy to her! Do they call you crazy without reason?'
>
> The manager stayed long and talked about much else. ... He would never be able to come to grips with Kumud. Would Kumud desist until he had ruined the manager! [p. 191]

The stark realism of the description following Haru Ghosh's death in the opening lines of the novel bears testimony to Manik's outlook of a dispassionate observer, albeit one filled with empathy for the mortality of man:

> Haru Ghosh stood under the huge banyan tree by the canal, leaning against its trunk. The god of the sky glared at him sharply and scowled.
>
> The black-and-grey hair of Haru's head and the rough, pockmarked skin of his face were singed and burnt, of which, though, he was unaware. The sensate world he had built up assiduously over fifty-one years in self-love and attachment had been obliterated in the twinkling of an eye, together with the mute sensibility of the century-old tree. [p. 1]

In this novel centred round the introvert and reflective character of Shashi, incidents by themselves are not as important as their subtle and complex repercussions on the protagonist's mind. It is not through the directness of happenings and deeds but down the interior alleys of introspection that Shashi strives to understand life in its infinite wonders and mysteries. The author does not make events the mainstay of the novel, and so a structured storyline with a defined beginning, middle and end is not to be found. The flowing narrative captures, as it were, the stream of life ruffled by discreet ripples and not agitated by tumultuous waves. The ruminations and reflections of Shashi on apparently disjointed episodes run through the novel to impart to it a unity.

In the final analysis we observe that compassion for the mortal limitations of man and his subconscious propulsions under ineluctable natural laws runs as an undercurrent throughout *The Puppets' Tale* and illustrates an aphorism from the Gita which succinctly expresses a profound truth, focused on the compulsive behaviour of humankind under the spell of delusion embedded into its psyche:

> *Ishwarah sarvabhutaanaam hruddeshe'rjuna tishthati*
> *Bhraamayan sarvabhutaani yantrarudhani maayayaa*
>
> The Lord dwells in the heart of all beings, O Arjuna
> Rotating through Maya all creatures as though mounted on a machine
>
> (*Bhagavad Gita* 18:61; translation mine)

This Bengali fiction classic has been translated earlier into English (in 1968, now out of print), and other languages. In the present attempt, as part of Orient BlackSwan's series of translations of major works of Indian literature, I have paid close attention to conveying the moods and undertones of the text, appending endnotes on some words and expressions to clarify certain nuances of Bengali language and culture; some English words used by the novelist in Bengali transliteration are shown in italics; and a list of Bengali pronunciations of some Bengali / Indian names and words is given in an appendix. The translation is based on the authoritative first volume of Manik Bandyopadhyay's works published by Paschimbanga Bangla Akademi, except for an additional passage (unaccountably missing in the Akademi version) in the final chapter (Chapter 13) that forms a crucial part of the penultimate encounter between Shashi and Kusum, respectively the male and female protagonists of the novel; this passage is taken from the book published by Prakash Bhaban, Calcutta (12th reprint, 1974, pp. 211–12).

Coming to Acknowledgements, the idea of translating this novel was suggested to me by my sons Rajib and Somnath. I deeply appreciate the role played by the two brothers in providing me with critical inputs to capture the contextual connotations of the dialogues, descriptions and reflections; immense labour was put in particularly by Rajib, my elder son, through all stages from inception to proofreading. I must also express my appreciative gratitude for the meticulous copy-editing done by Mr Suranjan Roy. Finally, my heartfelt thanks go to Prof. Samantak Das who has put me in his debt by contributing an elaborate Foreword.

Ratan Kumar Chattopadhyay
Kolkata

Pronunciations of Bengali and Indian Names and Words

Spelling	**Pronunciation**
Aghran	Aw-ghhrahn
Agnidev	Ogni-dheb ['dh' *pron. as in 'than'*]
Agrahayan	Aw-gro-hah-yon
akash-kusum	ah-kahsh-koo-shoom
Amulya	Aw-mool-lo
Ananta	Aw-non-tho [*soft* 't']
Arjuna	Oar-joon
Asharh	Ah-shahrh
Ashokbon	Aw-shoke-bone
Ayodhya	Aw-jo-dhhah
Babu	Bah-boo
Bagdi	Bahg-dhi ['dh' *as in 'dim'*]
Baishakh	Boi-shahkh
Bajitpur	Bah-jith-poo-r
Bamunpara	Bah-moon-pah-rah
Banbihari	Bono-bi-hah-ri OR Bon-bihah-ri
Bangshi	Bo-ng-shee
barbela	bahr-bal-ah
Barishal	Bori-shahl
Basanta	Baw-shon-tho [*soft* 't']
Basudeb Bnarujje/ Banerjee/Banerji/ Bandyopadhyay	Bah-shoo-dheb-bnarooj-jey/Ban-er-jee/bon-dho-pahdh-dhhah-ey ['dh' *as in 'than'*, 'bna' *nasal sound*]
Benarasi	Benah-roshi

bhai phnota	bhah-ee-phno-tah [*nasal sound after* 'ph']
bhaddarlok	bhhawdh-dhor-lok ['dh' *as in 'than'*]
Bhadra	Bhah-dhro ['dh' *as in 'than'*]
bhoot	bhooth
Bhujangadhar	Bhoo-jawng-go-dhhawr
Bhupaticharan	Bhoo-pothi-chaw-rone
Bhutho	Bhoo-tho [*soft* 't']
Binde	Bin-dhey ['dh' *as in 'they'*]
Bindhyabasini	Bin-dhho-bashini [*soft* 'd']
Bindubasini	Bin-dhoo-bahsh-ini ['dh' *as in 'than'*]
Binodini	Bin-o-dhini ['dh' *as in 'than'*]
Bipin Moyra	Bip-in-moy-rah
Bishbriksha	Bish-brikkho
bnoti	bno-tee [*nasal sound after* 'b']
Bnuchi	Bnoo-chi ['bnoo', *nasal sound*]
Borogaon	Baw-ro-gna [*nasal* 'g']
bou	bow-oo ['ow' *as in 'low'*]
Boudi	Bow-oo-dhi ['ow' *as in 'low'*, 'dh' *as in 'than'*]
Brahmachari	Brohm-mo-chahri
Chait	Cho-ith
Chaitra	Choith-ro
Chandi	Chone-di
Chandraketu	Chawn-dhro-kethu ['dh' *as in 'than'*, *soft* 't']
Charaka	Chaw-rok
Charan Datta	Chaw-ron-dhawth-tho ['dh' *as in 'than'*, *soft* 't']
Charitraheen	Cho-rith-ro-heen
Chhoto-babu	Chho-toh-bah-boo
Chhoto-mami	Chho-toh-mah-mi
chil	cheel
chnira/chnire	chnirah/chnirey [*nasal*]
chyavanprash	chaw-bon-prahsh
Dada	Dhah-dhah ['dh' *as in 'than'*]
dakath	dah-kahth
Debata	Dhey-bo-thah ['dh' *as in 'than'*, *soft* 't']
gamchha	gahm-chhah
ekadoshi	ack-ah-dhoshi ['dh' *as in 'than'*]

Gaodiya	Gah-o-dhi-yah [‘dh’ *as in ‘than’*]
Ghosh-mashay	Ghhosh-maw-shy
Gita Govinda	Geeth-gobindho [‘dh’ *as in ‘than’*]
Gobardhan	Go-bore-dhhon
Gopal	Go-pahl
Gora	Go-rah
Gurugati	Goo-roo-go-thi [*soft* ‘t’]
Haranchandra Ghosh	Hah-rahn-chawn-dhro-ghhosh [‘dh’ *as in ‘than’*]
Hari	Hori
Hari bol	Hori-bole
Harishchandra	Ho-rish-chawn-dhro [‘dh’ *as in ‘than’*]
Haru Ghosh	Hah-roo-ghhosh
Jadab	Jah-dhob [‘dh’ *as in ‘than’*]
Jadu	Jo-dhoo [‘dh’ *as in ‘than’*]
Jagannatha	Jawgon-nahth
Jamini	Jah-mini
Jana	(here) Jaw-nah
jarda	jawr-dhah [‘dh’ *as in ‘than’*]
Jaya	Joy-ah
Jayadeva	Joy-dheb [‘dh’ *as in ‘than’*]
Jogesh	Jo-gesh
kadam	kaw-dhom [‘dh’ *as in ‘than’*]
Kalighat	Kahlee-ghaht
Kartik	Kahr-thik [*soft* ‘t’]
Kayetpara	Kah-eth-pah-rah
Keshab	Kay-shawb
Khanta	Khahn-tho [*soft* ‘t’]
kharish	kho-rish
kholshe	khol-shey
Khuki	Khhoo-ki
knathalichnapa	knah-tthahli-chnahpah [*nasal* ‘k’ *and* ‘ch’]
koi	koh-ee
Krishna	Krish-no
Kumud	Koo-moodh [‘dh’ *as in ‘than’*]
Kunda	Koon-dho [‘dh’ *as in ‘than’*]
Kunja	Koon-jo

Kusum	Koo-shoom
Lakshman(a)	Lawk-khon
Lakshmimani	Lokkhi-moni
lattha	lat-hah
Lochan	Lo-chon
Madanmanjari	Maw-dhon-mon-joree ['dh' *as in 'than'*]
Magh	Mah-ghh
magur	mah-goor
mahakapiladi	maw-hah-kopil-ahdhi ['dh' *as in 'than'*]
makaradhwaja	maw-koro-dhhhawj [*soft* 'd'] OR maw-kor-dhhwaj
mashay	maw-shah-i
Mathura Saha	Mo-thhu-rah-shah-hah
Mohan	Mo-hone
Mokshada	Mok-kho-dhah ['dh' *as in 'than'*]
mongol ghawt	mongol-ghawt
Moti	Mo-thi [*soft* 't']
Nabin	No-bin
Nandalal	Nawn-dho ['dh' *as in 'than'*] -lahl
Nandanpur	Nawn-dhon-poo-r ['dh' *as in 'than'*]
Narayana	Nah-rah-yon
Nayeb	nah-yeb
Nitai	Nith-ah-i
Niyogi	Neo-gi
paan	pahn
Pagal-didi	Pah-gole-dhidhi ['dh' *as in 'than'*]
Panchanan Chakraborty	Pawn-chah-non-Chawk-ro-bor-thi
Pandit-mashay	Pone-dith-maw-shah-i
panjabi	pahn-jahbi
Paran	Paw-rahn
Paraner	Paw-rahn-aer
Paush	Poh-oosh
Phalgun	Phahl-goon
Pnachu	Pnah-choo [*nasal sound after* 'P']
poithey	poh-eethey
Prabir	Pro-bir
pronaam	pro-nahm

Puja	Poo-jo OR poo-jah
Purna Talukdar	Poo-r-no-thah-look-dhahr [*soft* 't', 'dh' *as in 'than'*]
Rajani Sarkar	Raw-joni-shawr-kahr
Rajatala	Rajah-thaw-lah [*soft* 't']
Rama	Rahm
Ramayana	Rah-mah-yon
Ramtaran	Rahm-thah-ron [*soft* 't']
Rasik	Ro-shik
Rasulpur	Ro-shool-poo-r
Rath	Rawth
Ravan(a)	Rah-bone
Saatgaon	Shahth-gna [*nasal sound between* 'g' *and* 'a']
Saha	Shah-hah
sajano bagan shukiye gyalo	shah-jah-no-bah-gahn-shoo-kiye-gal-o
samadhi	shaw-mah-dhhi
Santra	Shn-ah-thra [*nasal sound between first* 'h' *and* 'a']
Saroj	Shaw-roje
Satyahari	Shoth-tho-hori
Sealdah	Sheyal-dhah ['dh' *as in 'than'*]
Sen-didi	Shen-dhidhi ['dh' *as in 'than'*]
Shakta	Shahk-tho [*soft* 't']
Shakti Peeth	Shokthee Peeth
Shashi	Sho-shi
Shashe	Sho-shey
Shetala	Shey-thaw-lah [*soft* 't']
Shital-babu	Shi-thawl [*soft* 't'] bah-boo
sholmachh	shole-mahchh
Shravan	Srah-bon
Shyamacharan	Sham-ah-chaw-ron
Shyamal	Sham-ol
siddha-purush	shidh-dho-poo-roosh
Sindhu	Shin-dhhoo
Sita	Shi-thah
Srinath Das	Sri-nahth-dhahsh ['dh' *as in 'than'*]
Sudeb	Shoo-dheb ['dh' *as in 'than'*]
Sujan	Shoo-jawn

surjobigyan	shoor-jo-big-gan
Sushruta	Soosh-rooth [*soft* 't']
taalpukur	thahl [*soft* 't'] -poo-koor
Teishgachha	Thay [*soft* 't'] -ish-gahchhah
Thakurda	Tthah-koor-dhah [*hard* 'th', 'dh' *as in 'than'*]
'thetar'	*thhey-tar*
tumi, tui	thoo-mi, thoo-i [*soft* 't' for both]
upobeeth	oopo-beeth
Ukhara	Oo-khah-rah
ulu	oo-loo
Urboshi	Oor-bo-shi
Urmila	Oo-r-mi-lah
Vishnu	Bish-noo
Yama	Jo-m

The Puppets' Tale

1

Haru Ghosh stood under the huge banyan tree by the canal, leaning against its trunk. The god of the sky[1] glared at him sharply and scowled.

The black-and-grey hair on Haru's head and the rough, pockmarked skin of his face were singed and burnt, of which, though, he was unaware. The sensate world he had built up assiduously over fifty-one years in self-love and attachment had been obliterated in the twinkling of an eye, along with the mute sensibility of the century-old tree.

Immediately after the scowl the god let out a roar that reverberated across the horizon. And then the rain came down hard.

Even the thick foliage of the banyan tree could not keep out the rain for long. Haru's body was soon drenched. The pungent marine smell of ozone gradually faded from the place. The sweet fragrance of *keya* flowers permeated from a nearby bush. A thread-like green snake entwined round a screwpine tree lay comatose. Lashed by the rain it uncoiled leisurely and came out of the bush; staring at Haru with its fixed deceitful look for a while, it slithered through the gap between his feet, disregarding him, into the hollow of the banyan tree.

There was little chance of anyone discovering Haru easily in such a place. There was no human habitation around. People scarcely ever needed to come to these parts, nor did anyone normally want to. Village people love to fear. The dense woodland and the deep desolation on this side of the canal outside the village provides the setting for that. Ghosts and apparitions probably dwelt in the imagination of the fearful villagers, but there is no doubt that the place was a veritable den of snakes.

As long as daylight persisted, an intrepid traveller or two from Bajitpur, after traversing the field, would take a short cut using the footpath faintly visible through the grass. Then one just had to cross the canal in someone's boat—never mind the pleading—and one would be right on the Gaodiya road. From there, it was hardly half a mile's walk to the village. The mother of one Chandi occasionally came to this place to gather firewood. Jamini Kabiraj's[2] assistant came once a week to collect herbs. During the months of Kartik and Aghran,[3] snake-catchers from distant villages sometimes came here to catch snakes. Otherwise hardly anyone ever crossed this path.

The day was almost over when the rain stopped. In one corner of the sky a tinge of red appeared like a timid blush. A flight of birds descended on the banyan tree; when they noticed a freshly fledged swarm of termites soar into the sky from a nearby mound, they flew in that direction. Encouraged by Haru's permanent stillness a squirrel on the banyan tree skittered down at an opportune moment. Meanwhile, a chameleon on the branch of a *bnudhi* tree quickly overpowered quite a few insects. A jackal, carrying the dead young of a *shalik*[4] in its mouth, while splashing through the field turned back repeatedly to look at Haru. They can sense. Goodness knows how they can!

Shashi said, 'Take the boat that side, Gobardhan, near that *shyaora*[5] tree over there. It can't be lowered from here.'

The bank of the canal near the banyan tree was very steep; it was slippery as well after the rain. Gobardhan punted the boat away to one side. Seven miles down from here, the water level of the river had risen by three arm-lengths in twenty-four hours. The current in the canal was strong enough. Grabbing hold of a branch of the shyaora tree, he stopped the boat and said, 'You come into the boat and sit down, Babu. Let me do it.'

'You wretch, you aren't to touch.'

'What if I touch? Who would know? How can you bring down that bulky corpse all by yourself?'

Shashi saw that he had a point. If the body fell, it would be smeared all over with mud. Instead, if Gobardhan touched it, it would hardly be a greater insult to the corpse. His was an unnatural death: in any case, there was no salvation for Haru, whether Gobardhan touched him or not.

'All right then. Let's bring it down together. Fasten the boat tightly to the tree; if it slides, we'll be in trouble. And light the lamp first; it's getting dark.'

Gobardhan lit the lamp, fixed the boat to the shyaora tree, and went up on the bank. The two of them together carefully lowered the body into the hull. Shashi let out a sigh and said, 'Now, untie the boat. And look, don't touch him again.'

'Why should I!'

Shashi had been returning from the town. He could see even from the boat that on the deserted bank in the dim light of the evening a man was leaning against a tree like a spectre. Nobody except a madman would stand like that in a snake-infested spot at that unearthly hour. Shashi was filled with surprise and curiosity. He had raised an alarm, called out. When there was no response, he had asked Gobardhan to moor the boat. At first Gobardhan had demurred: why should a man come here at this hour? Might be an optical illusion. If Shashi had indeed seen something, there was no need to investigate that 'thing'; it was better to return home alive and in one piece. But Shashi was a qualified doctor from a college in Calcutta. He had paid no heed to Gobardhan's protests. 'If it is a ghost,' he had quipped, 'I will bind it hand and foot and take it home to tame. Now row the boat back.' Light lingered in the sky. The silvery glint of the water lodged on the arum leaves around Haru had not died out yet. Going near, Shashi had immediately recognised him.

'O Gobardhan, it is our Haru! How on earth did he get here?'

Gobardhan could not utter a word for a long time. At last in a muffled voice he said timorously, 'Is he dead, Chhoto-babu?'[6]

'He's dead. Struck by lightning.'

'Oh, his hair is scorched!'

If it had been anybody other than Haru, Shashi would perhaps have laughed to hear Gobardhan lament about the hair of someone who was dead. But he was deeply pained to discover Haru in this condition outside the village. Haru had sons and daughters, he had friends and relatives; what a tragic end it was for him to die under a tree all alone out of everyone's sight! Gobardhan's words left him even more saddened.

Gobardhan's heart was pounding.

'What's the use of standing here any longer, Chhoto-babu? Let's go and inform the village people.'

'Shall we leave him like this, Gobardhan?'

'What can you do about that?'

'What if the jackals begin to tug at him by the time we come back?'

Gobardhan had shuddered. 'What do you want to do then, Chhoto-babu?'

'Call out loud so someone may come.'

But who would be around in this foul weather to come running on hearing shouts? Gobardhan was startled to hear his own yell; nothing else had stirred the silence. Normally a good many boats used to ply down the canal on Rasulpur's *haat* days. Today it was not certain how soon another boat, if any at all, would be seen.

It was then that the thought of taking Haru down into the boat had occurred to Shashi.

As soon as the boat was unfastened, it moved swiftly along with the current. Standing on the prow, as he dropped the pole with a plop into the water, Gobardhan asked out of curiosity, 'Tell me one thing, Chhoto-babu. He has no salvation, does he?'

Shashi was at the helm. With a yawn, he said, 'How can I say, Gobardhan? I don't know.'

Taking his yawn to be a sign of annoyance, Gobardhan did not dare ask him anything more. Shashi was not annoyed; he was distracted. This accidental association with Haru's death had left him deeply moved. But what was far more shaken was his attachment for life. Death stirs individuals variously. Shashi was not like those who, at the demise of anyone related or unrelated, mourned for the deceased mortal. When he saw someone die, he never fell to brooding over the truth that everyone must die someday, whoever it was, known or unknown, including himself. At the burning *ghat*,[7] he was never overcome by any sense of detachment. Life would suddenly seem to him very desirable, something to cherish; he had so far not utilised such a life properly. It was as if life lived unmindfully until death would mean that a great deal of life would be wasted. Not his alone, but everyone else's. This loss was irreparable.

This is how the propinquity of death disturbed Shashi—from this angle.

After running straight for some distance where it touched the extremity of Gaodiya, the canal turned to the east. At the bend was the ghat of the village. Gaodiya was a small village. Trade and commerce did not concern it much. As for the ghat too, it was nothing to speak of, just a couple of steps notched with the spade. On the ghat was a tin shed. During the jute season, bales were stacked there, and then shipped to the warehouse of Shashi's brother-in-law Nandalal in Bajitpur. After three or four consignments had gone, it would be all over with the jute despatch business of Gaodiya. For the rest of the year, the shed would lie vacant. Whether it was a cow, a goat, or a human being, whoever wanted to would use it; nobody would come to object. In front of the shed, Chandi sat all day with a few packets of *biris*[8] wrapped in coloured paper and a few rolls of *paan*[9] covered with a wet cloth in a saucer, laid out on a wooden box.

A number of boats, big and small, were anchored at the ghat. But in none of them was there a lamp or anybody at this time.

Gobardhan feared that Shashi might want to go to the village himself, leaving him alone to guard the corpse in the boat. So, as soon as he anchored it, he said, 'I'll go and inform the villagers then, shall I, Chhoto-babu?'

'All right, go. Walk fast, Gobardhan. First you go to Goalapara.[10] Tell Nitai, Sudeb, Bangshi and the others that they should come running. Tell them I am guarding the body sitting alone in the dark. You take the lamp; it will get pitch-dark as you go. The road is slippery.'

Gobardhan went away with the lamp. By now it was evening. If one watched keenly, perhaps one might still discern a pale glow in the sky, but darkness was fast descending. Shashi thought that if he had come to the banyan tree fifteen or twenty minutes later, he would not have seen Haru. In the course of his journeys along the canal, he used to look up at that haunt of ghosts and snakes. He would have looked up today as well, but Haru would have appeared like a part of the tree trunk. Perhaps, observing the similarity of the part of the tree with the human figure, and not realising the mysterious contrast of whiteness presented by Haru's dhoti, he would have merely felt a shiver. And Haru would have been left out there. How long after, who knows when, someone might have come across a few bones of his body, cleaned out by jackals' teeth and vultures' beaks. Just as Chandi's mother had discovered Pnachu: patches of decayed flesh, here and there bones laid bare, and one hand still grasping a large *kharish* snake that had withered into a rope.

The boat was swaying gently in the current. The pitching caused a wave-like motion that ended in the prow, like the agitation of a living creature. Shashi shuffled in his seat and sat erect. He sensed an itch to light a biri but he seemed to lose interest. A dense gloom gradually settled all around before his eyes. The trees on the banks looked like darkness solidified. The lonely boats kept bobbing like flimsy shadows on the water. An almost invisible flight of birds swished past overhead. Fireflies began to flicker everywhere.

Even though Haru was so near, his face became a blur. As Shashi could not have a good look at him, the fact that Haru was dead seemed to sink in all over again. He wondered what Haru might have been thinking at the time of his death; what images, what feelings, what thoughts had suddenly been cut short?

Shashi knew that Haru had gone to Bajitpur to interview a groom for his daughter. He had set out by that perilous route to shorten the distance. Shortened indeed it was—he had embraced his fate.

After about two hours, seven or eight of Haru's kinsmen arrived, some carrying lanterns. The silent ghat at once became abuzz.

'Has Nitai come, Nitai?' Shashi asked eagerly.

'Yes, here I am, Chhoto-babu.'

Nitai's sense of responsibility was a byword. Shashi was greatly reassured.

'Has Haru's family been informed, Nitai?'

'Yes, Chhoto-babu.'

They crowded round and, raising the lanterns, stared at the body. They had heard about the entire matter from Gobardhan and now they heard it again from Shashi. Then squatting on the steps of the ghat, they started talking among themselves.

Soon enough, it seemed to Shashi that Haru's death was now at last acquiring a tragic dimension through their conversation. In the misty yellow light cast by a sooty lantern on a rain-washed gloomy night, fragments of Haru's life-story came drifting before his eyes like stills from a film. The true perception of the loss and pain to Haru's family now seemed to dawn on Shashi. He understood that the vast space Haru had left vacant could only be measured by the emotional yardstick of these illiterate people. Until now, Haru's unnatural death had not left a mark on Shashi. He had imagined Haru to belong to his own world where he had hardly ever occupied a place that would be missed.

Shashi listened intently to their talk for a long time and then finding that it was already late in the night, he said, 'So then, don't keep sitting any longer, Nitai. Go about making a bier; get the bamboos from Rasik-babu's grove.'

Nitai asked, 'Do you mean to take the body straight to the burning ghat, Chhoto-babu?'

'No, we have to stop at his house.'

Going directly to the burning ghat would have saved a lot of trouble. But Haru's daughter Moti was laid up with fever. So even if all the others went, she couldn't. Shashi could not think of cremating Haru without Moti getting to see her father for the last time. It was also doubtful whether anyone in the house would be prudent enough to keep the news from her, at least for a few days. Moti would come to know that it was to find a groom for her that Haru had gone out and that on the way back he had died an unnatural death. Maybe, sick as she was, she would rush to the burning ghat braving the rain. And if she were to be forcibly restrained, she would probably forgive everyone, even her fate, but she would not forgive Shashi so easily.

She would lament, 'Alas, you were there, but they burned Baba's body without showing me!'

Bamboos were brought from Rasik-babu's garden. A bier was made and the corpse was laid on it. Raising a chorus of *Hari bol*[11] they hoisted the bier onto their shoulders.

'Don't utter Hari's name now,' said Shashi. 'Haru hasn't set out on his last journey yet: he is going home.'

Shashi had not wittingly said this in the way he had. His eyes moistened at his own words.

The road was wide enough, but muddy. During the monsoon, at some places it would be knee-deep in mud, at others dangerously slippery due to the clayey soil. Cart-wheels did the most damage to the road. When the mud dried up after the monsoon, the entire stretch would look like it had been turned over with a plough. By the time winter set in, the path would indeed level up, but the ridges of innumerable potholes trodden on would produce enough dust for one's feet to be covered. In Phalgun-Chaitra,[12] the clouds of dust whipped up by the winds would blanch the trees on either side.

Before entering the village, one had to cross a culvert over the ditch fed by the canal. Below it, Nabin the boatman had been standing in chest-deep water since afternoon, casting his net at the mouth of the current.

Nitai called out, 'How's the catch, Majhi?'[13]

'Where's the fish, Ghosh-mashay?[14] The water is too deep!'

'Is there any catfish, Nabin? Give me one if you get any. My son will have his rice diet[15] tomorrow.'

Nabin had lied. 'Do you think I'm telling lies standing in water?[16] Such deep waters are no good for a catch, you know. There's a three-arm-length gap here—have you noticed?'

Nabin received the news of Haru's death calmly. 'A very good man he was. He had no enemy in the world.' He added, 'This year, you know, Ghosh-mashay, everyone's unlucky. Not three showers old yet, and already the water has become a menace!'

Day in and day out, Nabin had to struggle hard on land and in water. His mind too had become mouldy like his chilblained body. He had no time to feel perturbed by Haru's sudden death.

And yet he knew how to be affectionate. His ten-year-old son had been standing on the culvert since afternoon without budging; he too wished to catch fish standing in the water like his father. But Nabin would not allow him. 'Not at night, *baap*,'[17] he tried to dissuade him, 'You'll catch a cold. Tomorrow morning.'

'Tomorrow morning there'll be no water, Baba.'

'Who says so? Enough water to drown you, to be sure.'

After the culvert, both sides of the road up to a certain distance were only tilled land. Beyond lay the village. Population was sparse on this side. To the south of the road, within enclosures of hedgerows, were scattered several dilapidated huts, soaked through and through in the rain. Seven Bagdi[18] families lived there. Of the residents of the village, they were the poorest, the lowliest, and the most given to thieving. The house the roof of which they repaired by day they would burgle at night. Someone or the other among them was forever serving time for anything between six months to a year. On coming back home after release, they would proudly announce, 'Returning from father-in-law's house, brother. Had a good time there, you know!'

A little farther on one could find gradually denser population; a better standard of living was evident in the dwelling places. One could see bypaths branching out towards different localities on either side of the road. At intervals of some distance would appear banana groves, areca groves, or small bamboo clumps. The mango grove appeared in the dark to be a jungle. Feeble attempts to contrive gardens of *kamini*, *gandharaj* or *jabaphool* could be seen in front of some houses. By and by, one or two brick houses could be seen, not entirely brick-built though; if two rooms in one segment were of brick, the others were the typical traditional village dwellings made of thatch-of-flax or wattle and daub. The 'pall-bearers' were the only ones to show any sign of life on the deserted road. Shashi was sunk in a bleak melancholy. He walked ahead of the others with a lantern in his hand. Nitai, Sudeb and the others, everyone was talking; only

Shashi was not. If he noticed a light in any house by the roadside, he would call out and wait to hear them respond, stopping for a minute to ask after them, even if unnecessarily. He seemed to lack the strength to proceed towards Haru's house without talking to a family which, on hearing the news, would not burst into a loud wail.

A little further on was the bazaar. Here was the hub of the village. There were quite a few shops and establishments. But as it was a rainy day, all the shops had shut down before the night progressed. In an open space on the left of the road were several tin sheds where the market sat on alternate days.

A *sannyasi* from somewhere had taken shelter under one of the sheds, a censer burning in front of him; he was baking thick rotis in the fire. A mangy, depilated dog, its mouth resting on its paws, was watching from the shed on the other side. Shashi proceeded briskly, his feet often landing in puddles; he was unable to follow the drift of his mind today.

The path to Kayetpara[19] branched out from near Srinath Das's grocery shop. Haru's house was at the end of this path. After that, there were no more dwellings; a two-mile-long open field stretched out, devoid of life.

At the bend of the road was a *bakul* tree; its foot was paved. Everyday in the afternoon people used to gather here to gossip. Shashi put the lantern down and lit a biri. He noticed a doll wrapped in rags lying among the dry leaves and twigs under the tree. Shashi recognised it. This was the doll he had bought at the Bajitpur fair in the month of Baishakh[20] for Srinath's daughter in consideration for resting for an hour at Srinath's shop. This afternoon, after the rain stopped, the girl had come out here to play and left the doll behind.

The girl would cry at night for the missing doll. She would come to search for it in the morning and not find it. She would not know who had taken it. Only Shashi could guess that Jamini Kabiraj's wife, who used to come early in the morning to sweep the base of the bakul tree, had found it and picked it up.

Jamini Kabiraj's wife was neither a thief nor off her head; a clay doll held no attraction for her. But after bowing before the tree—one of which the bottom is paved has some divine quality—if on looking up she found such a big doll lying on the ground, there would be little doubt in her mind that surely this must be the work of a god and that this is his dispensation. Shashi pushed the doll further towards the trunk of the tree, picked up the lantern and moved on.

'Tread carefully, Nitai,' said Shashi. 'Walk slowly. Take care not to drop Haru and get him all muddied. What a road!'

The bamboo clumps on both sides of the narrow path across Kayetpara swarmed with buzzing mosquitoes. At the back of Jamini Kabiraj's cattle shed, cow dung dumped for three months had started rotting. In the stagnant pool, a year-long growth of weeds now submerged under rainwater had grown toxic.

A little distance ahead, the wail of Haru's bereaved wife reached their ears.

2

There were two distinct sides to Shashi's character. While he had no dearth of imagination, emotion, and a sense of humour, he had considerable practical wisdom and attachment for wealth and property as well. The imaginative aspect was covert and mute. Unless one mixed with him intimately, one would never know that he also had a deeply sympathetic discernment of the aesthetic sense of life. It was his intelligent, restrained, and frugal nature that generally came to the fore. For these qualities, which are essential for survival in the world, everyone treated him with awe and respect.

This trait of Shashi's character had been developed by his father Gopal Das. Gopal Das's profession, as they say, was to hold a knife to people's throats. What he actually did was buying and selling property and money lending; that is, he was a middleman and usurer. It is also rumoured that in the past, on at least three occasions, he had acted as a tout in the transaction of live human beings as well—that of procuring brides for three old men. That was a long time ago. Two of the old blokes had since died. Now, after Jamini Kabiraj's eventual demise, the entire matter could be consigned to history. But Jamini Kabiraj's wife, whom Shashi called Sen-didi, the son-less woman who loved Shashi very deeply, used to tend to her husband so scrupulously and with such care that Jamini was not likely to die anytime soon. But Jamini wished to die. Idlers given to scandal-mongering were so numerous that if there was the slightest slip, tales about the wives and unmarried daughters of the village would circulate across the length and breadth of the land. Some believed; some did not. In either case, neither the credulous nor the sceptical ever cared to verify if they were true or not. To believe or not to believe is a matter of an individual's whim. Among the tainted women of the village, Shashi's Sen-didi's disrepute was the most extensive. It was with Gopal Das that her name was associated most of the time. Tongues wagged. Shashi did not believe. Jamini did. He was a doddering old fellow. He was singed by the deadly flame of suspicion. If his wife went out to visit a neighbour, he would even give way to weeping in anger and sorrow on some days. He didn't believe her excuse that she went to the Kayet family to help them make some condiment. Yet, Shashi's Sen-didi spoke the truth. Any immoral act she might have ever committed was mingled with the past mesh of truth and lies, virtue and vice. No one but a lunatic would suspect Sen-didi today. With growing age Jamini was losing his senses.

He would curse Gopal whenever they met, 'I gave you a pile of money, and you did me a great deed in return, Gopal! You'll go to the dogs; you'll be ruined; your house and homestead will be burnt to ashes.' The talk about Gopal involving Jamini's wife was perhaps false; still, Gopal Das was not a good man. It was he who, for the sake of petty pelf, had procured the angelic, youthful girl as the bride for the old, eccentric Jamini Kabiraj.

Shashi was Gopal's only son; he had three daughters. The eldest, Bindhyabasini, was married to Mohan, the eldest son of the Borogaon *nayeb*[21] Shyamacharan Das. Mohan was lame in one leg. The second daughter Bindubasini was married into a family in the heart of Calcutta—to Nandalal of Nandalal & Co. of Burrabazaar.[22]

Really, that was an achievement of Gopal's one would never forget!

Nandalal dealt in jute. Once, some seven years back, he had come to this area looking for an intermediate village with adequate warehousing and shipping facilities. Gopal had invited him to his house and treated him cordially like a member of the family. And then, nobody knows quite how it happened. Maybe Nandalal was at fault, maybe not; but three days later, the villagers loyal to Gopal, standing guard with sticks in hand, got Bindu married off to Nandalal. Nandalal's servant had fled to Bajitpur overnight. Next day, he arrived with the police to rescue his master. If only he had wished, Nandalal could have meted out some punishment to many of them. But it was he who had with a sullen face dismissed the police. Then taking his wife he went away to Calcutta once and for all, never to maintain any contact with Gaodiya thereafter.

Be that as it may, Bindubasini was perhaps happy living with Nandalal. People of the village did not exactly know. In these seven years, Bindu had come to her father's house only once. Everyone, old and young, had then looked at her with envy: she was covered with ornaments, like a nautch girl as it were. And yet, she may not be happy. Nandalal was quite aged; he had another wife; perhaps his character was not good either. People of Gaodiya, whose married daughters stood in rows bathed in tears, would prefer to think that perhaps Bindu was not happy! And they were content. Some even made no bones about expressing their feelings. If Gopal happened to hear, he would curse them under his breath: a bunch of no-gooders!

So this was the sort of father under whose thumb Shashi had grown up. When he went to Calcutta to study medicine at the Medical College, his mind was narrow, his imagination blunt and his sense of humour coarse. A sketchy impression of the self-centred, narrow-minded lifestyle of a village householder was all he could fancy for his future. What brought refinement in his emotional domain were books, and a friend. The friend's name was Kumud; his place of domicile was Barishal;[23] he was tall and dark-skinned; and he was rather reckless and idiosyncratic. He frequently skipped classes. Occasionally Kumud wrote poems too. Sprawled on his bed in the hostel he would read whatever English and Bengali novels he could lay his hands on; in the manner of a narrator of myths he would declaim on religion, society, God, and teenaged girls; and he would borrow money from Shashi. To begin with, Shashi had fallen for Kumud much as girls fall in love; he would feel privileged to lend him money. Kumud did not much care for him initially. But after swallowing much insult and injured vanity in silence, Shashi did ultimately win Kumud's intimacy.

Shashi was then of an age when one tends to imitate. It was thanks to the influence of this one friend that Shashi changed altogether. Kumud could not break entirely the fortress in which Gopal had incarcerated his son's mind, but by providing a number of doors and windows to it he let in the light and air of the outside world and taught his mind to emerge from its dark recesses and roam freely in the open.

Shashi was somewhat baffled and overwhelmed at the outset. Man has made such a big affair out of life, blowing it up to fantastic proportions! So many aspects to learn, so many ways to enjoy, so complex and teeming was life, so piquant with the intermingling of science and poetry! Later, when he came to start his career as a doctor in his village, initially Shashi had almost felt suffocated. In Calcutta, life had been flowing like the lilting music at a friend's wedding; now it seemed to have stopped all at once. Would he have to spend the rest of his life here—amidst these illiterate people, these ponds and ditches, these bushes and fields? O Lord, there's not even a library here! By and by, his mind had calmed down. He was essentially a son of the village; he had grown up rubbing shoulders with men and women of the village, covered in its clay, imbibing its air and water; the elemental mould of his heart and mind was indeed rustic. The impression the city had left on his mind was not easy to erase; yet it was a mere mark, not a brand. Retaining as much of the urban habits as possible, he could discard the rest. Many greater hopes and aspirations that he owed to books and to Kumud he transmuted into his thoughts and dreams as well.

In this remote village, never perhaps would that spring come—the spring whose cuckoo is the piano, whose fragrance the scent of perfume, and whose south wind the breeze of the whirring fan. Yet, who could possibly tie down Shashi's mind? A long life lay ahead;

so did the vast world. Today, sitting on a camp chair by the kamini coppice, let Shashi be distracted by the gentle breeze rustling the bamboo leaves and carrying a whiff of the marshy pool; let the desired life lie confined between the covers of the book on his lap. One day, in his red-tiled bungalow set in the middle of a well-laid-out garden, Shashi would watch a canary sing in its cage; a breast covered in an expensive blouse would throb next to his: what then would he lack—light, song, laughter, joy, or aristocracy?

After crossing three-fourths of the Kayetpara path, one reached Shashi's house. Haru's house was at the farthest end of this path: Haru, who had been struck dead by lightning under the banyan tree by the canal.

There was no remission of Moti's fever. Shashi went to see her in the evening; he had had no time all day.

No lamps were lit in Haru's house this evening. Haru's widow Mokshada was furious with Kusum, the wife of her son Paran and Haru's daughter-in-law. Just think: this is a traditional household; evening has descended; there is a son's wife present. Yet, the evening lamp has not been lit! Why doesn't the woman go hang herself?

Kusum had gone to the ghat. She came back, put down the pitcher, and took her time to change. Then she went to light the lamp. Her shameless tardiness enraged Mokshada further. Snatching the lamp from Kusum's hand, she went to the kitchen and kindling a jute stalk lit the lamp. And then walking across the courtyard hurriedly, she stumbled and fell on the dry ground, heaven knows how!

Kusum burst into a laugh. Gathering the sari-end round her waist, she heaved Mokshada into her arms and lowered her gently onto the veranda in front of the bedroom. A barren woman of twenty-three years, she was strong.

Absolute bedlam followed. Mokshada kept cursing at the top of her voice. When Bnuchi came to enquire about the matter, her son in her arms, the child started crying. In her room on the far side, Bnuchi's moribund aunt sat up in bed, anxiously asking, 'Hey, what happened? O Bnuchi, O Kusum, what on earth has happened? O God! Isn't anybody listening?'

Moti lay in darkness in the main room. Raising her feeble voice as high as she could, she too wanted to know what the matter was.

The only one to remain unconcerned was Kusum. She stood quietly listening to Mokshada's vituperations for some time. Then she fetched a burning piece of wood from the kitchen and made for the bedroom.

Mokshada began to scream, oblivious of her pain, 'What's this, O Bou![24] What are you doing? Will you set fire to the house now?'

'Why would I set fire to the house, Ma?[25] I'm going to light the lamp.'

'Do you mean to use an oven cinder to light the lamp? Just look, Bnuchi, look. The godless, misbegotten wench goes to light a pyre in the room, just watch her.'

Rolling her eyes Kusum said, 'Don't you curse, Ma, I tell you, don't. Can't you see the mango leaves in my hand? If I am to light the lamp from wood, what am I taking the leaves for then? To chew?'

Mokshada scaled down her voice and said, 'No, child, it wasn't you I cursed. It was Bnuchi.'

Everyone in the family looked upon Kusum with a degree of awe. All of Haru Ghosh's property except for this homestead had been mortgaged to Kusum's father for seven years now. If she ever went to him and fell weeping, he would file a complaint right away. Where would these people go then? That does not mean, however, that Kusum adopted a domineering attitude over them all the time. On the contrary, she kept up a rather innocent bearing. If rebuked, she wouldn't always take it to heart either; instead she kept doing her chores at her own pace. If she didn't feel like working, she would simply go out by the postern door into the palm grove and keep sitting there quietly on the grounded palm tree by the *taalpukur*.[26]

Sometimes before going out, she made it a point to put something on the oven, rice or lentils or some such. The members of the family were then made aware of her absence by the burning smell from the kitchen.

Nobody could quite gauge Kusum's temper. Till now unable to ascertain how far she might be tolerant or just when she might flare up, everyone would remain on tenterhooks.

Neighbours would say, 'So this Bou of yours seems to be a bit eccentric, isn't that so, Paraner Ma?'[27]

'Why say *a bit*, child? She's quite eccentric,' Mokshada would remark. 'Theirs is a family of lunatics, you know. Wasn't her father stark mad for two years—he was kept bound in chains.'

Kusum went into the room and lighted the lamp. She had barely finished blowing into the conch for the third time when Shashi's voice was heard from the courtyard. Going near Moti's bed, she said, 'It's scarcely evening yet, and he's come to see you!'

Moti made no response. Kusum said again, 'O Moti! Are you listening? The evening lamp has just been lit and he has come. What a lot of affection!'

Picking up the heavy stool easily, Kusum placed it in the veranda for Shashi to sit, and said, 'Moti's fever has come down; she's sleeping now.'

'Has Moti gone to sleep, Bou?' Mokshada interjected. 'Didn't I hear her voice just now?'

Shashi quipped, 'Even the sound of your conch did not disturb her sleep, Paraner Bou?'[28] He sat down on the stool, cast a quick glance into the room, and said, 'Paran had come in the afternoon and said that the temperature has risen quite high since the morning, isn't that so?'

Kusum said, 'He lied, Chhoto-babu. He gets nervous so easily, you know. Where's the fever?'

Mokshada said, 'What nonsense are you talking, Bou! Why don't you go to the kitchen, child?'

Kusum went into the kitchen without a protest. There was no playful smile on her face, nor was it grave.

Shashi asked, 'Wasn't she given the medicine that I had sent in the morning?

'That I do not know, son,' said Mokshada. 'Let me ask my daughter.'

Kusum responded from the kitchen, 'She did receive her medicine; don't worry, she did. Why are you making so much noise and disturbing her sleep?'

From inside the room, Moti spoke in a feeble voice, 'I haven't taken any medicine, Ma.'

Looking towards the kitchen with a frown, Mokshada said, 'Did you hear that, son? How barefacedly Bou lied!'

Shashi smiled slightly and said nothing. He had often noticed Kusum utter such white lies. It seemed she indulged in them knowing fully well that she would get caught. It was a kind of joke with her. Calling black white, she chuckled unseen.

Shashi went into the room and asked, 'What's troubling you, Moti?'

Moti did not know. She guessed, 'Body's aching. I feel thirsty, Chhoto-babu.'

Bnuchi had entered the room after calming down her aunt. She said, 'Today she's coughed a lot all day, Chhoto-babu.'

Shashi examined her chest with his stethoscope. This was one examination that always put Moti to great embarrassment; her heart would keep pounding, which found its way through the tube to Shashi's ears. Surprised, he said, 'Who told you to hold your breath, Moti? Breathe deep.' Bnuchi held the lamp aloft; Shashi looked at Moti's face.

Moti's complexion seemed to have blended with the yellowish glow from the cracked glass of the lantern.

Kusum had come in silently and stood behind them. 'What's wrong with her chest, Chhoto-babu?' she asked. 'What's all the testing about?'

'It seems a slight cold has settled in her chest, Paraner Bou. Give her a hot oil massage.'

Kusum asked solicitously, 'Are you sure it is a simple cold, Chhoto-babu? Dear me! The way you were examining her made my heart shudder! Maybe it's TB, I thought. Moti, didn't I tell you not to sit in the open when you have fever, that you'll die of cold?'

Shashi went out of the room and sat down when Mokshada began to tell him how she fell. 'Bou gave me a push, my son. Bou will be the death of me!' She spoke a load of rubbish for some time in a low voice. Haru had been dead for about a week now. She didn't whine over him any more, only wiped her eyes at intervals, her voice caught. While grieving for her husband in a tearful voice, she blamed Kusum off and on. As one listened, one would think she only spoke the truth. Bnuchi listened quietly, neither agreeing nor protesting. And Kusum, who was in the kitchen, sang *jatra*[29] songs for Shashi's benefit in a continuous soft, indistinct hum. Was Kusum really insane?

Later Kusum left the kitchen and went out, who knew where.

Shashi took his leave after a while. Haru's house was not exactly on the Kayetpara path; a pathway three arm-lengths wide flanked by aubergine fields led to it. Shashi was briskly crossing this track when from the other side of the fence of the aubergine field Kusum called out, 'O Chhoto-babu, listen!'

Taken by surprise, Shashi said, 'What are you doing there, Bou? You could be bitten by a snake.'

'No snake is going to bite me, Chhoto-babu. I'm not fated to die.'

'What is it?' Shashi asked with a smile.

'Why did you call me Paraner Bou today? I get angry when I'm called by that name, Chhoto-babu. Aunt—Bnuchi's younger aunt who departed last year—also used to do that. One day I gave her such a piece of my mind—'

'Why don't you give me a bit of it too?'

'Did I say that, O Chhoto-babu, did I? You are a venerable person; we earn grace by honouring you.'

She reeled off a string of such flattering phrases as fluently as if quoting from memory, which didn't sound unpleasant to Shashi's ears. He had been observing such eccentric behaviour of Kusum's for many years now. There seemed to underlie some sweet rhythm in these random words and conduct of hers.

'Now go home, Bou, or the rice will get burnt,' said Shashi.

'Will you come to see Moti tomorrow, Chhoto-babu?'

'I think so. Just send me a word in the morning how she is doing, all right?'

'Can't you come once daily? The girl is down with fever; shouldn't you see her everyday? The few days you didn't come people in the family said so many things: that our Shashi has become a big doctor. He won't pay a visit unless called. Do you know what Moti said? That Chhoto-babu has grown vain!'

Shashi walked on ahead, saying, 'I've work to do, Bou. I'll listen to your lies tomorrow when I come.'

'Not lies, truly not lies, Chhoto-babu!'

After Shashi had left, Kusum, standing alone in the aubergine field smiled to herself in the darkness. Around the top of the tree in front of her, a faint glow appeared. Kusum knew that the moon would soon rise there. When the moon appeared or even before it actually did, Kusum seemed to hear:

A look at the stranger's moon-like face brings
A blush to the cheeks of the girl in her teens.

Who's that teenage girl who blushed with a surge of love at the sight of a man from a distant land? She's not Kusum, O God, surely she's not Kusum.

Peering into the darkness Basudeb Banerjee said, 'Isn't it Shashi? O my son, Shashi, it's you I'm looking for. Bhutho doesn't seem to be well at all. His mother is crying. Please come and see him.'

'Okay, let's go.' They started walking. Shashi said, 'Baba was telling me that day, "Shashi, you've been to the Bnarujje[30] house quite a few times; have they made any payment?" Uncle, if you do not pay for at least one or two calls, I'll be in trouble. How long can I keep lying to Baba? And you're well aware what money means to Baba; no one can cheat him out of a single paisa.'

Embarrassed, Basudeb said he would go the next day itself to pay Shashi's dues. Why not today, Shashi wondered, but said nothing. Basudeb's house was quite some distance away. One had to go past Srinath's shop, past Rajani Sarkar's brick house, from there till the middle of the serpentine path up to Bamunpara, then along the narrow path which runs about a quarter mile before disappearing into the field; close to its end, lay Basudeb's house. It had not rained for the last couple of days; the monsoon had perhaps ended for this year; the mud had not dried yet though. Shashi took off his shoes and carrying them in his hand entered Basudeb's house and washed his feet. Basudeb's younger son Bhutho was about ten years old.

Seven or eight days back, he had fallen from the top branch of a tree, fracturing both his arms and legs. He subsequently ran high fever, occasionally passing into delirium, and lay unconscious in a critical state. Shashi had told them to shift him to the district hospital; they wouldn't. Bhutho's mother had burst into a wail at the mention of the hospital: if her son is taken across the threshold, she would take poison. Thereafter, Shashi was treating him as best as he could. He came visiting twice or thrice a day.

Bhutho's mother Lakshmimani was weeping in a low moan sitting by his bedside. Two elder sons, two married daughters, three daughters-in-law all stood crowding in the room. The eldest daughter-in-law was a widow; she was fanning Bhutho, her veil in place. Perhaps in the family she loved this unruly boy the most, next only to his mother; tears were streaming down her eyes.

Shashi's face went pale on seeing Bhutho's condition. He wondered whether the boy would survive. Yet, when he saw him last at about noon, he was definitely hopeful. He could not imagine that his condition would turn so serious in just a few hours. He had left the boy swathed in bandages. It was impossible for the boy to make any movement; only his face was contorting from time to time. Shashi's voice was naturally low; now it sounded even lower when he said, 'I want some fire for fomenting and a piece of flannel if you can manage.'

The widowed daughter-in-law brought fire in a crucible. She fetched a shawl and started applying warmth to Bhutho's chest according to Shashi's advice. Shashi gave him an injection and waited. He repeatedly examined his pupils, felt his pulse; and then he quietly got up to go. Everyone was holding their breath; Shashi's withdrawal triggered a chorus of lamentation.

The widowed woman came running frantically and obstructing his path said, 'No, you can't leave, Shashi! You must bring back my Bhutho before you go, you must. It is to pluck berries for me that he had climbed the tree.'

What could Shashi say? He remained grim. He somehow managed to come out of the house. Shoes in hand, he stepped on to the path. Even when he had barely gone as far as the end of the path, he could hear them wailing.

A few men were gathered on the bench of bamboo strips in front of Srinath Das's grocery shop. Perhaps because they had been engrossed in talking among themselves, they had not observed Shashi when he went with Basudeb to his house. Now Srinath noticed him and said, 'Chhoto-babu, please will you come and sit here. Niyogi-mashay, may I ask you to leave the stool? Please make room for Chhoto-babu.'

Panchanan Chakraborti asked, 'Where did you go, Shashi?'

'To Basudeb Banerjee's house. Bhutho died just now.'

'Indeed? So he didn't survive? Let me tell you something, Shashi. The day Bhutho fell from the tree was a Thursday. When I heard the news, I had misgivings. I went straight home, consulted the almanac, and lo, it said just what I had guessed: the boy fell and with it ended the *barbela*![31] People keep talking about barbela, and I tell them, "Well, is the entire barbela inauspicious?" In fact, any danger it signifies comes only at the moment it ends. When the barbela ends, you know, even if a mere thorn pricks your foot, it will ulcerate and fester, ultimately leading to death. That year, when Nabin the fisherman's eldest son was dragged away by a crocodile, that day was a Thursday too. That time too, the moment the boy got down into the canal, the barbela had ended. Or who had ever heard of a crocodile straying into Gaodiya canal?'

Not just the crocodile of the canal, talking of Bhutho[32] naturally led to discussion on ghosts. Thereafter it drifted into a whole slew of topics: the holy man at the bazaar, market prices, differences between past and present times, abduction of women, the scandal of Purna Talukdar's daughter, son of the soil Sujan Das who held a high post away from the village, you name it. Had Shashi risen too high for all this rustic talk that he listened silently with indifference? Not so: with half his mind he contemplated the amazing similarity in the thinking of so many people. No one had any individuality or originality; the strings of their minds were all tuned to the same pitch. Their joys and sorrows were the same; their feelings were the same; their fears and superstitions were the same too: judging by their meanness and generosity, no one was the least bit inferior or superior to any other. Panchanan was a clerk at the zamindar's estate; Kirti Niyogi a pensioner head peon; Shibnarayan a teacher at a Bengali-medium school; Gurugati a farmer: everyone had a different trade; so how could their minds have developed in the same mould? Only Bhujangadhar seemed to be different; he had been a clerk to a lawyer at Bajitpur and served a two-year term for defalcation. He did not talk much; his small crafty eyes wandered about restlessly giving the impression of some deep, clandestine design. Kirti Niyogi had a bald pate that had once been covered with the yellow turban of the postman; now the large potato-sized tumour on the hairless scalp provoked laughter. Srinath had great respect for this man, nobody knew why. He seemed to be devouring whatever Kirti had to say. Kirti took out a paisa and said to Srinath, 'O *Chhinath*,[33] give me sago for a paisa.' Srinath gave him so much sago in a fold of paper that it excited the others' envy; Bhujangadhar's snake-like eyes forgot to blink for a couple of seconds. The light from the hanging kerosene lamp was adequate; the graceful signs of prosperity lay over the articles on display. In small rectangular wooden boxes were kept rice, pulses and spices; there was a sack of flour, a measuring can layered with oil scum lying on the wooden tray; in two large jars were *muri* and *murki*;[34] a pack of matchboxes carrying the picture of deer; on one side in a row of glass-fronted tin boxes were sago, barley, round lozenges, and so on. Bhujangadhar looked around as a pretext for having a good look at Srinath's square stool-cum-cashbox. A stray pedestrian carrying a lamp walked past his shop; another passed by without a lamp. One or two customers came. To one customer, he gave the news of Bhutho's death. Whatever topic they might discuss, they had not forgotten the news about Bhutho.

Shashi was about to get going when more or less to the surprise of all, Jadab Pandit[35] stepped into Srinath's shop. He had a canvas bag in one hand, a walking stick in the other, an umbrella under his arm, slippers on his feet, and a scarf wrapped round his head. He was an old man; his body was shrivelled, but his bones were strong.

As for learning, Jadab Pandit had not acquired much; neither had he any reputation as a scholar. Any respect he commanded was as a pious man with supernatural powers. He was a householder yogi, an ascetic who had not renounced the world. Those who were permitted to touch his person used to take the dust from his feet; others fell prostrate on the ground keeping a distance. Nobody knew how many stages of penance he had surmounted, but those who had overwhelming devotion would straightaway speak of his attainment of the ultimate goal. Jadab neither admitted nor denied anything. He lived in a small single-story house halfway between Jamini Kabiraj's house and Shashi's house by the Kayetpara road. There wasn't another house in these parts as old and dilapidated as his. A portion of the house had crumbled. At one time perhaps there had been a compound wall. Moss-covered blackish bricks were still strewn about. If he had not been living here, the house would have earned notoriety as a haunted house long ago. Jadab had no one in the world except his wife. For her eccentric nature, Jadab's wife was known as Pagal-didi[36] to all and sundry.

A few days back, Jadab had gone to Calcutta. He was not supposed to return today. Everyone stood up respectfully and offered him his seat. Panchanan asked, 'Why did you have to return suddenly, Pandit-mashay?'

'I'm a man rooted to the village, son, I just couldn't settle my mind in the city,' said Jadab.

Srinath effusively joined in, 'Do such feelings come even to you, O *Debata*!'[37]

Jadab smiled at this word. This was his manner of accepting overflowing devotion. He asked about the well-being of all one by one. He felt sorry at the news of Bhutho's death and uttered, 'Alas!' but he was not much moved. Neither was it expected from one who was indifferent alike to life and death to be moved by the death of a mischievous boy. Still, it seemed to Shashi that he ought to have been a bit more sympathetic. He may be hard of hearing, but was he not sensitive enough even to imagine that grief had overwhelmed a family? After about ten minutes, Jadab rose to go. 'Will you be going homeward, Shashi?' he said.

'Let's go,' said Shashi.

Jadab used to make his way by tapping the path with his stick. Shashi knew that such loud tapping was meant only to ward off snakes. Was he afraid of dying then—he to whom there was no difference between life and death? Or was it exclusively death by snakebite that he was afraid of?

As they walked on, Jadab said, 'Shashi, so you are a qualified doctor, right? Casting aside Charaka and Sushruta,[38] you have taken to blighty medicine. You use knives and needles to save people from death. So what do you people actually do, would you tell me? Is there really something in your medical science?'

'Of course there is, Pandit-mashay. You see, medical science is not any one person's fanciful thoughts; hundreds of scientists have experimented throughout their lives; that's how they have made discoveries. Otherwise, the whole world—'

Jadab interjected, 'A bunch of scientists ignorant of solar science! Unless one has the primary knowledge, how can one acquire any subsequent knowledge, Shashi? Just like you and the modern-day doctors, so also the Kabirajs—all insensible, blind fellows. They make their medicines by extracting sap from tree leaves, but where does the medicinal quality of leaves come from in the first place? One who knows solar science does not look for roots and leaves, Shashi; all he does is transmute the sun's rays into a powerful medicine with a magnifying glass and focus on the patient's body—instant relief. What use are fat books and all those surgical instruments?'

Shashi got irritated inwardly. He too had no less respect for Jadab, if out of the unshakeable values of his rustic mind; so even though he did not agree, he could not argue with him. At the entrance of his house, Jadab said, 'I've brought grapes from Calcutta. Come and have some.' Did Jadab, who made no distinction between affection and hate, have a soft corner for Shashi despite being critical of him? Shashi could not very well say that he did not wish to have grapes; he went inside with Jadab.

On the right side of his house lay a heap of rubble; behind it was the ancestral place of the Sahas, lying abandoned for a decade. Jadab tapped with his stick on the ramshackle door of heavy panelling. Pagal-didi ascertained from inside who it was, and opening the door, said, 'You weren't supposed to return today, were you? O Shashi, you've accompanied him? Come, come on in.'

With her toothless mouth, sunken cheeks and grey hair, Pagal-didi looked even older than Jadab. She had also acquired a slight stoop. Yet, with her emaciated, decrepit body and feeble heart Pagal-didi would keep smiling all the time with her hollow cheeks. This crumbling old house, Gaodiya village with its ponds and copses, her life afflicted with old age—everything seemed to amuse her; savouring her impending death, Pagal-didi bubbled over with merriment.

After Shashi took his seat, Pagal-didi came up to him and, lifting his chin, said, 'The old master wasn't home these few days; I suppose you didn't know, my little master? Why did you not come, my dear? I had put on my striped sari, done up my hair; complete in the make-up of a bride I'd been waiting for you all the time, my dear!'[39]

Jadab had brought the grapes stuffed in his bag. On unpacking, it was found that half the lot had got squashed. A shirt, two dhotis, a *gamchha*[40] and other such articles in the bag were all soaked with the juice. Jadab smiled in embarrassment. Pagal-didi said, 'Just look at the dotard's lack of sense, he's filled his bag with ripe fruits! Why, couldn't you bring them separately in the gamchha?' And she laughed, her face wreathed in a thousand lines. Shashi looked at her face as he tossed the grapes one after another into his mouth. The lines seemed to him to be the marks of time—an encrypted history. What was Pagal-didi's life like in her youth? Shashi had not been born then. When this bent, scrawny body of hers was firm of figure, and there was grace in the taut skin of her face, how did she look then—could Shashi read from these lines today?

Pagal-didi's was an organised household. Cleaned utensils were neatly arranged upside down, pots and pitchers lidded; the wooden chest wore a freshly washed tidiness; the flame on the lamp stand was bright, and the room still redolent of incense. And there was placidity. Everything here was placid; a mild, unruffled tranquillity pervaded the room. The amiability permeating the room was something one could inhale. It was not the sad stillness of a *broken haat*.[41] Here was a home where for ages no cries of life's stinging pains had entered; here no one had ever revelled in the pleasures of living: someone who only slumbered all their life had put this house to sleep. Shashi was fascinated. He was a doctor; the sick and the wounded were his only concern all day. He was busy day and night with harsh realities. In this dwelling of the old couple, he felt as peaceful as if he were sitting with a tired mind in a lonely temple in the evening. Not just today but whenever he came here, his heart seemed to be soothed. And yet surprisingly, he did not feel the least attraction for this room once he was outside it. In fact, unless he came here, he did not even realise that there was any anguish or discontent in his mind. The agony that gradually subsided on his coming here aligned so well with his workaday life outside this room that he did not feel it at all.

3

Haru Ghosh died an unnatural death under the banyan tree by the canal when he went to search for a match for Moti. Couldn't a suitable boy be found in the village? Haru had high hopes. In his youth Haru had gone to school. He had become a rich man. Later on, though he was reduced to poverty his mindset did not change much. The milkmen's community of Gaodiya teasingly called him *bhaddarlok*.[42] Especially Nitai. Nitai was well-to-do; his manners were also much like a gentleman's. Yet, Haru had scant respect for him. Nitai had a nephew named Sudeb. Sudeb had a house, land and property. He had a modicum of learning as well—in English and Bengali. Only, he was no spring chicken; he was nearly thirty-six. How doggedly Nitai had tried to get Sudeb married to Moti! Haru had not agreed. It was then that he had gone to negotiate about the Matriculate boy from Bajitpur. And that led to his untimely death.

Haru was no more, and his son Paran, unlike his father, was neither clever nor headstrong. The milkman community of Gaodiya once again began to take an interest in Moti's marriage. They tried to persuade Paran using various arguments. A girl of the village staying back in the same village was eminently desirable. If married into a known family, she would live happily. They were not even proposing a milkman's family for his sister—Sudeb's family was almost like an aristocratic one. 'What makes you hesitate, Paran, when you know well that the Bajitpur boy has slipped through your fingers?'

Moti's marriage with Sudeb—would that be ideal? Moti, whose complexion was tender like a succulent fruit and her face flawless like a goddess's! The proposal was not to Paran's liking. But neither did he have the strength of mind to say no to the face of so many people. Reluctantly he said that if his family and Shashi approved, he would not object.

The question of seeking Shashi's opinion did not go down well with them. Nitai said with a grin, 'Chhoto-babu is a good man. But when there are respectable well-wishers in your own community, why do you choose him as your arbiter, Paran? Calling in an outsider in a family matter?'

Then someone said, 'Chhoto-babu comes visiting frequently, doesn't he?'

Paran disliked this remark. What the discord between the two sides would have ended in is anybody's guess. But Paran had been greatly demoralised after Haru's sudden death. Without going into altercations, he left the place on the pretext of illness at home.

Moti's fever had, however, subsided. At the beginning of the rainy season, she had contracted malaria; she would be all right for a few days, only to come down again shivering with fever. Shashi's costly quinine could not effectively control it. This time, after giving her several injections, he had assured her that she would not have any further attacks. Moti did not look like one particularly pulled down by the fever. Before the onset of malaria, she had been putting on weight; the frequent bouts of fever had checked it. It would be a matter of great regret if her graceful figure were to put on fat.

Shashi was still giving her an injection every week. In the morning, he used to tend to the patients waiting at his house. By the time he went to Haru Ghosh's house, his black bag in hand, it would be quite late in the morning, the courtyard flooded with sunlight. Seeing Moti's pale, nervous face, Shashi would say with a smile, 'You've taken it so many times and still you've not got over your fear, Moti? Which arm is it today?' On rubbing it with spirit, dirt came off her arm. 'You lack cleanliness, Moti,' deplored Shashi. 'Can't you use soap?'

After administering the injection, Shashi sat in the veranda. Paran said, 'I need to consult you on a certain matter, Chhoto-babu.' When he heard that it concerned Moti's marriage, Shashi settled down and lit a biri. At a sign from her son, Mokshada came closer. Bnuchi, son in her arms, also came and stood near.

Not seeing Kusum, Shashi was surprised. The shadow of the east-wing room had retracted into the room itself. While listening to Paran, Shashi expected every moment that perhaps Kusum would suddenly emerge from that east-side room, her eyes dark and laden with shadow, and keep standing like an outsider in this assembly of the nearest ones.

How could Shashi know that becoming aware of his presence, Kusum had picked up the pitcher and gone down to the ghat? Towards the end of what Paran had to say, Kusum returned in wet clothes and, leaving wet footprints across the sunlit courtyard, receded into the shadows of the east-wing room. She did not come out again even after the air had grown thick with the smell of burnt pulses from the kitchen.

The stream of harsh words flowing from Mokshada's mouth swept away the topic of Moti's marriage for some time. The guilty pot of pulses flung through the open kitchen door falling with a thud onto the courtyard signalled there was no probability of that matter arising again today. Shashi wondered what rebukes from all were in store for Bou.

Mokshada, Bnuchi, Moti and the others raised a clamour; the bedridden Aunt screamed from her room, 'What happened, Bnuchi? What happened, Moti?' Shashi kept silent. Paran trying to quieten the others only added to the din.

But how unperturbed Kusum was! One who in the heat of the moment had flung the burning cooking pot came out with a smiling face. She stood before Shashi and said, 'Please examine me, Chhoto-babu, am I going to get fever?'

Shashi felt her pulse and said, 'There's no sign of fever, Bou.'

'Why do I have a headache then?'

'You alone know how long you ducked yourself in the pond; how is the head to blame?'

Kusum, signifying dissent, said, 'No, I must be having fever. I'm going to lie down. O Moti! Go to the kitchen. You'll cook today.'

Kusum went to her room and lay down.

But how could this restless woman so much as keep lying down? Leaving her bed after a while, she got up to make Paran a chillum of tobacco unasked, and then sat down nearby. Hearing of Shashi's disapproval of the proposal of Moti's marriage with Sudeb, she said, 'Why, Chhoto-babu? In what way is Sudeb unsuitable as a groom? A man's age doesn't matter—particularly when there's no thorn of a co-wife in the way. The man has a lot of money; our girl will live in bliss.'

Shashi said, 'Haru Uncle was unwilling; you can't ignore that, can you Bou?'

'He has gone to heaven.'

Kusum did not say anything more. Shashi tried to explain: Sudeb was not a good man; he and Moti did not make a good match. It was not clear whether Kusum understood what he meant. Reacting to a sharp glance from Mokshada, she pulled her veil a bit lower over her head and kept sitting motionless like a statue. When Shashi got up to go, she spoke again, 'Just have a look at Aunt before you go, Chhoto-babu; the old lady has started crying.'

Shashi felt a little ashamed; he often forgot to come and have a look at the dying woman. Her imminent death was too certain to admit of any further treatment at this stage. Is that why Shashi forgot that Aunt was still alive?

Aunt cherished a great desire to live.

The pyre wood that would be used for burning her body had been kept stacked, occupying half her room. In a corner of the room behind her head stood a bundle of jute stalks from which the old woman still got the smell of jute; Paran would take a sheaf out of it to apply fire to the corpse's mouth and light the pyre. Half the hair on her head had fallen; there was barely any flesh under her wrinkled skin. She was still determined to live. She told Shashi in a whisper, 'Baba[43] Shashi, consult books before giving me medicine; it must be a costly one. Don't worry about the price, my son; just let me get well and then I'll pay you. All I have will be yours; you just give me the proper treatment.'

Yet, Shashi often forgot that Aunt was still alive.

Every time Shashi gave Moti an injection, he reassured her, 'You aren't going to have fever anymore, Moti.'

If Shashi's assurance was true, malaria had let Moti off the hook for that year. Meanwhile Jamini Kabiraj's wife, whom Shashi called Sen-didi, had come down with fever.

Jamini was a famous Kabiraj. His services were requisitioned from distant villages. The *chyavanprash*[44] he concocted with a punch of hemp leaves was billed as a revitalising potion for old men. Jamini's branded *makaradhwaja*[45] was claimed to *resurrect the dead*. Thereafter, to sustain that life, it was advisable to take Jamini's original and genuine *mahakapiladi* pill. This pill took three nights to prepare; it was never available readymade. For once it was made, the sun's rays sucked out the medicinal property of this extraordinarily potent nostrum. So, even if life were to be imparted to the dead body thanks to his makaradhwaja, in the absence of the all-important mahakapiladi pill, life might not be sustained in all cases. But was that Jamini's fault? Blame it on the patient's fate! By the time the mahakapiladi pill would be ready, the resurrected man would have *died again*; that's why Jamini did not apply his famous and special makaradhwaja either. 'What's the use after all,' he would explain, 'the mahakapiladi pill is not ready. Suppose I revive the patient, what shall I apply thereafter to keep the man alive for three days?'

Nobody had ever seen him impart a moment's life to the dead. Yet, people—not just one or two, but many—believed in his power to heal.

Even so, Jamini Kabiraj's wife never took her husband's medicine. So far, whenever she was ill, she recovered without any treatment at all. This time, coming down with fever, she sent for Shashi.

Gopal was at home then. On Shashi's behalf, he said to the messenger, 'Go tell her he's coming.' He then forbade Shashi to go.

Shashi said, 'Why? Why should I not go?'

'I can never make out, Shashi, when you're going to attain maturity!'

Neither could Shashi. He kept silent.

Gopal then said, 'Jamini Uncle is such a big *Kobrej*.[46] Do you understand what it means to send for you when he is there?'

Shashi said, 'With respect, no.'

'She's a young woman; one hears many scandals about her too.'

For Gopal to say such things! Shashi shrank in shame. 'You've made it all up, Baba,' he said in a mild voice.

Gopal did not get angry. He said, 'I can't understand what has happened to you these days, Shashi. If I say a word for your good, you begin to argue. You're yet to learn how carefully man has to take his steps in the world. This is the time for setting up your practice; if you get a bad name now—do I have to tell you all this too? Well, if you take up her treatment, won't people wag their tongues? And with Jamini Kobrej around, why are you, a mere stripling, so bothered about her? There are women in every family; who will ever call you after this?'

Shashi was getting angry. But it had become ingrained in him to fear this Yama[47] of his childhood and adolescence. Looking at Gopal's penetrating stare, he lowered his eyes. 'Jamini Uncle too does not like you to go there,' Gopal added.

Gopal was pleased at Shashi's silence. To bring a grown-up and well-placed son under control—there was no greater victory in the world. Of late, frequent conflicts had been arising between Gopal and Shashi—no quarrels or altercations but arguments and differences of opinion, conflicts of instruction and disobedience. But today Shashi had realised how unskilled and inexperienced he was in worldly wisdom compared to his father; Gopal could still give him directions.

Gopal said much more, which Shashi listened to in silence. In the end, noticing his stern expression, Gopal thought it best not to press the point any further.

After taking his meal, Shashi went to Jamini Kabiraj's house.

Jamini Kabiraj was not happy to see Shashi. In the outer house, he was then giving two students oral instructions on the method of preparing a certain medicine. In the nearby shed perhaps some broth was boiling, the odour of which had filled the air. Jamini removed his spectacles and said, 'What brings you here, Shashi? Take your seat.'

'Sen-didi is sick, I heard, *Thakurda.*[48] I thought I should see her.'

'Sick?' Jamini laughed. 'Whom did you hear it from? Perhaps she had a slight fever yesterday, didn't she, Kunja? Where's the trace of any illness today?'

'Then perhaps she has called me for some work,' Shashi said, and went inside.

Sen-didi lay in bed, a sick, half-conscious, half-dead Sen-didi.

Her bright complexion had turned ruddy, almost indistinguishable from the colour of her armlets. There were more spots all over her skin which Shashi could recognise. His face turned pale. From where did Sen-didi contract this disease at the advent of autumn? In Gaodiya or Calcutta or any other place, nowhere had Shashi seen such a matchless beauty whose very looks had perhaps given rise to baseless infamy. And what a deadly disease had struck her!

As she heard Shashi's voice, Jamini Kabiraj's wife opened her eyes and said, weeping, 'You've come at last, Shashi? I'm all but dead. I don't know what the disease is. I lie unconscious with fever. There is unbearable pain all over my body.'

'I didn't know, Sen-didi.'

'Whom could I send to inform you? Does anyone come near me?'

Sen-didi could not keep her eyes open; tears kept rolling down from the corners of her eyes. Shashi sat beside her, took her temperature, and did not know what to do. Jamini had clearly tried to suppress the news, and until now, possibly no steps had been taken for her treatment either. But what had happened to Shashi all these days? Why didn't he bother to get any news of her? Who knows for how long his Sen-didi had been lying on this shabby, smelly bed-sheet, without any treatment, with no one even to attend to her. Shashi could not fathom: the kind of beauty that could excite universal awe, beauty in a wife not attainable even through penance was all Jamini's. At his age, he was expected to be at his wife's beck and call. Then why this perverse and cruel neglect? Who knows, perhaps it is only centred around a woman with the exceptional loveliness of a Sita,[49] a Helen, or a Cleopatra that such arbitrary things can happen!

After a while Jamini came into the room and with a long face said, 'You're still here, Shashi? I thought you had gone.'

Shashi said, 'Thakurda, would you please come outside for a minute?' Then he said, 'Could you not detect Sen-didi's illness?'

'You really make me laugh, Shashi! It is forty years since I've been in this profession. There is not a fellow across three districts who hasn't heard Jamini Kobrej's name. And you're asking me if I couldn't detect the disease? It takes just one look to know—she's got malaria.'

'Not malaria, Thakurda, it is pox.'

'Pox, indeed! Pox in autumn too!' Jamini scoffed.[50]

Jamini did say that, but then why did his face turn pale? Almost as if he was play-acting before Shashi, the pretence involved in concealing an enervating fear and dark worry. In a stern voice Shashi said, 'I take the responsibility of Sen-didi's treatment, Thakurda, here and now. For shame! You haven't done anything so far?'

'Does she take my medicine?'

Shashi went inside and sat in the room. Something made Jamini too go inside and keep standing there. Shashi felt greatly imperilled. And despondent. A few days back, he had gone to visit a pox patient at Saatgaon. Shashi could not save him. He could not even try to save the man; he was called in at the last moment. Until then, the treatment had been done by Kabiraj Bhupaticharan of Saatgaon, a former student of Jamini's. Shashi suddenly recalled that after that patient had died, Jamini had said with a snigger: one whom my student gave up as a lost cause, fancy Shashi trying to save him! Our *Shashe*![51]

Shashi began to treat as well as nurse Sen-didi with the utmost effort and sincerity. His other patients could scarcely obtain his services. If anyone in his own house had a cough or cold, he made short work of their treatment, and did not keep himself posted on their progress unless they reported. He ignored everyone else—friends, relations, outsiders. He did not go to Haru Ghosh's house either, whether casually or to give Moti her shot. Kusum thought that perhaps Shashi was annoyed. Going to pluck lilies at the taalpukur in the palm grove Moti hoped that Chhoto-babu would surely come today so she could present him with a basket of lotuses. However, Kusum's anger towards Shashi did not abate. The seeds of the lotus flowers made a curry that day.

If Shashi were only to take care of Sen-didi, he might perhaps have found the time to look at others. After taking Sen-didi's charge, Shashi found himself in a helpless and embarrassing situation, having to cope with advice, criticism, and hindrance from Gopal in this house, and from Jamini in that house. He could not understand the matter very well. At times it occurred to him that they had no faith in his treatment and that this message was somehow being conveyed to him. But there was no alternative arrangement for her treatment in sight either. Whether his treatment was good or bad, what was their logic for doing away with it? Jamini was unwilling to treat his wife himself because she refused to take his medicine. Then what did they want? To kill Sen-didi? But why would they want that? Besides, why was Gopal so actively supporting this shameful madness of Jamini? What would he gain by it?

Whatever the mystery and conundrum, Shashi continued to cope with the three perils of Sen-didi single-handedly.

He asked Jamini, 'Where's the big round phial of medicine, Thakurda?'

Jamini said, 'There were three doses in it, weren't there? I got her to gulp it down. Really, what are all these medicines of yours—each smells either of alcohol or of syrup!'

Shashi said apprehensively, 'Got her to gulp it down? I mean the medicine in the round phial?'

'Yes, of course! She was tossing and turning. I thought it's your patient and your medicine, and I went ahead.'

Shashi was angry. 'The patient is not mine, Thakurda. I am off. Do whatever you like.'

He as good as left. But as he walked out of the house, his steps slowed down and halted. Sen-didi's timorous, anguished look of utter dependence came back to his mind. Shashi went back.

He said, 'That medicine is for suppressing the eruptions; she was given it seven days ago. Did you not know?'

For some days now, Jamini's face had looked shrunken and pale, perhaps from worry. He blinked and said, 'I'm a Kobrej; what should I know about your medicine, brother? I don't know anything.'

'If you know nothing, then why did you administer the medicine without asking me? It is you who is going to kill her, Thakurda. The pustules are suppurating, and you fed her the medicine for suppressing at this stage?'

Jamini remained silent.

Relenting somewhat, Shashi said, 'You've done a great wrong, Thakurda. Don't ever do anything like this again.'

'Will you give her a medicine of mine, Shashi? For the quick maturation of the pustules.'

Shashi, at once suspicious, said, 'Have you given her anything else? Your medicine?'

'No, she doesn't take my medicine.'

'Which means that you tried?'

Jamini, already bewildered, now turned almost wild.

'What if I did? Yes, Shashi, what even if I did? I have no faith in all those wines and syrups of yours, lad. Do you call it treatment? If this is the nature of your treatment of pox, then you better throw your books into the canal and go sit at home.'

Even as he said this, he lost his courage. And still he said almost desperately, 'Don't come again, Shashi.'

Neither could Shashi keep his cool. He said, 'From the very beginning, you've been doing all sorts of things that can get you ten years in jail, Thakurda.'

Jamini said with an ashen face, 'What did I do? The treatment is yours; I never fed her a single pill of mine!'

Shashi desisted from further altercation. What was the use of bickering with this madman?

'Is this the time to quarrel, Thakurda?'

'Who's quarrelling, boy?'

When she regained consciousness, Jamini's wife said, 'Who is in the room, Shashi? Who are you talking to?' She could not see; her eyes remained shut. When she heard that Jamini was in the room, she grew restless, saying, 'Tell him to go, Shashi, tell him. He will surely kill me by poisoning. And you, why aren't you going away from here? Please go!'

When Jamini was gone, she said, 'Will I live, Shashi?'

'Of course you will!'

Sen-didi seemed reassured, and she lay quietly for some time. Didn't Shashi know how unbearable her pain was? He was staggered by what she could endure. No complaints, no groaning; only asking occasionally if she would survive.

Sen-didi said, 'You have to handle me so often; there's no risk for you, I suppose?'

'What risk? I was vaccinated six months back.'

Then she said, 'In a sense, you are my son. I love you more than I would my own son.'

The words agitated Shashi. The fact that Sen-didi loved him was something he had known since he was twelve. But the way in which it was now conveyed left him overwhelmed. A sense of childishness arose in him at the emotional outpouring of an ailing village woman. More than her own son? What did it even mean? Sen-didi was never known to have any son or daughter.

One day, after keeping awake all night at Sen-didi's bedside, while on his way back home in the morning, Shashi found Moti plucking flowers beneath the *shiuli* tree in front of his house. Since he had not visited them recently, she had perhaps come to assess what the matter was.

As he shook the tree to shed its flowers for her, Shashi asked, 'When were you vaccinated, Moti?'

'Why? I wasn't.'

'You weren't vaccinated? Why? What was the problem in getting it? Wait till I go and get the whole family vaccinated. Do you know that pox has broken out in this part of the village?'

Moti laughed in disbelief. 'What will your vaccination do? If Ma Shetala[52] blesses you, you will get pox, Chhoto-babu, that is certain. There's no escape.'

'Rubbish!'

The ground was wet with dew, as if after a shower. Moti's sari with its faded border looked soft like a half-wet cloth. Shashi thought Moti must be feeling a comfort in the cool, tender touch of her sari. To his sleepless eyes after the night's vigil, Moti seemed far more grown-up than her age. As he kept looking at her, the leisured smoking of a biri early in the morning seemed even more blissful to Shashi.

Moti went on, 'Boudi says you're like a sahib who does not believe in gods. Is it true, Chhoto-babu?'

'Not at all. I do believe in them very much.'

Moti seemed relieved to hear this. Then she said, 'Boudi keeps saying all sorts of things about you.'

'Really? What does she say?'

Moti smiled slyly and said, 'She says so many things!'

Shashi said with a smile, 'Why don't you tell me, Moti? Maybe it is from you that Paran's wife has picked them up.'

Moti's face turned pale. 'To think that I would say things about you! If I have ever said anything in your name, may I be stricken with cholera! Cholera, cholera, cholera! I repeat it three times so that it comes true. Let God witness me swearing this.'

Taken aback, Shashi said, 'What a girl you are, Moti! Early in the morning while plucking flowers, you are talking of cholera!'

To this, Moti only reiterated her oath angrily.

When the sun was up, Moti went home. Shashi thought to himself: so rustic is her nature; but she doesn't look it at all.

And Moti pondered: how Chhoto-babu was looking at me towards the end? What was he thinking of then?

The aubergine trees in front of Haru Ghosh's house were vibrant now. Some had grown a few tender fruits as well. Looking past their spacious room into the fields beyond, one could see sheets of mist hovering in the distance—as if the very distance loomed as mist; the fog was unreal. Moti felt contented: not because in the golden sunshine of the morning their small village limited by the horizons of her eyes had assumed an exquisite ethereal beauty. Nature, the nature of this their very own village she knew so intimately that nowhere except in the rainbow of the sky could her eyes and mind discern any colour. The swaying of shiny, tender new leaves might set some immature heart aflutter, but not Moti's. Ducks, absorbing the mysterious shadows of the palm trees into the whites of their feathers, swam unconcerned in the deep black waters of the taalpukur, cleaving their way through clusters of red and white *shapla* plants, which bobbed up and down in their wake. The flowers of the bindweed overgrowing the banks waved in the wind. Bright white clouds and flocks of wild doves sailed through the sky. A lone shalik in flight suddenly gave out a shrill note. A little distance away, a council of sparrows sat in deliberation. The breeze carried the scents of myriad flowers, soils, and pools.

Moti saw nothing, heard nothing, smelt nothing. She enjoyed the solitude of the taalpukur only when she removed the sari-end from her upper body and wrapped it round her waist. That nobody could see her in this state—her body laid bare—amused Moti no end.

If she skipped housework, Kusum rebuked her. Moti used to enjoy the leisure earned by avoiding work sitting by the taalpukur, pondering over her future. Unless she began by praying for Sudeb's death, Moti seemed unable to contemplate the future properly. Her cherished desire was to get married into a rich family, with a groom like Shashi. There would be no work, no rebuke, no quarrel, no vulgarity; everyone would be neat and tidy, would say sweet things, play cards, listen to songs on the gramophone, and—and only love the bride of the family; lifting her face by the chin, they would keep saying: our dear sweet bride, our darling bride; if a bride is not like this, she is nothing!

They'll say: she has brought light into our family!

Endless were her dreams: she is sitting in a corner of a big room, sparkling all over with ornaments, wearing a colourful sari, Moti's sandalwood-bedecked face under the veil blushing in coyness. Her breath is short from elation; the noises of the big household of a rich family reach her ears. Someone from the neighbourhood looking like Shashi's sister comes and makes her acquaintance. A woman as beautiful as Jamini Kabiraj's wife, perhaps Moti's sister-in-law, placing a paan tray before her says: Make paan, Bou. O little Bou, do make paan.

Then someone said: One of you, serve *Bouma* her food.

While returning home from the great festival of nature near the taalpukur, Moti vehemently wished for that accursed Sudeb to die.

Of late, Kusum had been frequently picking a quarrel with Moti. Without anybody knowing, she had started teasing and taunting Moti mercilessly, making references to Shashi.

She would say, 'Do you feel unwell, Moti? Is that why you're sitting quietly? Alas, tch-tch! Shall I send for Chhoto-babu? He will examine you and give you medicines.'

'Why do you pick on me, Bou? What wrong have I done you?'

'Your eyes are brimming with tears. If Chhoto-babu happens to see this, his heart will break!'

Moti said, 'Even Yama won't take you! Death to you, die!'

Kusum went on, regardless, 'Do you know, Chhoto-babu loses his sleep thinking of you? Sitting up all night, he keeps calling your name over the prayer beads—Moti, Moti, Moti. If you're married to Sudeb, Chhoto-babu will surely drown himself in the taalpukur!'

'You wretch, you go drown yourself in the taalpukur! Then keep hovering as a *shakchunni*!'[53]

Moti made to leave the place; how could she be a match for Kusum in a war of words? But Kusum would not spare her. She caught hold of her hand. Then bending over her face, fixing her with a sharp gaze and uttering each word through clenched teeth, she said, 'Don't you have any shame? You're such a big girl—aren't you ashamed? You scarcely get to eat. You're an illiterate daughter of a milkman: compared to Chhoto-babu, you're nothing but scum. Why do you try to act so clever then? That's exactly why Chhoto-babu is so annoyed that he has stopped coming altogether.'

A furious Moti bit Kusum's hand. Kusum let go of Moti and turning the bitten hand over and over kept inspecting the marks left by the teeth.

'You bit me! You dared to bite me! Just wait and see what I do to you.'

What would she do? What would Kusum do to her? Moti's heart kept pounding. What if she were to tell Chhoto-babu?

Moti thought that if Chhoto-babu came to know, he would be very angry with her.

A little while later she began to hover around Kusum. At one point she plucked up enough courage to ask her, 'Did it hurt, Bou? Let me see.'

Kusum was unforgiving. Mimicking Moti, she said, '*Did it hurt, Bou*? After biting me, she's come to act coy!'

Moving to the veranda Moti stood holding the bamboo pillar of the house, and thought: what a terrible woman Bou is! She will surely tell.

Aunt could be seen through the open door of her room. Of late she had lost her voice; any attempt to speak ended merely in low sounds producing no articulate word. When she saw Moti, she motioned to her to come near. Raising her head and frantically pointing her finger into her mouth, she indicated her thirst. But Moti made no move for quite some time even though she saw her.

She kept saying, 'Wait, wait, I'm coming. What's the hurry?'

Mokshada asked, 'Who's calling, Moti?'

'It's Aunt; she wants water.'

4

The Durga puja[54] of that year was due in the month of Kartik. By the time Sen-didi's pustules started to suppurate, the festivals were knocking at the door. They were no simple matter. At the house of the village *zamindar* Shital-babu there would be a three-night jatra, a puppet show and fireworks display; then there was the fair of Saatgaon, to say nothing of the puja itself. An intense excitement had enlivened the somnolent life of the village. Only Shashi was too busy this year, tending to Sen-didi.

The jatra began on the first day of the puja. The troupe used to arrive well in advance. At the time of booking every year, Shital-babu said to their manager, 'Make it a point of coming one or two days early so you can sleep off the exhaustion of the journey, and then take the stage.'

This year the assigned party was not a local one. The headquarters of Binodini Opera were in the heart of Calcutta. Mathura Saha of Bajitpur had to visit Calcutta frequently in connection with his business. On his son's marriage sometime back, he had hired this company. Hearing of its much-acclaimed performance, Shital-babu had made an advance booking at that time.

The Binodini Opera had arrived the previous evening. The big company that it was, it carried a good many large wooden trunks. The public was satisfied. The manager of the company was *BA-failed*; but when people heard that there were two *BA-passed* actors in the party, they got excited.

'*Thetar*![55] Eh?'

'No, it is jatra. Notice the opera tag in its name!'

'That's good, jatra is of course better!'

The estate office at Saatgaon had been vacated to accommodate the party. Not all of them had mosquito nets; but Kumud had one. He had a good sleep at night. In the morning he came to meet Shashi.

Shashi was dumbstruck. 'Kumud! You!'

'No, not really,' laughed Kumud. 'I am Prabir.'

Shashi couldn't quite follow. 'Prabir? Who Prabir?'

'Binodini Opera party is right in the village. There's great excitement all around. Didn't you get the news?'

'You've come with the jatra party? You are in jatra?'

It was almost beyond belief. Kumud had changed a lot. He didn't have the old lustre in his face, nor the careless unruliness in his hair. Even at this early hour of the morning, he had applied some cosmetics before turning up to meet Shashi. Nevertheless, for all the changes, there was no mistaking that this was indeed the same Kumud who had on one occasion explained, without the help of a guide book, an abstruse poem by Shelley in their prescribed anthology—and who had interpreted Mona Lisa's smile!

'Yes, I am in jatra,' said Kumud. 'I play the role of Prabir, I play Lakshman, I play Chandraketu,[56] and many more. I speak my lines at the top of my voice. I have won seven hundred medals.'

Shashi was amazed. 'Let's go in. Sit down and I'll listen to all you have to tell.'

Shashi took Kumud into his room and once again said, 'I just can't believe it is you, after so many years, Kumud! We are meeting after so long! It's incredible!'

Kumud said as he looked around the room sitting on the bed, 'What's so surprising about it? We've been touring the villages of Bengal, goodness knows how many, for three years now. This time, it's your village.'

'Why did you join a jatra party?'

'That's a long story, Shashi. My family threw me out one day. I found myself a job. They too chucked me out—would you want a chap in your office to show up every other day? I roamed about aimlessly, until I came upon this Binodini Opera in Berhampore. Drawn by their performance, I made the acquaintance of the manager. He is a good fellow, Shashi. After a test, he took me in on a salary of seventeen rupees a month. After playing the part of an army chief on a couple of occasions, I found the range of my voice; I learned to declaim emotionally. In one year, I was made the main actor. Now they give me eighty rupees a month—for up to eight shows; and for each extra performance, a bonus of five rupees. You don't know how cordially I'm treated by them! A grand success, isn't it?' Kumud laughed.

Shashi grinned too. 'You'd end up in a jatra party—I could scarcely ever have imagined it, Kumud.'

'Could I have imagined it myself?'

Finding a lull in the conversation, Shashi said, 'Today you must have your meal here and stay all day.'

'All right.'

Deep inside Shashi was very happy. Not simply because of their reunion after so long as because of Kumud's climbdown from his high pedestal. He did not have that careless, unthinking arrogance anymore; he no longer regarded himself as different from and superior to others. This much Shashi had observed from the very beginning today. He had all along felt small and inconsequential before Kumud. Ever since he had heard the stories of Kumud's delinquencies, he had felt with envy that he did not have as much courage of conviction, strength of mind or daring as Kumud did. He had thought that lacking such an extraordinary personality, his life was a waste. Today, Kumud's slight unease, his forced ease of manner, and his steep descent into a jatra party seemed to have dragged him even lower than Shashi. His friend no longer seemed to him a venerable elder.

'Your room is quite neatly done up,' said Kumud. 'Although you're living in a village, you haven't turned countrified, I see.' He smiled again. In contrast with his old smile, this one seemed timid, even contrite. 'Do you know, Shashi, how long it is since I have been inside anyone's house? Four years. The domestic ambience is charming. Did you marry?'

'No.'

'You didn't? The tidy room proclaimed itself as the handiwork of a housewife. Who has done it, then? Your sister? The one I saw in the courtyard?'

'No, she's not my sister; she's my niece, granddaughter of my aunt. I do have a sister, though; she's small, eight years old. Far from tidying things, she makes a mess. Under my bed is her playroom. Look, the dolls are all sleeping there in rows. Now it's time for them to wake up. Khuki's[57] due to come in any moment. Make an effort to be friendly with her; she's a clever girl, very intelligent. I'm her teacher, so I know. She's very quick to learn. I will get her admitted to school next year.'

Then Shashi shook his head, muttering, 'I say I will, but God only knows whether it will happen. My father doesn't approve of all this. He might just say, "Look at my son; with all his learning, he has turned disobedient. Who knows what the daughter will turn out to be? No, no, you had better not put her in school. Do teach her, but only at home."'

Kumud was watching the expression on Shashi's face. He said, 'Convince him that one just can't afford not to send girls to schools these days.'

'Convince whom? Baba? He's old-fashioned.'

Changing the topic, Shashi said, 'Did you ask who cleans the room? There's no dearth of helping hands. Remember this is Bengal, where one man earns and a host of others live off him. There's always someone to do the tidying up. But then'—he paused here to give his friend a meaningful look—'my room I do all by myself.'

Shashi would have to visit Jamini Kabiraj's wife. There was no neglecting this work. So after treating his friend to some sweets, he took his leave.

The custom of purdah was not strictly observed in the village, but that applied only to the known faces. In the morning, the women of Shashi's house were used to going about all their chores within the inner quarters. Kumud looked through the open door with eager eyes, watching the activities and movements in the large household as closely as he could, when a small boy came and shut the door. Kumud was hurt. He thought to himself: I was of course not looking at them? I was only watching them work, what they were trying to do together.

Putting on his shirt Kumud went out to take a round of the new place. It was difficult to keep sitting all alone in a room of the inner quarters bearing the guilt of having witnessed the private heartbeats of a family.

Once he was outside the house, the first object to catch Kumud's eyes was the high mound of earth on the far side of the palm grove behind Haru Ghosh's house. He proceeded in that direction. It is beyond the ken of mortals to figure out who in this deep loneliness of the palm grove rewarded Kumud richly for all the virtues he had acquired in his life, ignoring for the time being the tally of his sins. Perhaps the insult meted out unfairly to him by the women of Shashi's house was made good by the impartial deity of life in the form of the morning breeze, the chirping birds, and the age-old secluded peace guarded by the tall palm trees. Kumud did not know that there could be such a place in the world except the inner rooms of a happy family that could so easily make one *sentimental*. But again, did he also know that this unaccountable joy was perhaps the ultimate curtain-raiser to his death?

When he came up to the bank of the taalpukur, he suddenly felt he had trod on something soft but firm like rubber. Instantly, a yellow-coloured creature rose up to his knee and dug its teeth in, its lower part coiling around his leg.

The tally of his sins in life was also not small; after a few minutes of the extraordinary reward for his virtues, this was his punishment. Kumud removed the head of the snake from his knee by clutching its neck.

'Snake, snake!' He raised an alarm.

Moti was the first to arrive, somehow wrapping a dry sari over her dripping body.

Kusum could not run like her; she came later.

Moti said, 'That's a *dhnora* snake. It lives in water; it is not poisonous.'

Kumud was terribly afraid of death. He did not trust Moti's words, until Kusum came and confirmed them. Even so, he made a tourniquet with his handkerchief above the knee and said to Moti, 'Go call Shashi, khuki. Let him check in case there is venom. You know Shashi, I suppose? He lives in the same area as you; he's a doctor.'

Kusum smiled slyly and said, 'Go, then, O khuki. Call Chhoto-babu.' Kumud did not like the way she smiled.

So when Kusum asked him, 'How are you related to Chhoto-babu?', he answered briefly, 'No relation; a friend.'

Kusum said, 'In a sense, Chhoto-babu is like one of our own; he comes visiting every morning and evening.'

Even after hearing this, Kumud was in no mood to end up taking Kusum for a relative. He said, 'Why does dhnora not have venom?'

'Do all snakes have venom? Dhnora is a water snake. It bit me once. Maybe it was this particular snake. One day, very early, I was bathing in this pond, when Chhoto-babu came walking to the bank casually and stood chatting. The snake bit me here,' and Kusum pointed to her liver, possibly under the impression that her heart was there. "A snake has bitten me, Chhoto-babu," I cried out. Hearing this, his face—.'

'What about his face?' Kumud was curious. 'It turned pale?'

'It became ashen.'

'And nothing happened to *you*?'[58]

Kumud had used the familiar '*tumi*' for Kusum. Kusum took umbrage at being so addressed and retorted, 'You haven't learnt how to talk to people, I see. Sure you're a gentleman?'

After this, both of them being restrained, there was no further talk. The palm trees stood silently. A kingfisher plopped down into the taalpukur.

After spending the whole day talking to Shashi, Kumud took his leave in the late afternoon.

'The play starts early in the evening. You will surely come, won't you, Shashi?'

'Of course! I certainly will.'

The vast paddy field stretched out from behind Haru's house up to Saatgaon. Walking past the taalpukur bank along the ridges of the field, Kumud reached the estate office of Saatgaon. He had been expecting Moti at the taalpukur. But as she was busy with preparations for going to the jatra show, she had found no time to come to the pond. Kusum was cooking; all the meals had to be completed before the evening. Moti silently did all her bidding.

Paran was indifferent in all matters. With the arrival of evening, the busier his wife and sister got the more languid Paran felt, his spirits drooping. He had tried to chat with Kusum, sitting in the kitchen. As she had no time to chat, she had not indulged him, saying, 'Why don't you go and sit smoking in the veranda, my dear sir? I can't stand the sight of men hanging around their wives.' Paran had always felt bad at Kusum's rebukes. But the low spirits got transformed into a stoic detachment and drowsy languor too soon to allow him to get angry. At times, Kusum seemed to him to be very childish. It was as though she had grown only physically and not mentally since becoming his bride at the age of fourteen.

When he saw Mokshada put on a clean sari, Paran asked, 'Are you too going to the jatra show, Ma?'

'No. To think that I'll go to the jatra!'

If pressed insistently, Mokshada was more than willing to go. But no one there would so much as ask her, which was a foregone conclusion to her. So she had already arranged with the old aunt of the Santras[59] that the two of them would go to watch the show together. Then, she would have the excuse after coming back home that she was not in the least interested to go, but what could she do if someone prevailed upon her and virtually dragged her away?

'Then where are you going dressed in clean clothes?' Paran asked.

'To the Santras', my son. Jadu's aunt has sent for me.'

Kusum burst upon the scene. 'You can go there tomorrow, Ma; make it tomorrow. You know we'll be out, and you're on your way to the Santras! Who's going to stay back then?'

Was that Mokshada's concern? Whoever liked could stay.

She said, 'You're going to the jatra; why don't you arrange for it yourself, child? What do I know about that? Why do you drag an old person into everything? I have a host of personal problems to worry about.'

Kusum replied sharply, 'Look, everyone has problems in family life. Why do they not sit back at home worrying about their problems? Why act hostile? I knew there would be a spanner in the works at the last moment.'

Perhaps Mokshada felt slightly ashamed. Maybe it struck her that an elderly person should not make such fuss over going to a jatra show. She agreed to stay back, and sat down in glum silence.

After finishing the cooking, Kusum served food to her husband and then sat down with her sister-in-law, eating together off the same plate. While Paran ate his fill, to Kusum and Moti it seemed as if the food wouldn't go down their throats. They somehow finished their meal, picking and choosing and wasting. The more the day wore on the more anxious they grew, lest the show should begin. Asking Moti to go and dress up, Kusum wound up the work in the kitchen. There was no time now to go to the pond. Sitting under the mango tree in a corner of the courtyard, she quickly scrubbed the plates with a dump of cinders at the foot of the tree. This facility she had arranged early in the afternoon. There was no telling how much water she had drawn today carrying a pitcher at either side of her hip to fill all the pots and pans.

Moti said, 'Let me lend a helping hand, Bou; that'll hasten the work. Shall I?'

'No.' Kusum did not believe that Moti was prompt at work. She would spend ten minutes doing the work that needed one.

'Do as you're told, will you? You'll take a good hour just to put on your sari!'

At some point of time, even before the dusk had ended, all the work was finished. What was left was just a bit here and there, and it would make little difference whether it was done or not. Pursued by Kusum, both Paran and Moti had finished dressing up. Going to get dressed herself, now at last she smiled slightly to see the two of them. In his shirt topped with a scarf, Paran looked almost like a Babu[60] while Moti in her striped sari looked lovely. Kusum envied Moti's light, youthful body. It would perhaps have been better if she herself was not so plump. Striped saris she too had. But these days she felt shy to wrap her body in a sari with coloured lines.

When they reached the venue, the jatra was yet to begin. Behind the curtain of laced bamboo-strips the scramble for vantage positions had begun. Everyone wanted to sit closest to the curtain, be it an eleven-year-old girl, whose social movements had just been restricted by custom, or her fifty-year-old grandmother. Kusum was an expert in such matters. At one point she slipped into a ten-inch slot in the first row near the curtain by pushing and shoving, and once there, there was no dislodging her. Behind Kusum, Moti, who had followed her *as the thread follows the needle*, to quote a Sanskrit metaphor, ended up practically on the lap of Charan Datta's wife, brushing against Kusum's back. When the lady started pushing her, Moti hugged Kusum's waist desperately.

Kusum turned around and with flashing eyes told Charan Datta's wife, 'Why are you pushing the girl, pray? Want me to curse and swear? Move a bit, leave some space. Everyone will sit and everyone has to see—the show isn't for you alone, is it?'

Moti found Kusum so lovable at such moments! She felt so grateful to her! A little before the show began, Kusum said, 'Look, Moti! There's Chhoto-babu.'

'I've seen him.'

So many people, lights all around, so much sound, the festive ambience went to Moti's head like the rapture of intoxication. With his folded silk chuddar placed across his shoulder, Shashi looked every inch a Babu. The moment he arrived, Moti spotted him. When she saw that no less a person than Shital-babu called him to his side, Moti's honour, along with Shashi's, knew no bounds.

The spectators had spilled onto the ground outside the canopy under the open sky. Sandwiched between two corpulent women, Moti felt uncomfortably hot. Meanwhile, the music had started. *Concert*—symphony! Oh the excitement! The anticipation of something delightful about to happen. Then the music stopped and the play began. A troupe of sixteen *sakhis*[61] came and started to dance. They wore long, upcountry skirts.

Moti said in a whisper, 'It's a man made up as a girl, isn't it, Bou?'

After the sakhis had trooped back, enter Jana[62] and Agnidev.[63] Moti had her doubts about the identity of Jana. 'She's definitely a female, isn't she, Bou?'

'Unlikely. Quiet now, let me listen!' said Kusum.

Enter Prabir in Scene 2, just after a one-page soliloquy of the goddess Ganga swearing to mete out condign punishment to her son's killer Arjuna.[64] The whole assemblage was thrilled to see him. How smartly dressed! What a charming figure of youthfulness! And the glinting sword! His dialogue delivery sent thrills rippling through the spectators. Prabir's performance was sure to click. No doubt about that! It'll bring the house down—such a princely appearance, such a resonant voice. Prabir's sweetheart Madanmanjari was there too. In the midst of so many people, Prabir went on pouring out his love in such a voice—free of inhibition and unmistakably charged with emotion—as though they were alone in the solitude of a royal garden. In a jatra, physical expression of love beyond holding hands was prohibited. That seemed to be no impediment to Prabir. Merely by words, merely by acting, he succeeded in convincing so many people that the two of them were one entity in body and mind.

Kusum and Moti were surprised.

Kusum said, 'O Moti, it's that very man.'

Moti said, 'How well he's doing it! Just like it was real!'

Kusum said with a smile, 'As if it's with you he's doing it, isn't it?

Moti said nothing; she was all ears.

Prabir was speaking:

Are you angry? Why, my innocent lass? Why do you sulk so? Why so much rebuke in the two eyes? The cloud has descended on your face; your breast heaves and swells; it seems I've scolded you, addressed foul words to you! Does this sullenness, this unsmiling sternness befit a flower, my darling, does it befit a blossom? I love thee, my dearest. I swear I love thee with all my heart. Witness, my Lord! Witness, my heart's—

Moti felt a quiver in her bosom. Kusum got impatient inwardly and thought: What prevents you, wretched girl, from saying 'I'm not angry'? Can't you force those words out of your mouth? Blessed indeed is your heart!'

Having watched the show till three in the morning, naturally they were all late in getting up the next day, everyone except Shashi and Paran. Jamini Kabiraj's wife had reached a critical stage of the disease. Rising early Shashi had his bath and went to see her. Paran could not afford to put off harvesting a couple of *bighas*[65] of crops. Moreover, if he was not present at the spot personally, half the sap of his twenty-seven date palm trees would be pilfered.

Except for the palm trees, Paran had not leased out any other trees this year. He would make his own jaggery by boiling the sap. He had decided to cultivate some radishes too on the high land this year. Shashi had told him that compost of bone added to soil gave a good harvest of radish. Paran had ten *seers* of bone dust brought for experiment; it was still lying unused. He had a lot to do.

At about noon Kumud came to Shashi's house. Shashi was not home then. Gopal had come to know that Kumud was an actor in a jatra party. He did not allow Kumud to cross the partition of the inner quarters and kept him waiting in the outer room.

'Can you play chess?' Gopal asked Kumud.

'No, sir.'

Gopal then went inside to get some sleep. Kumud—last night's conquerer of a thousand hearts male and female, Kumud—considering himself forlorn and friendless went out to the taalpukur. There he found a friend, Moti.

Did Moti visit the taalpukur ever so often on some poetic impulse? Did the lazy hours of a calm midday hang heavy on her? That was anybody's guess; but today at least she had come here on purpose. Somewhere on the bank she had lost one earring. In the excitement of the jatra, she had forgotten about it yesterday; she discovered the loss only today during her bath. She could not tell anyone out of fear. At about midday, when everyone had gone to sleep, she had come to search for it.

It was not silver or copper but gold. She was scared of the consequences.

Moti did not find the earring. What she did find was Kumud. Each felt fulfilled. Kumud was no ordinary flesh and blood of the world; he was a fairytale prince, of great prowess and virility, the quintessential lover. Yes, Kumud was not an earth-bound mortal. The best man on earth was Shashi. Kumud was not like Shashi either. Which facts about Chhoto-babu did Moti not know? She knew everything, down to the items of food he relished. Who knew anything about Kumud's food habits? The shirt-wearing Kumud was Prince Prabir. Who was Shashi after all?

'What are you looking for, young girl?' asked Kumud.

Moti told him. In fact she loved to tell, as if to lose a gold earring was an act of bravado. She said, 'If they find out at home, they'll kill me.'

'Kill you? Do they often beat you?'

'Not ordinarily, but they do when I lose something expensive. What role are you doing today?'

'Ravana,'[66] Kumud said with a smile.

'You can't be Ravana; he's so ugly!'

Kumud was pleased. 'Today I'll play Lakshman.'[67]

'And who's going to be Urmila?'[68] Moti was eager to know. 'Is it the one who acted as your wife yesterday? By the way, that person is a man, I suppose?'

'Of course, a man.'

Kumud joined Moti in searching for the earring, on both sides of the mud track from the dilapidated ghat of the taalpukur to the middle of the palm grove.

Fearing that walking further down they would be approaching their house, Moti said, 'It can't be on that side; I've searched the place thoroughly.' She thought that after Prabir was gone, she would herself search the rest of the path up to their house. Together they retraced their path to the ghat.

Moti said, 'Who knows where it fell. There's no hope of finding it anymore.'

'If it's not found, they'll beat you, won't they? Who'll beat you?'

Was Moti supposed to know who'd beat her? Someone surely would.

'Then you're in trouble.' Kumud sounded worried. 'Well, where's the other earring? Let me have a look at it.'

Moti had kept it tied to her sari-end; she handed it to him. A very ordinary earring: just a crescent with a speck of a star in its lap, the crescent dangling beneath the star.

'Don't tell anyone that you've lost your earring, Khuki.'

Unless it was detected, she would of course not tell on her own. 'But why?'

'Tomorrow I'll bring you one.'

Moti was dumbstruck. 'Where will you get it?'

'Why? Is there no goldsmith's shop in your village?'

'You'll buy one!' It seemed as if she was Prabir's even before he bought the earring!

When Kumud was gone, the ring in his pocket, Moti kept musing on this, sitting on the ghat. Giving her a gold earring was not a matter of any moment with Prabir. He had probably given so many items like this to so many other girls. Perhaps there weren't many; weren't there even one or two such girls in the jatra party?

Yet, how fantastically good Prabir must be for wanting to give an earring particularly to her!

Today they were forbidden to go to the jatra show; it was Paran's order: why should they go to the jatra every day? They went yesterday; they'll give it a miss today; tomorrow they could go again. Paran did not like their going to jatra shows. There was no reason why. It mattered little to Paran whether they slept on till ten in the morning after watching the jatra. Every day when he went out to work in the half darkness of dawn, no one in the house woke up. No one in the family was in the habit of looking after his comfort. If he had to spend half a day eating puffed rice in lieu of cooked rice, Paran was not one to complain. Still, he did not like the women of his family going to the jatra show—and going on two consecutive days at that.

'Aren't you going?' Kusum asked. 'Or is it a different rule for yourself?' She was disgruntled.

'What have you got to do with me? Are you a man?'

'If you go, I will go too.'

'I won't go then.' Sometimes Paran could be stubborn too.

'It doesn't matter whether you go or not, but I will go.'

'Go to hell.'

Whatever she might have said, Kusum made no preparations whatsoever for going. The women of a number of families in the neighbourhood would be going; Kusum could go with them. But her anger and pique would be signified more effectively by staying put than by going; thereby her obstinacy would be better preserved too. So she spent the early afternoon sleeping.

In the evening, the sounds of the music made Moti restless. Prabir was slated for Lakshman's role today. She was thrilled to imagine how he would look today. If she could, Moti would have gone all alone. Even two years ago she had gone in this way; but it was no longer possible. She was startled to think how she had grown in the last two years. But what could she do? With the enticing beats of the drums and the instruments playing, it wasn't possible to remain at home either.

Then she said to Kusum, 'Even if we don't go to the jatra show, why don't we go to see the idol?'

Paran was sitting in the veranda brooding over his financial problems. He called out, 'Come here, Moti. Listen to me.'

Moti went near. Her brother asked, 'What were you saying?'

'We'll go to see the idol.'

'Go to see the idol? All right, let's go. Then you can listen to a bit of the jatra also.'

Thus, Paran almost directly conceded defeat. But Kusum was no longer willing to go. By the time dinner and paan-making would be completed, wouldn't the play be over?

'This drum-beating is for the idol worship,' Paran said without enthusiasm, 'The play is still a long way off.'

Moti urged Kusum, 'Please, Bou, let's go. Why do you act this way?'

Kusum said, 'Where will you sit? Do you think there is any room left for you? Better to stay at home than watch jatra from the last row.'

Paran said, 'If Chhoto-babu is requested—'

Kusum flared up even more at the mention of Chhoto-babu. 'What will Chhoto-babu do? Will he create space?'

Paran said, 'The women of Chhoto-babu's family sit together with the women of the Babus' family. Didn't you notice, Moti, it's separated by a netted curtain? Chhoto-babu is treated cordially in the Babus' house. If he's approached, he'll seat you there.'

Kusum suddenly grew calm and said, 'I won't go.'

There was no persuading her. The Babus were zamindars; Shashi's family was well-off. The women of their families had so many gorgeous saris, so many costly ornaments. If Kusum were to go there wearing a coarse sari from the weaver's loom topped with a jacket bordered with a cumbrous lace, sitting in their midst (perish the thought of sitting *in their midst*—she would have to sit like a maidservant in a corner), Kusum would feel suffocated.

Finally, Moti alone went with Paran. Shashi did not need to be sought out. He was in his house. He said, 'Moti, you make such demands!' But he did not refuse to accompany them and get Moti a good seat. Rather, he felt especially proud that he could arrange a seat for Moti behind the netted curtain where the women of the Babus' family sat.

The women of Shital-babus' house used to wear silk blouses with Bombay-brand saris. Shital-babu's brother, Bimal-babu, was a resident of Calcutta; his wife and daughters even wore shoes. And the women in the two families were not few either. In the world where there is more money, there are more women and more beauty. Moti did not know this rule of the world. Which worldly rule was she aware of at all? She was an immature, foolish girl. Finding herself huddled on a twenty-square feet area of a clean cloth cover amidst a throng of dolled-up species of her own tribe, she seemed to be at her wits' end.

'What are you looking at my face for, child?' Bimal-babu's wife asked Moti.

'She's looking at your specs, Ma,' said her daughter.

Moti's heart began to pound. She had been seated at a respectable spot in the front—not among the dependent relatives. Shital-babu himself had ushered her into their midst and said, 'Sit in front. She's from Shashi Doctor's family.'

The previous day, the women from Shashi Doctor's family had put on gaudy dresses and make-up, no matter how odd the overall effect was. What a shabby dress this girl has put on today! This is what the women of Shital-babu and Bimal-babu's families thought to themselves. They were familiar with the varieties of saris and ornaments; they used to scrub their bodies until they shone. This girl was practically grimy.

Last year, when Shital-babu's daughter-in-law went into labour, she was compelled to submit her life into Shashi's hands, pending the arrival of the Civil Surgeon from Bajitpur. What a punishment it was to keep lying in bed, reading novels! Anyway, the baby boy was now sleeping peacefully under the care of a nursemaid on the first floor. The Civil Surgeon had done precious little; the baby was virtually Shashi Doctor's gift. So Shital-babu's daughter-in-law asked Moti out of curiosity, 'How are you related to Shashi Doctor?'

'He is not a relation.'

'Dear me! Not a relation? And you've come out with a stranger so late at night?'

'Why do you say stranger? I've come with my Dada.'[69]

'Who is your Dada? Which house do you belong to?'

'I'm from the Ghosh family. My father is the late Haranchandra Ghosh.'

The word soon spread. The women of Shital-babu and Bimal-babu's families were much displeased with Shashi at his audacity to thrust Haru Ghosh's daughter into their midst.[70] Those who had been sitting near Moti excused themselves on the pretext of going inside the house, and on returning took their seats elsewhere. Even though Moti now had the opportunity to be comfortable, she felt out of sorts. After all, she was not so stupid as not to perceive social slight and insult.

Meanwhile Shashi made frequent visits to the greenroom to praise Kumud, 'You're doing well, Kumud! Why didn't you join a theatre group in Calcutta?'

Pleased, Kumud said, 'You like it? I was on starvation diet for fourteen years, brother! Still, I have not yet been able to retrieve my sister-in-law from the clutches of Ravana.[71] Only after I have taken her back to Ayodhya, and made Dada king, shall I be relieved!'

Kumud laughed. 'A little later I've to go to rescue *Boudi*[72] from Ashokbon. The killing of Ravana isn't too far away. Don't miss that scene. By the way, is there any jewellery shop around?'

Shashi said, 'Jewellery shop? There's none in the village. Two goldsmith's workshops are there; they supply orders. Sometimes they may keep one or two small readymade pieces but nothing like setting up shop. Why, do you mean to buy ornaments?'

'Buy ornaments? Me? Why? Why would I buy ornaments?'

Shashi was intrigued: why did Kumud ask about a jewellery shop? That too, all of a sudden while talking about something entirely different. What was he thinking about? Kumud was a headstrong boy, and quite out of the ordinary; there was nothing under the sun he couldn't do if he really wanted to, and he did precisely what made him happy. But why did he suddenly enquire about a jewellery shop?

Shashi planned to make enquiries whether, during Binodini Opera's play at Bajitpur, anything had happened at any jewellery shop there.

The suspicion continued to prick Shashi's mind. At the same time it also occurred to him what an absurd thought he harboured! How was it even possible? Still, he decided that he would try to get news about the jewellers' shops at Bajitpur for the last two months tomorrow itself. And in advance atonement for this unfair snoop, before returning home at midnight, he also invited Kumud to lunch with them the next day at his house.

Shashi told Paran, 'Why don't you take Moti back home? How long will she keep awake?'

Paran was feeling drowsy too. 'Will she agree to go?' he said.

However, Moti came along as soon as she was called. Today she felt little pleasure in watching the show. The women of the zamindar families had soured an uncorrupted mind, which was always full to the brim with joy without any reason and which bubbled over with excitement at the slightest pretext. Moti returned home like one with a guilty conscience. Still, she wondered how beautiful those women were—each one a picture, as it were!

The place where Haru Ghosh was struck by lightning was a den of venomous snakes. Those in the palm grove near his house had no venom. Had no venom? The one that bit Kumud had no venom; it was a water snake, a dhnora. But were all snakes of the palm grove water snakes? All dhnoras? Who could tell? Moti did not know that. In the end, she had to admit that if any other snake had bitten him, he might have died.

Moti wore two dangling earrings. In the lap of the two crescents, the two stars swung too. Kumud had put the earrings on her ears with his own hands. One of them was new and shining; the other one old and faded. That was of course a problem. But however stupid Moti might be, she wasn't a complete fool—she had noticed this discrepancy. The very sight of the new earring would be a telltale sign. What would she say? What explanation would she give? If they were told that Prince Prabir had put it on her ear with his own hands, standing by the taalpukur about noon, she would be beaten to pulp to be sure. Kumud had solved this problem too.

Before reaching home (as if her home was far away!), Moti would take off both earrings; at night she would dab them with tamarind and leave them like that; in the morning if scrubbed with washing soda, both would look the same old pair, only cleaned and polished. If asked, she would say she had cleaned them with tamarind and soda. This is the explanation Moti would offer—the unalloyed truth.

Moti was startled by Kumud's presence of mind.

'If a different snake had bitten me, would I have died?' Kumud asked, 'What would you do if I had died?'

'I? What would I do? I don't know.'

She was an immature girl, totally immature. But deep inside, Moti knew everything. What did she not know? If Kumud had died that day from snakebite, she would do nothing at all: this was point number one. Moti knew. Point number two: she also knew that Kumud wished to hear from her that on his death, she would weep a little bit. Moti knew that much. The truth that she would do nothing at all and the lie that she would weep a little bit and that neither of the two ought to be uttered: if Moti did not know even this much, why did she feign ignorance by giving that intermediate reply? All things considered, Moti was by any account immature.

'And if I die now?'

'Then I would—if you die now? Forget it, one shouldn't talk of dying.'

Goodness knows where Moti had learnt all this! She must have learnt this as a matter of course, like talking, eating, and wearing clothes. No one teaches these things. Who would teach this? After this, Kumud asked Moti about many different things. No more childish questions but questions about herself, her kith and kin, their village, which Moti answered eagerly. At times, she asked him her own questions in turn. At times again, she told Kumud many unnecessary and irrelevant things on her own. Her simple look never once grew crafty; her trust never wavered. No, Moti had no worries. She knew nothing, understood nothing; everything in the world was novel to her, beyond her experience. What did she know about whether she ought or ought not to let Kumud hold her hand? Let those matters be left to the care of Kumud, to the care of Prince

Prabir. Moti did not seem to feel too bashful either. But that she suddenly lowered her eyes and smiled slightly was not something to make much of.

Of the day and the night, the progress of time around midday is the slowest. The period is seemingly endless. There is no knowing how much and in what time the sun drifted across the sky shining over the two of them. They got up and began to slowly walk towards the mound. There was plenty of dense shadow in that direction.

5

Jamini Kabiraj's wife survived the disease, thanks to the mercy of the Almighty and her good fortune, and it redounded to the credit of Shashi.

Gopal had almost stopped talking to his son of late. Not because Jamini's wife had survived, but for a different reason. At least that should be the general view. The fact of the matter was this: Shashi had been doing well in his profession. It took a fair sum of money to call in the government doctor of Bajitpur. There were many who opted for Shashi. In connection with the treatment of Jamini's wife, Shashi had not only stopped visiting distant patients but had even refused to attend calls from Nandanpur three miles away. This was at a time when Jamini Kabiraj's wife was at death's door. Provoked by Gopal, Jamini had tried, unsuccessfully, by quarrelling and insulting, to prevent Shashi from visiting her. Having failed in his attempts to send him on distant calls, Gopal had been furious with his son. Yet, neither Jamini nor Gopal had the courage to escalate tensions; both of them had begun to fear Shashi. This is one sign of a sinful mind; it tends to think that perhaps everyone knows everything. Lest a snake should come out, one hesitates to dig the earth even for an earthworm. The sun rises; so does the moon. The world is forever the kingdom of the Lord. This instinctive faith of man is not easy to wear off. Not even after one has committed a thousand sins.

'Is this how you mean to keep up your practice?' Gopal had asked Shashi. 'Won't you go to attend any calls? Will you keep refusing clients?'

He had further said, 'Will Jamini Uncle ever do you the least bit of good that you should be doing so much for him? What wisdom is there, my son, in going about doing good for others while destroying your own prospects?'

'What if my mother had been struck by such a disease?' Shashi had asked. Who knows why he had said this!

'Your mother isn't alive, right? She was lucky to escape ahead of us. Or she would have to suffer your great feats! Shame on you! You'll go to ruin, Shashi.'

After Jamini's wife got a fresh lease of life, Gopal said with an ominous gravity, 'Now then, Shashi, pay attention to your work. Jamini Uncle doesn't want you to go to their house anymore.'

'Thakurda should be handed over to the police.'

'My goodness, Shashi! What's this you're saying? What is it that you want, pray? Yes, my boy, what is really in your mind? If I proceeded to Kashi[73] leaving everything behind, would that please you? *Gurudeb*[74] was telling me just this: "Why keep dithering, Gopal? It is time you came over." And I was telling myself: Let me see Shashi somewhat settled. If I go away all at once discarding everything, he'll be saddled with too many responsibilities. But if you keep doing things like this, son, how can I stay even for another day?'

To think that Gopal would renounce the world, that Gopal would go to Kashi! Shashi had long been used to encountering this kind of ambush in preference to direct assault from Gopal. He did not weaken one bit.

'What wrong have I done, Baba? Why don't you tell me?' Shashi asked.

'You want to know? You've brought slurs upon yourself. What everybody is saying doesn't reach your years; it does reach mine. What makes you melt with pity at Jamini Uncle's wife's illness? You're a doctor; you'll go once, give medicine and come back, that's all. If you keep staying beside the patient day and night, night and day, won't people say that unless there was something from before—'

'This is a figment of your imagination, Baba.'

Since the allegation was true, it enraged Gopal even more. Gopal exchanged no further words with his son.

Not one word. Sitting in the outer room, opening journals and ledgers on the carpet, Gopal looked over the accounts, talked to debtors, intending borrowers, and seekers of counsel or favours. When Shashi crossed the room and went past, Gopal, suddenly stopping in the middle of a conversation, looked up to glance at his son. If he won't talk, let him not; would he not even let his son hear his voice? Not that really. When he saw Shashi, Gopal wished to call him and say, 'Listen, Shashi.' Suppressing this wish, Gopal couldn't utter a sound; he remained speechless.

When Shashi was gone, Gopal told one of his favour-seekers to go and ask where he was going.

If he brought back the news that it was to Jamini Kabiraj's house, Gopal simply went wild.

'Being flippant? Joking with me?'

The client looked on unblinkingly.

It took the whole of Kartik and some days of Agrahayan for the pustules of Jamini's wife to heal and fall off. The sight of her now aroused one's fear as well as pity. The small scars all over her body had left ugly reddish cavities. In due course of time, through scabbing and sloughing a number of times, some of the cicatrices would largely blend with the skin, and some would stay. At any rate, Jamini's wife lost her claim to fame. Her looks themselves were gone, not to speak of her famed beauty!

One of her eyes was damaged too.

This one loss had demoralised her most of all. The disfigurement by scars was no trivial matter to her either. Beauty was her kin, and a habit of thirty-three years. A woman is mortified even to cut off a lock of her own hair. And this was about overall beauty, her cherished possession! Even so, she could have borne it: she might have been able to console herself that hers was no longer the age of playful romanticism; what use had she now for seductive beauty? But to turn blind in one eye! Surely this was not just a loss of beauty; this amounted to turning ugly, loathsome! Now that people would snigger to look at her, what to do about that? And she had such beautiful large eyes!

'My eyesight is gone, Shashi. I've turned one-eyed.'

'What can you do after all, Sen-didi? Your life has been spared,' Shashi consoled her.

'Death would have been better than this, Shashi. Don't you think I look repulsive?'

'No, no, why repulsive? It isn't repulsive.'

What the sight of Jamini Kabiraj's wife excited in Shashi was sorrow, not repulsion. No, it wasn't repulsion.

Shashi was not that sort.

But there was no doubt that Sen-didi's worth had fallen. Shashi did not however perceive that the loss of Sen-didi's charm had been made good by his sympathy for her. Sen-didi's smile was no longer dazzling; her single eye did not adequately express deep affection any more; nobody could possibly keep looking at her face in wonder now. Words from Sen-didi's mouth, her affection, and her partiality towards him were no longer invaluable. Shashi felt sad for her, but she could no longer draw him the way she used to.

Shashi did not find time these days to come daily to see Sen-didi. Even if he came, he could not spare much time. Following his successful treatment of Jamini's wife, his practice had quickly soared. He no longer refused patients; he regularly went to attend calls, and returned with money in his pocket. He had even spent an entire night at Nandanpur: travelling expenses plus ten rupees for his visit. In the village, ten rupees would mean calling on ten patients; all of ten rupees in a single night was no trifle.

Jamini Kabiraj's wife would say, 'Have you discarded your Sen-didi, Shashi?'

'Not at all, Sen-didi. There's a huge rush of patients; I just don't have the time to come.'

'Ah, God bless you! So be it. Let there be more and more patients; be a millionaire. This is all I pray to God for day and night.' It would seem she would burst into tears. Hers was a debilitated body; emotion easily gave way to tears. 'Get married and set up house. Let your name spread throughout the land. I wish that I may live to see it.'

She would look on at Shashi, her vision of one large sunken eye misting over in intense fondness. From the other side could be heard Jamini's acolytes pounding herbs using the mortar and pestle. Jamini smoked tobacco, coughing and brooding. He did not even cross the threshold of his wife's room. He did not speak with Shashi. There was no end to his worry. Nor was it meant to be. At his age—he was over sixty—how much more could one bear? What a state! His long-married divinely beautiful wife had survived but turned so ugly one could hardly bear to look at her. And an absolute pest had descended in their midst—Shashi. Would he not even let people die?

The villagers, however, heard a different version from Jamini.

'Shashi's cure? Cure indeed! With that kind of treatment, no patient has to worry about how soon to set out for heaven. He'd all but killed her. What did he know of treatment for pox? It was I who ultimately, with lots of medicines—'

He continued, 'And how do you think she lost an eye? She took two doses of that rascal's medicine!'

All this talk reached Gopal's ears. Many villagers went and reported to Gopal that Jamini Kabiraj was an ungrateful wretch, going about slandering Gopal's son. Many chuckled to themselves as they supplied this information. The imaginative faculty of village people is sharp. By gazing at the sky in the morning they can predict rain in the afternoon. If it does not actually rain in the afternoon, the fault, of course, lay with the sky. If what people had surmised for four or five years after Gopal had brought a bride for Jamini was false, then the whole world itself was false. That is to say that the fault was everything else's except of their power of guesswork. So at the time of giving Gopal any information relating to Jamini Kabiraj, they would look at him with serious expressions while laughing inwardly.

Gopal would get angry. He went and said to Jamini, 'What's all this I hear, Uncle? Why are you slandering my son?'

'Slandering whom? Shashi?' Jamini looked surprised. 'I will slander Shashi? Do you believe this, Gopal?'

'Do it in your own house. Do it to me, I won't mind. But be careful, don't ever do it before outsiders again, Uncle.'

But Jamini was unable to restrain himself. He smarted from malice, and he ended up maligning Shashi again.

He said, 'The village will go to ruin because of that lad. Have you noticed how the fellow has had his hair cut?'

Sometimes he would even insult Shashi. But Shashi would pay no heed. Earlier, he would not tolerate anyone insulting him. These days he had attained a strange kind of patience. He did not feel at all angry at Jamini's words. The trait that Jamini had betrayed of himself during Sen-didi's illness was enough to convince Shashi that besides the clearly insane, there were many others in the world who too were mad to some extent in that they had a fantastical mania in some matter or the other. Jamini was also one of them. If Shashi were to be annoyed at his meaningless insults, he would only be enlisting himself in their tribe.

Apart from that, Shashi's mind had calmed down and attained poise in another aspect as well. It was his thirst for *intellectual romance*: something like the wisp of smoke from a steaming cup of tea, nothing more than water vapour, not tea either. Having learned to look at life, having countenanced it very incompletely and superficially, he had perceived to his amazement that life was by no means shallow or less complex here in this pond-, woodland-and mosquito-infested village. Even though he had begun his career as a doctor most reluctantly in the village, the fact that gradually he was coming to like this life was primarily and pre-eminently due to this realisation. Then there was the arrival of Kumud in the garb of a jatra performer. Kumud, the authority on the *Mona Lisa*, on Venus and Cupid, on Shelley, Byron and Whitman; whisky-drinking, waltz and foxtrot-dancing Kumud; Kumud, the lover of blue-eyed girls; Kumud his senior and superior in learning, worldliness and cleverness: fancy his appearing as an actor of a jatra group! Were all these to go in vain? Shashi's mind had become calm and composed. Somehow he had realised that the *kidskin* shoes, the splendid sari, and the gorgeous blouse were what mattered. Another thing that counted was Kumud's present earnings. As for looks, he definitely had them. That too was somewhat necessary, as also an *I-don't-care* attitude. The stage was set for romance.

Shashi had realised this. But it was no simple calculation. Neither was the co-existence of so many criteria easy to bring about; he admitted this as well, and also that it was not a bad idea. It was an indication of the tremendous progress of human civilisation: a splendid enjoyment, something to covet. He would definitely have been the gainer had he achieved it. But just because he had been deprived, there was no justification for nursing regret either.

Shashi had also realised that if life was not given due respect, it gave no joy. Exchange of honour for joy: that was the edict of the *jiban-debata*, the deity of life.

Hence Shashi respected life to the utmost. Be it a constricted life, a pallid, weak and crippled life—the whole of life. He respected his own life more than any other.

Meanwhile on another occasion Shashi had quarrelled with Kusum.

One night, Kusum suddenly had a pain in her stomach; unbearable, excruciating pain. There was no alternative but to call Shashi. At night, particularly on winter nights, to be woken from sleep and called upon to attend patients was something Shashi had not got quite used to yet. His immediate reaction was annoyance, no doubt. Stomach pain! For stomach pain, whoever in Haru Ghosh's family had ever called a doctor? Could they not massage hot oil? But seeing the intensity of her pain Shashi could not persist with his ire.

Colic? Who knows?

'What did you eat, Paraner Bou?'

The reply came from Moti. 'Bou hasn't eaten anything today. After a tiff with Dada, she's fasted all day. A married woman, her husband alive, fasting on *ekadashi*[75] day! Won't she suffer?'

This was terrible, this fasting on the ekadashi day. No one other than Kusum would probably have had the guts to do such a thing.

'Haven't you eaten anything, Paraner Bou?'

'I have. Why wouldn't I? I've eaten fish scales.' Kusum was wilting in pain as she said this.

So she had not fasted on ekadashi day. That she had quarrelled was the truth; Moti had unnecessarily mentioned ekadashi. Shashi was suddenly irritated. Why did Moti make such irresponsible remarks without verifying the facts? But what had happened to Kusum? Colic? Stomach pain is a very puzzling ailment.

There's no way you can check it; you can't find out whether it is true or false; no thermometer or stethoscope can help. You have to take the patient's word for it: if she says the pain is on the right side, you accept it; if she says it's a stabbing pain, it is that; if a dull nagging pain, likewise; you can't doubt her. Hearing Kusum's report, Shashi had understood nothing. He had called Paran to one side.

After some time, back home, he had sent the medicine; he did not go again himself.

That was his fault. Next day, going to enquire about her condition, he found that Kusum was livid.

'I didn't die. Here's your fee.'

Kusum did indeed take out the two rupees she had tied to her sari-end and put them before Shashi. It took Shashi no time to realise why she was going about her chores with the money tied to her sari-end.

Moti said, 'What audacity, Bou!'

Bnuchi was not in the house; she had gone away to her in-law's house quite a few days ago. Had she been present, she would have said something different, something harsher, more acerbic.

Kusum said quietly, 'Ma is cleaning the cowshed all by herself; please go, Moti, my good girl, go help her. Let me take Chhoto-babu's advice on your marriage with Sudeb. See that Ma doesn't come running, leaving her work. Finish what you have to do, go straight for your bath and then come. Chhoto-babu will wait till then.'

Kusum knew how to give orders too. And why should she not? Hadn't the whole family, coming together as one to flatter her, extracted her pair of bangles for buying cows? Why should she then relent? Occasionally, at times of some pressing need such as now, when she would quarrel with Shashi, everyone must obey her orders.

When Moti was gone, Shashi said, 'Didn't your stomach pain subside with my medicine yesterday, Bou?'

'Medicine indeed! Just a couple of tiny white pills—not medicine but rubbish! Couldn't you come yourself? What if the pain did not subside after the medicines?'

This is called ingratitude. So the pain had subsided. Getting up at night, coming in person and examining her, he sent medicine; taking it she got relief too. Yet Kusum was not content. Shashi felt vexed.

'You carry everything to excess, Bou.'

'What was that? Excess, is it? Yes, Chhoto-babu, I do things in excess. Say whatever you like, but examining the chest for all of an hour, for a malaria case, I'm not one to do that.'

She would examine the chest—was she a doctor? It was beyond Shashi to fathom Kusum's mind. For her bellyache yesterday, if he had listened to her heart beats, pressing the stethoscope to her chest for an hour, would she have been pleased? The treatment for Kusum's headache was perhaps to massage her feet. He was a doctor worth his salt. Could he afford to indulge such whims?

'Where did you get the money, Paraner Bou?'

'No matter where, I'm paying for your visit. Take it.'

'I can't, Bou, if you don't say where you got it from.'

'Why? Do you think I stole it?'

Shashi thought: this was the opportunity. If I make a joke out of this utterance, maybe she will laugh and calm down.

'It would hardly be strange if you did. Unless you steal, where will you get any money? Do you have an income?'

Kusum said, 'My father earns a lot. Even so, can we compare with you? It is not through putting a knife to people's throats that we are rich. So if you call us poor, we're poor; call us thieves, we're thieves.'

Shashi returned home in low spirits.

He felt morose all day. Kusum had dented the shell of education and culture that he had carefully preserved around himself. She was not wrong. Had his father not been poorer than Haru Ghosh once upon a time? It could also not be denied that Gopal had made his pile by usury and unfair deals alone. Kusum's father was far more cultured than Gopal. He occasionally wrote her letters. It was beyond Gopal's ability to write such fine letters in so beautiful a hand. On the envelope he wrote Kusum's name in Bengali and the rest of the address in English. Gopal did not know even A, B, C, D. While snubbing Shashi, Kusum had perhaps remembered all this too.

That the people of the village called Shashi 'Chhoto-babu' scarcely did him any credit. It was just a title, a mere name, not an honorific. In his childhood, Gopal's clients used to call him Chhoto-babu out of affection, which name somehow had spread in the village and stuck. Overlooking all this, had he been growing conceited? Had he begun to behave with everyone like a young master?

Shashi's self-esteem was seriously wounded. He wondered if Kusum might laugh to herself to see his ways. Maybe she thought this was how an upstart behaved. Having conducted his studies with his father's ill-gotten money, why did he go about with such supercilious nonchalance?

Kusum came to seek his forgiveness some four days later; about noon, stealthily, like a thief!

At the rear of Shashi's house was an orchard. Litchis, mangoes, jackfruit, cauliflowers, strong-smelling *knathali chnapa* and red-calyx shiuli grew there. She crossed the garden and standing outside the window said in a whisper, 'Listen, Chhoto-babu!'

Coming round into the garden, Shashi saw that by trampling upon it, Kusum had almost buried the rose sapling he so cherished.

'Why did you trample the plant, Bou? You have to watch what you're going to stand on.'

Even though she had battered Shashi's cherished plant to start with, Kusum's purpose was served. Shashi ended up forgiving all her faults, all the wrongs Kusum had so far done him. Kusum said she had not slept well for four nights. Shashi took her at her word. He believed her even though he knew that Kusum was used to telling lies without batting an eyelid. For the proof was manifest in her face, and there were tears in her eyes. Kusum further said that she would be going away to her father's house in a few days. Her father had written to her. She had been feeling extremely bad about going away after needling Chhoto-babu. That's why she had come to ask his forgiveness.

'Nobody can stand the sight of me because of this nature of mine. I have no control over what I say.'

Shashi asked, 'What exactly had happened to you that night, tell me? Be honest.'

'I had stomach pain.'

'Show me your tongue.'

Kusum stuck her tongue out shyly.

'Why, it's clean.'

'Why should the tongue not be clean, Chhoto-babu?'

No, there was no reason why her tongue should not be clean. Kusum's health was no external show; she was quite robust internally as well. Shashi liked Kusum for this. Once in ten years, one night she might have just a pain in the stomach, and that was all. This was ideal. If the womenfolk of all Bengali families possessed such good health, the race would not be about to sink, thought Shashi.

Looking through the window with eager eyes into the room, Kusum said, 'Can I have a quick look around your room, Chhoto-babu?'

'Let me call Sindhu or someone else.'

'No. Let me do it alone.'

Kusum saw Shashi's room all alone. Shashi knew that it was not proper. But he did not object either. He thought: if she has no fear of a scandal, I couldn't care less. After all, I didn't call her.

Having seen Shashi's room, Kusum complimented it on its decoration. But unlike a museum, what was there to see in one's bedroom? The two big cupboards had five shelves each. One cupboard was packed with books but could not accommodate all, the rest being stacked on top. On the upper three decks of the other, medical books were arranged and on the lower two were surgical instruments, all sparkling clean. Which one was for what, asked Kusum. It seemed as though she was in no hurry; she could spend as much time in Shashi's room as she liked. The walls were hung with a few pictures and photographs, which Kusum looked at casually. The photographs were of members of Shashi's family, requiring no comment. Pointing to the one of Kumud, she asked, 'It's that man, isn't it?' Last year, Shashi had kept a sheaf of inflorescence of paddy hanging on the wall, which Kusum was very pleased to see. 'What's in the wooden box? Medicine? Let me have a look. That small cupboard is stacked with medicines; then why in the box again?

'Do you sleep alone in this room, Chhoto-babu?'

'Yes, I sleep alone.'

'When is a wife expected? Soon I'll be going to my father's house, Chhoto-babu. I won't come back again.'

'Won't come back again? How can that be?' Shashi was taken aback.

Kusum pondered for a moment. 'I will come, but much later on. It could be the next year or the year after; nothing is certain. Well, I'll go now, Chhoto-babu.'

'How will you go? Baba is sitting in the far side veranda. He has woken up from his nap.'

'So what do I do?' She didn't seem particularly worried, though. She was used to keeping her head in times of danger; she was neither agitated nor perplexed.

Shashi said, 'Sit down for a while. Baba will soon be going to the outer room.'

'Then close the door. In case he happens to see.'

Who would have known that Fate would make Gopal, on waking up, sit in that particular veranda—today after seven years?

After the autumn festival season, the state of health of Gaodiya gradually improves. The incidence of malaria becomes less frequent, cholera stops altogether; people's appetite increases; fish and milk become cheap. A few people die of pneumonia and influenza; that's not a big deal. In the months of Agrahayan and Paush[76] the water level in the canal goes down considerably. Towards the end of Magh[77] the small ponds dry up. In Chaitra, the water is just one or two arm-lengths deep in most ponds. If there is no rain in Baishakh, they began to dry up. Then there would be great scarcity of water in the village. The people of Gaodiya, Saatgaon and Ukhara survive on the water of the big pond in front of Shital-babu's house. In that pool of the Babus, none but their family members are permitted to dip their bodies. A sentry guards the pool, a stick resting on his shoulder. When Shital-babu's sons, nephews and the small girls begin to bathe, stirring up the water, resting on his stick he beams a smile. Dipping pitchers except at the ghat is strictly prohibited for the villagers. After Shital-babu's children finish their bath, the water at the ghat is left turbid for two to three hours.

Someone coming to collect water might say, 'Can't you tell the boys to be a bit careful, *Darwan-ji*?

The Hindi-speaking sentry would say, 'Whose lake is this? Yours?'

He was right; the lake was indeed the Babus'.

But the month of Baishakh was still some time away. Who could tell whether there would be much rain and storm this year? People of the village used to spend the winter happily. *Koi* fish, various species of *magur* and the tubular *sholmachh*[78] were available in plenty. Those who had small ponds would wait until they dried up when they baled out water and scrabbled up a basketful of fish, among which fry such as *kholshe* and *lattha* predominated.

In this land which is a maze of canals and ditches, there are no good roads. But deciding to spend the winter in his native home, Bimal-babu arrived in the village with his family in a car.

Bajitpur had its cars, but for Gaodiya to have one!

Kusum said to Shashi, 'I remember the year I rode a car—the year before my marriage when I had gone to Calcutta with my father.'

'Do you remember that?'

Kusum was surprised. 'Why should I not remember? How long has it been since after all? Eight or nine years. How old am I do you think?'

'Twenty-five?'

'No! Twenty-two.'

The negotiation of Moti's marriage with Sudeb had fallen through. Of late, Kusum had not been making any reference to the matter. It looked as though it did not concern her at all whether Moti got married or not. Even if occasionally Paran broached the subject at night, Kusum would yawn, saying she had no opinion.

On some days, she fell asleep without saying anything. Meanwhile Nitai was pursuing the matter so insistently as if it was not Sudeb's marriage but his own. After consulting Shashi once more, Paran finally told Nitai that he was not going to marry off Moti to Sudeb. Nitai could not accept the rejection lying down. He held out carrots, counselled that this was for the best, and then lost his cool. No, Paran wouldn't agree.

'Chhoto-babu said no, is that it? When Haru-da died, who went to burn him, eh? Who lent his shoulder to the bier? Was it Chhoto-babu? When Chhoto-babu has forbidden, no questions asked, there ends the matter, is it? Chhoto-babu's word is gospel, indeed!'

'Can't I reason myself? I'm going to get Moti married to someone from the town—into a cultured family.'

This one thing Paran might as well not have said.

Anyway, thereafter Sudeb filed a suit against Nitai at Bajitpur. The charges were serious: defalcation, unlawful confinement, and physical assault. To vent his ire he did complain indeed, but whether he could prove anything is doubtful. Nitai was a prudent man with self-control. He was not one to do anything on the spur of the moment; never one to commit a misdeed leaving incriminating evidence.

One day on his way back from Bajitpur, Nitai came across Shashi on the road. In connection with this suit, in spite of suspecting Nitai as guilty, it was Sudeb whom Shashi was angry with. Nitai was Sudeb's uncle; instead of going for litigation, could Sudeb not have taken some other course of action? Moti's name would crop up in the court; Paran would be required to stand witness: it would be a nasty affair.

But Shashi did not discuss the case with Nitai. He said, 'You owe me some money, Nitai.'

'I shall pay up, Chhoto-babu; once the month of Magh ends, I'll repay it in full.'

Shashi looked worried and said, 'Magh? All right, do that. But why did you not give Lali's calf to Paran? Lali has stopped milking, I'm told?'

'Why should I give Lali's calf to Paran, Chhoto-babu?'

'Why, was it not agreed at the time of selling Lali that Paran would get the first calf?'

'No, Chhoto-babu, there was no such talk. Paran has told you a lie. I had bought Lali from Haru-da; what would Paran know?'

Shashi said indifferently, 'Anyway, if there was no such talk, then there is nothing to say. Day after tomorrow send us six seers or so of milk. They'll be preparing something at home, I was told.'

Shashi was gone. Nitai called him back and said, 'Listen, Chhoto-babu. At Bajitpur I met *Jamai-babu*.[79] He will be coming to this village tomorrow morning.

'Which Jamai-babu?'

'The second one.'

Shashi did not know this. That Nandalal was coming to this village without any intimation to them was no surprise to him either. Immediately after marriage, Nandalal had cut off all connections with his father-in-law's house. He never wrote letters or replied to any. In the beginning, Bindu used to write occasionally, and secretly, against her husband's orders. After Nandalal had found out, she had to wind up even the correspondence with her own people. Once she had come here for two or three days, that too unknown to her husband, when Nandalal was away in Bombay on business for fifteen days. Such matters are not something to remain under wraps for long. On returning from Bombay, one day Nandalal asked his wife, 'Did you go to Gaodiya?'

Even as she trembled in fear, Bindu tried to shrug off the matter with a slight smile. 'I went for a day; just one day. I heard news about Baba's grave illness. Are you angry?'

'*Are you angry?*' He mimicked. 'Daughter of a lowborn!'

A wife foisted on him, a wife accepted on pain of death, a wife who knew nothing of studies, singing or dancing meant a wasted life.

But Nandalal had not abandoned Bindu—who knows why! Maybe from a sense of duty; maybe from some fancy; maybe because Bindu was pliable at will she had a value of sorts for him, who knows! Why Nandalal gave her so many saris and ornaments was another mystery. Had Bindu come to her father's house wearing borrowed ornaments? Was it to pretend that she had indeed got what she hadn't? Who could tell! An unknown mystery of life had engulfed the Bindu of Gaodiya—the indefinable mystery of Calcutta, which Shashi had not been able to unravel even during his stay in that city for studies. Nandalal used to insult him in a way; but Shashi would not desist from going. On *bhai phnota*,[80] on several occasions Shashi had gone to participate in Bindu's ritual. Did he not see ornaments all over her body then? No. The explanation that Bindu did not like to go about the day-to-day mundane life in the women's quarters bearing the burden of ornaments was falsified by what he saw and heard. Shashi used to think: so is Bindu happy? One thing he did not understand, however; nor was it a matter that one outside the family could understand. Nandalal kept Bindu in a different house, alone. If Bindu was asked how long she had stayed in the house where Nandalal's family had been living for twenty-five years, she avoided the question; neither would she tell how long she had been living in the new house. 'We had frequent quarrels, so I came here,' was all the explanation she would offer. 'I'm quite fine here and independent; there, they keep on quarrelling!' and then she smiled in a manner that suggested as if what she had said was the whole truth. There was no dearth of servants and maids; a doorkeeper on duty too. The rooms were filled with costly furniture—immoderately so. Nandalal had provided utmost luxury for Bindu. The entire house was redolent of perfume.

Did Nandalal love Bindu then? On so many occasions on his visits to Bindu's house, Shashi had found that Bindu's demeanour was amiable; she was ordinarily dressed. On enquiring, he would be told that Nandalal would not turn up anytime soon. Then again on other days, he had found Bindu was not at ease; her behaviour was enigmatic. She would be engaged in decking herself up elaborately with cosmetics, and could spare no time to talk. Nandalal was due in an hour.

The unknown mystery of life had indeed engulfed Bindu.

Next day, Shashi went to the canal ghat, the ghat where he had spent an evening with Haru's dead body in a boat. It was morning.

Shashi had not told his family that Nandalal was coming. Nandalal would never go to their house. But Shashi had had no news of Bindu for a long time. He had come to the ghat only to get news of her from Nandalal. It would be impossible to have any conversation with his completely alienated and arrogant brother-in-law in the village.

Shashi also had another desire in his mind. That was an impossible dream. The affair of Bindu's marriage was known to Shashi. But it was not a matter of just the other day—it was almost history now. For so long now, Nandalal had been nursing his anger. All right, perhaps it was natural. But what was the point of continuing to brood over past incidents forever? Nandalal could easily bring himself to forgive Gopal today, could he not? He could think that there had not been any coercion but that he had willingly married Bindu, after inspecting and approving her personally. For Gopal's fault Nandalal was nurturing his resentment, while for no fault of hers Bindu was suffering, which was not right.

To have to sever relations with her father's family was a punishment for Bindu: this was Shashi's view. Today he would request Nandalal to stay at their house. He would convince him, indirectly, that for seven years now Gopal had been contrite. So, 'Why go on with it any longer, brother? Make it up now.'

Then Nandalal arrived. He had grown older, and more of a dandy than ever. If compared in relation to their status, the servant accompanying him was even more so. To traverse this small canal, for the two of them Nandalal had hired a boat with a capacity of ten. Perhaps he was afraid of drowning—a Calcutta dandy!

Shashi made no complaint for not being informed earlier. 'What day did you leave Calcutta?' he asked.

Bindu was younger than Shashi by one year. On that count, Shashi was Nandalal's social senior.

'The day before yesterday.'

'Is Bindu well?'

'Why should she not be?'

What a reply! Meeting Nandalal face to face and hearing his words, Shashi's goodwill was ebbing. One for whom anger and vindictiveness are the mainstays is not easily persuaded to discard them. If he did, what would he live on?

'News reached me that you would arrive this morning. Baba said, "Go to the ghat, Shashi. Take the Babus' car along; escort him home." He would have come himself as well. I dissuaded him. He is a rheumatic patient; how long he would have to keep waiting at the ghat was not certain either. There's a flurry of excitement at home that you're coming, Nanda.'

'Hmm,' grunted Nandalal. 'Whose car is it?'

'Shital-babu's brother Bimal-babu's. They are the zamindars.'

'What sort of a man is Shital-babu?'

The question left Shashi rather surprised.

'Quite good. Very religious-minded. Why do we keep standing here? Tell your servant to put the luggage in the car. Release the boat; you'll return in our boat.'

Nandalal shook his head. 'I'll return before evening, Shashi. Besides, after finishing my work, whether I can make it convenient to go to your house—I mean, perhaps I won't find the time. No, why perhaps? I won't find time.'

Shashi swallowed this insult too.

'Who's going to let you return today? Everyone is expecting you, Nanda.'

'Return I must. I left work unfinished at Bajitpur. Immediately after seeing Shital-babu, I'll set sail.'

Asked about his purpose with Shital-babu, Nandalal gave some vague reply: that he would purchase some plots of land at Bajitpur from Shital-babu. Even talking seemed painful to him. Shashi asked no further questions about it, nor sought any details. He seemed to himself to be a steward of Nandalal's.

'All right then. I won't insist if you have work. Stop over for now, have your meals and then start in the afternoon.' Shashi added, 'Baba would have come personally, Nanda. I forbade him.'

But it would not be convenient for Nandalal; he had no time.

'Oh, all right,' said Shashi finally.

He was growing angry and seething under the surface.

On one side of his tin shed, the lad Chandi had laid out a saucer full of paan and a few packets of biris wrapped in red and blue paper. Going near the car, Chandi was gaping at it in wonder. A motor car in Gaodiya! Nandalal had been glancing at the car every now and then. But he had just now practically ceased to be on speaking terms with Shashi who had brought the car. Nandalal therefore said, 'How far is Shital-babu's house?'

'At the end of the village.'

'Then it is quite a distance. Is any hackney carriage or a taxi available? My servant can then go and get it.'

'Hackney carriage is available. This car is going back to the Babus' house. You can take a lift if you like.' Shashi had kept his gaze fixed on a tree in Rasik-babu's garden; now he turned to look at Chandi's kiosk.

There is no knowing what Nandalal thought, but he said, 'If I had time, I would have gone to your house, Shashi.'

'If you do not have time, what more is there to say?'

There ended the matter. Nandalal went to his boat, taking out a mirror and comb from his suitcase arranged his hair neatly, popped into his mouth two rolls of paan and two pinches of *jarda*[81] from the containers, casting aside the costly shawl he had been wearing put on an even costlier one, and got into the car.

'Come, Shashi. I'm in a bit of a hurry.'

It looked as though now at last he had acquired the ownership of the car. Well, that was no surprise: Nandalal was used to riding in cars. Shashi rode bullock carts.

Shashi said, 'You go ahead; I've some work to do here.'

The city of Calcutta! Calcutta goes to Gaodiya riding in a motor car! Nandalal had put up Bindu in a separate house and provided her with all the trappings of a luxurious life besides a retinue of servants, maids and guards. The part of the city where Bindu's residence was located had no good repute either. Was Nanda mad? Mad or whatever, Shashi could easily have thrashed him—rained slaps and punches. How long could he have borne it? Five minutes at most. Before that Nanda would have been rolling at Shashi's feet. An unconscious Nanda in a faint.

Still, perhaps Nanda loved Bindu.

Winter was intensifying.

The Paush festival[82] was not far off. In the village, the continuous pedalling sounds of the husking lever could be heard. The sun shone less brightly. In the fields, the *rabi* crop[83] was resplendent. People's skin had begun to chap; those whose skin had gathered layers of dust found it coming off in flakes when rubbed. Rugs and quilts had begun to be taken out; chinks in walls made of bamboo strips were being stopped up with rags and paper. Moti had escaped fever by a whisker. Kusum had had another bout of bellyache. Paran had despatched a consignment of treacle. He intended to produce some jaggery this year. Borrowing money from Shashi he had bought another lot of forty date palm trees. Nitai had come one day and on his own returned Lali's calf to Paran.

'It is thanks to Chhoto-babu, or you'd never have got your calf back,' said Kusum. She had shown great reluctance to let Paran borrow money from Chhoto-babu for purchase of the date palm trees. Paran had not paid heed to her words on the logic that it was not practicable in household matters to always honour her likes and dislikes. Mokshada had not been well for some days. A dependent girl in Shashi's house, a niece of his of some kind, had contracted a cold during parturition and died of pneumonia.

This incident gave Shashi a big jolt. As was the practice, in the courtyard of the house, at a very low cost, a lying-in room was built by raising a temporary tin-roofed shed and cheap walls of raw bamboo strips. When the purpose had been served, the room except for the tin roof was abandoned. The same arrangement had been made in the case of the deceased girl as well.

This was the age-old custom in Shashi's family. Shashi himself had been born in such a hut. He had come into the world naked. Now he was a doctor, one with a good practice. Why did he allow such a thing to happen?

Had he learnt medicine merely to earn money? Would he apply his knowledge only where it would fetch money and just as much as was necessary for that? Well, leave aside teaching hygiene to the whole village—that is a big affair—but what about his own household?

No, he was no doctor; he was a businessman. He ran after money; he was a mercenary to combat death. In his own home, the atmosphere was unhygienic, haunted by death.

Thereafter for some days, in his attempt to introduce a code of healthy living, Shashi harassed the entire household no end.

'What are you brushing your teeth with?'

'Charcoal.'

'Use *neem* twigs.'

'It's bitter. Charcoal makes teeth whiter.'

One who used charcoal was by no means willing to use neem twig.

Had Shashi gone mad? It was a simple question of brushing one's teeth; why make such a fuss about it?

'Why did you give him muri on the floor to eat from, Kunda? Is there no bowl?'

'You give it in a bowl, and he'll eat it all up in one scoop! Then he'll begin to cry again. I've scattered it so he can pick it up one by one and take time over it.'

Kunda watched her son proudly. A plump child, he had caught Shashi's fancy. Couldn't he pick him up in his arms? He explained, 'Do you know that your son is eating germs along with his muri? There'll be worms in his stomach; he will get dysentery, cholera—'

What inauspicious things to say! God forbid! Kunda prayed. She thought to herself: if indeed the child happens to get those ailments, I'll know it's all due to your accursed tongue! Do you think just because you're a doctor, you can say whatever you like? You're his elder. Aren't you aware that your word may even come true and that his fate may be sealed?

Kunda's son kept crawling and picking muri from the floor mornings and evenings day after day. Kunda did not believe Shashi's words. How sweet the infant looked putting each grain into his mouth with the tips of a finger and thumb!

If Shashi rebuked her angrily, Kunda said, 'Do stop it, Dada. The child isn't yours. When Uncle dies, you'll drive me away from the house, I know that for sure.'

Shashi could not see how the question of driving her away from the house arose. Yet, it did not sound irrelevant. For, except Kunda, who else was suitable to be driven away from the house?

Addressing another member of the family, Shashi said, 'Listen, Aunt, don't feed your son so much milk. He doesn't have the capacity to digest even a quarter of that.'

Aunt thought: Alas just my bad luck! The house is flooded with milk; my son takes just a few sips, and no one can bear to see it. And what a small quantity he takes after all! There's no knowing when the allotment of milk for her son would be reduced: afraid, Aunt began to feed him a little more milk.

In the early afternoon, Shashi would go about saying, 'Get up, get up, all of you, don't keep sleeping. One doesn't sleep in the early afternoon in winter!'

They would comply for one or two days. Sitting up with a smiling face and yawning, they would say among themselves, 'What's happened to Shashi? He needs to get married now.' But within a few days, they rebelled. Those who were young and had husbands thought: if you had to keep awake at night, you'd realise why we sleep in the day. Those without husbands thought: what will we do in the afternoons if not sleep? Shashi must be mad, really; what are we to do with so much good health? The women who were elderly thought: perhaps, not all that he says is wrong. If you do not sleep in the day, you possibly have less heartburn. But once the rice is in the stomach, you feel so drowsy—what of that?

When Gopal heard, he said, 'Has he finally begun to apply his medical science within the house itself?'

In the evening, Shashi made a door-to-door call at the dwellings in the compound. To those living in brick-built rooms, he would say, 'What's the matter with you? Do you want to die of suffocation? All the windows are closed: where will the air come from?'

They laughed. With the windows open, won't they catch a cold? Let these creatures inhale a roomful of air first; only then they would suffocate, wouldn't they?

To those living in huts of bamboo strips, he said, 'Even the gaps in the walls you've sealed with paper! The air has already become foul. Do open one window at least. Or tomorrow I'll cut an opening in the ceiling so at least the foul air can escape through the gap between the ceiling and the wall.'

Kunda said, 'Dada, do you mean to kill us too, like Khemi who contracted pneumonia? I'm living with a slip of a child in a thatched room; what will you know of how cautious I have to be? This is no building, you know. Is a brick house ever to fall to our lot so that we can—'

In every single matter, Kunda would voice some such murmurs of dissent. That was her nature. Shashi had given up all attempts to improve the health of his family. At the beginning he had been extremely angry. Gradually he acquired wisdom. He had realised that if they were to follow the codes of healthy living, the very rhythms of their life would be lost; they would be unhappy. Suffering from disease and dying unaccounted-for deaths, that is how they found great delight in living; not exhilaration, but bliss, a calm subdued sense of contentment and happiness. Their lives were in utter disharmony with health, with abundant vitality. Each one of them was a depository of morbid sentiments; the upheavals of their lives went on within narrow confines; in the world, they were but poetic excrescences of marshy land: musty smells, wispy mist, darkish lichen, poisonous toadstool, and bindweed flower. A warm vibrant life would not suit their constitution.

So Shashi would ponder, and pondering thus, would be surprised. Kumud had once delivered a *lecture* of this kind to establish just how foolish the people of the world were. In his view, we ascertain the colour of the sky with a cloth-measuring yardstick and gauge our mental happiness or sorrow in relation to the status of our lives; we say man is a suffering lot and we seethe with rage. Kumud wasn't wrong, thought Shashi. In the realm of cogitation, we really make no stratification. Object and the existence of the object are one and the same thing to our mind. Do we ever care to think that there is no relation between man and his staying alive? When an individual laughs or cries, we associate the laughter and the tears with the individual itself; in our mind, we affix a *label* to the individual: happy or sad. Affixing labels is not wrong. Everything ought to have a definition. To indicate who laughs and who cries it is convenient to use words, which may be few or many. Why do we proceed further than that? Why do we seek change? Why do we want to bring in noisy cheer by wiping away the silent tear? What would be the gain if instead of illness, bereavement, sorrow, pain and gloom, there were only health, oblivion, happiness, joy and festivity? There is more fun in it. Perhaps there is no gain; but what is the loss either?

As he went on musing, Shashi indeed became nonplussed. He cured diseases; he restored the ailing to health. Yet, in the ultimate analysis, one arrives at just this truth: suffering from illness and coming round to health, curing the disease and not curing it are one and the same thing—to the patient as well as to Shashi. As he pondered over all this, numerous extra-sensory feelings arose in him! The workings of these mysterious feelings was not unique to Shashi. In every human being there dwells a child who loves to play at any hour with the poetic perceptions of the mind, with its imagination, its bizarre unreality, and its craziness.

One day Shashi climbed up on the mound near the palm grove not far from Haru Ghosh's house. After the rains, the mound used to be overgrown with weeds and bushes. Why did Shashi need to go there, making his way through the jungle? He would see the sunset. And he would see it by peering through the chink in the row of trees forming the arched horizon.

What a childish whim! Shashi felt no shame in being a child to himself. Only if he had known beforehand what price he would have to pay to satisfy the whim, he would not have been willing. Climbing up to the top when he stood facing the sun in the west, his mind was filled with peace; he found himself reinforced with a simple faith and courage—to do all the work, good or bad, allotted to him in the days to come. But before sunset, Shashi got frightened, just as he used to on some days in his boyhood, waking up suddenly at midnight. A shiver ran through his body. It seemed to him that he had not even a few minutes of future left; he was so helpless, so fragile. Up above the earth, very high over the earth buried under layer after layer of fear, on top of a mound of earth thick with undergrowth, Shashi was suddenly lost. Before him lay the embodied infinite. He did not know what boundless, inconceivable object or idea having concentrated around him had all at once become bounded, but he would never be able to breathe freely again.

For several days after this, Shashi remained deeply distraught and melancholy.

6

Once again Shashi developed an aversion to rural life. In the intervening days, he had lived here as if distracted. With half a mind he always contemplated on his desired existence: a bright, clamorous, enjoyable life in an educated, cultured and aristocratic ambience. He had become inured to the mosquito-bitten, mud-sullied life of this place by seeking consolation from the prospect that whenever he liked he could leave this village, and going wherever he pleased start his life anew in any manner after his heart. Meanwhile, of course, the vastness of the world had not diminished; neither had anyone robbed Shashi of his freedom. Still, it seemed to Shashi that he had been branded a village doctor forever—he lacked the strength to go outside this village. No doubt Kusum was to blame for this. It seemed as if she had forever blocked the source of his imagination. A life bright as the incandescent light which he fancied for himself was no nomad's life—Shashi's attachment to home and family was boundless. At the heart of his imagination was the impression of a wondrous ethereal woman, but in no way unreal: Shashi was not given to wild fancies. Kusum had debunked, as it were, the idea of that superwoman.

Shashi did not like the company of anyone except his younger sister Sindhu, and Moti. In this big village, only the two of them were his dearest female friends. Sindhu sat on the floor playing with dolls; on the bedstead Shashi sat watching the game intently.

'Khuki, what will you do when you grow up?'

'I'll play with dolls.'

This single answer seemed to lighten Shashi's mind completely for a while. He looked out of the window. The rose sapling Kusum had trampled the other day had reared its head once again, thanks to Shashi's tending.

Moti asked him, 'Has that friend of yours written to you?'

'Whom are you speaking of? Kumud? No, he hasn't. Why?'

'I just asked.'

'Why would you ask just like that?'

'He acts so well in the jatra, that's why.'

That's right, of course. Because Kumud acts so well, Moti was indeed within her rights to ask whether or not he had written letters. Shashi smiled and said, 'You liked his acting very much, didn't you, Moti?'

'Why I alone? Everyone did. Well, why don't you arrange a jatra show, Chhoto-babu? Will you? How much does it cost?' Ignoring Shashi's chuckle, with a grave face Moti said, 'If I had money, I would have hired that party, Chhoto-babu; putting up a *shaimana*[84] in front of our house, I would arrange a show—there would be plays for seven days!'

Moti had become a little pensive these days. When she talked, her eyes betrayed a timid curiosity. After having her say, she seemed to brood. Shashi thought that perhaps she had gradually come to muse about herself, as she must. She was after all a village girl; no wonder she would by now begin to cross the age of a carefree life.

Basudeb Banerjee made preparations for leaving the village with his family. His second son was employed in Calcutta; recently, his third son too had joined some office. Basudeb had no landed property. Thanks to Gopal's enmity, no one came to borrow money; even if anyone ever came, at Gopal's counsel he tried to appropriate it, interest and all. So what was the point of remaining rooted to the village any longer, if not to suffer from malaria? Several other families had left Gaodia too; deserted homesteads looked starkly vacant here and there throughout the village. Learning of his departure plans, Shashi went to see Basudeb. The sight of the household packing up enraged him all of a sudden. It was as if having surrendered himself forever to the mire of the village, he deemed it patently unfair of anyone else to leave the village.

'You owe me some money, Bnarujje *Kaka*.'[85]

'When I reach Calcutta, I will send it up, son. Matter of a few rupees, isn't it? After my sons get their salary at the end of the month, I won't delay even a day.'

Shashi shook his head, 'No, it's long overdue. Please pay up before you go.'

Why was Shashi in such urgent need of money, who knows! An ugly quarrel ensued with Basudeb. His two sons came rushing in a challenging mood. Neither party bothered about any niceties of honour and dishonour. Still, Shashi stood his ground; he did not desist until he had realised all the dues on account of medicines and fees recorded in his small notebook. Putting the money in his pocket, he said, 'Not one, but two earning sons of yours—why do you quail when it comes to paying a doctor's fees, Bnarujje Kaka? When in Calcutta, mind that you never behave in this way with a doctor who comes on a call, or he will grossly insult you.'

Shashi felt in no mood to turn back—he wished to revile them in an even stronger language; he deeply savoured a bitter glee. Suddenly, Basudeb's widowed daughter-in-law, who had once stopped Shashi on his way out urging him to revive the dead Bhutho, caught his notice, startling him somewhat. Even three months after Bhutho's death, while going past the vicinity of this house, Shashi had heard her lamentation. Today too, she was weeping silently. Not surprising: if the doctor under whose treatment Bhutho did not survive were to come and make such a row over his fees, anyone with a tender heart would certainly shed tears. Shashi slunk away, ashen-faced.

That he had not included Bhutho's treatment—that the money he had realised accounted to the last paisa for the treatment of others of this family who were still living and in good health—was something the woman would never take into consideration. Whenever her heart pined for Bhutho, she would shudder to think of Shashi Doctor of Gaodiya. Maybe someday while recounting stories of her village to her women neighbours in the city, alluding to today's incident she would remark, 'Even the doctors of the village are such mean fellows, Didi! Did we leave the village simply because we felt like it?'

A few days later, Shashi had occasion to go to Calcutta; he would buy some books and medicines. Paran came and stood near him somewhat diffidently. 'Moti insists on going to Calcutta and she is sobbing her heart out.'

'Moti will go to Calcutta?' Shashi was surprised. 'With whom?'

'She says she'll go with you.'

Shashi smiled and said, 'So you've come to sound me out if I'd agree? You have no sense, Paran. I can take her along, but what will people say?'

Paran had not come to suggest that Shashi alone should take Moti along to Calcutta. Paran would go with them too, of course. Mokshada had hinted several times that she wished to take a dip in the Ganga—it was unlikely she would let such an opportunity slip; which means Kusum would accompany them as well. Because of Moti, Paran would go bankrupt: was it easy to bear the travelling expenses of so many people to and from Calcutta? But not going was not an option either—Moti had given up meals and ablutions for the last two days.

Shashi asked, 'Why is she bent on going to Calcutta all of a sudden?'

Paran did not know the answer to that. Shaking his head in supposed wisdom he only said, 'Chhoto-babu, father has spoilt her by going on pampering her, I must say.'

'Talking of pampering, you do it no less, Paran!'

Shashi tried to dissuade Moti, saying, 'Tell me what you want; I'll buy it for you. What will you do going all the way for nothing?' Moti was usually timid and docile; she had always obeyed Shashi, but today she paid him no heed.

In the end, Shashi said angrily, 'All right, let's go then. We'll come back leaving you out there. Then you'll know what is what.'

One has to go by boat, then by steamer, then by rail, and at last reach Calcutta. All along the route Moti was restless and excited. Kusum looked around enjoying the thrill of travelling. But Moti seemed to find nothing worth seeing in the river or on either side of the railway track. A slip of a girl, she was going for the first time in her life to a far-off place; it was only natural for her to remain tense lest the path should end in a trice before arriving at her destination. But her utmost eagerness was noticed only in reaching Calcutta early. Perhaps she had thought that as soon as they set foot in Calcutta, she would get to meet Kumud: Prince Prabir would welcome her to the city!

On the way she asked, 'Where are we going to stay in Calcutta, Chhoto-babu? In the house of that friend of yours?'

Shashi said, 'Then you can see a lot of jatra, is it? So you're going to Calcutta for the attraction of jatra, I suppose? I'll take you to the theatre one day—that is far better than jatra.'

They stayed in Calcutta for five days. They went about seeing whatever was worth looking at in the city. They took dips in the Ganga; offered prayers at Kalighat;[86] travelled around by tram for the heck of it. But where was Moti's Prince Prabir? He was Shashi's friend; he lived somewhere in this city. But Shashi neither once mentioned his name nor called him over. If the interminable wonders of the city had not held her in thrall, her eyes would perhaps have filled with tears. They had rented two rooms in a hotel near Sealdah.[87] One room Shashi occupied alone. Shashi spent one night in the house of one of his doctor friends. Peeping into his hotel room at night, and finding it empty, Moti thought that he must have then gone to Kumud, only for them to return together in the morning. Moti did not know that Shashi had any friend on earth other than Kumud. Next day, it was past ten; since morning Moti had been watching the comings and goings of people along the stairs; but neither Shashi nor Kumud turned up. That day they were supposed to go out with Paran to visit the museum—they ought to have had their meals early and got ready. Moti was unwilling to stir.

'Let Chhoto-babu return.'

'Chhoto-babu is not likely to return soon, or he'd have come by now.'

'Could we not go in the afternoon, Dada? It's very chilly.'

Covered in Paran's chuddar, Moti was shivering from cold.

'Get lost then, you spoilt child,' said Kusum. 'Chhoto-babu is not going to give you a car ride today, understand? Why keep waiting and hoping? That day since it was late he came by car; it costs a lot. Now have your bath if you will or come and have your meal; it is served.'

Moti had to go. After seeing the exhibits in the museum, returning in the evening she found Chhoto-babu having tea in his room—alone. Kumud must have come; annoyed at having to wait, he had left.

Moti asked meekly, 'When did you come, Chhoto-babu?'

'Just a short while ago. Where did you go—to the museum? Tomorrow is the last day, Moti; we're going back the day after.'

Moti had no objection to that. What was the point of staying any longer in Calcutta?

Next day, in the evening, Shashi went out to get news of Bindu. If Nanda was at home he would be angry; perhaps he would insult him too. Let him. Even so, there was no question of going back without knowing in what state his sister was. Shashi had extra sympathy for those who had suffered on account of Gopal's whims. For the latter's misdeeds, Shashi considered himself guilty as well in some way; it seemed he too was responsible.

It was an area of ill repute. The street, at about the end of which stood Bindu's house, was one where if anybody was found after dusk known people would slander that person. The redeeming feature was that the house was at some remove—adjacent to the respectable neighbourhood. To the east of the house a plot of land lay vacant. Virtually entombed beneath the mass of brick and mortar, Bindu, perhaps looking in that direction at times, released her pent-up sighs.

Nanda was not at home. Shashi saw Bindu after about two and a half years. She looked almost the same. The furnishing in her room had not changed markedly either.

'How are you, Bindu?'

'Quite all right, Dada. When did you come? Hope all of you are well?'

Shashi smilingly replied, 'Why? Can't you find out by writing to us?'

'I feel very lazy writing letters, Dada.' Shashi knew this was evading the issue. Nanda did not permit her to write. Laying out food for Shashi, she sat down, asking him about various things.

Even today, Bindu was keen to know about goings-on in Gaodiya. Which of her old acquaintances were alive and who had died; which of the boys and girls she knew were married; which of them had had children and how many: as Bindu listened to all the news from Shashi, tears appeared in the corners of her eyes.

Shashi asked, 'What about your children, Bindu?'

Bindu shook her head, but said, 'It died, don't you know?'

'Died? When did it die?'

'Last year.'

The previous occasion that Shashi had come, it had seemed that perhaps Bindu was expecting. So that baby had been born and was dead? Bindu stood, looking at the picture of Radha[88]-Krishna on the wall. Suddenly it occurred to Shashi that physically Bindu looked all right, but her face had become strangely thin. Underneath her features there seemed to be a sort of dryness, as if the natural grace of her complexion had been blotted out.

'Are you ill, Bindu?'

'What illness? I'm fine.'

Bindu went out and, after a round of the place, came back.

'Then you are quite well, Bindu, are you?'

'Indeed I am.'

It all seemed so odd! Bindu's face concealing a wizened look and her listless words marked by ennui appeared mysterious. She was his sister, not some factitious relative. They were blood relations. And yet it was as if he could not recognise, could not understand Bindu.

Shashi said in a kindly voice, 'Why do you sit so far away? Come here, sit near me.'

Bindu curtly asked, 'Why?'

'Come closer, dear, let me ask you a few questions.'

After some hesitation, Bindu came near, tears suddenly rolling down her cheeks.

'Why do you cry?'

This question triggered a paroxysm of sobs.

'Have you ever called me near! Has anybody!'

Shashi was stunned; he could say nothing. True, whenever he came here, he had sat for half an hour like an outsider and then sought her leave to go. But what could Shashi have done? Even for the small duration that he came, he was apprehensive lest Nanda should get angry and behave harshly with Bindu. Did Bindu feel so upset by that—that constrained neglect? But she had never told him anything, never spoken her mind.

Out of a prolonged sense of hurt and injured pride, Bindu wept for a long time. When at last she calmed down, Shashi said, 'What is the matter with you, Bindu? Tell me frankly.'

'It's nothing, Dada.'

Shashi coaxed her, saying, 'If you don't talk today, you will never do in future, Bindu; some other day you will feel embarrassed and regret it. Does Nanda treat you badly?'

'Yes, he torments me, a lot.'

Extreme torment? Nanda was tormenting Bindu a great deal? She had such a fine house, such an impressive stock of saris and ornaments, such arrangements for luxury!

'Doesn't Nanda love you, Bindu?'

'He does. Not as a wife. As a kept woman.'

'What? As *what*?' Understanding seemed to finally dawn on Shashi. The nameless secret of Calcutta that had engulfed Bindu of Gaodiya gradually unfolded before him.

Bindu said, 'Do you want to see? The room he sits in when he comes here—will you see it, Dada? Come, let me show you.'

Shashi had no wish to see; Bindu dragged him by the hand. Going to a big room on the other side, she unlocked it and pressed the switch.

What a blinding light! A chandelier holding three or four lamps was sparkling from the ceiling. It seemed to dazzle Shashi. On the wall hung eight or ten indecent pictures. The entire floor was covered with a carpet, on which lay a couple of big dumpy bolsters. A harmonium, tabla and other such musical instruments were also there.

Bindu said, 'He's taught me some songs. He plays on the tabla, and I sing.'[89]

Shashi had no wish to see or hear anything more. Benumbed, he said, 'Bindu, let's go to the other room.'

Holding his hand firmly, Bindu said, 'No, see the real thing before you go.'

There was a small cupboard in the room. Bindu swung the door open and said, 'Look.'

Shashi had guessed without even seeing. The shelves were stocked with bottles of various sizes and labels.

Shashi felt sick. Even such things happen in the household! What a brave girl Bindu was! She had kept it all to herself for so long? If death had not snatched away her child, if Shashi had not called her affectionately to his side today, perhaps even today she would have said nothing.

'Do you drink?'

'If I don't, will I be let off, Dada? Look at me: this one is a false tooth. The first day, he forced my teeth apart with pincers and poured it down my throat. From then on, I take it myself.'

Going over to the other room, Shashi said, 'All this because he was forced into marriage, wasn't it?'

Bindu said, 'No. Because I seduced him in a way; that is why.'

'But surely you didn't do that? You were small then!'

'That is what he believes, Dada.'

Bindu's dry eyes, which had shone until now, again grew dim and moist. She said, wiping her eyes, 'Why did I tell you all this?'

Shashi was startled at Bindu's words. He was thinking: she has been reduced to such hopelessness. As he reflected on this, his face stiffened and grew dark. Looking in another direction, he asked, 'Does Nanda bring others—his friends?'

'Oh no!' recoiled Bindu. 'Don't even mention it; he has no such intention. Whatever punishment he wants to mete out, he does it himself.' Then in a low voice, she said, 'When I fall sick, he worries a lot, Dada, even takes care of me.'

Shashi thought things over at length.

'Will you come with me, Bindu?'

She said eagerly, 'Where shall I go with you?'

'We'll go back home tomorrow—will you come?'

'I will. Let's go right now, Dada—in case he suddenly turns up!'

She seemed to be in no mood to wait even a minute. How was it possible for her to have lived here so long, who knows. Shashi asked Bindu just this question in the car.

'I thought he would forgive me,' said Bindu as her eyes wandered over the decked-out wayside shops.

After so long, what sort of a homecoming was this for Bindu? Where were her ornaments, her saris, her bag and baggage? The people of the village were puzzled. They harassed her quite a bit too; everyone was eager to know what the matter was. Outside the house the men, and inside it the women of the family, were pestered by endless interrogation. No one except Shashi and Bindu knew anything, nor did they get to know. So various versions spread by word of mouth.

It was Sen-didi who distressed Bindu the most. To Shashi's surprise, Sen-didi was frequently coming to this house for some days. Apparently she had arrived at a truce with Gopal. Gopal sat smoking tobacco, his belly covered in a long shirt; sitting on a low stool not too far, Sen-didi kept talking to him. Seeing Sen-didi's scarred face and blind eye, Gopal too seemed to have been cured of a certain disease. These days he had been looking rather contented and composed. True, Sen-didi, with the passionate affection of a village woman, did attract Shashi; and since a man naturally prefers the affection of a woman with charm, it was valuable to Shashi as well. But he never believed that Sen-didi had the least desire to avenge herself on Gopal by captivating his son with the matchless beauty of her evanescent youth resplendent like the setting sun. Gopal's crooked mind looked for dishonest intentions. So it was not hard for Shashi to understand Gopal's exultation at Sen-didi's present ugliness. What he failed to understand were her comings and goings. Shashi seemed to feel ashamed that she could bring herself to sit chatting with someone who had forever been hostile to her and caused her irreparable loss. At times, perhaps, Gopal could be humorous too, as evident from the exquisite smile that occasionally wreathed Sen-didi's face. Shashi knew that when she was very young, Sen-didi's responsibility had fallen on Gopal. Thereafter, in exchange for how much money Gopal had sacrificed her to Jamini was also known to him—one hundred and fifty rupees. To think that the same Sen-didi could laugh so unabashedly at Gopal's rustic humour made Shashi feel even more disgusted with the village itself.

One day, for nearly three hours, Sen-didi alone grilled Bindu. There is no knowing what deluge of words she inflicted on the reticent girl. Bindu did not even respond to most of them. Sen-didi was not one to be daunted by it. Framing questions of her own, she herself found their choice answers, thereby proceeding unchecked to enrich her imagined knowledge about Bindu. The upshot was this: Nandalal, after marrying again, had driven Bindu out. 'So Nanda is thrice married, isn't he? What sort of a man is he, really! Now I see why all of a sudden Shashi went to Calcutta. How could I have known, dear, that such a disaster had fallen to your lot?'

So deep and passionate was Sen-didi's affection! Her blind eye brimmed with tears.

Ever since Kusum had inspected Shashi's room, Shashi had not met her again in private. One day at dawn Kusum woke him up from outside the window. Shashi got up to find that today also Kusum had trampled his rose sapling. Wasn't she afraid even of being pricked by thorns?

'Once again you've stepped on the plant, Bou! It took me so much effort to revive it last time.'

'I did it quite willingly, Chhoto-babu. Why do you have so much feeling for a sapling? There is something to be done; still I have to come personally to call you: wouldn't one get angry?'

'What is it, Bou?'

'Please come to the taalpukur, I'll tell you.'

Shashi went to the taalpukur. In the biting cold, even the palm trees seemed to be lifeless. A long distance away to the north of the pond an uprooted palm tree lay, to which Kusum led Shashi. Sitting down comfortably on the bole, she almost seemed to command him, 'Sit down, Chhoto-babu. There's a lot to say; it'll take time.'

Shashi said nothing; he sat quite some distance away from Kusum. She seemed to be a bit surprised to start with, and then suddenly a blush of shame covered her face. Kusum had called Shashi here to find out about Bindu. Overcome by curiosity, until now she hadn't even been conscious of the fact that calling Shashi secretly over here amounted to acting blatantly like a woman soliciting for an assignation.

Then, by asking him about Bindu, Kusum perplexed Shashi somewhat. She was so whimsical: so much ceremony just to hear Bindu's story? That was something he could have told her just anywhere.

'What's the use of listening to her story, Bou?'

Taken aback, Kusum said, 'Won't you tell me?'

As though there was nothing as strange as Shashi not confiding his secret to Kusum. Today for the first time, Shashi was overwhelmed to discover an unexpected side to her nature. A girl dwelt in Kusum who was even simpler than Moti, even more foolish. This girlish Kusum resided in the shadow of that part of her which had grown and matured with the experience of the world. When she forgot about the world, when she was too aloof to be affected by the responsibilities and complexities of life, this wondrous side became apparent. Shashi suddenly realised that for so many years all the caprices that he had noticed, which would never go with her quiet, tolerant and grave nature, were all deeds of the child Kusum of a distant past—whose existence in the mature mind and body of today's woman was difficult even to imagine.

Shashi gradually told Kusum everything about Bindu. While doing so, he was also distracted at times. How enigmatic Kusum seemed to him today. The day when she had come to inspect his room was the first time it had occurred to Shashi that the instances of her incoherent behaviour that he had noticed for the last few years were all flirtatious acts of a mature woman. Shashi had been quite upset that day. He regarded his heart as something precious; that heart seemed to have been sold off at the price of a dud coin. Now Shashi found comfort. Had it been so—he argued to himself—when he had spent year after year in close proximity to Kusum, would he not have sensed even once what she was after? If a woman wants to beguile the mind, does it take a man all of seven years to understand such a simple thing? The teenaged girlish entity that was latent in this woman just used to play with him. But Shashi never recognised her; and so he thought that even at this age Kusum was not free of her caprices.

Shashi returned home that day from the palm grove with a carefree mind.

Bindu also came to like Kusum. Kusum's curiosity was satisfied. She did not raise any further questions about Bindu's life in Calcutta. Bindu had come to her father's house as a matter of course; there was nothing surprising about it: Kusum kept up such a posture. She often came and sat with Bindu and tried to divert her by talking on various matters. She was adept at this. Kusum was peerless in weaving engaging stories with an intermingling of fact and fiction. She excelled in the art of creating an aura of delusion. She said, 'You took a fancy to coming over from the town to the village, sister; you're sure to die of malaria here. Two bouts of shivering with fever, and you'll run for dear life to your master, bidding farewell to the father's home!'

Gopal made angry noises; he had a quarrel with Shashi. He screamed and ranted, saying he had never in his life seen anything so absurd. A man keeping his wife in any manner he wished to was the way of the world. It would be a different matter if he had physically assaulted her. Nandalal had done none of that. For what he had done instead, Bindu ought to have been happy. If someone wished to satisfy some curious fancy by keeping his wife in a separate house, swathed in diamonds and gold, and posting servants and a sentry at the gate, the woman should reckon it as nothing but her fortune. A husband must have that right. Nandalal drank? Was there one rich man in society who was not addicted to alcohol? Shashi ought to have spoken out in the beginning; instead of obtaining a rich son-in-law after so much effort, Gopal would have given his daughter's hand to a destitute wanderer; people would then have had to face the music!

'Why did you bring her here, Shashi? What made you act as her guardian? Is all this just something to trifle with, do you think? Go take her back—go today itself.'

'That cannot be, Baba. You do not know the details; if you did, you would have realised that it is not possible for Bindu to stay there any longer.'

'How did she stay there all these years?'

That was something that perplexed Shashi himself no less.

Gopal asked his daughter, 'What arrangements did you make about the ornaments and other articles?'

'I haven't brought them.'

'Why? Why didn't you?'

'What did I own that I could have brought? If I did bring them, he would have sent me to jail for theft.'

Gopal burst into a rage to hear this. 'Send you to jail? No one can send Gopal Das's daughter to jail so easily. Both of you are immature; you're inexperienced fools! You will suffer a lot in life, I tell you.'

The result of the altercation was that Gopal and Shashi once again ceased to talk to each other. This kind of difference of opinion with his son was devastating in Gopal's realm of parental affection, causing him much anguish. Days would pass by without reconciliation. Gopal would keep fidgeting: the son seems to have become a god of the heavens—difficult to access. Finally, one day in desperation, Gopal on his own went to Shashi's room. When Shashi had put down his fat medicine book, Gopal pulled it near, leafing through it and feeling visibly proud of his son's superhuman talents for mastering such voluminous books. He said, 'All the time that you are at home you are busy reading books; your health is declining. Why do you read so much? There's no exam ahead, I suppose? Previously you never read day and night like this, did you?'

'A doctor must always know the new developments.'

'What you know is more than enough for practising in a village.'

'If I ever decide to practise in a town—'

What a curious turn of conversation! Having come to talk about Bindu, what did he end up bringing to the fore! Town, did he say? Did Shashi have any plans to go and practise in a town? Was that why he was studying so hard? Gopal went pale. He was born in a hut in this village. Here, at one time he had had to scrounge for a meal.

Today he had a brick-built house; thirty meals were laid out each time. There was plenty of money invested all around and so much land and other property. Here was his ideal Bengali life, at home and outside. He was ordained to die here. Would Shashi not stay on here, not follow in his footsteps? Anxiously Gopal said, 'Don't let those terrible thoughts enter your head, Shashi.'

Shashi replied, 'Sometimes it occurs to me that if I practise in town I could make more money.'

'Rubbish! There are so many big doctors in the town; you'd count as of no consequence there. How badly are you doing here after all? Apart from that, you can very well do even without any money coming from the medical line. Look after the property; count the interest. If something comes from your profession, well and good; if not, so be it. There's not another doctor in the village; people die without treatment: shouldn't you consider that side too? You're very selfish, Shashi.'

Then Gopal left the room; there was no knowing what he might end up saying without meaning to; maybe once again there would be no talk with his son for fifteen days. A little later, he went back to Shashi's room. 'Did I leave the key here?'

'Key? What's that in your pocket then?'

Weighed down by the bunch of keys, the pocket of his shirt indeed bulged. Gopal was embarrassed. He is put out of countenance at every step: what sort of a son is he! He sat silently for a while. Then changing tack, he adopted an intimate tone and asked, 'Well, Shashi, my son, tell me why isn't your mind settling in the village where you belong?'

'Did I say that?'

'Why then do you talk of going to the town?'

'I haven't decided anything. I think about it, that's all.'

Watching Shashi's calm manner, Gopal felt disconcerted for a second time at his own agitation. When the son is grown up, what a difficult task it turns out to be to interact with him. Not a friend, not a debtor, not a boss—God knows in what relationship a man stands with his adult son.

One day a letter came from Nanda—for Bindu. He wrote that if she went back within three days of receipt of the letter, he would forgive her this time. Shashi went ballistic: 'Forgiveness? There's no knowing who would forgive *him*—how dare he speak of forgiveness? You mustn't reply to the letter out of courtesy, I tell you, Bindu.'

'Won't I reply?'

'Do you wish to?' Shashi was surprised. 'You came away after breaking all ties with him; how can you reply to his letter?

Bindu said, 'I won't, Dada; I only asked if I should.'

'Was this too something to ask?'

Bindu said with a wan smile, 'I can't be firm, Dada. I have completely lost my courage. I can't decide anything on my own. Otherwise, don't you think I would have come away earlier?'

After that one letter, Nanda did not pursue the matter any further. The winter days passed by, briskly. Shashi rarely met Kusum. There was apparently no urge on the part of either to meet. Moreover, Shashi was very busy. Of course, in winter, the incidence of diseases in the village was low, but that was only compared to other times. A few days back, Shashi had gone to Bajitpur Hospital to make the acquaintance of the doctor there. While studying in Calcutta, he knew the doctor by sight. Shashi had told him that if any unusual patient turned up, he might please be sent word: one couldn't learn merely from books. He used to go to Bajitpur often. If there was an opportunity to oversee a major surgical operation, he halted there for a day or two, forgetting his own patients.

Kusum had not been making complaints of late. Something had come over her; perhaps she had forgotten how to complain. Such spells of absentmindedness do come when one forgets to do even one's habitual work.

At the beginning of Phalgun, suddenly one day Kumud arrived.

'How long will you let me stay, Shashi?'

'As long as you like,' said Shashi happily. 'Will you really stay?'

'That's why I've come. If I like it, I will stay.'

Shashi smiled, 'What is there in the village to like after all? Ponds and undergrowth and ignorant people. Even if you do not like it, do stay here for some days, Kumud. Lack of company has made me introspective.'

'Lack of company? Why don't you marry?'

Seeing Shashi smile, Kumud turned serious, 'I'm not joking, Shashi; you really do need to marry. You are an ordinary homebound, laid-back, frugal man. You too should live the same life as ordinary people. You can't be happy trying to live differently, Shashi.'

'But you weren't like this, Kumud; what is all this counsel you're giving? Will you stay in my room or shall I arrange a separate room for you?'

'A separate room isn't a bad idea, Shashi. How can one do without being alone for a few hours?'

'You mean you write poems?'

'No. I don't even know how to live properly; to think that I'd write poems! I feel shy to write.'

It seemed surprising that Kumud did not write poems out of shyness. Had he not realised yet what he wanted in life? Was he still going on experimenting with life? Had he been sailing over the seven seas scouting around for the one to collect pearls from? There is nothing stranger than the fact that no man, tame or wild, can penetrate the mystery of life to attain a state of perpetual stability that he can accept as absolute, where no more novelty remains to be desired. Today Kumud wished to slow down the pace of his life like Shashi's, while Shashi aspired for the torrid, exuberant vortex of Kumud's past life. Shashi knew that it would not bring him much happiness. Yet he felt a yearning within.

Shashi could not exactly ascertain why Kumud had come to Gaodiya. How long he would stay was not known either. If asked, Kumud gave the same reply: *as long as you let me*. This made no sense. If he were to stay, say, for six months or even a year, would Shashi tell him, 'It's time you left'?

Shashi observed a novelty in Kumud's manner. Last time there were clear signs of the descent into the ranks of a jatra party in his face, eyes, words and demeanour. This time round, he seemed to have turned poetic and given to cogitation as in the days long gone by, with the difference that he did not have that insolent, rebellious nature. He seemed to be musing, thinking of something piquant, his eyes growing eager in anticipation, and quite incongruously, his face a picture of deep contentment. Besides, he alone knew what other interest he had in wandering through the fields of Gaodiya—at any given hour of the day he would go off somewhere.

One day Shashi asked, 'How's Binodini Opera doing, Kumud?'

'I've left that group. In Baishakh, I'll join another party named Saraswati Opera: it's settled. They've offered a much higher salary. They were insisting on my joining right now. But having to keep repeating the same lines day after day, I developed a sort of loathing for it. So I thought of taking a break for a few months.'

Who knew if this was true or not? A suspicion crossed Shashi's mind: perhaps Kumud has been sacked from Binodini Opera. Unable to make any headway anywhere, he has come here for shelter; and the story of Saraswati Opera is a sham as well—probably he has no money.

One day, Shashi said, 'Can you give me fifteen rupees or so, Kumud? I'm short of cash; I have to give it to someone.'

Kumud opened his suitcase, and after a search, said, 'Where's my purse?'

'Hm,' Shashi thought to himself: your money bag has to be stolen right now of course! Shame on you, Kumud; at last you've started playing tricks with me too!

But no, it was there. Once the suitcase was emptied, the money bag turned up. Kumud said, 'I'd thought of keeping it with you and then completely forgot about it. If it had been stolen, it would be terrible! Take what you need and keep the bag with you.'

Shashi hesitated.

'How much is there?'

'Who knows? Count it.'

Eventually, the reason behind Kumud's self-imposed banishment in the pond-and-jungle-filled Gaodiya was discovered.

Shashi went pale and said, 'What is all this you're saying, Kumud? Marry Moti? Such a small girl!'

'Not too small. Besides, small is good. If I must marry, why on earth shall I marry an overgrown girl?'

Shashi was now getting angry. He had been smarting from indignation as well. 'So then, Kumud, this is why you came, to your friend's house, on the pretext of taking rest?'

Kumud was confounded. 'You seem perturbed, Shashi? Is it such a grave offence that I'm going to commit? I was wandering about like a vagabond; my getting married, settling down—you should be delighted at this.'

'So, you found no other girl in the whole of Bengal?'

'Why? What's wrong with Moti?'

'That tiny, ignorant, rustic girl!'

Kumud smiled. 'I can't make out whose side you are on. Moti is an uneducated country girl, indeed; but I too am a jatra party clown!'

Shashi grew even angrier to see Kumud's smile. Nothing in the world seemed serious to Kumud: as if whatever fancy comes to mind can be realised playfully; as if there were no code of life, no method in living. Suppressing his annoyance, Shashi said in the manner of a judge pronouncing his verdict, 'Get over this folly, Kumud. Who told you to keep playing a jatra party clown? Better not join Saraswaṭi Opera; go back to your uncle. He has such a flourishing business in mica; won't he give you a good job there? Then you'll get many eligible girls from families of equal status to choose from; one of them can make a suitable companion for you. Marrying a village girl on the spur of the moment, why should you suffer for the rest of your life?'

Kumud said, 'Uncle has two Great Danes; did you know this?'

'No,' said Shashi, surprised.

'If I enter Uncle's house, he'll set the dogs after me!'

They were talking in Shashi's room in the evening. A seven-rupee-worth table lamp was shining in the room. To look at each other's face in such a bright light seemed to hurt the eyes. Anger did not last long in Shashi's mind. After a brief silence, he said, 'That you came to like Moti is something I find hard to believe, Kumud!'

'Neither did I at first. That time when I went away, who knew that I would have to come back for her sake?'

Kumud then told Shashi in detail the story of the origin of his love for the innocent village girl. Kumud had no idea that such a small girl could possess a heart of her own where the blossoming of unfathomable affection was possible. Moti had impressed upon Kumud that everything in a person's life except the love of an ingenuous mind was a hollow sham. Frankly, Kumud had never even imagined this exquisite experience. As he listened, Shashi's wonder knew no bounds. *Moti*? Did that slip of a girl, slovenly too, love Kumud so deeply in secret? Shashi seemed to think that all this was a figment of Kumud's imagination, a reverie, a fanciful thought. Could Moti ever be the heroine of the epic which Kumud went on composing extempore like the *Gita Govinda*?[90]

After listening to Kumud, Shashi could not sleep till late that night. The marriage of Moti and Kumud? How could it be allowed to happen! All along Kumud had lived the life of a bohemian wanderer. Even if he had developed a liking for domesticity for the time being, it was hard to believe it would last. Besides, it would possibly take Kumud not even six months to outgrow his patience over Moti's crassness and rusticity. What would befall her then? If Kumud were to torment her or abandon her, the life of the docile, foolish girl would be laden with sorrow: who would take that responsibility? It was, after all, Kumud's nature to get rid of the one-time favourite objects from his life.

Next day he quizzed Kumud on this point. He said, 'How can you continue to like Moti for a long time, Kumud?'

'I will like Moti forever.'

'I was thinking how it will be possible.'

'Shashi, do you think that even after marriage Moti will remain like this? Won't I mould her after my heart? I accept her as a freshly mined diamond that I myself will cut, grind, polish, and brighten. Her mind has no definite form; and that's why I'm so keen to marry her. I'll shape her mind. There is no girl in the world, brother, who can be my partner: I have to myself create my companion.'

One half of Shashi's mind was family-oriented, calculating and cautious; such high-flown words annoyed him. Had Kumud not the minimal awareness that going to mould someone after your heart you do not end up with the one after your heart? The development of mind brought about by another's efforts is abnormal and unpleasant. It was doubtful whether Kumud would have the patience to transform Moti into a weird creature by casting her in a mould; and even if he did, would he like the altered Moti? And how was he going to shape her mind? Reading and writing, singing, playing an instrument and painting were all he could teach her; what else could Kumud possibly do? If he were to impart to Moti even her identity, what worth would Moti then have as an independent, complete human being? Did Kumud who knew such a lot not know even this much that man cannot create his own lover? That one who could be raised by training like a daughter could not then also be enthroned as a lover?

Shashi pondered without reaching a definite conclusion. At one time, he noted to his own surprise that Kumud's romantic overtures to Moti did not seem all that incongruous—only the talk of their marriage seemed out of place. If Kumud had deflowered Moti and left, Shashi's sorrow would have been profound; yet it might seem that nothing unnatural had happened: given the gulf of difference between the two, what relationship was possible other than the reprehensible intimacy of a couple of days? Their marriage would be absurd and meaningless.

Shashi felt uneasy at this thought. For Moti he had a strange sort of attachment laced with parental affection; he was pained to think of Moti as unsuitable to be Kumud's bride. Shashi came across Moti in the afternoon; she had arrived at their house with a basket of pumpkin flowers. Perhaps Kumud had told her that Shashi had been informed of their affair. She blushed to see Shashi and then smiled slightly; a sudden feeling of coyness at this age does light up one's lips with a smile. Moti's face today seemed to Shashi to be extraordinarily beautiful. He thought that perhaps Kumud had made no mistake; perhaps one day he would indeed make Moti unmatched in both beauty and accomplishments.

Once she was gone, no longer did Shashi hold his trust in Kumud's capacity for doing this. Moti was indeed like an uncut diamond in the mine; it was possible as well to carve her into somebody matchless and resplendent; but that was not something Kumud could do. He had the knack of dreaming about the future, but not the perseverance to realise that dream. He would end up rendering her delicate facial complexion lined with sorrow.

Shashi remained morose. He was thoroughly disgusted with Kumud. Did it behove a friend, after coming to his friend's house, to secretly dally with the latter's object of affection? If it were possible, Shashi would have driven him away. But after all that Kumud had told him, he no longer thought Moti had any hope of help from any quarter. Her anxious questions about Kumud, her eagerness to go to Calcutta hoping to see him, everything now kept coming back to him. Was it love? Had so much love for Kumud dawned in Moti's heart? Besides that, perhaps not only the upsurge of love in Moti's heart, there was no believing Kumud: his life was entirely fraught with contradictions.

Shashi could not make up his mind. In this matter his decision would be final and binding. If he consented, only then would the marriage take place. To broach the matter to Paran would be his task as well. Shashi felt that no matter what might happen, he should tell Kumud to leave the house this moment: let their friendship end forever. Let him go back to his nomadic life, and Moti the daughter of the village remain in her village. How could Shashi consent to this marriage even when he knew that Moti would suffer all her life?

In the evening he had the opportunity to consult Kusum in this regard. The moon was up in the sky then. Standing in the shadow cast by the eaves of the roof, after much talk, Shashi said, 'There is a way out, Bou.'

'What is it?'

'I could marry Moti.'

'So that is the way out?' said Kusum, and had a good laugh.

Shashi, however, did not smile. He said, 'This is no laughing matter, Bou. I'm really worried about giving her away to Kumud.'

Kusum said, looking serious, 'That's because you love her like your younger sister. It's only natural for people to be anxious when it comes to giving their daughters and sisters away in marriage.'

Still Shashi said, 'If I marry Moti—'

'*If* you do! If!' After saying this in a sharp undertone, Kusum again laughed. 'One can't carry on, Chhoto-babu, with so many ifs in the practical world. You will marry Moti? Wouldn't your life be ruined?'

Shashi reconsidered. 'Of course, Kumud is not absolutely inhuman; he also earns a tidy sum.'

Kusum said, 'Moti is fortunate to be liked by Kumud-babu. Otherwise, she would surely have found herself in a farmer's family, flogging logs of wood morning and evening; life would have been made unbearable for the girl. She must have done many good things to find herself such an enviable groom.'

'Let it be so then. What does Moti say?'

'What will she say? She's counting the days.'

Counting the days! Let her.

Shashi kept fuming with anger at Kusum. Where did that simple girl disappear today, the one whom he had discovered to his delight within Kusum in the palm grove that morning? How astute was her reasoning! How tactfully she had diverted his bent of mind about Moti's marriage! What he had failed to decide after pondering for two days was settled so easily by Kusum within half an hour by presenting two worthless arguments. As he stood near her, what made him so nonchalant about Moti's well-being that he could casually utter: let it be so then? Moreover, what was all this that Kusum was saying today?

'On a moonlit night like this I wish I could run away with you somewhere, Chhoto-babu!'

In deep misery, Shashi felt this was something concocted by Kusum. Lest he should himself marry Moti to save her from Kumud's grasp, she had uttered these words to please him. Let her talk. Shashi was not Kumud after all; all Kumud said or did in life was mere play-acting. Yet, bathed in moonlight, how blissfully the landscape all around was indulging in dreams! Shashi did not like to believe that he was ordained to suffer such agony from the poison of Kusum's deviousness at such an hour. But why was he still standing here? Why could he not go away? Who knows—perhaps the allure of the moments of aversion and mortification in life was so intense to him alone? Kumud would perhaps have run away, saying, 'To hell with you, Kusum!' Or perhaps extracting the poetry of the moonbeams with his own joy, he would have glorified even these gross moments!

Kusum spoke under her breath, 'Why does my body feel like this when I stand near you, Chhoto-babu?'

Body! Body!

Don't you have a mind, Kusum?

7

After the wedding, Kumud went away with Moti.

Where? On their honeymoon. Saying, 'Lend me some money, Shashi,' Kumud set out on a honeymoon with Moti the rustic girl of Gaodiya.

Paran had found this matter quite inexplicable. To proceed on an indefinite journey with one's newly married bride! What sort of a custom was this? Paran knew that Kumud had no friend or relation with whom he could put up in the company of Moti. He had expected that Kumud would stay at Shashi's house itself for a few days. Thereafter, providing for Moti's maintenance, he would set up house in a town or village. Where did Kumud vanish with his sister overnight?

This marriage was not to Paran's liking; he had given his consent only in deference to Shashi. Always in every matter, he had depended on Shashi. Paran might be a poor village householder, but he was Moti's elder brother, and Kumud's social senior. And yet, how rudely and insultingly Kumud had behaved with Paran all along! Shashi had observed this too, and he was no less angry: if Kumud could marry Moti, could he not respect her elder brother? But he had not said anything to Kumud openly. All he did was be amiable and respectful to Paran in Kumud's presence—as an example for the latter to learn from. This effort of Shashi was of little avail. Kumud had accepted Moti, while showing profound contempt for her near ones.

In the field Paran's men were engaged in heating date palm sap. Because Shashi was never free except around midday, Paran came walking a distance of one and a half miles, incurring loss of labour, just to meet him. His broad strong shoulders seemed to droop with fatigue. He said, 'Why does he not write letters, Chhoto-babu?'

Shashi replied, as if he was the culprit, 'As a matter of fact, you know Paran, Kumud is not in the habit of writing letters. When he was in college his father used to get news of him by writing to the hostel superintendent.'

'But should he not let me know where they've put up or how they're doing? Meanwhile, mother has begun to cry.'

Mentally cursing Kumud, Shashi said, 'It'll come, Paran, the letter will come. He'll certainly send word. Today or tomorrow, he will surely write.' Paran kept gazing at Shashi with a sort of glum, subdued look, seeming to convey some complaint silently like a dumb creature. Shashi felt extremely uneasy. No one had entrusted Shashi with the welfare of Haru Ghosh's family; but since he had always wanted to do them good, a responsibility seemed to have automatically devolved on him. But what good had he been able to do them? It wasn't his fault; yet it was because of him that Kusum seemed to have changed. Moti had an unsuitable, fraught marriage! Perhaps Paran was reckoning all this and taking stock; perhaps he was troubled by the consequences of their unequal friendship; perhaps he was now contemplating what other harm, for all his good intentions, Shashi would end up doing them.

Shashi knew that Paran would never openly blame him in any matter; only keep looking at him with a sad, worried face like a child staring at some inscrutable mystery. Shashi's heart filled with compassion for the tall, trusting, simple man. He resolved that whatever it takes, he would compel Kumud to make Moti happy: let Moti be transformed, let Kumud mould Moti any way he likes—but Paran must get to see the glow of happiness in her face.

Not for Moti alone, Shashi's worries had multiplied in different directions. Of them, the anxiety over Bindu was chief. She was turning unrecognisable by the day. To divert her mind, taking away the responsibility of the huge family from the hands of aunts, Shashi had entrusted it to Bindu's charge. Bindu had never in her life conducted the affairs of a household: how could she bear this burden? She did not like it either. One by one, she handed all the tasks and responsibilities back to the aunts. When it came to doing work, Bindu felt lethargic. She did not like the company of others. She did not talk much with anyone at all. She sat in a corner of the room silently by herself all day. And she dozed. She would yawn all the time as if she were sleepy after keeping awake at night at a stretch for an indefinitely long time. And yet she slept very little. She did not want to eat anything; she was steadily growing thin. She spent her long days and nights in a languid and enervated way as if half-dead.

Shashi, being a doctor, called Bindu to his room, examined her tongue, checked her heart, and queried her about her health. Then shaking his head doubtfully, he said, 'I can't make out anything. I'm just a village doctor; I don't know enough. I'm giving you a medicine; take it for a few days, then I'll examine you again.'

'No, I won't take any medicine.'

'You will,' said Shashi. 'If you don't take it orally, I'll inject it. Coming to your father's house, Bindu, if you die despite my presence, can you imagine what dishonour that will mean to me?'

Bindu broke into tears. Even as she wept, she said, 'What can I do, Dada? I can't find the mental strength to do anything. Day and night, a fire keeps burning deep inside.'

'Do not cry,' said Shashi. 'As soon as you take my medicine you'll feel cheerful.' He seemed unable to diagnose Bindu's malady. A fire burned in her mind without ceasing? Whom did she yearn for? Why? Because one's life has gone to waste, does grief leave one drained of energy and more dead than alive? Why, intense hate towards Nanda alone should have been enough to restore Bindu to fitness and health in no time. Even if it wasn't hate, why was her towering sense of slight not reinvigorating her? Given that Bindu had spent so many years expecting that Nanda would forgive her, today if her heart went out to the same Nanda, Shashi wouldn't be surprised. The world has a few uncommon girls like her. Then again, if she felt a longing for Nanda, wasn't she supposed to be restless and flighty, to fidget on the pretext of work or even a travesty of it? Why should she grow so lazy and languorous instead and about to go out like a lamp without oil?

One day Bindu said, 'Dada, give me the key of the cupboard; I want to take out some books.'

Shashi said, 'There aren't many Bengali books there. If you wish to read, I can have some books brought from the town.'

'First let me read the ones in the cupboard. Then bring others from the town when you can.'

Shashi handed her the bunch of keys. Bindu opened the cupboard, took out a book, locked the door, but didn't hand him back the keys. 'Let me keep them with me,' she said. 'You are busy visiting patients; if I need to take out another, I may not see you for the whole day.'

'What will you do with the bunch? Just take out the key of the bookcase.'

'Better leave the bunch itself; if I like, might I not spend some time rummaging through your trunks and suitcases as well? I'm not going anywhere; just call me when you need the keys.'

Bindu spoke so casually that not an iota of doubt entered Shashi's mind. Perhaps because he was also absentminded that day, it did not occur to him that in the medicine chest there were four or five phials with '*bish*'[91] labels in red. On many occasions he had seen Bindu avidly looking at the chest, which he would have recalled if he were attentive.

That day, Shashi went to visit a patient in a village some five miles away. It was about nine at night when he returned. Nearing home, he could hear a hubbub coming from the inner quarters. The outer rooms were dark and empty. Only Sindhu stood in the darkness weeping softly. Alarmed, Shashi asked, 'What has happened, Sindhu?'

'*Mejdi*[92] is dying, Dada!' Sindhu sobbed.

Shashi was transfixed. Bindu was dying? Why? Sindhu could not tell him anything coherently. Still it did not take Shashi long to guess. In the evening Bindu had eaten something and now she was dying. The blood in Shashi's heart went cold. Being a doctor, he ought not to remain rooted to the spot after hearing such news: Shashi was aware of this, but he could not stir for a few moments. Bindu had taken poison. Did she wish to die? For a moment it seemed to him that it wouldn't be such a bad thing to let Bindu have her wish. Shashi knew what poisons there were in the chest; if Bindu had taken it in the evening, it was possible to save her. But what was the point of saving her? Bindu was no child; what she had experienced in life was obtained the hard way. If it was her deliberate decision to resort to an extreme means of escape from her misery, would it be right to stand in her way?

Wiping the sweat from his forehead and walking across the large courtyard past Kunda's room, he came into the inner courtyard. Bindu was sprawled there over her own vomit, her clothes in disarray. The entire family and many from the neighbourhood stood crowding round her. They raised a clamour on seeing Shashi. The garrulous Kunda was heard above the others, 'O Shashi-dada, just look at what Bindu-didi has done!'

The pungent smell of alcohol was in the air. Shashi nervously asked, 'What's happened, Kunda?'

Kunda said, 'What strange things Bindu-didi has been doing since afternoon! If only you had seen her, Shashi-dada. Now she laughs, now she cries, then she starts singing: it scared the life out of us! Do you know what she's done? Opening your medicine chest—'

Shashi did not need to hear anything more. He went and sat near Bindu. After examining her pulse, he said to Kunda, 'She's been lying here like this; couldn't you give her a wash and take her inside and lay her on the bed?'

Kunda said defensively, 'How could we? She came at us, trying to bite if we tried to hold her!'

'Now she is not even conscious, Kunda. Bring a pitcher of water.'

Shashi bathed and cleaned Bindu, and then helped by others he took her to the room and laid her on the bed.

This was a scandal, indeed!

There was much uproar for a few days in the village. What an untoward incident it was in the inner quarters of a respectable family! Men drink, indulge in drunken sprees, and throw up profusely; people disapprove but take it in their stride. That a daughter of the household could go to such horrifying lengths was even beyond imagination! Those who were not present to witness

Bindu's drunkenness lamented the missed opportunity; others were blissfully exasperated having to go on endlessly recounting the details to all.

When it happened, Gopal was taken unawares; all night he kept smouldering without doing anything, and next morning the flame of his anger was almost palpable. He reviled Shashi for the crime of bringing Bindu over. In unspeakable language and shouting at the top of his voice Gopal told Bindu repeatedly to go away: there was no place for such a wretched daughter in his house. Shashi kept silent; Bindu bolted her door; she too made no response. After ranting and raging all morning, then beating a day-labourer with his wooden slipper, and finally putting on his shirt and chuddar, Gopal walked out of the house, umbrella under his arm. He said he was going to Calcutta because there was no way he could show his face in the village. If he found Bindu still there after he returned, he would set his house on fire.

Shashi was in no good humour either. He did not get angry with Bindu, though. She did not come out of her room for nearly three days; day and night she kept herself completely shut up. Only at Shashi's insistence would she come out, take a dip in the pond, nibble at her food sitting with her eyes downcast, and then going back to her room bolt the door again. If spoken to, she would neither make any response nor raise her face. After three days, whatever she might have thought, she came out; she even spoke a few words normally with Kunda. But she could not bring herself to mix with anyone. Her days went by in the same way as she had been spending her apathetic and lonely life ever since she came here.

Shashi went around with an unwarranted hurry and performed the tasks dictated by duty. Hitherto he had visited his patients as one of the friends of their family and relatives, giving assurance besides medicine. Now he examined them with a grim face, flaring up over trifles. He would be greatly annoyed to have to repeat anything he said.

It was the month of Chaitra. Under the searing sun, Shashi's palanquin took him across the fields from one village to another; hot air kept blowing relentlessly. The torrid and passive leisure Shashi had in the palanquin he exhausted in contemplation. He thought about Bindu, about Kusum and Moti. Concerning the latter pair, there was nothing to start thinking over anew. As for Bindu, he found no way out howsoever hard he pondered. He himself had snatched her from the clutches of Nanda; her responsibility was entirely his. He considered himself guilty for Bindu making herself a laughing stock with her misadventure, giving rise to unsavoury rumours across villages. He was to blame. Whatever he entrusted himself with fizzled out. An irresistible, invisible power seemed to be constantly at work against him. He had once been enamoured of the affection of the beautiful Sen-didi; today because he wished to give a wide berth to an unsightly Sen-didi, he deprecated himself. Ever since Haru Ghosh's family had fallen on hard times, Shashi, by way of giving them counsel out of compassion, had been on close terms with them. Thereafter, when he was automatically elevated to the position of their guardian, he came to know Kusum's mind, and spoilt Moti's future. And now Bindu had come to this state. What bright prospects he had dreamt for her when bringing her home! That by and by he would heal her spirit; the tranquil surroundings of the village would restore her peace of mind; his affectionate care and company would bring her all the joys and animation that are possible in the life of an estranged woman; teaching her to read and think, he would build her a wonderful inner world. Shashi knew now what an impossible task it was.

It was painful for Shashi to acknowledge, yet it is true that it was solely for her addiction that Bindu had drunk wine that day. Once Nanda might have had to use pincers to force her to drink; today Bindu could not do without it. Not merely the addiction to alcohol, but the tumultuous, abnormal life Nanda had offered her for seven years had become indispensable to her as well. The profound and perverse sorrow at her parting was not only for Nanda but also for the shameful luxury, the music and the feverish thrill of it all. The monotonous, low-key, torpid village life did not suit Bindu.

What was to be done now with Bindu? Going back to Nanda—no, that would not help anyway. Even if she were to return to the warped way of living she had become habituated to, and which she was now pining for, her problem would not be solved. It was under duress that Bindu had become accustomed to that abnormal life, and so the traditional domesticated side of her being had not died within her. She would be unable to do without that wild, turbulent and degrading life; but because of that, she would also suffer unendurable anguish out of shame, sorrow and remorse. Along with her unquenchable thirst for wine, Bindu harboured such a deadly hatred for it that the return of sobriety left her half-dead in mortification.

What was in store for Bindu?

She had overcome her sense of shame. The mean courage of a cornered, timorous beast had been aroused in her. Waking at midnight she came to knock on Shashi's door, roused him and asked for sleeping pills and a cure for headache.

Shashi said, 'Go and lie down quietly; you'll get some sleep; the headache will go too.'

Bindu was crying. 'No, Dada, give me the pills, I can't bear the pain.'

In the dead of night her lean, trembling body and the dire want in her glowing eyes made Shashi anxious; he couldn't make her understand. Bindu would not listen; like a simple-minded child she went on asking for sleeping pills.

Shashi said, 'Don't you have any strength of mind?'

'I'm dying of pain! Where will I find the strength of mind?'

Shashi prepared a mixture for her. Bindu poured it on the floor and, clutching Shashi's feet, she implored, 'Give me some good medicine, please, some *good* medicine, won't you?'

Shashi had locked away the brandy in a box; he had not dared to keep it in the cupboard: without a key, it would not be impossible for her to get at it by breaking the glass. He looked at the prostrate girl for some time. Then he said, 'Let go of my feet. I'll give it.' Taking the sleeping shot from the medicine glass, Bindu went to her room to sleep. Shashi stayed awake sitting quietly; swarms of mosquitoes stung him without respite. He wondered why he was so incapable, so helpless. Why did he have to serve alcohol in the dead of night to one he had brought along with the resolve to give her a new life of repose?

After staying some ten days in Calcutta, Gopal returned. He did not raise the topic of his daughter, seeming to have forgiven Bindu her trespasses of that day. But Shashi knew him; he alone was left a little worried over Gopal's calm exterior.

Three days or so passed without event. Then one morning Gopal called him and said, 'I came across Nanda, Shashi.'

Gopal had chanced upon him on the street quite unexpectedly—he had not on his own gone to meet him. Unable to fathom the workings of Gopal's mind, Shashi grew vexed.

'Bindu has been here a long time, Shashi. Meanwhile Nanda is losing his temper. He told me to send her in a few days.'

Shashi asked categorically, 'Did he tell you to send her or did you guess it from what he said?'

Gopal said emphatically, 'He told me—he told me to send her back. Can you escort her back home?'

Shashi said he could.

'Tomorrow is an auspicious day; start tomorrow itself.'

That's settled then. If she must go, there's no harm in going the next day. He informed Bindu rightaway. She smiled slightly.

'Let's go, Dada. This is better.'

'If I had known, I wouldn't have brought you, Bindu. You only suffered. On the other hand, Nanda grew angry; it wasn't worth it.'

'Not exactly, Dada! If I had not come away, how could I have known that I had no alternative but to lead that sort of life there? From now on, if nothing else, I won't be pointlessly pining for freedom. Now perhaps my mind will settle down. And maybe I'll be happy as well.'

Possibly because her departure was finalised, Bindu cast a good long look at the village at last; she mingled with friends and relatives. After creating a scene that day, Bindu ought to have felt embarrassed to establish an intimacy with others. One day she had wallowed in her own vomit in the courtyard of this house: judging by her sudden transformation to free and confident behaviour with everyone, it did not seem that Bindu remembered it. Sitting in the kitchen with

Kunda's son on her lap, she chatted away with others for quite some time and even laughed. It looked as though after a long spell of a simple and ordinary housewife's life in her husband's house, she had come on a visit to her father's: there was no mortification, no abnormality in life; pure joy filled her heart.

Hearing the news of her departure, women of the entire neighbourhood gathered to have a look at Bindu. Many among them had been there when she was born. Today Bindu was to them even more enigmatic than the fairies of the sky. On one occasion long ago, she had startled the village by her visit; she did this time too. Once again, Bindu—a daughter of their village—was going back to her unknown, mysterious exile. Kusum and Paran came too. Kusum whispered into her ear, 'You seem to be on cloud nine, Didi!'

'I am going back to my hubby, that's why!' An ineffable smile lit up her emaciated face.

'When will you come again?'

'Never again, don't you know, Bou.'

Paran asked Shashi, 'Will you try to get some news of Moti and Kumud, Chhoto-babu?'

'I certainly will. It is Baishakh, you know. And in Baishakh Kumud had said he would join Saraswati Opera. I don't yet know the address of the group. But I don't think it will be difficult to locate.'

'If you happen to trace them, Chhoto-babu, please bring Moti along. It's been two months; she's a mere child, after all; perhaps she's been pining away.'

Two months had already passed? Yes, indeed! Shashi could not look Paran in the face. Moti had been away from the village for two months, and there was no news of them at all meanwhile! If only Kumud had written even to ask for money! If he met Kumud he must thrash it out with him. He must be made to realise what an irresponsible rascal he was.

Well, Moti could have scribbled a letter in her inept hand. Why did she not? Was it because she found no time after dallying with Kumud? Kumud did have this knack; he could make one oblivious of oneself. Besides that, perhaps exactly as Kumud had perceived, an impossible unreal love had actually dawned in Moti's heart; perhaps, as extolled by poets, in the ecstatic joy of conjugal union she had forgotten the world. Shashi laughed to himself: he had begun to imagine Moti in the role of a fictional heroine—he was letting his imagination run away with him.

The next day Shashi departed for Calcutta with Bindu. The journey took a whole day as well as the night; they spoke little to each other. Who could have thought that Bindu would have to be returned to where she came from in this way? That room of Bindu's house—carpeted and cluttered with musical instruments and vile pictures—flashed through his mind. Shashi was thinking: in his cupboard, next to the wine bottle, there were poison phials; why did Bindu not take poison that day?

At about ten in the morning they reached Bindu's house. The watchman bowed in a deep salaam to Bindu as she alighted; Bindu's maidservant smiled from ear to ear. Nanda came downstairs—a shameless, brash Nanda. He received Shashi with a smiling countenance. 'Come, come. Most welcome.'

'I can't come in, Nanda; I have work.'

Bindu implored him, 'Won't you stay for a while, Dada?'

'There's work to do, Bindu.'

Shashi, who had alighted from the carriage, climbed back into it.

Bindu did not again urge him to step out, only saying, 'If you can make it convenient before going back to the village, please come once to see how we're doing.'

Bindu went into the house. The carriage had started to move when Nanda bade the coachman halt; he came near. It seemed to Shashi that Nanda had grown very thin, his eyes showing signs of sleepless nights.

'You won't be coming back to look us up, I suppose?' Nanda asked.

'How can I say? Possibly I won't have the time.'

Nanda considered this and then said, 'You'd do well to come, Shashi. I'm thinking of taking her to our home tomorrow—where my mother and all the others stay. I will sell off this house. She'll perhaps feel a bit out of place to find herself amidst new people. If you go and meet her there, she'll be comforted; it will help her settle down.'

Shashi was surprised. 'You've decided to take her home?'

'That's what I was thinking. Since she does not like to stay here, let her come home. Once she went away with you; what if next time she decides to leave me forever? You know, Shashi, these hassles are a bother to me at my age. Here she had a comfortable life—no crowd, no trouble, independent in every way. If that does not please her, let her be where she'll like to stay; it doesn't matter to me. I'm a man of work; I'm busy with my own work.'

'Why did this good sense not dawn on you earlier, Nanda?'

Nanda had no ready answer to this. And then he said almost like a child, 'How could I have known earlier that she would run away? She seemed quite happy.'

It struck Shashi that he would persuade Nanda to give up this plan. Why was Nanda trying to set right at an inopportune moment the wrong he had been doing for seven years? And when there was little chance of that effort being successful either. How could Bindu, after so many years, suddenly behave like a docile wife covering her head in a veil in the household of her mother-in-law, sisters-in-law and co-wife? If she could, the bland, leisured life of Gaodiya would not have grown so unbearable to her.

Finally Shashi decided that saying nothing at all would be best. This could not be discussed with Nanda.

This time too Shashi put up at the same hotel where he had lodged with Kusum's family. He remembered how restless Moti had grown in eager expectation of seeing Kumud. Moti. That little girl Moti. What a spell Kumud had cast over her—the spendthrift, cruel, nomadic Kumud!

Next day Shashi went out to track him down. A shop dealing in theatrical outfits was able to supply the address of Binodini Opera; about Saraswati Opera, no one could give any clue. Kumud had told him that he no longer had any connection with Binodini Opera; it was doubtful if knocking at their door would yield any result. Still, in the late afternoon, Shashi met the manager of the company on the first floor of a house at Chitpur.[93]

The manager who had just risen from his siesta said, 'Kumud? We too have been after that scoundrel since the month of Aghran, sir. He bluffed me into giving him three months' salary in advance, and then he simply vanished. We had a booking for a performance two days later at the royal palace of Sripur; he has completely let us down.' Glaring angrily at Shashi, the manager said, 'May I ask just what disaster the rascal has brought upon you, sir?'

Shashi smiled slightly. 'What's the use of hearing that? Can you please tell me the address of Saraswati Opera?'

'Saraswati Opera? I haven't even heard the name.'

So was this the end of the search for Kumud? Shashi had got up to go when the manager said, 'Is there any chance of your meeting Kumud?'

'Can't say. It's possible.'

'If you meet him, kindly ask him whether such behaviour was proper for a gentleman's son. Well, forget it; you need not ask him all that. The Babu is quite conscious of his self-esteem. Just tell him that Adhar Mallik cares not a whit for a petty two hundred or four hundred rupees. Why did you need to run away, pray? If you had asked for it, would I not have given you that trifling sum? You have been in my party for three years; I looked upon you as a son!'

His voice caught, who knows whether from phlegm or emotion! Blinking rapidly he said, 'I have no children, you know. I had a daughter. Being the father I shouldn't say this, but she was truly incomparable in looks and accomplishment; as for complexion, she was very fair. I had intended to marry her off to Kumud. But has the lad ever had any plans of getting married—a complete blackguard! That's why I was compelled to give my daughter's hand to a man from Krishnanagar, who turned out to be a most wicked fellow. They tortured the girl to death. I don't know what's come over me since then but I've lost the zest for life. I launched a jatra company, true, and I go to perform on bookings, but my heart is not in it. As it is I'm half-dead with a hundred and one troubles, and it is I whom the fellow left to drown—he has not an ounce of kindness in him. In his place, I couldn't have brought myself to exploit a grieving man, I really couldn't. What sort of chap is he really?'

The manager kept shaking his head for quite a while in disbelief and deep feeling. Then getting more intimate, he went on, 'Let me tell you frankly, Dada, ever since Kumud disappeared, the company has been left crippled. His acting was excellent. I've been in this line for twenty years; never seen one like him. If you see him, tell him I don't mind the money; let him come back, let him work. Adhar Mallik is not one to rake up the past. Does he want a rise of ten or twenty rupees? Did I say I wouldn't give it? What sort of chap is he!'

For three more days Shashi enquired of some other jatra companies, but to no avail. Back home, he had many patients waiting for him, so he could not afford to linger in Calcuta. He decided to go back to Gaodiya the next day. He could not of course spend the rest of his life in Calcuta searching for Moti. This internal urge for returning to the village rather surprised Shashi that night. His room in the hotel overlooked the road. Late at night, he was sitting at the bedside window; pedestrian traffic had thinned and shops and markets were shut. He would have to go back to his village the next day. He used to spend his days dreaming of when he would leave the village and begin to live a more meaningful life encompassing a wider spectrum. And now he had reached a state where he could not stay outside for a week. When he thought of all the patients of cholera, pox, kala azar, typhoid and many other diseases that he had left behind, any plan of remaining in Calcutta even for a day made him consider himself negligent and barbaric. Who knows which of them had died in the meanwhile or whose condition had turned worse! Unless he returned and sat by their bedside again, he would certainly not find his peace of mind. What ties were these? Was it bondage?

Shashi grew angry. He spurned this responsibility; why must he so bind himself with ethics? He would not go back to his village at least for a month—was he the arbiter of life and death? As long as he was in the village, he had visited and treated whoever needed his services. Now if lacking his treatment patients were to die, let them. Three years back, when he was not yet a doctor, what did the villagers do? Let them do that today as well; Shashi knew nothing about it.

8

The vow of not returning to his village for a month did not last more than two days: Shashi's helpless patients in different villages were after all eagerly waiting for him.

He did not wish to meet Bindu anymore. On the eve of his departure, suddenly overcoming his unwillingness, he found himself on the way to Nanda's house. Nanda was home. Where was Bindu? No, she had not yet been brought over here.

Nanda said, 'I was getting ready to go to that house. If you wish to see her, come along with me.'

'I won't have the time, Nanda. I'm going back home today; my train is at seven.'

'Going today itself? Stay a while and have tea and snacks.'

Did Shashi cherish the hope that even though Bindu could not stay at her Gaodiya home, she could still remain the mistress of Nanda's house? When he heard that Bindu had not come, he seemed deeply disheartened. He was a bit surprised to see Nanda's house and its ambience. He had never come here before; he had no idea that there were such distinct and pleasant imprints of aristocracy in Nanda's house. An assortment of antiquated, heavy, solid furniture, costly curtains for doors and windows, life-size oil paintings on the walls, and other fixtures and fittings lent a marvellous and dignified grace to this room of Nanda's. The inner quarters were perhaps not detached: conversation in soothing voices and laughter reached Shashi's ears; he could sense the presence of a large happy family inside. Then at some point a good-looking boy of seven or eight coming to say something stopped short on seeing Shashi, and stood close to Nanda. How beautiful his two curious eyes were! And how affectionate were Nanda's!

'You're covered in sweat!' As he said this, he took off his son's shirt, seemingly to Shashi's surprise. Did this mark a contradiction between Nanda and his surroundings? Was this ancestral home an abode of peace? Did waves of joy and contentment undulate in this circumscribed domestic setting?

When Nanda's son was gone, Shashi said, 'Did you tell Bindu to come here?'

'I did. She won't come.'

Won't come? It was not unexpected; yet Shashi seemed put off.

The servant had laid the hookah, and the smoking tube lurched like a snake in Nanda's hand. He said absently, 'I've never seen such an obstinate person in my life. If you say something to her, she laughs it off. What trouble I am in! I admit that what I had done was not right to begin with; in the heat of the moment I had lost my bearings. But honestly, Shashi, towards the end, it was she who drove me on, never letting me stop. Of course, I did not say anything clearly so far: I never quite realised until now how much my mind had changed, Shashi. This time, when she suddenly went off to Gaodiya, since then some kind of—'

Even a man like Nanda today coughed on the pretext of inhaling tobacco smoke.

'I've been coaxing her so much to come here—it's a long story. I've been telling her every so often: Enough is enough. Now let's go over to that house; you can be happy staying together as one of the family. Khoka's[94] mother has been bedridden for a year; if she were to die, this huge family will be yours. Or do you think I will be taking another wife at this age? At this, she laughs as if I was joking.'

Shashi said, 'Such words in your mouth perhaps do sound like a joke, Nanda.'

Nanda's sentimental spell broke; a cloud of disgust seemed to descend on his face. Putting down his smoking tube, knitting his brow, he said, 'If you've come to make fun—'

'Fun? Of you? If you were not so lacking in common sense, how could you have possibly acted the way you did?'

Shashi did not stay any longer. Nanda did not rise to see him off. Staring at the tea and snacks which Shashi had not touched, he was lost in thought.

After his return to the village, this time Shashi's days went by in uneasy disquiet. In the hot weather, his health too suffered somewhat. This year there had been no rain. Scorched by the sun the lush green appearance of the village had turned almost nut-brown.

This was the season when cholera was rampant; the cremation grounds knew no respite. Having had to work overtime, Shashi was on edge. He scarcely had any time to eat or bathe; yet, he earned little. Such hectic practice in Calcutta would perhaps have made him a *lakhpothi*[95] by now.

Paran had expected that Shashi would bring him news of Moti from Calcutta. The moment he heard of Shashi's return, he made a beeline for him. Shashi could not look him in the eye. As for Paran, after sitting silently for some time, he left. That was in the morning. Then around noon came Kusum. She said, 'I can't see why he's worrying himself to death. After all, no one has kidnapped his sister! She has only gone with her husband; so what's the point in agonising day and night? What did you bring for me, Chhoto-babu?'

'For you? Nothing, Bou.'

'Goodness, how forgetful he is! How many times did I tell you to bring it?'

Surprised, Shashi said, 'What did you ask me to bring? When?'

'Dear me, didn't I tell? Maybe so! I thought I would and ultimately didn't. Even so, should one not bring anything unless told?'

What ingenuous childlike behaviour on part of Kusum, and what an unsullied smile! Thereafter for a few days Shashi did not meet Kusum, but her smile stayed with him. He consciously preserved its memory. The sultry weather, the dried-up ponds, the arid landscape of the village and the revolting proximity of cholera patients: amidst these disturbing phenomena, except for Kusum's singular smile Shashi found nothing worth calling to mind.

Nothing was to Shashi's liking—neither the village nor its people. The sound of the husking implement awakened him before dawn. From then on, until the birds gathered on the branches of the banyan tree by the wayside of Kayetpara began to twitter before the evening silence descended, the various sounds of the wild and the domesticated life that reached Shashi's ears seemed to be drowned by the thumping of Jamini's mortar and pestle and the deep sound of Gopal's cough. Within the house the men and women laughed and cried and quarrelled; outside, the young and old played cards and made idle gossip. Farmers, labourers, milkmen, potters, goldsmiths, fishermen, shopkeepers: except these people, those who had any respectable profession other than idle worthlessness could be counted on one's fingers. In the reddish light of Srinath's shop if Shashi happened to see the oil-smeared growth on Kirti Niyogi's head glistening, the glory of the stars and the moon of the night sky seemed to pall! In the Bagdi quarters, some ex-jailbirds engaged in a brawl at midnight, resulting in broken heads. Their bandages wrapped by Shashi were opened in the jail hospital. Sudeb went about spreading that Moti's marriage was a sham, a pretext and just a ploy of Shashi's to make Moti his own. Remember the gentlemanly person Moti was married to? Do you know how much hush money he's exacted from Chhoto-babu? Shashi has kept Moti hidden somewhere, maybe at Bajitpur, maybe somewhere else. That Shashi did not stay at the village and often went elsewhere on the pretext of going to visit patients, who else but Sudeb knew what that meant! One dark night, eight or ten urchins of Goalapara poured two or three bowls of cow dung water over Shashi—cow dung was plentiful in the colony. Next day when word reached the milkmen's colony that Gopal's steward had gone to file complaints for non-payment of dues at the district headquarters, the headman of the colony, Bipin, did of course come and fall weeping, brought along eight or ten innocent chaps, made them tweak their own ears and rub their noses over a stretch of ground as penance. But that could hardly assuage the mind.

Then there was Sen-didi. While making her escape stealthily in the dark, to stop short on encountering someone had become a favourite histrionic act with her these days. Not far away, the glowing blob of the hookah suddenly vanished somewhere; soon after, Gopal's voice could be heard coming from the inner quarters.

Of late, Sen-didi had been badgering Shashi in a different way. He had recently restored the eyesight of an old man in the village suffering from cataract. From then on, Sen-didi gave him no respite. 'Oh, Shashi,' she would plead, 'now you must take up my case, my son; cutting, stitching, giving medicine, whatever way you can, do heal my eye, dear.'

Shashi said, 'Your eye is permanently damaged, Sen-didi; it won't heal anymore.'

At this Sen-didi said even more desperately, 'It certainly will, in your hands, Shashi. I was not born blind, was I? Where has all the affection that you had for me vanished, son?'

It was difficult to convince Sen-didi. She wouldn't see reason. Clutching Shashi's hands she burst into sobs. 'Everybody calls me one-eyed; I can bear it no more, Shashi. O my son, I'm one-eyed!'

Helpless, Shashi pondered long and then said, 'Will you have a glass eye, Sen-didi? An artificial eye? You can't see with it, true, but it'll look like the real eye; people won't be able to detect easily.'

'What shall I do with a glass eye, Shashi?' She flared up. 'You're a worthless doctor, Shashi; you know nothing about treatment! Now I see what my husband says is not wrong. You've permanently damaged my eye with your wrong treatment; if it had been any other doctor, would I have lost it? You want to deceive me today with a glass eye? Wicked scoundrel, rascal, cheat! Death to you, die!'

Shashi kept quiet. How deeply Sen-didi used to love him; how completely she once trusted him! Still, nothing surprised Shashi anymore. That the love and affection founded on sentimentality was transient like bubbles Shashi had known since long.

Some days later, Sen-didi said, 'Tell me Shashi, if a glass eye is fitted, won't people come to know?' No preamble, no regret for the abuses of that day—a straight, clear-cut question!

'No, they won't know easily. And what even if they do? Now it looks odd because of the eye; at least, that'll be rectified.'

'When will you fit the eye?'

At the mention of a glass eye the other day, Sen-didi had flown into a rage. Today look at her eagerness! Calmly Shashi said, 'But I can't do it myself; I don't have the instruments. I do not even know whether it can be done at Bajitpur. It has to be done in Calcutta; it'll take time. Perhaps the eye will have to be made to match the colour of the healthy eye.'

'When will you take me to Calcutta?'

Sen-didi had no hesitation, no embarrassment in saying this, as if she had all the claim in the world on Shashi. At first he got angry and then he laughed to himself. He said, 'It is not certain when I'll be able to go, Sen-didi. You can see how busy I am with my patients all day. It is doubtful if I can make it before the Pujas. Why don't you go with someone else?'

Sen-didi, on the verge of tears, said, 'Who is there, Shashi? Who'll take me? Everyone will be relieved if I die; who'll go to all this bother? Please make it convenient for my sake, son, so I can get the eye corrected.'

Shashi was also obliged to give her medicine to heal the pitted scars of her face. In less than two days she came back to complain, 'Look, the scars aren't disappearing at all, are they? What kind of medicine are you giving me, Shashi?'

Shashi said in a tired voice, 'They will disappear, Sen-didi, they will. You have to be patient. Do pockmarks go away so soon?'

As the days went by, Shashi's aspiration for launching a new life in a new world beyond the limits of this village grew increasingly stronger in his mind. He realised that unless he forcibly extricated himself, he would never get out of his narrow confines. If he carried on continually deferring it for the future, he would have lived his life never confronting his future. Moreover, if he were to realise the vast splendour that he sought to embrace in life, he needed not merely to quit the village, but to forget the inner ties with his friends and relations as well. If the ripples of the joys and sorrows of their restricted, narrow lives were to keep agitating him like the shell of a banana cone on the river, how could he possibly muster the necessary strength to rebuild his life? The ambience as well as the style in which he aspired to live was tantamount to bringing a revolution in his personal life. A revolution he would have to bring in all by himself, and then live in the newly created world all alone—certainly, there was no room for them there. If thinking of Bindu were to leave him perpetually grief-stricken, whether Kusum wept secretly or what Moti's whereabouts were constantly occupied his mind, and he lamented his inability to mould Sindhu after his heart, when would he organise his own life, do his own work? Those whose company was disturbing, those whom he did not want near him must be removed from the mind ruthlessly if he were to make his life fruitful.

Jadab would say, 'Exactly so, brother! If you wish to renounce the world, you need to have detachment in your mind. At the age of twenty-two I came to this village and set up house; nobody knew anything about where I came from or my antecedents. Earlier I had everything, Shashi: house and homestead, friends and relations. It is forty years since I've stopped concerning myself with them. My parents died: I didn't get the news; I didn't perform their last rites either. Of siblings, I did have some: I don't know whether they are alive or dead. I don't grieve for them either. Shashi, if you are to have a new setup, won't you have to discard the old material?'

'Didn't you feel sad to begin with?' Shashi asked.

'For how many days does one feel sad? Man has a forgetful mind; in a matter of days he forgets. Isn't it because I couldn't stand them in the first place that I renounced them all?'

Pagal-didi laughed and said, 'We're quite happy and peaceful here, aren't we, dear?'

Forty years of peace and happiness! Who knows what Jadab's earlier life was like, and in which village? What inducement made him renounce home at twenty-two? Was this life of a home-bound ascetic desirable to Jadab even then—holding the highest rank among all, in the reverential awe of villages far and near? If so, it must be admitted that he had achieved incomparable success in life. He was known far and wide as a *siddha-purush*;[96] everyone was avid to touch his feet for his blessings.

Shashi could never truly understand Jadab. A detached and dispassionate man, he did not accept any *pronaams*;[97] he remained unperturbed by words charged with obsequious devotion; so many people were eager to be his disciples, but he had not made a single person his disciple so far. Yet, Shashi felt that Jadab seemed to crave for pronaams. He did not give the dust of his feet, did not bless, and he ignored devotion like a soulless god. Shashi was sceptical; he thought that all this was only a clever ploy to arouse fear and reverence in the minds of people. But then, what difference did it make? The habit of being held in the esteem of people as possessing supernatural powers formed an integral part of his forty years of peace and happiness. An abstemious, righteous, peace-loving and harmless man, even Jadab's desire to be regarded by people as possessing supernatural powers was not motivated by any worldly gain. It was, as it were, a mere fancy, a whimsy.

Pagal-didi treated Shashi to a dish of mangoes, while Jadab, sitting with a scripture lying open before him, wound his thick, white *upobeeth*[98] round his finger. This insignia of Jadab's Brahmanhood Shashi never once found soiled. To the unspoken question in his eyes, Jadab smiled and said, 'I never scrub my thread, Shashi.'

'Don't scrub?'

'No. That task I've entrusted to the sun.'

'The sun?' Shashi was astonished.

Jadab said with a grave look, 'Yes, to the sun. You have no faith in *surjo bigyan* and so you look askance; otherwise, you'd know it's elementary. Can the sacred thread of one who is versed in solar science ever be unclean? Do you know what I do? Everyday after my bath, I spread it under the sun and it turns snow-white. Today, a part of it had somehow gone unnoticed: look how dirty it remains.'

Jadab held out his thread and Shashi carefully noticed that like shadow beside sunshine, a segment of the thread indeed looked faded and pale. To inspire Shashi's faith in solar science as well as in his own astounding power, with what care had Jadab dipped this segment in thin watery ink so that the ruse couldn't be detected. Shashi felt amused and at the same time, pity too. Why this frantic effort on Jadab's part to convince him? Even though he had no faith in supernatural powers, his respect for Jadab was no less.

Jadab said, 'How often did I tell you: learn, Shashi, learn; learn at least the preamble to the solar science and you won't have to move about carrying your medicine box while visiting patients. But you did not. You stayed engrossed in a science whose very foundation is false. One can't impart this knowledge to just anybody; in all my life I haven't found one deserving disciple to whom I could teach the science. Meanwhile, my time to depart draws near. Only you could learn a bit, but certainly not the whole of it; even you aren't competent for the whole, just the introduction. But then how many get even that much? Only because you are a devout celibate even today—'

Shashi listened, embarrassed and amazed. Jadab often used to say words to this effect; Shashi neither approved nor disapproved. He came to Jadab's tranquil dwelling with the aroma of incense that relieved his jaded state for a while: why should he be made to listen to all these incredible stories? Was he a Srinath Mudi[99] that he would be overcome by emotion and froth at the mouth?

Jadab could sense Shashi's disbelief. Perhaps that was also the reason why he was so eager to win Shashi over.

He said, 'What is impossible for one who knows solar science? The past and the future are at his fingertips: what will happen in one's life; and, when everything is within his knowledge, he can even foresee ten or twenty years in advance the day of his death.'

While saying this, Jadab kept alternately winding and unwinding his holy thread round his fingers, his eyes shining brightly. It was not for nothing that the fearful villagers were in awe of him! Nobody had the courage to disbelieve whatever he might say with such a luminous gaze and such force of conviction.

'Do *you* know?' Shashi asked.

'Don't I? I've known it for twenty years now.'

Lest he break into a laugh, Shashi blurted out, 'When?'

Jadab also promptly replied, 'On the Rath[100] Day. I shall die on the day of the Rath, Shashi.'

Which year on the Chariot Day, as predetermined, Jadab would discard his mortal body Shashi refrained from asking because immediately after uttering the words, Jadab abruptly fell into such a nervous silence and Pagal-didi gave out such a muffled scream that Shashi felt embarrassed. Provoking him with the pressure of scepticism, he ought not to have made Jadab inadvertently utter those words. Jadab knew that Shashi would not be staying in the village for more than another six months to a year. Even so, within that time in case he should be struck by a life-threatening illness, and Shashi himself were to come to treat him, the poor fellow would find no satisfaction even in dying.

To defuse the situation Shashi broached a different topic. 'You know, Pandit-mashay,[101] go away I must, true; but at times I feel apprehensive. If I only wished to go and practise in the city, there would be no problem. But I think so big! Of going to foreign countries; after returning, to set up practice in Calcutta, carry out researches into the various diseases of the human body and mind, make a name in the country and abroad, make money—'

The way Jadab had been talking of solar science Shashi now spoke about his own dream.

That marked the beginning. What Jadab had said forecasting his death on the Rath Day Shashi knew was just an incidental remark uttered at an unguarded moment. Shashi did not know why, on going to Haru Ghosh's house, he had narrated this story to Paran in course of a conversation, perhaps to let it be heard by Kusum. It had become a sort of habit with Shashi to recount in the hearing of Kusum, on the pretext of telling Paran, whatever curious things he witnessed anywhere.

Then somehow the news spread! And it spread far and wide, across villages. Who could have known that the meaningless words Jadab had impulsively told Shashi would cause such a stir!

Shashi was preparing to set out for Bajitpur when Srinath came running. 'Is it true, Chhoto-babu, that Debata will give up the ghost?'

Shashi said, 'Are you mad, Srinath? What he said or didn't by way of conversation—'

'That is just what he would do, say it casually by way of conversation, or would he go about spreading it on his own! Just tell me, Chhoto-babu, did Debata himself state that he will cease to live on the Rath Day?'

'He did, indeed, say so, but you know—'

'Alas, calamity!' A visibly moved Srinath rushed out.

Even at that time, Shashi did not imagine that the matter would snowball in the manner it did. Or he would have called Srinath back to clarify that Jadab had indeed said it, but it could be any Rath Day, not specifically the coming one. Shashi was on his way to Bajitpur along with a difficult surgical patient to get him admitted to the hospital. The patient's condition was critical. Shashi forgot to tell

Srinath because he was preoccupied with the thought whether it was wise counsel to decide on hospitalisation or not, for if the patient did not survive the journey it would be a matter of great regret.

Shashi had developed a familiarity with the government doctor at Bajitpur, who was going to be transferred soon. He persuaded Shashi to halt for the night. Next day, on returning to the village, Shashi was surprised to see crowds of people on the Kayetpara path. Many of them had gathered in front of Jadab's dilapidated house. Jadab had come out and was sitting in the open, devotees scrambling for a grain of his foot-dust. Srinath, his voice moist with tears, was intermittently uttering, '*Hai, hai!*'.

Someone said to Shashi, 'On the coming Rath Day, Pandit-mashay will leave his body.'

'The coming Rath Day? Who said this?'

'The blessed tongue has uttered it. People from distant villages are coming, Chhoto-babu. Just now Shital-babu paid a visit.'

Shashi took the back door to go into the house. Women had begun to come in throngs; Pagal-didi had not opened her door. At Shashi's persistent call, she finally did; she wept and said, 'O Shashi, why did you bring such ruin upon me? Why did you spread the word?'

With a pale face Shashi said, 'But I did not spread it, Pagal-didi!'

'Srinath came with a horde of people and fell crying, Shashi. Srinath said that you told him you had heard from his own mouth that this year on the Rath Day—'

'*This* year on the Rath Day? I had not said this, Pagal-didi. Did Pandit-mashay admit this?'

Pagal-didi assented.

Shashi anxiously said, 'Why did he do that? What madness is this? Could Pandit-mashay not say that he had not meant this Rath Day?'

'At any rate, he did not do so; on the contrary, he affirmed it with a smile. What's the way out now?'

The noise outside was coming in; Shashi put the door on the latch. The entire matter seemed quite baffling to him. Such hearsay about Jadab was by no means surprising; various strange rumours about him did occasionally circulate. Why did Jadab confirm it? Jadab was certainly not eccentric, nor by any means a madman! With a troop of blokes Srinath came and fell weeping; instantly, without a thought Jadab ended up admitting that he would court voluntary death on the coming Rath Day? Should he not have paused to ponder the consequences of such a public avowal? There was no knowing what would happen now! If on the Rath Day Jadab did *not* die, he would be deemed by people to be a liar; they would lose faith in his spiritual fulfilment, in his extraordinary power: to Jadab, that would be a hundred times more frightful than death! Except for the blind faith of man, he had no other resource to fall back on for survival! Why did he admit the truth of the words attributed to him? He could well have said that it was mere hearsay, a baseless rumour! Who would have disbelieved Jadab's utterance? The Rath Day was not too far away. How could he die on that day? And if he did not die, how could he possibly face the villagers afterwards?

After a long time, a weary Jadab came inside for rest. A few devotees were also making their way into the room in his wake; rudely pushing them out, Shashi closed the main gate. Perspiring profusely from the heat and the crowd Jadab had gone pale; Pagal-didi quickly brought a hand fan and started fanning him with it. The constant smile on his toothless face had been snuffed out; tears filled his eyes—two dim eyes of old age.

'What is this you've done, Pandit-mashay? Why did you do it?' Shashi was solicitous.

'Why did I do it? I will die on the Rath Day, that is why. Did I not tell you?' Jadab replied placidly.

'But you didn't tell me about this year's Rath, did you?'

'Of course I did. This year's Rath is what I said. Why are you so troubled, Shashi? Is there any difference to me between life and death? By the mercy of my Guru, the day I mastered the solar science, the day I attained my spiritual goal, that difference was wiped out. Even by normal reckoning, am I not old enough to die?'

'It is all because of me,' said Shashi. 'If only you knew how terrible I'm feeling about it!'

Pandit-mashay smilingly went on to quote from the Bhagavad Gita: *Just as after discarding worn-out clothes, man takes on new ones…*

Shashi remembered the night when Jadab, just returned from Calcutta, was making his way home from Srinath's shop, tapping the path with the tip of his staff in fear of snakes. Where had that pusillanimous attachment to life disappeared? And where had this serene detachment vis-à-vis death come from? Had Shashi got it all wrong about Jadab? Did Jadab indeed possess the supernatural power that people spoke of? Perhaps the knowledge acquired by reading a couple of medical books was not sufficient for explaining such abstruse matters. Perhaps Shashi's incredulity was the mere murkiness of ignorance!

No amount of arguing, requesting, pleading or imploring could make Jadab retract. He did not admit that he had *not* mentioned the coming Rath. Shashi had done him no harm. Even if the word had not spread, Jadab would definitely give up his life on the Rath Day. If Shashi had caused Jadab any inconvenience by whipping up a public frenzy, it was only because people were pestering him for his foot-dust, and nothing else.

'Aren't you going to give up this plan, Pandit-mashay?'

'How can that be, Shashi? It's been predetermined for twenty years.'

'How is it then that Pagal-didi knew nothing of this?'

'Did I ever tell her that she would know? The time has drawn near and so I told you in the course of our talk that day. Otherwise, I would have announced it right on the day of my departure.'

With frenzied imploring Shashi said, 'By sheer will power you can defer the day of your death as well, can't you? Why don't you make a public announcement to that effect? Say that you have much work left to do, so after some deliberation you have deferred the day by two or three years.'

The proposal seemed to take Jadab's fancy. He looked on eagerly at Shashi's face. It seemed to Shashi as if a trapped animal had suddenly spotted a small opening in the fence. Then, restraining himself, Jadab shook his head.

'People will laugh at me, Shashi. They will taunt me.'

Saying this, he at once added, 'That is not the only reason, though. The power one acquires by practising yoga one is forbidden to apply for circumventing God's decree, Shashi.'

After making enquiries in different quarters throughout the day, Shashi came to understand to some extent why Jadab had acknowledged the rumour without protest. The word had spread taking on many appendages along its course; many among the devotees knew that Jadab had for long been trying to win Shashi over as a disciple—a good fortune of the latter they envied. Kusum reportedly went around yesterday telling people hurriedly and excitedly that when she had gone after her bath to offer her pronaam to Pagal-didi, she had herself heard that since he was going to die on the Rath Day, Jadab was insisting on Shashi being initiated as a disciple. Other rumours had gained currency too. Still, even at that point Jadab might possibly find out a way to deny the basis of the rumour. What Shashi told Srinath before going to Bajitpur turned out to be the greatest bane for Jadab. People did not disbelieve Shashi's words easily. Besides, he was known to be a special favourite of Jadab's. Even so, if Shashi had been in the village, Jadab would perhaps have sent for him and told him, 'Just listen to what these people are saying, Shashi.' But he was not found. Whipping up a commotion in the village, he had left. And then fearing a dent in the extraordinary devotion built up with the endeavours of a lifetime, and lured by the temptation of enhancing that devotion, Jadab was carried away by the tide of public perception.

Shashi could somewhat guess the condition of Jadab's mind when Srinath and the others came and fell crying at his feet. Jadab remembered what he had told Shashi about his death. He was also well aware of the considerable faith that people had in Shashi's words. When told that Shashi was not in the village, Jadab had calculated that if he now denied having told Shashi about dying on the Rath Day, on Shashi's return, people would cross-check with him. Maybe, some enthusiast unable to restrain himself might rush to Bajitpur to meet Shashi. In all probability, Shashi would not perceive the gravity of the matter and end up repeating what he had said. People would then conclude that either Shashi was a liar, or Jadab himself was.

Perhaps Jadab had thought many other things too. Perhaps unable to fathom the nature and strength of the rumour, it frightened him to think that if he contradicted it, what was dearer to him than life itself would be ruined. Perhaps the exuberance of the crowd had befuddled him like an intoxicant. He had had no time to think.

Shashi asked Kusum, 'Why did you go around telling lies, Bou?'

Kusum said, 'Somehow I felt like, Chhoto-babu; that's why.'

'I sometimes wonder whether you're mad, Bou. You are a strange person.'

Days passed. People from near and distant villages thronged the Kayetpara path to see the great man of imminent-voluntary-death fame in this *Kaliyuga*. Srinath the grocer and Lochan the confectioner between them made a lot of money. Srinath did brisk business selling puffed rice and beaten rice, put away the coins in his wooden cashbox and kept wailing all the time. Pagal-didi seemed to rapidly grow thinner. A heavy weight bore down on Shashi's mind as well. He could not imagine what would happen on the appointed day. Could Jadab indeed by will power give up his life on that day? This was scarcely believable. And what would Jadab's plight be if he didn't die after all?

Wherever Shashi went, he could hear this one topic being discussed. Few regretted the prospect of Jadab's death; they were eagerly awaiting the Rath Day. Shashi had to keep silent. There was no way to disclose that such a serious affair was based on a lie. He was the source of this public opinion, but he had not the power to correct this canard. A single spark had set a dry thatch on fire; no one had the power to extinguish it. Shashi felt a strange sort of helplessness. He realised for the first time today that the collective opinion of people with whom we have no relation whatsoever in our daily lives could grow into an ineluctable, blind and ruthless force.

Shashi would often visit and spend time at Jadab's house, observing the man's emotions and expressions. Jadab seemed to have been overwhelmed and stupefied by some insuperable addiction. The whole affair seemed to be gradually growing into something highly enjoyable to him. He would come into the inner rooms briefly for rest and then go out again and sit in the open before the devotees, his mouth spurting like a fountain words of religion, philosophy, yoga, and spiritual exploration. Shashi was amazed to listen to those marvellous deliberations. It was as if some miraculous spell of inspiration had come over him. To hear him speak was to be stimulated, to be filled with a unique delight, to feel a limitless yearning for being elevated to an unattained spiritual realm.

Pagal-didi said piteously, 'What's befallen us, Shashi?'

Shashi kept pondering in silence. One day he said to Jadab, 'If you have indeed decided that you will leave us on the Rath Day, why must you stay here? Why don't you go over to Puri?[102] That is the place where the real festival of Rath is held; here, virtually nothing happens. The Rath of the Babus is the biggest; even that chariot is not more than three arm-lengths high. Going to Puri is what you should do.'

Jadab seemed to be startled out of a stupor. 'You're suggesting that I go to Puri?'

Shashi feared that Jadab had perhaps not got the real purpose of his suggestion to go to Puri. He had pondered a great deal before coming up with this solution to Jadab's predicament. It didn't matter whether Jadab did go to Puri or not. He would declare that he was going to Puri, then go away anywhere he liked in this vast country and live among unknown people at unknown places where even if he did not die on the Rath Day there would be no cause for shame. A sensitive matter like this could not be spelt out for Jadab. As for pretence, Jadab had kept it up for Shashi too. The latter threw a hint. 'It's best that you go off to Puri, Pandit-mashay, taking Pagal-didi along with your possessions. The people of the village are giving you so much trouble and making such a lot of noise; you're getting no respite in your last days. There nobody can catch up with you.'

Pagal-didi was sprawled on the floor; she sat up all at once. Jadab looked on in wonder at Shashi. Shashi again said, indirectly, 'You just say that you're going to Puri. Of course, it doesn't mean you have to go to Puri itself. If you wish to go to any other holy place, very well, change your decision on the way and proceed accordingly. Then you can spend the last few days peacefully amidst unknown people.'

Shashi nodded gravely. 'Save for this, I don't see any other way for you to get away from the clutches of the people.'

'What are you saying, Shashi? In the end, I shall run away?'

'Why run away? You're going on a pilgrimage.'

Jadab thought over it. Suddenly he flew into a rage. Trembling in anger he said, 'You're mocking me, Shashi! You've started joking! You presume that all these are pretensions, don't you? Not for a day have you believed me. You have always thought that all I say or do is humbug, that I've spent my entire life deceiving people! With a modicum of English knowledge you've grown into a know-all; what will you understand of all this? What would you know about yogic practice? You're an atheist, an unbeliever in Hindu customs! Because I have a soft spot for you, I've never said anything hurtful; rather I've tried by counselling you and talking about scriptures to change your mind. The real devil dwells in you, Shashi; it is beyond me to do you any good. Now get out of my sight; to see your face is to commit a sin.'

Who could have known that Jadab could scold Shashi so harshly! In the world, next to Pagal-didi, he was the object of Jadab's deepest affection.

To see his face was to commit a sin! He was an atheist, an unbeliever! What a grand prize for giving advice on how to escape death to one who must choose between death and infamy in just a few days! Jadab's rebuke left Shashi afflicted by a deep sorrow and injured pride like a child.

Was it then true that Jadab would be courting wilful death on the Rath Day? So Jadab had indeed foreseen with his yogic power long ago the certainty that the day of his death was preordained? If that was the case, Shashi was no doubt a sinful infidel: even now he did not believe that man could die of his own free will or know when death would come.

Even though he did not believe it, the rustic superstition hidden in a corner of his mind had been stirred. At times he would tend to think that perhaps there did exist something; something beyond the ambit of rational judgement known only to Jadab and men of his ilk.

Throngs of people were prostrating themselves at Jadab's feet: was everyone's belief false? If indeed Jadab did not possess something more than an ordinary man did, was it without reason that so many people were behaving so crazily? Householders with their families had come from villages some twenty or twenty-five miles away and were camping under trees. Shashi had noticed tears rolling down the eyes of so many people. Getting down to the Kayetpara path, he felt as if he had come to a place of pilgrimage. Men and women of different ages who were wandering about had left behind the accumulated filth of envy, malice and selfishness of everyday life, had forgotten their desire for worldly pleasure, their calculations of petty losses or gains. Maybe all this was temporary; once they went back, maybe they would once again wallow in the meanness of their workaday world. Still, the eager intentness writ large on their faces right now was entrancing.

Everyone else being preoccupied with Jadab, it was easier for Kusum to meet Shashi. She said in an anxious voice, 'Why do you look so depressed?'

'All's not well with my mind, Bou.'

'Ah me! What's wrong with your mind?'

Irked, Shashi said, 'I don't have to give you an explanation, Bou.'

Proudly raising her head, Kusum said, 'Nobody asked for your explanation. I just felt sorry to see your pale face, so I came to ask if you were ill. In this world, you know, Chhoto-babu, if one goes out of one's way to express sympathy, there's insult to expect at every step. Meanwhile, I'm leaving this place for my father's house; and I'll call for explanations!'

Shashi softened a bit. 'There's so much going on in the village, but when we meet you say nothing about that; only about the two of us. Is there nothing else in the world to speak about?'

'Why not? There's loads of claptrap and there's no end to it!'

Kusum laughed as she said this. Shashi said, 'Try to be a bit serious, Bou. You're going to your father's house—this I've been hearing for a long time; only, it doesn't happen.'

Kusum smartly said, 'I just can't get away.'

Then she said, 'What funny goings-on in the village! A seventy-year-old man will die and people of a dozen villages are making a big fuss over it. I suppose I'll live to witness much more!'

Not that Shashi particularly liked this kind of talk from Kusum. Even so the stuffy atmosphere that had been created in his mind by brooding all alone seemed to lighten somewhat with a draught of fresh air. Indeed so! Why was he so agitated over a rustic matter? If Jadab was going to die, let him; what did it matter to him? After a few days, would he even find the time to recall having once lived in this village?

That day in the afternoon, Srinath came and called him. Pagal-didi herself came the next day. Shashi had to go.

Pagal-didi said, 'It was all very well for you to tell us to go on a pilgrimage, but what would come of it? The people of the entire village will follow in a procession. So many are keeping watch day and night; where does one escape evading their notice?'

Pagal-didi seemed to have shaken off her inertia; had she found any ray of hope from any quarter, who could tell? She looked very sad yet calm; signs of fear and anxiety had gone. On the way, she said, 'What would we gain in the end, tell me, even if we fled? How many years more will we live? In another land we would have to suffer living among strangers; it would only bring regret. The point is—what happiness is there in living one or two more years in this manner? Rather, it is far more glorious to depart in this way.'

'But can anyone really depart of one's own sweet will at any time one chooses, Didi?'

'You know he has attained the spiritual goal, you crazy boy. Is there anything impossible for him?'

Perhaps Pagal-didi had come when no one was looking; as soon as they spotted her, they came crowding around her. With great effort making her way with Shashi into their house, she shut the door. She could not bear a crowd. People clamoured to have a look at her also, but she never came out. Oil and vermilion in their hands, women had to turn back from her closed door.

Coming into the room, Jadab said, 'So you've come, Shashi? Because I spoke one or two harsh words that day, out of pique you didn't show up even once these several days? I was thinking of you, Shashi. You have no idea what harm you caused me that day. Out of a misplaced compassion, you gave me bad counsel; it distracted me from time to time. I cannot easily ignore what you say.'

Jadab said much more. He was leaving the world behind; Shashi should look after his Pagal-didi. So far, whenever she fell ill, it was Jadab who had cured her by his solar science; from now on perhaps she would have to take Shashi's medicine. 'Shashi, you could do with taking lessons in solar science. You're not a Brahman's son, so I cannot initiate you as my disciple; but then, I could impart the knowledge. Are you willing?' Jadab smiled. 'But there's no more time to learn, Shashi!'

Two days before the Rath, there were heavy rains. *That day* too, during the morning, sometimes it drizzled, at other times it remained cloudy. A session of devotional songs had started the previous evening and continued through the night without pause. In the morning, new groups had taken over, lending greater panache to the choir. Jadab, after taking his bath, had put on a silk cloth; devotees had decked him in garlands. Pagal-didi too had not been spared today; many garlands had found their way to her neck as well. But women with living husbands refrained from offering her oil and vermilion; one who was ordained to be widowed today ought not be offered those marriage insignias. As the day progressed, the area in front of Jadab's house and the Kayetpara path swarmed with people. A band of boys from Gaodiya, Saatgaon and Ukhara villages worked as volunteers controlling the crowd; their enthusiasm was the greatest. Bamboo fences had been put up demarcating separate passages for men and women. Jadab's seat was laid out on the rickety veranda of his dwelling. In the courtyard the leading lights of the village sat chatting on some charpoys that had been spread out. The manner in which they smoked their hookahs and talked portrayed the prevailing mood of a ceremonial house as though they had come to supervise a wedding or sacred thread ceremony. Both Shital-babu and Bimal-babu had paid their visits once in the morning and came again around noon. The women of their families came in the afternoon. Jadab and Pagal-didi had by now reached a moribund state.

Shashi kept a close watch on the two all through. Finding that from around eleven in the morning both were gradually sinking and growing drowsy, he felt a great turmoil within. Later Jadab, opening his drooping eyes to look just once at Shashi, beamed an inscrutable smile; Pagal-didi's eyes were closed. Jadab's face was covered in a clammy sweat and a darkling hue, and the pupils of his eyes had contracted. In a gathering of three or four thousand eager and excited people, Shashi was the only doctor; he shuddered. Yet he could hardly blink: he observed the successive appearance of the familiar signs of imminent death from a known cause in the bodies of both Jadab and Pagal-didi.

When everyone sensed that along with Jadab Pagal-didi too had set out for the other world and perhaps would breathe her last even before Jadab, a fresh clamour rose all around. Everyone, child or old, male or female, went berserk. Thanks to the volunteers, getting a glimpse of the unique couple and offering pronaam had been going on smoothly; now the crowd seemed to be on the point of going out of control. It looked like Jadab and Pagal-didi were going to be crushed by the crowd; Pagal-didi's feet were covered with several layers of vermilion.

Thereafter when the mob had been brought under control by the boys, a bier was made and the two were laid side by side. On the narrow path of Kayetpara, on no previous occasion had the Rath been drawn. By Shital-babu's order, at about three in the afternoon the chariot of the Babu family was, after much effort, hauled up to Jadab's premises. Pagal-didi could not be made to open her eyes at all; Jadab opened his eyes just once with difficulty: his pupils had grown even smaller now.

After that Jadab too made no response of any kind. People cried in unison: '*Samadhi*'![103] Pagal-didi died after about an hour; nobody could note the precise time. A Brahman housewife cleansed the froth of her mouth with Ganga water. Jadab breathed his last at dusk.

Shashi, a non-Brahman, was not permitted to touch the bodies. From a distance he anxiously said, 'Someone please sprinkle some Ganga water in his mouth.'

The world is a web of truth and falsehood. Falsehood has significance too. The fascination of it can drive thousands crazy. A lie can even reign perpetually as truth. Of those who had considered themselves blessed by taking the dust of Jadab and Pagal-didi's feet, who could have guessed the mystery of their death? The incident remained etched for ever in their minds—the memory of a unique, unearthly sight. It would come to mind in times of sorrow and pain! If ever life grew unbearably harsh and arid, one might still find the courage to hope that in the world there could be found such things that were greater than survival. By sheer strength of will man could overcome even death, not to speak of sorrow, bereavement or unendurable exhaustion. Shashi wondered how Jadab had left a yearning, whether faint or intense, for something vast in the weak narrow minds of scores of men. And when he thought this, he forgot about the clammy sweat over the skin, the gradual diminution of the pupils of the eyes to pinpoints, and the frothing at the mouth under the action of opium.

The rains came. Water rose in the canal; ponds and ditches filled up. It was muddy all around, and movement by road was difficult. The feet of palanquin bearers sank in the mud; they had to walk slowly. Amid such foul weather, one day Kusum's father came to take his daughter home. That day, near the taalpukur, Kusum fell down she alone knew how. She said she had injured her hip and fractured her hand.

'How will I go with you now?' She said. 'I can't go, Baba. Come back during the puja to take me along.'

Kusum's father Ananta lamented, 'It's so long you haven't been there; your mother often weeps, Kushi.[104] Let me stay back and watch for a couple of days, in case the pain subsides.'

'Is a pain like this going to subside in just a couple of days, Baba? I can't move from the pain in the hip. Who knows I might have broken a bone or two.'

She had indeed sprained her hand. Shashi came, and while examining her, privately asked, 'You didn't fall willingly, I suppose?'

'The things you say, Chhoto-babu! Does one fall willingly to break one's hip?'

'Your arm is all right then; only your hip is broken, isn't it?'

'My arm is broken too.'

Moving her hand about, Shashi said, 'But the swelling is not much?'

Kusum said with some irritation, 'How much swelling do you expect, Chhoto-babu? Will it swell like a drum?'

Next day at about noon, a dense canopy of clouds enveloped all sides in darkness. Shashi was sitting in his room. He had an appointment with patients in another village; seeing the sky overcast, he had cancelled it. When he was in a brown study, a downpour began. That was when Kusum came; unable to bear the pain in her hand, she had come to ask for medicine.

Shashi said, 'How severe can your pain be that you braved the heavy rain to come for medicine? And how did you come at all? Isn't your hip broken?'

Kusum mumbled, 'I had to make quite an effort.'

'Why did you have to come, even so? I would have gone in the afternoon myself.'

'I can't bear it, Chhoto-babu.'

Now Shashi went slightly pale. He knew that it would not do to go on like this forever; a day would arrive when matters would come to a head. Still, braving such inclement weather, she had come to settle scores with him? Kusum could not be blamed. It was cruel of him to have tried to keep evading the day under cover of light flirtation. That Kusum had borne this for so long was surprising enough. Whatever there might be in his mind, what did it matter to Kusum? Why should she keep indulging his timid silence indefinitely? Shashi felt ashamed to think how unfair he had been for so long in his conduct with Kusum.

In a mild voice he said, 'Don't feel bad, Bou. I should have understood it before.'

Kusum did not speak, which apparently made Shashi look more ashen still. Rain splashed through the window. He got up to shut it and now at last suddenly found himself making some awkward courtesies. 'Why don't you take a seat, Bou? Please be seated over there.'

Kusum sat down, much to her relief. In a still milder voice Shashi said, 'I've been thinking of telling you something for a long time, Bou. I was on the verge of telling you many times, but couldn't. But it needs to be told at any rate, isn't it? We are not children; can we do just anything simply because we wish to? We have to be prudent. For one, you see Paran is my friend; trying to be good to him I've always done him nothing but harm. Yet I wouldn't even have bothered about that. You've come braving this weather; the anguish of not being able to sit closer to you I would not have brought myself to bear for anyone's sake. But I am not going to stay on in the village, Bou. Today or tomorrow I will go away to some distant land, never to return. In such a situation, with a bit of determination—'

Abruptly lifting her face Kusum said, 'My hand is paining badly so I came to ask for medicine. What is all this you're telling me?'

Shashi was flustered for a bit, then he spoke dryly, 'Come for medicine, did you say?'

'Can't bear the pain in the hand, Chhoto-babu.'

His face looking pallid, Shashi said, 'I don't know of any medicine for pain in the hand. Go and apply the massage oil I left with you. How will you go back in this rain?'

'How did I come?' Saying this Kusum swung open the door and got down into the rain. Her gait wouldn't give one the impression that yesterday she had been confined to bed with an injured hip. A gloom like the rains descended on Shashi's mind. Kusum had to become so unfathomable in the end. How ardently had Shashi anticipated that Kusum would listen calmly to all that he had to say and understand the matter thoroughly. With nothing incomprehensible, no gaps left anywhere, there would linger no sorrow, pique or shame in their minds. Their mutual understanding would end in an atmosphere of deep cordiality and profound sympathy. Instead what happened? As he went on thinking, he felt that Kusum's was a rustic mind; she was completely unable to grasp anything.

Next day he heard from Paran that the pain in Kusum's hand and hip had subsided. She would proceed to her father's house the day after.

'How long will she stay there?'

'She says she will come back after the pujas. Let's see how long she stays ultimately.'

'It will be hard on you, Paran.'

Paran said gravely, 'How is it going to be hard? A handful of rice twice a day: this my mother can very well boil for me. It is my considered decision to send her, Chhoto-babu. Unless a woman gets to go to her father's house, her head goes haywire.'

There had been no plan at night. Towards dawn, deciding to go to Bajitpur, Shashi went and woke up Gobardhan and two other boatmen and set out. When going alone to Bajitpur, he never used a large boat; Gobardhan took him in a small boat all by himself. Today why he needed a large one was not apparent. Laying down the bedding, loading his water jug, tiffin carrier packed with home-made food, a basket of ripe mangoes, ingredients for tea, his medicine box, and so on Gobardhan arranged everything. But Shashi did not immediately give his order to untie the boat. He stood on the bank smoking a cigarette.

When it was light, Kusum's palanquin reached the ghat, Ananta and Paran with her. Surprised to see Shashi, Paran said, 'How come Chhoto-babu is here?'

'I'm going to Bajitpur, Paran. I was waiting for you all. They had better not go by that small boat of yours. Come up to Bajitpur with me; there I'll find a suitable boat for you.'

So be it. No one had any objection.

Kusum got into Shashi's boat, helped by Paran. When her trunk, bundles and other articles had been loaded into the boat, Shashi said, 'You go inside the awning, Bou, and sit on the bed. Take the front position so you can see the sights.'

9

The rocking of the boat made Kusum's father feel sleepy. Kusum made arrangements for him to lie down in the rear part under the awning. When he fell asleep, she called Shashi to her and said, 'Can I ask why you suddenly fancied escorting me to my father's house?' She smiled slightly on saying this.

Shashi said, 'So you think I've no work? I'm going just for your sake? I've got to consult my lawyer.'

'There is a court case, I suppose?'

'One or two cases are always there. That's not the reason. I don't know why he has written to me to go, but it is urgent. Of course, I might as well have not gone today.'

A faint smile played on Kusum's lips.

Taking an oblique glance at her father, she said, 'It is for my sake that you've come today, isn't it?'

'Yes.'

Kusum's face brightened up in great felicity. Yet, breathing audibly she said with a hint of sorrow, 'I had planned to stay at my father's house for a couple of months; that is not to be, I see.'

Kusum's was a strange character. At this point, Shashi felt a bit abashed. The other day she had woven no mystery: the manner in which she spoke her mind was convoluted like that. She wouldn't understand anything, wouldn't accept anything. Why did Shashi worry himself to death? That was the only meaning of her conduct that day. Shashi was surprised over another matter as well. That day he had said he would leave the village for good. Did Kusum have nothing to say about that? Had she not believed him?

Beaching his boat at Bajitpur ghat Shashi got down and went his way. He gave instructions to Gobardhan that after leaving Kusum at her father's house he should be back and get the boat made fast at the ghat in the afternoon.

In connection with his court cases, Shashi had often had to come to Ramtaran-babu who was a senior advocate at Bajitpur. This time too, he had received a letter from him two or three days back and there was no unusual expectation in his mind. So when Shashi heard about the matter, he was startled. Jadab had died stirring and intriguing a dozen villages; that he had stowed away more surprises Shashi could not even imagine.

Jadab had bequeathed everything he owned to set up a hospital in the village. All the arrangements were to be made by Shashi; all the responsibility was Shashi's.

What did Jadab own? Not much to be adequate contribution for setting up a hospital; but coming from Jadab, it was astounding, huge: some fifteen thousand rupees in company shares, about twelve or thirteen thousand rupees in cash, besides the house and the land where he lived. Jadab had so much money? Jadab and Pagal-didi's simple homemaking in the damp rooms of the old dilapidated house recurred in Shashi's mind: a couple of utensils, earthen pots and pitchers, a weather-worn wooden chest and the destitution due to lack of furnishing. Even that much was wonderful indeed; the cleanliness and incense-filled tranquillity of the rooms had always enthralled Shashi, but there had not been any hint of wealth in the home of that worldly ascetic!

Ramtaran was an elderly man. He had curtailed his visits to the court to a great extent. A pious man, he used to rise at four in the morning and sit in prayer. He said, 'Word had reached me that he would give up his life voluntarily. I thought it was a rumour and didn't believe it. Else, I would have paid a visit. Now I regret that I didn't. How often he had blessed this house with the dust of his feet! If I knew he was a man of such exceptional holiness, I would have improved my prospects for the afterlife. He came and he went. I never could sense his intrinsic greatness.'

Shashi added, 'Many said he had attained godliness.'

'Indeed he had. But he was so self-effacing there was no way to recognise his worth. Had I only known before!'

There was much talk, much discussion and much counselling. Ramtaran's son, son-in-law, clerks and officials crowded round and listened to Shashi's words in silent amazement. While hearing the detailed narrative of Jadab's passing away, Ramtaran, overcome by emotion, said, 'Man dies as he must; but how many meet with such a death? No illness, no mishap: he just wished and the soul left his body to merge with the infinite. What do they call this in your medical science, Shashi?'

'What would they call it? Nothing whatsoever.'

Ramtaran said even more effusively, 'How could they? Except India, where else in the world is this knowledge to be found? One gets gooseflesh even thinking about it. Once we have leafed through a few pages in English, we tend to disbelieve all this, dismiss it as a hoax. Well, can anybody come forward and point out any of it as sham? You're a doctor yourself; you stood watch over the entire proceedings. Go, Shashi—write out the whole story and send it to newspapers: let people know and have a change of heart.'

Shashi had been coming to this family since when he was small. He had his midday meal here and had some rest. A few days before his death, Jadab had come to the town and executed his last will. It was after the day when Shashi, daring to advise him to flee for his life and honour, had been reprimanded. Perhaps around that time Jadab had determined to die, not before. Today everything became clear to Shashi. How exceptionally beautiful and coveted death had grown to appear! Could man possibly overcome its allure? Standing nearby, Shashi had witnessed everything from beginning to end; death as well as the cause remained permanently etched in his mind, and his alone.

But why did Jadab have to involve him? Shashi was a heathen infidel who had disbelieved the man's miraculous power until the end; yet when it came to setting up a hospital, it was to his care that Jadab had entrusted the entire matter. It came to Shashi's mind how eager Jadab had been to convert him. How many wonderful sides to this man's character kept unfolding one after another! Not to have told him anything about this will was also remarkable on Jadab's part. If he had told him directly, Shashi could not have refused to accept the responsibility; that Jadab had nevertheless not done so was perhaps due to nothing else than a misgiving: suppose so much money left in his custody brought about a change in his normal behaviour? In case Shashi told him unctuous words out of gratitude or whatever? If during the last few days Shashi grew to believe in his yogic power, in case Jadab could not make out whether this belief was spontaneous and there was no motivation of any worldly consideration?

Gobardhan came in the afternoon. It grew dark when they reached the village. When he had heard everything from Shashi, an astonished Gopal said, 'Where on earth did the fellow get so much money from?'

'Perhaps he was the son of a rich family.'

'If there are legal heirs, after getting the news they may create trouble, Shashi; they won't let go of it easily without going into litigation. I hope you do not get into any danger in the end.'

'Why should I be in danger? The money has not been left to me! Wills of this kind aren't reversed easily.'

In a voice lowered without reason, Gopal said, 'Won't you be accountable to somebody?'

'It involves money; why won't there be any accounting? But then I won't be liable to anybody for explanation. There'll be a committee of three members of my choice; they'll just offer their advice; in every matter the authority will be mine.'

'You've to put in so much labour; won't you get anything in return?'

'As a doctor of the hospital I can take some salary if I wish.'

Gopal pondered over the matter all night, and next morning he said, 'Look, Shashi, you're a mere youngster. You'd better stay off such troublesome affairs. If you're engaged in all this, when will you practise medicine? The whole process will be hugely cumbersome! Rather, leave it entirely to me; I'll arrange everything. There's going to be a hospital in the village: so many elderly and wise men are there, where you're but a stripling; if you're in authority, everyone will take offence; out of hostility they'll spoil everything. You opt out, I say.'

'That can't be.'

'Can't be? Why can't it be, pray? I suppose you do not trust me?'

Shashi, now annoyed, said, 'How does the question of distrust come in? I'm not authorised to delegate powers. If I decline to accept the responsibility, it'll vest in the government.'

Perhaps Gopal did not believe it. Next day he went to Bajitpur. On returning he said, 'I had a look at the will. All the responsibility is yours; but as for the work contract, you can offer it to anyone you please; there's no restriction. So offer it to me; make me your agent.'

'Nothing has taken shape yet; why are you so anxious in advance?'

'Am I anxious for nothing? You're immature; going to do one thing you'll end up doing another—'

'Anything I do will be after consulting you.'

Someone has given away his all for a noble cause; another wants a share of it. Shashi was filled with chagrin. Many misgivings milled around in his mind. Meanwhile the rains had started, without respite. That was excruciating too. The village! How unsightly and repulsive this playground of Nature was! Soaking in the pure monsoon shower it was reduced to slush which mouldered into a foul-smelling mass. There was no knowing by how long the day of his escape was deferred. It would have been better if he could exit the village before Kusum returned. It was not possible anymore! There were so many respectable persons around and Jadab ended up plopping him of all people in such troubled waters.

The excitement over Jadab's phenomenal death had not died down yet; as soon as news of the will got around, there was a fresh wave of excitement. Shital-babu called in Shashi and heard everything. Then he said, 'Because it is Pandit-mashay and as he is in heaven, I accept it, Shashi. Otherwise, I wouldn't have tolerated the audacity of setting up a hospital in my village bypassing me when I'm present. Anyway, listen, I promise to deposit one thousand rupees as subscription to your fund.'

Shashi's fund! It sounded as if Jadab had left the money for Shashi's welfare. The reputable gentlefolk of the village too started visiting Shashi en masse. Everyone had taken umbrage like Shital-babu. There was a whole host of rich, respectable, elderly people in the village; yet, Jadab had entrusted the entire responsibility of such an important matter to Shashi: what a surprising act it was! How insulting to them all! Although they felt snubbed, they could not stay away; they swarmed around him. It looked like instead of three, a committee of thirty members as unsolicited advisors was going to be formed centring around Shashi. And Gopal kept chanting into his ears constantly, 'You won't be able to manage, Shashi, you won't. Leave everything to me.'

The key of Jadab's ramshackle house was deposited with Shital-babu as the zamindar of the village. One day it was found that the house had been broken into and things rummaged; deep holes had been dug with a crowbar here and there on the floor. That the few utensils had not been touched indicated that no pilferer had come; the one who had was fanciful and inquisitive—in quest of hidden treasure.

Srinath started howling curses. 'Death to the rascals; they'll be ruined! The hand that held the crowbar will fall off!'

The legal complications were not easy to sort out. For a young man to have control over funds donated for the public good, even though unambiguously granted by the will, seemed to be rather questionable in law. It was not quite clear which lobby was behind it, perhaps those very people who had been smarting from malice for Gopal Das's son getting a windfall: after pursuing the matter that led to pointing out a few lacunae in the will, they even tried to have it declared null and void. Thorough investigations followed; Shashi had to make frequent trips to Bajitpur; witnesses were examined scrupulously. Ultimately, Shashi was granted the right to establish the Gaodiya Hospital with Jadab's money and the proceeds of the sale of the property of Jadab who lacked a legal heir. Shashi encountered another problem when it came to forming the committee. Whom to take in and whom to leave out? The will provided for three respectable mature gentlemen. There was no dearth of them; but those whom Shashi acknowledged as such, if inducted, would themselves not heed Shashi; and if those who were loyal to Shashi were co-opted, those who were not would give vent to their ire. When Shital-babu was approached, he refused and expressed his resentment too. Shashi would boss around, and despite being the zamindar of the village Shital-babu would be limited to merely giving counsel, imagine that! Shashi's impudence to suggest this!

With all humility Shashi said, 'Why me? You'll be the *head* in every matter.'

'But there's no such provision in the will, is there, son?'

Considering the situation, Shashi said, 'Well, drop it then. You're so busy; you'd better avoid all this bother. When the hospital comes into being and the standing committee is formed, you've got to be its president of course. I'll come and take your counsel as and when necessary. If you're not there by my side, Shital-babu, how can I possibly manage such a big affair, tell me?'

'Do you mean I'll have to be the president?'

'When you are there, who else will be the president?' Shashi sounded as if he was surprised.

It was then that Shital-babu received Shashi cordially, offering him a seat and ordering refreshment to be brought. He asked, 'Who are the other persons to be on the committee?'

Shashi said, 'If you'd suggest who would be suitable—'

'Why not take in our munsiff,[105] I mean Satyahari-babu of Ukhara? He's well versed in the law.'

'All right, I'll tell him. So, we have two: you and Satyahari-babu. One more person is needed. Well, how about Keshab-babu, headmaster of Saatgaon?'

Now that Shital-babu had been won over tactfully, it proved easy to form the committee as stipulated. The members went on meeting and consulting in Shital-babu's house regularly. Shashi's fear of differences of opinion turned out to be almost unfounded. Concern over disagreement was no less theirs than his. Even in his politeness and humility, if in any matter Shashi's firmness was revealed, however subtly, Shital-babu discreetly refrained from making any objection, trying to avoid confrontation. Satyahari and Keshab were old and extremely harmless individuals. It was decided that a fund would be launched and donations collected; selling off Jadab's land and his dilapidated house, land for the hospital would be purchased at the common border of Saatgaon, Ukhara and Gaodiya. A general meeting was held one day under the presidentship of Shital-babu. Hearing his own speech at the meeting, Shashi was himself taken by surprise. Who knew he could speak so well! Much excitement and enthusiasm was created indeed, but towards the end a sudden sharp shower dampened the spirits to some extent. As soon as the boys began to make rounds of the venue holding the corners of a chuddar for collection, many in the audience on the pretext of the gathering clouds made themselves scarce as well.

There were many apprehensions and worries in the beginning; now Shashi felt buoyant and excited. The eagerness to do something great which had so far remained suppressed and made him restless now seemed to be liberated all of a sudden. After running about all day in mud and water, returning home, files and ledgers under his arm, he felt extremely tired and deeply contented. Some novelty, some variety had come to his life. He felt grateful to Jadab. The fact that rapid changes were overtaking the minds of the villagers in their opinion of him also gave him a taste of keen exhilaration. So long he had been a doctor; now he was growing, if unwittingly, into a leader of sorts. As he was known to be a workhorse, the boys of the village used to give him a wide berth. Now they turned up in droves to ask for a chance to make a big to-do in the name of work. Braving the rains, they rushed out to village after village as directed by Shashi to collect donations. In the village adjoining Ukhara a meeting had been arranged where Shashi was urged to say something. Not merely that; in an assembly on some social issue, now for the first time in his life the inexperienced Shashi was invited; the proceedings of the meeting were also put on hold till he arrived! Those who were elderly even seemed to have forgotten Shashi's age.

In social matters, however, Shashi did not participate. He knew that this was but a temporary impulse of old age, an expedient and fragile compromise with youth. The meeting resounding with the spluttering hookah and racking cough that would offer him an honourable position today and would hurl jibes at him tomorrow.

Meanwhile, Gopal became somewhat downcast. The fact that Shashi gave him no right to interfere in any hospital-related matter seemed to hurt him deeply. Gopal's was an arrogant nature, quick to take offence. Shashi was his only son. Such treatment from him was beyond his imagination. At times, he looked on with wonder at Shashi, seeming unable to make out anything. Gopal had not learned that to keep one's veneration undiminished, even a father had to keep his life ever worthy of his son's respect! Laying the blame therefore on fate, he lamented internally. A sense of repentance also seemed to come over Gopal. Sometimes he thought that this was the punishment for all the wrongs he had done in his life.

One day he told his son, 'You know, Shashi, because of many sins God has given me a son like you. Do you think I do not understand what all your greatness is about? You play a game of oneupmanship with me; you make a pretence of righteousness to put me to shame. Greatness! His father is sinful, he is a saint! Don't you feel ashamed, Shashi?'

Looking at Gopal's face, Shashi said somewhat faint-heartedly, 'I never criticise you, Baba.'

'At any rate, you distrust me!'

Shashi said in a mild tone, 'You don't understand a thing, Baba, only keep forming wrong notions and getting worked up. There's no question of trust or distrust here, is there? If I had done as told by you, would people not say that between them father and son are plundering the hospital funds?'

The words appealed to Gopal for the time being. But then, Gopal's grievance did not arise only from being deprived of the right to handle Jadab's money. As days went by, he could feel that in Shashi's mind, in Shashi's life, his place was gradually shrinking. It was not just that Shashi did not respect him; he seemed to feel no regret for it either. This was enough to nearly drive Gopal mad.

Gopal thought endlessly. He scarcely slept at night. Woken up at midnight Shashi could hear him puffing at his hookah. Here was a man, who, having spoilt others' lives for a little personal gain had never for a moment repented his misdeeds, and because of a deep-seated but strange sort of meanness, his hard and active nature was composed entirely of cruelty: did Shashi make him grow sentimental? Placing his hand on Sen-didi's shoulder, when Gopal said in a tired voice, 'You know, Saroj, not for a day did I get happiness from my own children,' if Shashi were present there at that time he would perhaps be startled: not because of his father's hand resting on Sen-didi's shoulder, but because of the expression on Gopal's face and the tone of his voice. Perhaps he might as well have realised the profound sorrow that today made Gopal desperately seek comfort from the one-eyed Sen-didi.

One day Gopal tendered all of five hundred rupees to Shashi.

'What is this for?'

'My contribution to the hospital fund.'

'Only five hundred? What will people say, Baba?'

What had Gopal expected and what did Shashi say! Gopal snatched away the notes and furiously said, 'How much am I to give then? A lakh? I won't give a paisa! You can go.'

Amidst such on-going discord involving Shashi, one day Kusum arrived, and a few days later, news of Moti.

10

Talking about Moti, well, let us recount her story from the beginning.

With Prince Prabir for her husband, Moti's happiness knew no bounds. When the time came to leave her village, tears filled her eyes; as she pondered over the unknown future a mysterious fear gripped her heart; still the girl seemed to melt inwardly in rapturous delight. At this tender age, such delightful aching of the heart! After the steamer had cast off, while looking through the parting of her veil at Paran who was standing on the dock, when she began to feel a mighty turmoil in her heart and everything went blurred through her tears, what thrill, what a reassuring comfort it was to feel the presence of Prince Prabir sitting by her side!

After arriving in Calcutta, Moti made no mention of the fact that she had once come to the city exclusively in search of Kumud. Sensing that Kumud wished to stun her by showing her the city for the first time, Moti indeed pretended to be appropriately stunned. She began to talk rather sheepishly; asking this and that she kept pestering Kumud to his great delight. How impeccable was her contrived exuberance!

'Where are we going to put up?'

'In a hotel. Staying there for a few days, after I have shown you around I'll decide whether to rent a place or proceed on a tour, all right?'

Let it be so. Let Kumud make whatever arrangements he pleased; Moti had no objection. She was a newly married wife; she would accept whatever way her husband wanted to keep her until he set up house, when she would start her homemaking. At present, what was her responsibility, what was her worry? Moti was ecstatic at her good fortune. Which girl of her village was as fortunate as she was? They were scarcely ever married to grooms after their own hearts; once in the in-laws' house, they kept sitting in a corner with their faces behind veils to start with; thereafter they had to scrub utensils, scour floors and swallow abuses. They had so much fear, so much worry; how dependent they were! In contrast, her husband was her own choice; immediately after marriage, she was romping in revelry, enjoying freedom in every matter. Moti rather liked the hotel room: there were two windows facing the road, looking out from which one could have a view up to a long distance on either side. Right in front was a narrow lane leading to the main road on the far side where trams plied. With the help of Kumud, Moti laid the bed and did up the room; had one or two necessary items brought by the hotel boy. Then she had her bath applying soap on her body; Kumud standing guard outside the closed bathroom door was so amusing! The old Oriya Brahman cook—a short, thin, brown-complexioned man, brisk in word and deed—came to serve their meals in the room. Looking at the heaped rice on her platter Moti said, 'Dear me, just see how much rice they have given me! Enough for seven like me!'

'This is how they serve meals at hotels and messes.'

'But it'll be wasted, won't it? Better ask him to take away some?'

'Let it be; what does it matter to us?'

Still Moti felt bad. Rice is *Lokkhi*;[106] should it be wasted? She lamented even as she went on eating. Kumud said, 'You're a strange sort, I find! You worry so much over a trifle? Rice would be wasted and that too rice of the hotel: I wonder how it can even strike one!'

After meals Kumud lighted a cigarette and even as he puffed away, he fell asleep. The burning cigarette having slipped off his outstretched hand, Moti picked it up, stubbed the end and put it away: not even half the length had been consumed; after waking up he could have a smoke again. Then from the fatigue of the journey Moti began to feel sleepy too. Kumud was sprawled across the bed so awkwardly that there was little room left beside him. A newly-wed bride, she was customarily supposed to lie beside her husband, wasn't she? Unable to observe the rule Moti, with a dejected heart, spread a rug on the floor and lay down. Kumud woke up at three. He freshened up, changed and then woke Moti up. 'Come, close the door,' he said. 'I'm going out, will just buy a few items and come back.'

After Kumud was gone, Moti bolted the door. It was hardly fifteen minutes when there was a knock on the door. Even as she unbolted it, she asked, 'You're back so early?'

But no, this was not Kumud! A bespectacled young man of about twenty or twenty-two had entered. He too looked surprised to see Moti. Taking a look inside the room he said, 'A friend of mine used to stay here. I didn't know he had left the room.'

Moti had nothing to say.

'The day before yesterday I saw him here; where did he go in the meanwhile?'

The man's eyes and the manner in which he was looking made one uncomfortable. Moti wished to slam the door in his face. But if his friend had indeed disappeared from this room, he might perhaps rightfully ask one or two questions. Moti was scared; she mumbled, 'We've come only this morning.'

At this point the manager suddenly arrived. Perhaps he had been in the room of a boarder next door.

'Whom are you looking for? Come this way, sir, come away.'

Moti now shut the door. She could hear the young man say he was looking for Shyamal-babu.

'Shyamal-babu? He's moved to the second floor, Room No. 21. Why, I saw you there in his room till a short while back, right? Would you tell me what's the matter, sir? After chatting half the day with Shyamal-babu, why have you come here to search for him?'

Moti could sense that one or two boarders from adjacent rooms had come out; presently a fracas ensued. In her closed room Moti sat stiffly, abashed and alarmed. What kind of goings-on were these?

What was the man's intention? What sort of a place was this where Kumud had left her alone?

A while later, the noise receding into the distance gradually grew fainter and finally stopped. About an hour later, there was another knock on the door; Moti's heart missed a beat. 'Who's it?' It was the hotel boy come to ask if she needed anything. Moti said no, she needed nothing.

It was late evening when Kumud returned. Narrating the entire incident to him, Moti felt apprehensive that enraged to hear it he would perhaps create a commotion, maybe even want to kill that ruffian. But Kumud only smiled slightly. 'A cunning chap indeed!' was all he said.

Cunning? Not a rascal, scoundrel or wretch? Just cunning?

'He gave me such a scare!'

'What scare? He would surely not have devoured you, I suppose? There were so many people around; would the lad have dared to do more than say a word or two to you on some pretext? Maybe he had wagered with someone that he would make your acquaintance. Those are all caprices of youth.'

Perhaps true; even so, why would Kumud tolerate that? Moti was greatly disappointed. Had it been Shashi, he would perhaps not have laughed off the matter in this manner; with a stick in his hand he would have dealt the guy a couple of blows. All at once, it struck Moti that it was cowardice on Kumud's part: the only reason he tried to make light of the matter and forget it was that he was afraid in case the matter took a serious turn or it brought him any embarrassment or harm. Was it a fact then that for fear of trouble, Kumud ignored small insults? In this context, was he like Kirti Niyogi of Gaodiya?

Kumud had bought a pair of shoes for Moti. This was his first gift to Moti after marriage.

One by one, seven days passed in this hotel. Once Kumud took her to see a film and another day for a stroll on the bank of the Ganga. So many things he had promised her: he would take her roaming across the city showing her the sights; go around visiting the cinema one day and the theatre on another; sit face to face with her like a pair of lovebirds in the cosiness of home. Where had all those promises gone? Moti was amazed to see Kumud's inordinate fondness for indolence. Far from taking her round, he seemed to be tired out even by dallying with her. So tender and light a body Moti's was; yet how brief was her shelter on his breast! He sat, he lay down, and he yawned, reading books. Pepped up by the comfort of idleness he would smoke away a whole tin of cigarettes a day; abruptly giving her a brief cuddle he would keep looking out of the window for ten minutes at a stretch; whistle some tune absently. And then he said, 'Make tea, Moti.'

'Aren't you going to take me anywhere today?'

'Where would you like to go? What after all is there worth seeing in Calcutta? One visit to the theatre is enough to make you lose all interest in it. Well, after that let's go out on a tour of Puri, Waltair and other places. Can decent people live here? Do you call Calcutta a city? It's a veritable bazaar! If you go out on the road, your head reels.'

'When are we going to those places?'

'Wait, wait, what's the hurry?' Kumud laughed and then pulling an embarrassed Moti near by her sari-end, cooed into her ears, 'We two are alone in a cubbyhole, just think! Don't you like it, Moti?'

'Yes, I do.'

Then with some apprehension she added, 'But the way you go on reading books all day!'

'You too will read, Moti, you too will.'

That's all: thereafter, a cup of tea, and Kumud was sprawled out again. She could never enjoy the complete playing-out of an emotion. A little while of desultory thought, a chapter of some book, ten minutes of togetherness with Moti—as if this was all a game of Kumud's in several parts: creating variety!

Moti did not like such serialised romanticism. But then, as for providing services big and small, Kumud gave Moti ample opportunity: she made tea, served food, offered water to drink; made arrangements for shaving, rinsed the razor and neatly put away the shaving implements; Kumud's fashionable parting of hair was also done by Moti, and she supplied cigarettes and matchsticks. And Moti did so much more.

One day Kumud told her, 'My feet are aching, bou.'

'Why?'

'Just like that. If only someone would give me a massage!'

Moti blushed and said, 'Why don't you call and ask the servant?'

'A hotel boy to massage my feet? Then I'm done for! Why, you can do it just as well, a bit gently!'

Ever since, when Kumud felt sleepy around midday, Moti would massage his feet too. At that time of day, a local lull would subdue the din of the city. Moti would feel very melancholy then. Mechanically she would massage his feet with one hand, and with the other wipe her tears. She felt like a prisoner. She was afraid Kumud would keep her confined in this pigeonhole forever to get her to massage his feet, with no one to keep her company for play, no one to call her own; she would never get to see the open country and the sky again, never again walk on the soft, silted village path.

Seven days. Moti had spent just seven days here!

Then Kumud's friends began to trickle in in ones and twos. Their number kept increasing by the day. Strange indeed were Kumud's friends, the likes of whom Moti had never seen in her life. They would come and knock on the door. Kumud would ask, 'Who's it?'

'It's me.'

Kumud would tell Moti to open the door.

Opening the door Moti would slip into a corner. On entering the room, Kumud's friend would make straight for the bed to sit down. If he was a newcomer, on seeing Moti he would keep staring at her for a while.

'Where did you find her?'

Kumud, even as he kept lying, said, 'She's my wife.'

His friend laughed, and striking a match he lit a cigarette.

Taking another look at Moti, he said, 'Make some tea, Boudi. Little sugar; I like my tea strong.'

And the next moment he was lost in chatting with Kumud. Coming as she did from a village, Moti could sense that his friend was not a good sort of man. Yet, when she noticed that he did not have a good look at her one more time, she was surprised. She told herself that whatever sort of man Kumud's friend may be, he knows his manners. He can behave as if there was only his friend in the room, not his friend's wife too.

Not everyone else was like him. Some of them tried to get friendly as well. Someone immediately on entering the room might try to make himself out to be an old acquaintance of hers; another would try to build up familiarity gradually. Someone's talk would be contrived, another's simple and straightforward. Moti would also receive an occasional gift of books and magazines. Of all Kumud's friends, Moti came to like one very much, his stout, sturdy figure and his stiff, black, bushy moustache notwithstanding. His name was Banbihari.

Making himself comfortable in his seat, he straightaway said in jest, 'What shall I call you: Khuki or Boudi?'

Moti responded, 'Why will you call me Khuki?'

Banbihari seemed surprised. Turning to Kumud, he said, 'Well, she's not all that rustic, I see. She needed no persuading to speak.'

Kumud said, 'She's somewhat overcome her shyness.'

'Wait and see; she'll overcome many other things,' Banbihari laughed. To Moti he said, 'I'm an old friend of Kumud's. Going by age, I'm your elder brother-in-law. But my wife has told me to ignore the age factor.'

Moti felt shy, and amused too.

Banbihari said, 'After I heard that Kumud has put you up in a hotel, I came to break his head. My wife too approved of this wish. All I now need to perform the task is your permission. Shall I do it?'

Moti's eyes brightened in mirth. Banbihari went on, 'I earn my living by painting pictures for advertisements. A single room with a slice of veranda is all I call home. Yet, it's a home, not a hotel. This rascal isn't aware even of that.'

Although he had made an untimely call, Banbihari spent a long time there, chatting nonstop and making others laugh. Towards the end, unable to contain herself, Moti often burst out into audible laughter. Ordering Kumud to pay a visit along with his wife to his house one day, Banbihari took his leave that day.

Kumud said, 'A frivolous type, quite hollow. He slaughters art for the sake of money. He had great talent for painting; just couldn't keep up the fight till the end to earn fame. He now ekes out a living by painting for monthlies and ads. He has no regrets for it either; utterly worthless.'

Moti could not make out just what Banbihari's fault was here. Neither did she wish to. There was a sneaking affection and sympathy underlying his words. That a mere child leaving her village, leaving her friends and relatives she found herself in an unknown, strange world was a fact which except for Banbihari no other friend of Kumud's had perhaps even noticed. Two days later, Banbihari called again in the morning. Expressing dismay over Kumud's not paying a visit yet, he said, 'Let's go, Kumud; today, right now; you'll have your meal with us.'

Kumud yawned and said, 'Wait, wait, we'll go; what's the hurry?'

Banbihari now looked grave. He said in a serious tone, 'What's the matter with you, Kumud? Come clean. It's nearly six months that you haven't been to our place. Now that I've come to call you, you're yawning. Earlier, if we didn't see you for seven days, we'd be worried. Have you suddenly abandoned us?'

'Abandon? That's not in my nature. I'm yawning simply out of exhaustion.'

'Exhaustion from lying down all day! I'll never ask you again to come, Kumud.'

'What's the need? Tomorrow or the day after we'll descend upon you without notice; just wait and see.'

Now Banbihari smiled. 'Probably, even before that, Jaya will arrive here any moment. I wonder what punishment she has in store for you. Perhaps she'll kidnap Khuki and hide her for a month.'

Moti seemed to like the word khuki uttered by Banbihari. Still she said pleadingly, 'Why Khuki again?'

After Banbihari left, she told Kumud, 'Why don't we go one day? He's been insisting so much!'

Kumud said with a wisp of a smile on his lips, 'Do you think it is he? Someone else gets him to insist. Her name is Jaya, his wife. Okay, we'll go one of these days.'

Meanwhile, by and by, the number of Kumud's friends who assembled in the evening went on increasing. There were regular chat sessions; the bedstead was not spacious enough for all of them to sit. So turning it on its side and spreading the mattress and the bedcover on the floor they made their sitting arrangement. Someone talked non-stop, another burst out laughing boisterously at intervals, yet another hummed some tune. Someone else leaning against the wall dozed from beginning to end. The air inside the room became thick with the smoke of biris, cigarettes and cheroots.

There was card playing also. From the exchange of notes and coins Moti understood that it was a gambling game.

Moti found herself on the verge of tears; she could not breathe normally. Kumud had told her not to feel shy; she didn't either if only one or two friends came. But this was quite different. There was just one room and she was constrained not to go elsewhere even for a moment; if that single room was occupied by Kumud with a horde of friends from evening till eleven at night, how could she possibly refrain from feeling shy a thousand times?

Moti supplied tea. The stove lit in the afternoon couldn't cool off until midnight. Perhaps, Kumud had briefed the evening friends; they completely ignored her. Even their demands of tea, paan, etc., were placed with Kumud, not her. Her duties ended with making tea and preparing paan, not extending to distribution. The rest of the time she kept sitting by the window. Its shutters opened inwards, providing Moti with a screen of sorts. Sitting there she sometimes felt a sort of thrill. She wished to cry but could not because of fear with so many men in the room. Mortified with anger, grief and injured vanity Moti wished to turn into a bird and fly off to Gaodiya. Night advanced by the hour. Pedestrian traffic grew thin. At the far end of the narrow lane, trams with glowing lights were no longer seen. The incandescent lamp of the stationery shop on the other side of the road was switched off and its shutters downed. In the room right above the shop, a girl of Moti's age, after doing her lessons at her desk, began to make her bed. Moti too felt sleepy as she looked on.

After his friends left Kumud said, 'Will you make the bed? So shall I put the bedstead in place? Or shall we have our meals first?'

Moti made no response. Kumud felt lethargic even to get up and go near. He said, 'Come, come here. I've something to tell you. Are you peeved? Ah, why don't you come?'

Moti had not the courage to disobey for long. Going near she sobbed and said, 'If so many men enter the room, how can I stay?'

Kumud said affectionately, 'Can I drive my friends away if they come, Moti? Surely, they don't bother you?'

Moti then suggested that Kumud could take another room. He said, 'Is the rent a small amount? Where's so much money?' Well, when there was such dearth of money, why did Kumud gamble? If a room in the hotel was too expensive, why did he not rent a small house at a cheap rate? Moti did not like this place any longer. If even that was not possible, Kumud had better shift the sessions to one of his friends' places.

'Shall I leave you alone till so late in the night? Won't you feel scared?'

'No, I won't. I'll keep the door bolted.'

Now Kumud did not put forward any argument that Moti could refute. To start with, he nuzzled and cuddled her so passionately that she felt limp and charmed. Then he tried to make her understand. 'Didn't I tell you that I would remodel you? Did I not tell you not to expect me to set up house? As for homemaking, everyone does it, from the coolie on the street to maharajas. I'm not that kind, Moti. If I'm to go by the rules, I'll die from depression in two days. I love to keep drifting about, never worry about what will happen tomorrow; do whatever pleases me. If you're to stay with me, you certainly can't do with the coyness of a new bride. "I'm a housewife; I'll do this, I'll live like that"—if you have this attitude, you can't get along with me. I'll earn money and you'll do the cooking and scrubbing sitting in the corner and raising children: didn't I tell you that's never to be? You're no wife; you're my companion. At least that is what you've got to make of yourself. If I have to take your responsibility in every matter, if you stay as a burden to me, I can't bring myself to like you at all, Moti. If for you I have to change myself, if I can't spend my days the way I like, how can I keep you with me?'

Moti panicked. 'Will you leave me?'

Kumud laughed and stroked her affectionately, saying, 'Don't be afraid. Everything will be all right, Moti. What's there to worry about? After you stay with me for a year, you'll be changed so thoroughly that I won't need to tell you anything anymore; wherever and in whatever condition you are, you'll find enjoyment in that. Because you aren't used to it yet, you have these initial hiccups. A few days later, you won't even notice such things or care. What do you think I'll do then? I'll ask them not to come.'

'Why?'

'I don't like anything for very long, Moti. I've come to Calcutta after many days, so I'm spending some time chatting with friends. It's just a matter of days before I grow an aversion to that.'

A couple of days later, Banbihari turned up with his wife. Jaya was rather fat, but beautiful: fair complexion, round face, glamorous looks and sharp, bright eyes.

She said to Moti, 'You didn't come, so I came to see you.' Then she said, 'What's the matter with you, Kumud? You married and then kept your wife hidden? I've sent him at least seven times. Still it did not occur to you that a creature called Jaya was bursting with curiosity? I was surprised and have been curious from the day I heard that you had picked your bride from a village.'

Jaya kept observing Moti with her piercing eyes. She said, 'I couldn't have imagined she was really so young. You simply puzzle us, Kumud! Had she been my daughter, I would have surely made her wear a frock![107] Just see how she stares. Come, child, come here. Let me have a good look at you.'

'Won't you sound her out first?' Banbihari asked.

Kumud said, 'Slow your pace a bit, Jaya. She'll get confused. She's not a doll after all.'

Jaya smiled and said, 'Is it attachment on your part then? So at last even you've learnt how to dote?' Looking at Moti she said, 'Why don't you come near? Come, sit here. I haven't brought any present for you; I was short of funds. I'll buy you one later. Let us become friends empty-handed today.'

She wore an ordinary sari, as though she were a queen in a maid's dress. Jaya's clothes, her words, her demeanour all struck

Moti as peculiar. Jaya addressed Kumud by name,[108] like she were his guardian, yet she talked with him flippantly: what sort of a woman was she? In their very first meeting, an adverse feeling about Jaya was created in Moti's mind. Jaya's conduct betrayed a strange attitude of condescension; she seemed to find Moti laughable! They went away after spending about an hour.

It seemed to Moti as if a magic show had been going on in the room for an hour—conjuring! Half the time Moti simply couldn't follow what Jaya said or why she laughed. Only, sensing that there was a close intimacy between Kumud and Jaya, she felt jealous.

'Why did she call you by name?'

Kumud felt amused at Moti's question. 'We're friends, Moti, long-time friends.'

Moti was taken aback. A woman friend? After remaining silent for a while she said, 'Tell me, she was behaving like that with you; won't her husband be angry?'

'How was she behaving?'

Moti was silent.

Kumud said, 'You're so mean-minded, Moti.'

Some time later, seeing tears roll from her eyes, Kumud suddenly put on a *panjabi*[109] and went out. He said before leaving, 'You're no less of a sniveller either.'

Moti had never heard such harsh words from Kumud before. The first rebuke from her husband dried up her tears.

The manager called one day to demand payment and left.

Moti searched in Kumud's bags and trunks and then said, 'Only seven rupees. You've kept the money hidden, I suppose?'

'Where's any more money to hide?'

'There's no more?' Moti's face went pale.

Kumud smiled and said, 'Do you think seven rupees is a small amount?'

'What will happen then? Where will you get the money? How will you pay the hotel dues?' Moti kept staring, fear in her eyes. 'You gamble and lose everyday. Why do you keep playing?'

Kumud seemed to be amused at Moti's worry. He made her sit by his side and said, 'Being my wife, you're worrying about petty pelf? Today I have seven rupees; let it see me through today; come tomorrow and I will think about tomorrow. Some arrangement will certainly be made; lack of money can't ever stop a human from living, can it?'

An agitated Moti said, 'How can seven rupees do?'

'It'll do well enough. You just see how it does. This is how I have been living all my life; wouldn't I know? Why do you worry so? You aren't supposed to worry about money!'

Still Moti said, 'How will you pay the hotel bill? You said you would pay it tomorrow?'

Out of profound tenderness, Kumud hugged the timid girl to his chest and said, 'You're still going on thinking about that? Don't make whining a habit, Moti; don't begin to sound like a matron. What I promised to pay tomorrow I'll think about tomorrow; why are you anxious today?'

At night, when his friends had gone away, Kumud laid down a handful of notes and coins on the bed. 'Do you see where money comes from? And you were worrying yourself to death!'

'Tomorrow you'll lose again,' said Moti sadly. 'At any rate, what can you do with this meagre sum?'

Lighting a cigarette, Kumud looked on steadily at Moti for a while. Then he said gently, 'I could never have imagined that you'd grow so worldly-wise at such a tender age. You are not supposed to understand the necessity of money in such a way! You're a mere child, Moti; you should be joyful and blithe; to think about what makes what should be irksome to you. Far from it, just because funds were short you looked downcast all day. You were such a greenhorn at Gaodiya; when did you suddenly mature beyond your years? There you understood absolutely nothing; whatever I said you accepted like a child and kept looking at my face open-mouthed. Did you then deceive me by pretending to be a child?'

Moti found no answer; neither could she understand Kumud's accusation completely; she only felt like crying. She pretended to be a child? Was she not still a child? There was no money and so she worried about money: did that mean the end of one's childishness? Next day the manager came to ask for his dues, and returned empty-handed. Despite having the money, why Kumud refused to pay him was something Moti could not understand; but she spoke not a word out of fear.

About a week later, one morning Kumud bought an inexpensive tin trunk. He told Moti, 'Pack up; I've just fixed up a house. After having our meals we'll shift there. I don't want to stay in this damned hotel any longer.'

Nothing was packed into the newly purchased trunk. Kumud said, 'Leave it empty, Moti.' All the items were packed up in bundles; only a clean bedcover was left out spread on the bedstead, along with a pillow. On the clothes rack hung a torn kurta, an old cloth, and a vest. Then he sent the room boy to fetch a carriage.

This brought the manager scurrying in. He said, 'Are you leaving, Kumud-babu?'

'Going to leave my wife at her father's house. I'll be back tomorrow about afternoon. My things are here; please keep an eye on the room.'

'You said you'd pay up today?'

'Tomorrow, you'll get it tomorrow—without fail.'

The manager kept watch. The carriage came, goods were carted and then, when Kumud locked the room, finding the new trunk, the bedding and the clothes on the rack, the manager was somewhat assured.

In the carriage, Moti found herself at a loss for words. Kumud smiled slyly. 'Do you think I've cheated the manager? No, Moti, I'll come and pay.'

'Will you come tomorrow?'

'Maybe not tomorrow; but as soon as I get some money, I will. Unnecessarily he'd have created a ruckus; that's why I adopted a bit of tact. Otherwise, I never cheat anyone, Moti. Within two to four months I'll certainly come and pay up.'

The carriage rattled down the road. Where were they going? Various wild thoughts came crowding in on Moti. She seemed to suddenly feel afraid of staying with Kumud, as if he was a terrible man. After a long journey, the carriage finally stopped in front of a small one-storey building in a narrow lane. Presently Banbihari opened the door; Jaya came too. She said, 'I didn't find the time to set up the *mongol ghawt*;[110] there's no conch shell in the house, neither do I know how to sound *ulus*.[111] Forgive me, Kumud.'

It was a small house: two bedrooms next to each other, a sliver of a porch in front and a small yard; a kitchen on one side and attached to it a pigeonhole of an extra room. When Jaya saw Moti standing in the yard looking around, she said, 'You don't seem to like the house?'

Moti replied doubtfully, 'It's not bad.'

Jaya said, 'We were in such a hurry when we came yesterday afternoon! The rooms have not been cleaned yet. Never mind, if we do it together, it won't take much time. I've taken this room; it has an extra window; a fat woman, I feel out of breath if it is stuffy. Your room is a bit small I admit. Let it be! You're small yourself; the items in your new household are few too; that much space is sufficient.'

The house and the premises were not cleaned; but Jaya had already tidied up her own room. As for Jaya's goods and furniture, they were none too few, but they were all of the cheaper variety. More than the furniture, the pictures in the room drew Moti's attention. All were paintings; a wide range of pictures large and small, framed and unframed, in water colour, in oils and so on almost covered the four walls. Moti blushed to see a large painting.

Jaya giggled and said, 'She is Urboshi,[112] my co-wife, dear. She's descending from the sky, you know, so her sari was swept away by the wind to hover as the cloud behind. A buyer offered seven hundred rupees; hubby asks for a thousand. I said, "You'd better agree. Seven hundred rupees isn't a small amount, is it, let's get rid of the pest." But actually, he doesn't want to sell it at all.'

Moti said, 'The face resembles yours.'

'That's why he demands a thousand.' Jaya laughed.

With Jaya's help, Moti arranged her room. Just a few articles; compared to Jaya's, her own room seemed rather empty to Moti, more like a playhouse. But that very afternoon, an assortment of furniture arrived. Kumud alone knew where he had got the money. He might have duped the hotel manager; but he was not a miser. A table, a chair, a clothes rack, and a double bed nearly filled the room. He had also bought an exquisite blue-shaded table lamp and for Moti a decent sari too.

11

At the advent of new hope, Moti began to fantasise again. She laid out their bed on the charpoy with great care; neatly arranged her small stock of cosmetics; put away the clothes pleated and tidied up on the rack; and filling oil, lighted the table lamp as soon as it got dark. She alternately lowered and raised the wick, unable to decide what would be right.

'Shall I make the flame bigger or smaller? I'd rather shorten it a bit, what do you say?'

Kumud smiled and said, 'Let it be. That's all right.'

Jaya had done the cooking for this meal. After dinner, when it was time to go to bed, Moti for the first time, because of Jaya, felt shy to enter the bedroom. While brushing her teeth, Jaya said, 'Why do you keep standing? Go to the room.'

'You go first, Didi.'

'Which room shall I enter, yours?' She began to laugh so much she had to stop brushing. Moti was surprised: what was so funny about it to excite such laughter? Then rinsing her mouth, Jaya led her by the hand into her room. 'Here's your wife, Kumud; she feels shy to come into the room.'

Kumud lay supine, reading a book. He said, 'But that's how it goes. Have a seat.'

'No, I must go; I feel sleepy.' Saying which Jaya sat down on the chair, not showing any sign of going. She sat chatting with Kumud. Moti could make neither head nor tail of what they talked about; English words spouting from Jaya's mouth struck her every now and then. Friend, Jaya was Kumud's friend. When Kumud had not descended in the form of Prince Prabir on the scene of Gaodiya, Jaya was his friend. Envy welled up in Moti's little heart; not a trace of the evening's delight remained.

Now freed from her captive hotel life and the gossip sessions of Kumud's cronies, Moti at last found space here; she only felt a yearning for Gaodiya. The little girl filled her heart with hope: the dreams she cherished were many; they might become a reality now. But she could not adjust herself here either. Here too, her inborn nature and lifelong habits were dented and hurt. Her eyes brimmed with tears when she thought of the familiar look of her village and the people she had known. How long since she saw them last. Maybe in the evening Paran talked about her with Mokshada and Kusum. Maybe Shashi came occasionally and joined in. Who knew when Kumud would take her to Gaodiya!

Moti said, 'So we're settled here. Why don't you now write a letter to Dada? They must be worrying so much.'

Kumud said, 'Have you forgotten already, Moti?'

'What? What did I forget?'

'Did you not tell me that you'd forget about Gaodiya, keep no connection with Gaodiya? Did I not tell you clearly before marriage that if you wished to come along with me, you had to come for the rest of your life? And I also told you that there should be no exchange of letters.'

Oh, that. That vow uttered in a moment of unreasoning infatuation in the palm grove! Kumud still kept it in mind? Moti got apprehensive. Whatever Kumud had told her she had indeed accepted; but she could not then anticipate that even when she lived with Prince Prabir, she would ever pine for Gaodiya; she had fantasised about a new life, a new world, dancing like a puppet at the movement of Kumud's hand: the dream of all this would benumb her power to think, to understand. Did Kumud mean to rigorously implement that promise now?

'But surely you did not mean it?' Moti said in a feeble voice.

'Did you think so? Was I joking?'

Days went by. Inured to the thought that she could never go to Gaodiya again, when Moti ceased to feel dejected, her mind, immature that it was, began to nurture a trace of joy and hope. In spite of a marked lack of discipline, life here was by and large regular. Moreover, however frightful, cruel and distant Kumud might at times seem to be, he kept her spellbound with some indefinable charm. Moti had learnt to rely on him to some extent. She knew that however impoverished Kumud might be after making meaningless expenses, he never seemed handicapped for lack of money. Rather, Kumud seemed to thrive only in a penniless state, having incurred debts left, right and centre! He was allergic to giving money, as it were; with money in the house, sleep seemed to elude him. Yet another thing Moti had gradually come to feel. Kumud loved just to talk about his dream to mould and remodel her; he scarcely had the urge to execute it. Kumud wished for nothing else in life—if only he could satisfy his whim, in whatever form and whenever it arose, he was happy. Discipline, responsibility, good or evil, propriety or impropriety were concepts as detestable to him as poison. He was all talk too. Realising that when he boasted, merely to keep assenting to his words was enough, Moti had been greatly reassured in some way. But then she was also tired and exasperated at having to constantly render him personal service. At times she felt she wasn't Kumud's wife but his maid: for getting her to perform innumerable services—from helping him light the cigarette to massaging his feet—Kumud had married her after making such a show of love. A little fun and games, a little personal comfort and luxury were what Moti wished for. That was not to be if only for the nagging demands of Kumud.

Moti would eagerly watch the lives of Jaya and Banbihari. They had limited their existence within the confines of this small segment of a house, never trying to import any variety or change from outside. Banbihari spent all day painting; only when it came to selling his work did he ever go out, keeping himself imprisoned for the rest of the time. He was sometimes solvent, sometimes hand-to-mouth. In money matters, he was the exact opposite of Kumud. Banbihari never borrowed a paisa. In this respect, Jaya was even stricter. Here were two families living in the same house; but Jaya would not tolerate even an exchange of vegetables. One day going to offer her surplus curry to Jaya, the bitter experience Moti had she would not forget for the rest of her life.

'It'll be wasted and have to be thrown away; still won't you accept it, Didi?' Moti had urged.

'No, dear, no. I don't like give-and-take.'

'All right, all right. If I am ever to take even a slice of lemon from you—'

'Who'll ever give you any, my dear?'

When Moti was angry, her rural upbringing was betrayed. She said, 'You're very mean-minded, Didi! You're bursting with pride!'

Jaya only smiled without saying a word.

Not only her temper, but Jaya would laugh at, and ignore, Moti's rustic nature and her narrow-mindedness too. The narrow-mindedness was not limited to a single matter either. That even before they arrived Jaya had seized the opportunity to occupy the better room was etched for ever in Moti's mind. Even though she stopped short of saying anything directly, she time and again betrayed her feelings unwittingly. They shared a kitchen; their ovens were side by side. The day when Moti cooked good dishes of fish and curry, the atmosphere of the kitchen was relaxed. But when Jaya surpassed her in the assortment of items, Moti's unease knew no bounds; she seemed to feel small. She took sidelong glances at the fare laid out by Jaya, and her face darkened. Banbihari loved Jaya deeply; however silent and hidden that love might be, Moti sensed it all the same. Therefore, trying in indirect ways to prove to Jaya how passionately Kumud loved her Moti created a ridiculous situation.

Jaya laughed silently.

'Why are you laughing, Didi?'

'How can I keep from laughing? You just make me laugh!'

Looking po-faced, Moti said, 'So much laughter isn't good.'

Try as she might, Moti could not get along with Jaya. She mixed with her, she chatted with her; but she could not achieve the rapport she desired. Even though Jaya behaved as if Moti was a younger relative, she seemed to remain an outsider; Moti was unable to repose her trust and affection in Jaya as an elder sister or friend. If a day was spent well enough in a congenial atmosphere, come evening the thought would occur with a mild sense of discontent: everything is there all right; but where is love? On her way to Calcutta, on the train Moti had befriended a housewife: this intimacy with Jaya too was, as it were, love on the road like that. Where was the joy of fellow-feeling and affection despite such closeness? Was it only from monetary and other considerations of expediency that they had set up house together? Was no other relation to develop between them? Jaya had no fault in this. What Moti wanted in the surging emotion of an immature mind was intense, unguarded affection and sympathy—was it not too much to expect from Jaya? Her upbringing and culture were quite different from Moti's. Even so, Jaya did not ignore Moti: she taught her to cook, did up her hair, gave her good counsel, offered her consolation. But Jaya was not sentimental. Moti regarded her as cold and cruel.

Apart from that, there was also a deep sorrow in Jaya's mind. Her husband's talents were about to be set at naught because of lack of money. She had married an artist whose future was bright; she was now the homemaker for a man who drew pictures for a living. Jaya's need for sympathy was no less. Yet Moti did not realise the nature of this sorrow of hers. One day while trying to tell Moti about it, Jaya was pained by her lack of comprehension. When Jaya became aware of Moti's inability even to imagine that a life of great promise lay thwarted next door, her mind indeed soured a little against the girl.

Even though Jaya had laughed off Moti's envy and suspicion regarding Kumud and herself, she sensed it at least to some extent.

Of late Moti had realised that the reckless Kumud feared Jaya to a degree. That here he had considerably restrained himself was entirely thanks to Jaya! Moti expressed this idea so cuttingly one day that Jaya felt offended. 'You can't be serious! Why on earth would he be afraid of me?'

'It seems he holds you in some esteem, Didi.'

'How do you know that?'

Moti proudly said, 'I can sense it, Didi. I'm not as much of a fool as you think I am.'

'I can see that.' Jaya sounded irritated.

The impression of Banbihari that Moti had formed during his brief visits to their hotel was completely overturned by what she saw of him here. He was a terribly busy man, always running short of time. Did he not get exhausted going on painting? You never saw him without the brush in his hand. Initially, Moti had thought perhaps he was very fond of laughs and banter; how he used to make her chuckle whenever he called at the hotel! Here he seemed to her to be a bit blunt, rather lacking in energy. Banbihari was not at all like the gifted and dynamic individual Jaya so wanted to make him out to be. Rather, he could be called cowardly. There was no doubt that he feared Jaya, more than Kumud did. Moti could not understand why Jaya entertained that sort of idea about such a simple and ordinary man! That Banbihari could have made it really big, that his fame would have spread at home and abroad and that only poverty stood in his way was in Moti's view a perception and regret engineered by Jaya. To think that someone could become great just by painting pictures!

Moti had no idea about concepts like genius, art or what it meant to be celebrated as an artist; still she could well perceive the incongruous aspect of the relation between Jaya and Banbihari. As for spiritedness, Jaya had it to some extent. She regarded her husband as a might-have-been governor! Despite giving evidence of his abilities, Banbihari, out of fear of Jaya, kept up the posture of approving this and in her presence pretended to be persecuted and deprived. He found himself in the same predicament as that of a poor householder who had to act like a deposed king before his wife.

'If only I had money, Moti!' Jaya would despair. 'If only he didn't have to paint for the sake of money!'

'But isn't whatever work one does for the sake of money, Didi?

'Worthless people do. Poets and artists can't afford to pay attention to such trifling matters.'

After some thought Moti said, 'Why don't you save money? The way you spend whenever some money comes rolling in, your nature is just like his (Kumud's), Didi.'

'You won't understand all this, Moti. An artist's mind has so many needs; I can't provide any. When there's money, I carry on smoothly for a couple of days; his talent gets nothing to thrive on.'

At times Moti would go and stand behind Banbihari and with wonder in her eyes watch him working away at his canvas. Whatever he painted—trees and plains, houses and homes, people's apparel, everything—seemed rather strange to her. Sensing her presence Banbihari would turn and look at her with affectionate eyes. He said, 'As soon as I find the time, I'll draw you a portrait, Khuki.'

'I don't want any.'

'Why? What makes you angry?'

'Did I not ask you not to call me Khuki?'

Banbihari laughed. He quipped, 'As long as a khuki is not born to you, I won't call you anything except Khuki, dear sister.'

Meanwhile Moti noticed that Jaya was beckoning her. When she went near, Jaya said with a serious face, 'Do not disturb him, Moti, when he is at work.'

Peeved, Moti thought to herself: hah, just listen to the fat woman's orders!

One day Moti could not find her gold necklace. It was a gift from Shashi; whatever could have happened to it, she wondered. The previous day Kumud had made some payment at the grocer's; the house rent he had tendered to Jaya. Moti remembered this. Still she searched each box and trunk, every nook and cranny thoroughly. Once she had lost her earring at the taalpukur, and Kumud had bought her a new one unasked. Would he today purloin her gift from Shashi, her wedding ornament?

Jaya felt uneasy when she learnt the chain was missing. This is one ugly side to two indigent families living together. If a costly thing goes missing from one family, the thought keeps pricking the other: god knows what feelings are arising in the minds of others. Whoever does not know that poverty can make everything possible!

'Search, Moti, search thoroughly. Are you sure it didn't drop at the washing place? Or in the kitchen?' Moti wept and said, 'I had not put it round my neck; it was in the box. It's lost forever, Didi.'

When Kumud returned, it was Jaya who gave him the news. Kumud said, 'It's not lost; I've sold it.'

'What did you say?' Jaya was startled.

Kumud said, 'What good would it do left to itself? The money came to use.'

Moti was weeping. Jaya said, 'Money does come to use; doesn't a chain do too?'

Kumud said, 'I can't stand the sight of women to whom ornaments are everything.'

Jaya was annoyed now, 'Do not call her a woman; call her a child.'

'A child should be all the more indifferent to ornaments.'

Jaya's anger was of a peculiar kind; it found no expression on her face or in her voice, yet it could be sensed. She said, 'If the world were as you would have liked it to be, Kumud, I wonder how I could live in it. The house rent you might as well have paid me later.'

Kumud said, 'Do you think I sold the chain only to pay the rent?'

'I've known you for long, Kumud. Don't try to pull the wool over my eyes.' Jaya stood there no longer. With tears in her eyes, Moti looked up to see that today for the first time, Kumud looked shamefaced.

It was morning. Moti remained sullen all day. Kumud did not call her to him even once. As the day wore on, Moti's breast swelled with indignation. What kind of neglect from Kumud was this? Her grief for the ornament was considerable; still he didn't bother to tell her even a soothing word or two? If he admitted his fault and planted a kiss on her she would have forgiven him. Maybe not a bit of sorrow would have remained for the necklace.

A little before evening, Kumud came out of the room and washing his hair in the running water from the tap said to Moti, 'If you'd like to go out with me, get ready.'

Moti was then sitting on the porch, cleaning her fancied table lamp; she spoke not a word. The shade fell and broke.

While drying his hair Kumud said, 'I told you to change, Moti, didn't I?'

'I won't go.' Moti's voice was tear-soaked.

'Come on, Moti, we'll go to the theatre.'

'No.' Moti went and lay down in her room. But hers was not the sulk that would hold good with Kumud. She had to eventually dress up and go to the theatre. On the stage, when a drunken Jogesh declaiming, '*Sajano bagan shukiye gyalo*:[113] the beautifully laid-out garden withered away!' pushed up a well of tears in Moti's heart, Kumud broke the news.

'I've got a job here, Moti.'

Moti turned to him to ask, 'What did you say?'

'I've got a job at this theatre; they'll pay me one hundred rupees salary.'

Jogesh's lament over the withered garden instantly seemed unreal to Moti. She said with bated breath, 'Are you going to act here? When?'

'In their next play.'

No trace of sorrow, hurt or regret now lingered in Moti's heart. It was all part of Kumud's bag of tricks: bringing friends to the hotel room, cheating the manager, intimacy with Jaya, selling the chain—everything—Kumud had done to test her; those were all acts of Kumud at play. So long he had been fooling around with her; now Kumud would build her the dreamland she had dreamed round him. Looking out at the illuminated stage Moti could no longer see Jogesh; she saw Kumud in the guise of Prince Prabir. Her mind filled with happiness and pride. Moti could barely wait till she returned home to give the news to Jaya. When Jaya heard it, she said, 'Such jobs he's been taking and leaving all the time; just watch how many months he sticks to it. Tell you what, without letting Kumud know, save a little each month.'

In her mind, Moti rejected the idea: saving money secretly indeed! What did she need to do it for? That Kumud would never get stuck for lack of funds she would unwaveringly trust from now on. Moti's eyes shone in excitement while she changed. She experienced a unique feeling of recklessness: what's the point of being thrifty? What's there to worry about? Who cares when and from what some benefit or harm might flow? What difference did it make whether she did or did not possess any jewellery? Just as Kumud had no comparison, Kumud's opinions were equally peerless. What could be more delightful than having a devil-may-care attitude towards money and rules and customs? Come what may later on. Moti embraced Kumud. Carried away with rapture, she said, 'Listen dear, will you teach me how to sing and dance as they were dancing today? I'll dance in front of you behind closed doors.'

'Take me everyday to the theatre, everyday. Finishing the cooking in mid-afternoon, I'll go there, okay?' Moti added, 'You can sell off the ornaments if you like, all of them. Let's make merry with the money.' Ah, the intoxication of shirking responsibility, the excitement of drifting with the tide! It was just the other day that Moti had married; Moti, a rustic girl of Gaodiya: had she already been infected with Kumud's disease then? Still, it was true that although their marriage was recent, her relation with Kumud went back a long way. Ever since he was bitten by a snake near the taalpukur, this *knachpoka*[114] from a far-away land had been hypnotising this village cockroach.

Kumud was glad. He said, 'What makes you behave so, Moti?'

Moti said:

'Binde[115] *says: Why do I find you so, Rai*[116]*/ Lurks a smile on thy lips, tho' Shyam*[117] *is not nigh?'*

'And what does that mean?'

Moti said, 'Wait a bit, wait a bit—

Rai says, O Binde, have you gone blind? / Look there! Beneath the kadam[118] *bough, we are closely entwined.'*

Kumud asked again, 'And what does that mean?'

Meaning! Out of sheer joy a village girl recites a rhyme; does she have to explain even that? However, Moti didn't know the meaning. She hid her face in embarrassment.

About a fortnight later, the new play started. Moti went to watch the show on three successive nights. She could not persuade Jaya to accompany her to see Kumud's performance even once. Only Banbihari went one day and watched it, without telling Jaya. He came back to express his appreciation secretly to Moti, saying Kumud indeed had histrionic talents.

If he had no acting schedule, Kumud went around noon or in the evening for rehearsals. In Kumud's absence at night, Jaya slept with Moti. Moti was not used to waking early. Returning home, he called her while removing the greasepaint from his face; after having his bath, he called her again; Moti awoke much later. It was Jaya who made tea for Kumud. Jaya did quite a bit for Moti, yet in many matters she stayed distant.

Days went by for Moti doing housework, visiting theatres and *bioscope*[119] shows, merrymaking with careless abandon, getting nostalgic about Gaodiya, and feeling at times envy and at times affection for Jaya. She had also begun to take lessons in reading and writing from Jaya. After seven days' effort she even finished reading the play in which Kumud acted. Hopes soared sky high once again in Moti's mind. There was no end to her imaginings; her old fancies while in Gaodiya were supplanted by newer and newer dreams. Moreover, after so long, she seemed to have begun to love Kumud anew. It seemed to her to be the true love: what they had experienced in the leafy shade of the palm grove in Gaodiya was mere dalliance; now at last was the real prospect of a deep romantic love growing between them. What had happened to Moti in the interim? Had her mind become enervated? Or why did she then not feel such ineffably unbearable ecstasy from Kumud's kisses as she did now? Then it seemed to be sorrow-laden and distasteful. Did this indicate the advent of spring for the first time in Moti's life in this springtime? When Kumud read a book, Moti felt such joy just to look at his face at intervals while performing her chores. When he was away, a strange shiver of delight would keep coursing through her body and mind ceaselessly for no reason. To sit drooping languidly was as pleasing as to move about and do some manual work. Even the cleaning of utensils seemed to have a piquancy. Every scene of Moti's tiny world seemed to be strewn with charm.

Jaya asked her, 'Hello there, what on earth has happened to you? There's a certain look in your eyes; often you wilt and slump, or you choke with emotion as you talk—what's the matter with you?'

Did Moti herself know what had happened to her? She shook her head as if befuddled. Jaya said with a smile, 'You're possessed by *chait*;[120] you've become fanciful like a poet, Moti.'

The village girl that she was, trying to make a point, Moti said, 'My mind seems to be about to take flight, Didi.'

'That's what is called being possessed by chait.'

Jaya turned grave and with special attention looked at Moti from a new angle. Moti felt a trifle discomfited before asking, 'How long have you been married, Didi?'

'Two years.'

'Just two? Then you must have married rather late, didn't you?'

'Compared to you, it was of course late. Come, Moti, let's go to your room; I've some things to ask.'

Jaya had never shown any curiosity about where and how Kumud had discovered Moti. Today, she quizzed her about it exhaustively. Just about everything: the most intimate and private matters which Moti could never imagine might be divulged to anyone. She was surprised at Jaya's sudden eagerness to know everything after all these days. Jaya did not let her curtail or conceal anything. It seemed that she would be even happier if the facts came with frills.

After that Jaya said, 'Then Kumud does love you truly, Moti.'

What did it mean to state an obvious truth in this way? Did Jaya think that Kumud did not love her? Moti looked at Jaya proudly, and thought: now at last you are disabused of your notions, right—you, Kumud's longtime friend. Don't again try to act smart with Moti, mind.

'So in the end, Kumud fell in love with you, Moti?' Jaya asked.

Hurt, Moti said, 'How could he not? Do you know for how many cycles of birth I've been his wife?'

'Do you know even that—that you were his wife birth after birth? You leave me floored, Moti. You, a slip of a girl, overpowered him—whom none else could captivate with beauty or skill, learning or intelligence, song and dance! You are someone to reckon with!'

'Who was it, Didi, that could not captivate him? Who is she? Do you know her?'

'I do, but I won't tell you.'

'Please tell me, Didi. I implore you, do tell me.'

A little disconcerted, Jaya said, 'I'd really have liked to tell you just to distress you a bit, Moti. Still I won't. What use is it anyway? There's no knowing where they have gone or in what condition they are now. Besides, what do you need to fear, Moti? No one can ever snatch him away from you. He had come back once, but for your sake he went back again to Gaodiya.'

Jaya's words frightened Moti a great deal: what had happened to Jaya suddenly? Was Jaya too one of those who could not tie down

Kumud? If true, she must indeed be suffering a lot. What reasoning led Kumud to set up house here under the same roof as Jaya? Gradually, Moti's heart filled with compassion for Jaya. Sympathy, rather than jealousy, was what now dominated her feelings.

Within just a few days Moti could begin to understand that what had happened to Jaya was no temporary phase. She seemed to have been permanently crushed. She appeared to find no interest in work; she had lost her previous eagerness to cater to the needs and comforts of her gifted husband; knitting her brows, she tried desperately to decipher the meaning of some incomprehensible matter. Occasionally Moti could sense that Jaya intently observed the open talk and exchange of feelings between Kumud and herself. What was on Jaya's mind? Why did she act hawk-eyed in this way? Moti's heart pounded in fear.

In his leisure, sometimes even neglecting his work, Banbihari painted something on a big canvas. This canvas Jaya had so far cared for like her family deity, treating it with the utmost precaution. This, she claimed, was not for sale nor a work to anyone's order; urged by his genius at moments of inspiration Banbihari applied colour to it; one day the work would find its place in exhibitions at home and abroad earning the painter lasting fame. Moti didn't bother her head over all that. She only knew that of all his paintings this one was something special; once finished, it would trigger a series of big events. Day after day, she heard Jaya and Banbihari discuss the painting. For some days now even these deliberations seemed to hold no interest for Jaya. Yet Moti often found her lifting the cover and looking probingly at the nearly finished picture. A woman slightly corpulent like Jaya, discarding her skeletal child on the ground, stretched out her hand to a fleeing beautiful cherub in eager expectation: this was what the picture showed. Moti could never discern what was so special about it. But she attributed it to a shortcoming of her own eyes. Who would deny Jaya's claim that there were not more than a handful of pictures of this standard in the world?

Some days later, one morning Jaya ripped this very painting to pieces. Moti had never seen such an act or such a mood of Jaya.

Kumud was not in the house then; it was about ten. Moti had nearly finished her cooking. Jaya looked ominously grave since morning; perhaps she had had a quarrel with her husband at night. Getting no reply to one or two questions she asked her, Moti had not dared to speak further. A little while ago, after putting the rice to cook on the oven Jaya had gone out of the kitchen. Suddenly hot exchanges between Jaya and Banbihari reached her ears. Moti quickly came out to see what had happened. In front of the remarkable picture stood Banbihari, paintbrush in hand, his face flushed. Not far away stood Jaya, her face also red, and she was quivering with some strong emotion.

'Throw away, throw away that picture! Inspiration! You don't know how to paint and you talk of inspiration? Aren't you ashamed to talk of inspiration?'

Jaya's voice was nearly choked. Suppressing his anger Banbihari said, 'Jaya, what does it mean saying all these things after so long?'

'I was blind till now. You spoke of conquering the world merely by bragging about it. You led me on with your big mouth—you're an impostor, a cheat!'

Banbihari was faint-hearted, but not so faint-hearted as to tolerate this slur. He said, 'That's possible. If you had so long been blind, where did you get your divine vision today? Who opened your eyes, pray? Is it Kumud?'

At that, Jaya went up to the canvas with her *bnoti*[121] and slashed it. After standing motionless for some time Banbihari went into his room, picked up his shirt, and went out of the house. Jaya went into the room and bolted the door. While picking up the knife, Jaya might have cut her hand; a few drops of blood were left on the porch.

What terrible, incomprehensible affairs were these! Had Jaya gone off her head? Moti could not complete her cooking. After a long time, gently tapping on the door of Jaya's room, she called her in a low voice. Moti called her several times before Jaya said, 'Go away, Moti; don't disturb me.'

Moti sat quietly in her room until Kumud returned. She felt herself in considerable danger. She could not understand such complex, arbitrary matters. Quarrels between husband and wife were quite natural; but what kind of a quarrel was this? What Jaya said, what Banbihari said: what did it all mean? It occurred to Moti that in all this she too seemed to have a place; the quarrel was not limited entirely between Jaya and Banbihari. What had Moti done? What was her fault? She wished someone would explain it to her. Kumud came back quite late in the day. Making him sit in the room Moti told him everything as coherently as she could in an undertone.

Kumud said, 'In that case, it spells disaster.'

'What disaster? What has happened?' Moti was anxious. 'For goodness' sake, tell me. My head is reeling, dear.'

'I'll explain later, Moti. I myself can't make out anything clearly. Isn't it terribly hot? Will you fan me a little?'

Moti was greatly agitated today; otherwise she wouldn't need to be told to fan. After cooling down, Kumud went to have a bath; then after his meal, he lay down on the bed and tried to get some sleep. Moti said, 'Won't you speak to Didi?'

'Now? She is angry and has shut herself up. Who'll dare to disturb her now? She'll rush out to beat me. Go and have your meal.'

After her bath, Moti was about to sit down to her meal when Jaya opened her door and came out. Going into the kitchen she helped herself to a glass of water from the pitcher.

Moti asked with some trepidation, 'Why did you have a quarrel, Didi?'

Jaya said, 'You'd better remain like a child, okay?' Then she walked into Moti's room; Moti had to leave her meal unfinished. She was afraid to get up; yet it was impossible to keep sitting in front of her plate. Unable to suppress her curiosity, she went and stood outside the door.

She heard Jaya say, 'Kumud, you are not to stay here any longer. You're earning a hundred rupees; arrange to stay elsewhere. Find yourself some convenient place in a day or two.'

Kumud had sat up on the bed; he said, 'Why don't you sit, Jaya? Sit down and tell me everything in detail.'

Jaya sat down on the chair and said, 'There's no use talking, Kumud. If you don't go, we will. And it'll be tomorrow itself.'

Kumud said calmly, 'All right, we'll leave tomorrow. That's not a problem. But if you don't tell me what happened, I wouldn't know what to think.'

'I have no objection in telling you, Kumud; I can't do without telling either. You want to hear it right now? Then listen, though I'm not sure whether you will understand. You know that I married him for love. I have suddenly come to know that that is not true.'

'How did you know that?'

'By observing the two of you, Kumud. You love Moti, don't you?'

Kumud smiled slightly and then became grave. 'I don't exactly know. Most probably I do. I can be sure perhaps after some more time.'

Jaya said, 'No, Kumud, you love her; she too loves you. A few days ago this doubt suddenly struck me. I had not noticed it earlier. After that, observing you closely for a few days I realised that my perception of love so far was itself wrong. I did not love him; I loved his genius. Kumud, do you know what I discovered the very day I realised it? That his genius was false too; it was all my imagination.'

'It is also possible that you are wrong.'

Jaya's eyes were moistening; the degree of her pain could easily be understood. Leaning forward a little, she said, 'One may be wrong in everything else, but never wrong in realising one's own wrongs. I want to die out of shame and sorrow. How could I make such a mistake? How did I sustain an imagined paradise of lies for so long? How great was my self-confidence! I thought I lived in a different world, that nobody could love like me; that only my love was true; everybody else's was childishness. I was so smug in my belief that by associating myself with the unsuccessful life of a genuine artist trying to help preserve his genius, I seemed to be doing penance by inflicting misery on myself. I smiled complacently to myself at the dull, ordinary lives of others. The lies of my own creation therefore have left me shattered. What would you say to this? I am ashamed to show my face to Moti! I do not know if you can get what I am saying.'

'Of course, I can. But then, there's a great difference between what you feel and what I understand.' After a pause, Kumud said, 'That's why I dare to suggest this: can't you just laugh it off?'

Jaya sat up erect. She said, 'How can that be? The very belief that sustained me till now has broken down.' Jaya seemed to have fallen into a stupor; she looked like a cadaver. 'Only I can't understand how I managed to deceive myself so full-bloodedly for so long. Can anybody make such a perfect blunder? I am no dunce either, Kumud.'

Kumud said, 'I tell you what, Jaya, we all deceive ourselves. We eat and drink when we are hungry and thirsty; we go to sleep when we feel sleepy: barring these, our lives are all made up, a fiction. Were it not for deluding ourselves, we would never take the trouble of making it all up. Most people are unable even to realise this. Neither does realisation of the errors of their beliefs ever come in their entire lifespan. If mistakes are not realised as such, what do the mistakes matter? There are some who happen to sense it; they are the ones who suffer. That is why those who want to understand and analyse their lives are condemned to suffer. Anything big they wish to embrace turns out to be false. That is why for such people to expect anything big from life is disastrous; the higher the expectation, the greater the misery. You know I am forever so whimsical and irresponsible; today I take to one thing, tomorrow another; there is no attempt to set my life in order; no anxiety to be of any use to the world. Why I became so I've never said to anyone. I've known this long since. If I ever aspired to anything big in life, I too would meet with the same plight as yours, Jaya; gathering up a pile of things, I would have discovered that they were all a sham. Instead, I want just what I wish and whenever I wish. I make no undue demands; I accept whatever comes my way, never nourish any expectation. If I ever strike a big bargain, even that I accept with indifference. You said I love Moti; well, if tomorrow we happen to separate for life, I'll overcome the shock within a matter of days. I get Moti to massage my feet, Jaya.'

'Massage your feet? That's fine. Unless you do something eccentric and out of the way, you won't survive. Had I been Moti—'

'You'd have done something else, something eccentric and out of the way. The very joy of living consists in being inconsistent. If you can't do anything inconsistent—'

Jaya said, 'Yes, I know all that. Enough of your lectures, Kumud. Fix a house later today and shift out tomorrow. I can't bear to see the two of you loving each other in front of my eyes.'

'Neither could you if it is out of your sight.'

'That's a different matter.'

Just after saying this, Jaya seemed to be suddenly surprised. 'What did you think, Kumud? What made you say that? You definitely know that you could never draw me like that; you never had that kind of attraction for me.'

Somewhat embarrassed, Kumud said, 'That I know. Neither did I mean that. We came and broke up your home; so I said that even when we are gone, our memory will rankle.'

With a faint smile Jaya said, 'How well you talk, Kumud! O Moti, come inside. Listen as much as you wish to; you won't understand any of this. We are tainted with modernism, always being enigmatic.'

Once again the hassles of moving house? Jaya won't let them stay here? Let her not. It was all for the good. They will live happily enough in the new house. An angry Moti wore a long face. Poor thing, she had not figured out yet what had happened or how, not even after Kumud's explanation. She told Jaya, 'You alone know what wrong we did you. What you've done is not right, Didi, it's not right driving us away like this. I'll remember and tell everybody.'

'What will you tell?'

'You're such a dangerous woman; that is what I'll tell; you say one thing and something else goes on in your mind. What a show of love you used to make! Where did all that go? I'm a tough girl too; if I ever utter your name again, *let vermin fall in my mouth*.'

'If you don't utter my name, how will you tell others about me?'

Moti was on the verge of tears; she fell silent.

Banbihari returned in the afternoon; he looked utterly crestfallen. Moti noticed that the morning's events had not made them stop talking to each other. Banbihari had his meal and even handed some money to Jaya. Still, the distance of strangers seemed to have come between them; the two looked despondent. After renting a house, Kumud came back in the evening. Moti said, 'Won't you go to the theatre today?' Kumud said, 'No.'

Next morning, a carriage was hired and goods were loaded. Jaya enquired only whether it wouldn't be better if they left after having their midday meal. Banbihari had nothing to say. Moti, without taking her leave of Jaya, walked determinedly into the carriage. Jaya came up to the door as she spoke to Kumud.

Kumud said, 'We will meet again someday, Jaya.'

Jaya said, 'Who knows if we will!'

'Shall I come to look you up from time to time?'

'All right. Come alone.'

The smouldering anger in Moti flared up: Come alone! Why? Did Jaya think that unless Moti came to see her, food wouldn't taste as good in Moti's mouth? When the carriage got going, she said to Kumud, 'You shall never go to see them. She drove us away!'

Kumud said nothing. Moti went on, 'How selfish she is. I had indications of it on the very first day. How blithely she had occupied the better room before we arrived.'

'Don't keep those trival things in mind, Moti.'

Kumud had rented two rooms on the second floor of a house; it had a separate kitchen too. Two rooms instead of one was a sign of progress: Moti was pleased.

Moti missed Jaya for a few days to begin with; she had learnt to depend on her in some matters. But then she did not have the time to spare too much thought on Jaya. In her newfound infatuation and delight she was almost on the verge of forgetting about Gaodiya. Material considerations and interactions with people had become secondary to her; except for the emotional demands on Kumud, all others had become insignificant for Moti.

Meanwhile, after coming to the new house, Kumud had stopped going to the theatre. He spent his days lolling and lazing, reading books and smoking cigarettes. One day Moti asked him, 'Why aren't you going to the theatre?'

'I have left the job, Moti.'

'Why?'

'The play flopped; they said they would cut down the salary, so I resigned. Those rascals, they'll choose worthless plays; if they flop, they blame the actors. Jatra is far better than theatre, Moti.'

'Did they say that your acting is not up to the mark?' Moti seemed incredulous.

'That's what it comes to, indeed. When the play did not click, it was surely due to bad acting. I'm no famous actor after all that even if one or two plays don't run, they would favour me. It's all for the good, Moti; I don't really like to stay in the theatre.'

Assuming the posture of a shrewd matron, Moti said, 'What will you do now?'

Kumud smiled and said, 'Something I will do for sure, something or the other. What's there to worry about? Won't you give me one or two ornaments if I need them?'

'Take them.'

Moti said this without any hesitation, without turning a hair. Here was our Moti, the village girl, who was unperturbed to hear that Kumud had resigned from his job, and whose face did not turn pale at the thought of having to part with her ornaments. What had brought about such a change in Moti? Kumud was a magician indeed. He was whimsical, self-willed and a vagrant; still he had an uncanny power to charm people. He might not obey the rules and customs of the world; but he did obey his own norms devoutly. He did not lack in spirit; the faculty of his mind was alive to opportunities. It was a tribute to his masculinity to be able to build with his own capacity a world of his own to live in. Kumud was that kind of man to whom one could go to forget one's anguish: he never worried; never wept; cared not for sorrow or misery; even a calculating, circumspect mind found repose in him.

Days went by. The rains came. Sitting by the window or standing in the narrow balcony with its railing, Moti could see only clusters of bricks; yet, even in that, she could discern the mark of Gaodiya. Across the two-storied building to the south could be seen the garden of a rich man; its tall trees seemed to remind her of the palm grove of Gaodiya. In the lane below, an Oriya man's shop selling puffed rice and sugared rice reminded her of Bipin Moyra's sweet shop in Gaodiya. The sight of an unknown man passing by in clothes befitting a villager brought back memories of her acquaintances in Gaodiya. The kites flying about resembled those in Gaodiya's sky! The gathering clouds overhead coming down as showers replicated perfectly the ever-familiar rains of Gaodiya.

One day Kumud did take Moti's ornaments and went to sell them off. Not that Moti did not feel a twinge for a while; but she felt nothing like she had when, having to part with her chain on the first occasion, she was almost reduced to tears. By the time Kumud returned, even the faintest trace of discontent had been wiped out from her mind. She was childlike when she said, 'Those were *my* ornaments you sold; what did you bring for me?'

'I brought nothing,' said Kumud.

'Why should you? It was absolutely right that you did not!'

With pretended pique Moti embraced Kumud; hiding her face in his chest she smiled slyly. No one who saw Moti clinging to her husband's neck in a small urban room up above the vast city would recognise her as the same old Moti of Gaodiya. A dangerous man was this Kumud; he passed his life severing one tie after another; he was irresponsible and ruthless: one would be surprised to see Moti's carefree and trusting dependence on that very person.

It was then that Kumud said, 'I have brought something for you, Moti.'

'Where is it, give me?'

He took out from his pocket the chain he had once taken from her, and also returned the ornaments he had gone to sell today. Long-time practitioner of the dramatic art, there was no limit to the histrionics Kumud could perform! He was not ordained to do anything in a plain, artless manner. In exhilaration, Moti seemed unable to utter her words distinctly. This was not merely returning her ornaments; together with this, Kumud had given her—his puerile child bride—so much more.

'Where did you get the money?'

'Borrowed it from a rich friend.'

Moti giggled. 'Borrowed? Hardly! I know what you'll do about repayment!'

Kumud also joined in the laughter, saying, 'He has lots. If I think I won't repay, I won't; it will not matter to him.'

Through a messenger, Kumud had sent word to the manager of Binodini Opera. Within two days it brought the manager to his house. Even as he entered the room, he said, 'You're a strange fellow indeed, Kumud. What made you run away like that, pray tell me? Vanished without a trace!'

Kumud received him with a smile. 'Welcome, Ghosh-mashay. Please take your seat. How are you? How is the company doing?'

'Doing fine. It's been doing even better since you left!'

'Very good, very good. It's a pleasure to hear that. You're very angry with me, aren't you'? In reply to this, asking Kumud himself to judge, the manager said, 'You yourself decide whether one should or should not be angry. You took so much money in advance and simply fled nobody knows where.'

'Why should I flee, Ghosh-mashay? I didn't flee. I just took a break for a couple of months; I got married; that's why. I was planning to meet you one of these days.'

The manager was surprised. 'Did you get married? So at last you got married?' He was sceptical at first. Then he became serious and said, 'If indeed you did, son, why did you not marry my daughter? What was her fault, pray?'

Kumud kept silent. The manager remained a bit distracted for a while.

'You would never have got such a girl, Kumud. Not that you hadn't seen her. Tell me, you tell me honestly, is a girl like her easy to find? But you never took a fancy to her! Do they call you crazy without reason?'

The manager stayed long and talked about much else. He also reached an understanding with Kumud. Kumud would rejoin Binodini Opera. The advance he had received would be written off; the manager agreed to consider it his wedding present. He would never be able to come to grips with Kumud. Would Kumud desist until he had ruined the manager!

'But mind you, you must reorganise the troupe properly, my son. It won't do merely to speak your part.'

'Does it ever do?' Kumud smiled. 'If the troupe as a whole is not good, how can my own role create an impact?'

The manager departed that day with a radiant face.

So Kumud would be acting again in the role of Prince Prabir and going from one place to another. What would be Moti's fate? Where would she stay? And with whom? This was by no means a simple problem. But Moti did not seem to be at all worried about it. Her power of thinking things over too seemed to be impaired with the intoxication of joy she was lost in.

In the end Kumud broached the matter. 'When I'll be away on tour, where will you stay, Moti?'

With a tilt of her head, Moti said, 'Why don't you tell yourself?'

'Will you go to Gaodiya?'

Gaodiya? Moti seemed startled to hear that. The man who had commanded her to wipe out the memory of Gaodiya from her mind was now suggesting of his own accord that she go there? Moti looked straight into Kumud's eyes. What did she look for there? Kumud was given to changing colours like a chameleon; what he might say one day he would reject the next. Even so, could he possibly possess some unchangeable trait whose originality overwhelmed even a girl like Moti?

'You are asking me to go to Gaodiya?'

'Yes, you'd better stay there for a few months. Meanwhile let me get a few things settled over here.'

'What things?'

Kumud said solemnly, 'I've to set up the group, look to my savings; just about everything is waiting to be put in place.'

It was prudent talk. Yet Moti seemed to be sad to hear it. Did such talk suit Kumud? Even three months ago perhaps she might have been happy to find such thrift and reasonableness in Kumud. No longer did she want that. She preferred Kumud just as he was, Kumud who would indulge in boasting, loll instead of work, love her yet get her to rub his feet.

'Write to your Dada to come and take you.'

'Why don't you write?'

'No, you do it.'

'All right, then write me the address, okay?'

In response to the letter from Moti, both Paran and Shashi came to Calcutta. The purpose of Shashi's visit was not only to see Moti, but also to attend to some personal work. He had thought to give Kumud a piece of his mind, but ended up saying nothing. He was speechless to see Moti. Was this the same Moti he had seen grow up in the bucolic ambience of Gaodiya? It looked as though she was a girl unknown to Shashi; having lived so long in a different world, today for the first time she stood before him. The one who would keep staring vacantly like a dullard now had a look which was so refreshingly bright like light filtering through rain! How imposing was her gait; how charming her posture! Today even the act of moving her fingers seemed sweet and suggestive. It seemed her whole being was biding every moment in keen anticipation of the attraction and call of someone.

Taking him aside, Kumud said to Shashi, 'How do you find Moti?'

'What have you done to her, Kumud?'

'I did nothing except talk and keep silent.'

Bindu too had undergone a change, and what a contrast that change was! Shashi said doubtfully, 'You're sending her to Gaodiya. I'm worried whether she will be able to stay there now.'

'What kind of worry of yours is this, anyway? Moti grew up in Gaodiya; and she won't be able to stay there?'

Bindu too had grown up in Gaodiya; she could not stay there when she went back. But Shashi did not say anything more. He remained bemused all day. When lightning sparked in Moti's eyes, he compared it with Kusum's eyes; this light was not there. Once again today Shashi felt himself small compared to Kumud.

The bright visage of Moti sparkling with joy and contentment as well as her graceful movements, languid with exhilaration today, seemed to completely wipe out the disdain Shashi had developed for Kumud in the intervening period. Shashi had never been able to identify the mainspring of Kumud's life; this one aspect Shashi pondered over today. What did Kumud possess; what was that cryptic hidden treasure that had filled his life with opulence even though he had flouted all the rules all his life?

At the outset Moti felt slightly embarrassed before Paran and Shashi for not having written any letter for so long. As neither of them complained, she forgot about it within a short while. Paran had become emaciated; his sad, withered face evoked great pity in Moti's heart. She repeatedly asked Paran what illness he was suffering from. She then meticulously collected news about the village, about Mokshada and Kusum too. She was a bit bashful and at the same time a bit daring. This was virtually her first appearance as someone's wife before her elder brother and Shashi; she was quite within her rights as well to behave a little in the matronly manner obtaining news about her father's house standing in the midst of her domestic set-up in her own home. It was the hot month of Bhadra: Moti picked up a hand fan and waved it to cool them; gave them cold water to drink. She was so perfect at her work today; how gentle her small services were! Moti cooked the food with great care. While eating, Shashi praised her cooking; Paran ate virtually nothing. When Moti complained, Paran said, 'I've got a sore in my throat. It hurts to eat soups and curries.'

'Sore in the throat? Why?'

Moti's anxious question made Shashi forget to laugh. Only one whose mind throbbed with surging emotion could be so solicitous about someone having a sore in his throat. Paran was not so discerning; he said with a slight smile, 'Do I know why one's throat has a sore? Chhoto-babu is a doctor. Ask him.'

Being even more anxious, Moti said, 'What will you have with your rice then? Why did you not tell me before so I would have put less of chilli?'

'I can't eat any curry even if it has a little chilli, Moti.'

'Then have some milk. Let me send for sweets.'

At this point, tears came to Paran's eyes. He was a farmer, a boor; never in his life had anyone treated him with such cordiality.

It was Paran in particular who was drawing Moti's mind to Gaodiya. With the sore in his throat he could not eat anything;

and only because he did not eat, a man of such large build as Paran seemed to have shrivelled. Once she went to Gaodiya, she would take special care of his food. Paran was so indifferent to his own happiness and comfort! She was also feeling tempted to show everybody how accomplished in housework and tending to people she had become, how smart and clever she had grown. Everyone would be taken aback. Wonder what Kusum would say! The girls of the village would come to ask where she had been so long, and what her story was.

Kumud was due to leave in two days. Binodini Opera had been booked for a faraway place. What role would Kumud play? That Prince Prabir? Oh, Moti would no more get to see Kumud in the guise of Prince Prabir and hear his thrilling declamations! What else could she do except worry and look morose? Was Moti not a woman, a housewife? Alas, if only one could transform oneself at one's sweet will—a male into a female, a female into a male!

Kumud said, 'It is happening, Moti; it does happen these days.'

Hugging Kumud tightly, Moti said, 'Absurd!'

Kumud laughed. 'Why? Did you not see with your own eyes? Jaya was a male and Banbihari a female! Right?'

Moti did not share his mirth.

'Won't you go to see Jaya-didi?'

'Yes, yes; what's the hurry?'

And Kumud let out a yawn.

The shadow of the imminent parting from her husband and the light of premature joy of returning to Gaodiya played alternately on Moti's face for two days. Finally the day of Kumud's departure arrived.

The train was in the afternoon. As the time approached, Moti grew terribly restless. She felt such a pang that she herself was surprised. At the time of leaving her village too, she had suffered and her heart had ached, but that pain was by no means like this. And what was the anguish for after all? It wasn't as if she was going to lose somebody forever? She wouldn't get to see Kumud maybe for fifteen days, maybe for a month. What was there to feel so upset about? Yet she remained disconsolate. Shashi and Kumud chatted away; looking with pensive eyes at Kumud, Moti felt a great turmoil in her heart.

At one point Shashi said, 'Let's go, Moti; we'll see Kumud off in the train. Will you come?'

Moti gave no definite reply. She dressed, put on her shoes and was ready. With wonder in his eyes Shashi was glancing repeatedly at her sad face and tearful eyes. He too was feeling agitated with a surge of emotion. Perhaps there were very many like her in the world; perhaps there were many too who loved like her: but from where did Moti learn? From where did such depth of feeling come to her?

That this was no sentimentality, no temporary impulse of an immature mind Shashi sensed from the presence of an uncommon forbearance in her anguish of separation.

When they reached the station, the sky was still full of light. The train was due to start some time later. It was not crowded. After sitting together in the compartment talking with Kumud for some time, Shashi called Paran and got down. He said to them, 'You two keep sitting; we'll be back soon.'

When they were gone, Moti, her face pale, said to Kumud, 'Do not go, for my sake, please don't. I won't be able to bear it; I'll die.'

Kumud said, 'Coming to see somebody off at the station one feels like that, Moti.'

'I've been feeling so since yesterday.'

'Since yesterday? But you didn't tell me anything yesterday? In any case, if you do feel like this, let it be so. That is no less fun either!'

Fun? Did Kumud not understand that the entire world was darkening before her eyes? Kumud, who understood everything? Even Kumud's cruelty Moti had learnt to love; yet today she was hurt. From the next platform a crowded train started moving: Moti's mind was getting crushed under its wheels. There was no more time, no more opportunity. There was no making Kumud turn back now. Once the train left, her heart would break; there was no preventing it. How could she make Kumud realise the intensity of her feelings? Did anybody who had boarded a train to leave ever turn back? Neither was there any way she could burst out crying clinging to his feet. It was probably she who the people in the compartment were gaping at.

Kumud, placid and unperturbed as ever, talked of this and that. Moti's voice was getting caught; yet with utmost effort she kept giving her responses. The minutes kept ticking by one after another. A little before departure time, Shashi and Paran came back. What an inauspicious moment it was when she wrote to them to come to Calcutta!

Then Shashi said, 'Come, Moti. Let's get down.'

'You get down; I'll just have a word with him.'

Both Shashi and Paran were stunned by this shamelessness of Moti. Shashi was apparently displeased as he got down. Just because she had experienced the advent of romance, was this slip of a girl to indulge in such excesses?

Kumud smiled and said in a mild voice, 'You acted like a mature housewife, Moti. What did you have to say?'

'I'll tell you; wait, I'm coming.'

With this, to the utter surprise of even Kumud, Moti went to the lavatory. The starting bell rang; the guard waved the flag; on the platform Shashi and Paran grew restless; still Moti did not emerge. When the train had started, walking alongside the moving train Shashi said, 'Should one of us get up, Kumud, to take her down at the next stop?'

Kumud refused, saying, 'No, no; there's no need. I will myself see to it.'

After the train had crossed the platform, Moti came out. 'What happened? But I couldn't get down!'

'No, you couldn't, could you?'

'What will happen then?'

Kumud smiled. 'Nothing will happen. Moti, sit down. Why did you have to play such a trick? You could very well have told me that you'd go with me.'

Moti sat down and said, 'They were here. They would have created trouble.'

Unbeknown to either, the other passengers watched them, amused. As the train picked up speed, the pallor of Moti's face faded. She breathed deeply a couple of times.

Kumud said, 'You just wished to go and you came along. Have you thought about where to stay, what to do and other things?'

Moti said recklessly like Kumud, 'What's there to think about?'

Along with her home-forsaking, nomadic husband, today Moti too had embraced the haphazard, restless life of the road—Moti, our rustic Gaodiya girl Moti. Maybe one day their love will look for a resting place; maybe one day if only for the sake of their child they will be compelled to build a nest and the ordinary rules of life will become indispensable even for them. Nothing can be said definitely today. In the chronicles of the puppets' dance, that episode will be an interpolation—here ends their story. If I have to tell, I will narrate their story in a different book.

12

The newly constructed building of the hospital looked really beautiful. The compact, attractive and elegant building in red-painted bricks made one lament that Jadab died before seeing it. Up front, below the cornice was written, in big English lettering: JADAB MEMORIAL HOSPITAL. Still, when referring to it, people said *Shashi Daktarer Haspatal*: Doctor Shashi's Hospital. That is not to say that people had forgotten Jadab. Jadab's connection to the hospital was not perceptible, while it was Shashi whom people had seen actively working to set up the hospital. And now it was he who distributed medicines to the patients with care.

The hassles of founding the hospital were over; there was no halt to the fame and honour of Shashi soaring higher. The collective psyche of people is forever unidirectional: the direction it takes at a certain point of time is the one it begins to move along swiftly and vigorously. That is also the reason why a molehill of a rumour rapidly grows into a mountain. By word of mouth do small events turn big; so do men. Shashi had done nothing extraordinary—he had only discharged faithfully the duty Jadab had imposed upon him. The result was something beyond all expectations. People installed him as their leader placing him on a pedestal. By making speeches at a few public places his faculty to speak had also developed surprisingly well. These days he often had to speak at meetings and gatherings; everyone listened to him with rapt attention. If Shashi spoke in an emotional vein, there swept a wave of emotion through the meeting; if he said something amusing, the resulting roar of laughter startled the birds and animals around.

At times it occurred to Shashi that because he had decided to go away from his village the numerous tentacles of village life had tied him down. This sudden popularity was to wheedle him into staying here. This was no prize but a bribe offered by fate. This was not what he had desired—honour and authority of this kind. This solemn aspect of life had affected him to some extent indeed; but what would he do with this kind of fulfilment?

One morning Paran came to Shashi's dispensary. He looked desiccated and withered; a muffler was wrapped round his neck; to see him was to feel pity. Shashi had no time to feel pity: he had so many responsibilities, so many tasks. How did Paran get so skinny even though he had a physician friend like Shashi? What had happened to Paran? He had a sore in his throat? He could not swallow food? But wasn't that a long time ago, when on receiving Moti's letter they had gone to Calcutta to bring her back? Had that sore not healed yet? Shashi was surprised: it was not supposed to persist; hadn't Paran applied the medicine he had given him? Had he been sleeping over it so long?

Shashi's demeanour was like that of a busy doctor of the hospital—as if even Paran had no special favour with Shashi anymore. As he talked, he went on writing a prescription. That is not to say that there were a great many patients to attend to. It would be some time still before villagers broke free of their fear of hospitals. Six or seven male patients were standing in a queue at Shashi's counter and outside the door sat a married woman, with a veil over her head, and an elderly woman, probably her mother-in-law, holding her in place with one hand on her back and the other in front. Perhaps each of them sought courage from the other. These were all the patients there were; yet Shashi found no time even to ask Paran to take his seat? Surely not because Paran had no shoes on his feet, his shirt was not ironed or his hair was not decently combed? Would Shashi, in the pride of building this tiny little hospital, ignore in this manner today one who had been his friend when, sitting in a corner of his room, he was engaged in conquering the world in imagination, one in honour of whose affection he had allowed Kusum to leave on a squally, turbulent midday? There was a chair on this side of the table; if not that, let Shashi at least offer Paran the stool lying a respectable distance away.

'There's severe pain in my throat, Chhoto-babu.'

Looking up, Shashi said, 'Come closer, let me have a look. Open your mouth.'

No clear view was possible from the chair; they had to move into the light near the door. After examining him closely, Shashi said, 'The sore doesn't look too good, Paran. Tell you what, wait a while; after I'm finished with these patients, I'll take another look.'

Paran kept sitting on the stool. After examining all the patients one by one Shashi took Paran along to the small room at the southern end of the hospital. This was his private chamber. In the context of this chamber, Shashi had had some disagreement with the committee members: fancy an ordinary, honorary doctor of a small village hospital being allotted a private chamber like a judge or a magistrate! Shashi had paid no heed to anyone; quite selfishly he had this room neatly arranged for himself. Who could follow the course of Shashi's mind? The old members of the committee were not supposed to know that the all-work-no-pay Doctor Shashi would love to stay back at the hospital even when it was not necessary. If anyone in the world sensed that Shashi could not find repose at home, it was perhaps Gopal.

The more closely Shashi examined Paran's throat, the graver his face grew. He said, 'Swallow, Paran, swallow. Why can't you do it? You should be able to. All right, take some water then. The condition is not so serious that you cannot swallow. It's out of fear that you can't.'

After taking sips of water, Paran felt better. He swallowed too. Forcing a smile he said, 'Suddenly I had such a fright, Chhoto-babu; my heart began to flutter.'

Shashi said, 'The way your life-force has dried up while you starve day after day, won't your heart flutter? Report everyday for a check-up. Here is a lotion; I'll apply it now; do it yourself once again in the afternoon.'

With the help of a swab Shashi smeared the medicine in Paran's throat and said, 'Do you think you can do it yourself? If you can't, leave it. I'll be going later in the day when I'll apply it for you.'

Paran left and Shashi stood at the open window, watching the short strides of his long legs. Then drawing a chair near the table he sat reading a thick medical book very attentively. At times he would look up and reflect, pull out another book and turn its pages or glance over all the names to pick a particular book. Finally he returned home hurriedly at an unusual time, took out a book from the cupboard and sat down to read.

When the day was drawing to a close, Shashi went to Paran's house on his way to the hospital. He had not been there for many days; not too many, though; some twenty days at the most. Depending on the situation, however, that too can seem to be long enough. Paran was not in the house; he had gone to the field. It was time now to sow the rabi crop; however feeble, he could not afford to stay back at home.

Kusum said to Shashi, 'I told him not to go; yet he did. He said he would return soon.'

'Return soon! Am I to keep sitting here waiting for him? Don't I have any work to do?'

'So you mean to say a man of work never sits for a while? If you sit down for even a moment or two of leisure, you feel disgruntled; this is no healthy sign, Chhoto-babu. Of course, you're no servant of anybody's, are you?'

'The house looks empty; where's Paran's mother?'

'Goodness knows where she's gone,' said Kusum indifferently. 'She's such a wandering gossip!'

Shashi was suspicious. 'You didn't send her away on some pretext, I suppose?'

'Me? And I will send her away?' Even as she blushed scarlet, Kusum smiled slightly. 'What a dangerous man you're indeed, Chhoto-babu! Well, even if I did, should you say it so bluntly? Doesn't it hurt one to hear it?'

'How sweet your words sound today, Bou!'

'Because I've eaten sweets, sweetness still lingers on my tongue.'

Delighted, Shashi said, 'To see your smile soothes one's heart, Bou! I'm harried attending to people all day; no one except you ever smiles at me like this. I don't have a single friend, Bou.'

'Neither have you a wife!' Kusum smiled one of her most perfect and complete smiles. Then she asked, 'What's the problem with his throat?'

'Not today; I'll tell you the day after tomorrow.'

'Why, what's the harm in telling today?'

'Let me first find out myself; only then can I tell you, isn't it? Don't give him anything but milk for food, Bou.'

'Can he eat anything else that I would give it to him! Even milk hurts.'

Shashi sat for some more time waiting for Paran. Kusum spoke no more and smiled no more. How long does the effect of an exchange of affectionate words linger? Kusum grew fidgety. Now she would get up and go into the northern room, now come out and look at the sky trying to ascertain the hour of day, and then again, while going past Shashi into the bigger room deliberately drop the bunch of keys on his back, saying, 'Oh, did it hurt?'

Now Shashi got up to go, saying, 'I've no time to sit any longer, Bou. When Paran returns, send him to the hospital.'

Kusum never got angry. Today, suddenly losing her temper and flinging the bunch of keys tied to her sari-end over her back, she said with a darkened face, 'You don't have the time to sit, do you?'

Shashi said with a bit of surprise, 'But you know that patients will be waiting at the hospital?'

These were no difficult words; still it seemed Kusum was getting at the meaning with some effort. She looked at Shashi as if he was a stranger.

Kusum said, 'But they wait everyday.'

Shashi smiled awkwardly and said, 'If you insist, I'll sit, but don't get unreasonably angry. If work is not done in time, the work is spoilt; to sit down and talk can be done in good time. You're here; I too am here—!'

'As I have been for nine long years, not just a day or two.'

With this, Kusum vanished in a trice. If she had not, there's no knowing what might have happened. She would never go off like this. She never lost the expectancy of something happening every moment. What happened to Kusum today that she suddenly broke off leaving Shashi high and dry, when intrigued by her anger he had been getting beside himself? The sight of distress on Shashi's pale face would have at least excited some exultation in Kusum. It had never happened like this before. One day, standing on the high knoll in the palm grove, while observing the sunset, Shashi's heart had grown restless; he was throbbing all over with a surge of emotion he had never experienced before. Today, standing alone in the shadow of the house in the afternoon, he seemed to be overwhelmed in equal measure—with a different kind of emotion. This is but a village, Shashi; a village where the house has a thatched roof and a cow dung-smeared floor; the woman who just left in a huff wore no blouse, had not smeared her hair with scented oil: it doesn't become you to pine for her with a pale face. Her impulse is but a ripple on the village pond; there are seas with waves in the world outside.

A visitor from another village was waiting at the hospital. Shashi must go right now! Right now? After taking Kusum's leave, was he to go to another village right now? But there were several points Shashi would now have to ponder over; he needed to first calm his mind down.

'You've to pay twenty rupees,' snapped Shashi.

'Twenty rupees!' The caller got a start.

'Don't whine. If you can't afford it, call in a quack.'

The man trudging his weary way returned to where he had come from. Today Shashi dealt his patients some harsh words together with medicines. Why was Shashi so angry? Why such meanness? What had made his language and behaviour so impolite and rough? Who could imagine in his presence today that Shashi was given to high thinking, that the urge to widen the domain of life was ever awake in his mind?

When Paran came to the hospital, Shashi said, 'I had told you I would come; still you were not at home?'

Paran said by way of excuse, 'I didn't anticipate that you would come so early in the afternoon.'

Even angrier at this, Shashi said, 'Should I have gone late in the evening instead of early in the afternoon? Can one examine the throat in the dark or can one apply a lotion? Today there's going to be nothing; come tomorrow morning.'

Paran did not come the next morning, nor in the afternoon. Remembering his own agitated state of mind the previous afternoon, Shashi got a little angry with himself. He didn't know why occasionally he had such spells of madness. Then he wanted to hurt whoever might be in front of him; he had the impulse to smash things and go on a rampage. At those moments he thought himself to be very unhappy. He thought he had got nothing after wanting so many things. Just as in the name of tidying up his room he had only cluttered it with junk, so was his life wasted in useless activities. What would he gain by leaving his village if he went on forever asking for something that was not available soon enough, and going on waiting for what he would meanwhile have even lost the power to enjoy? Shashi suspected that perhaps there was something wrong with his head. Those who wanted to live differently in the future did not regard the present as so dull, so meaningless. What did he lack? What was his sorrow really about? His was a healthy and handsome body; he had no shortage of money or honour; and if no one else, at least one person had a heart full of affection for him. As long as he stayed here, he could easily enjoy all these things, and keep up a semblance of romance in his life. What did it avail him to spend his days like one living in somebody else's home?

Next morning he went to Paran's house. No, Paran was not home today either. Mokshada was sitting in the veranda; she said, 'Paran has gone to Bajitpur to have the sore in his throat examined.'

In the village, close to home there was Doctor Shashi; in the village there was Doctor Shashi's hospital; but Paran had gone all the way to Bajitpur to have his throat examined! Shashi found himself smarting with anger. He couldn't imagine that Paran would insult him like this. Only because Shashi had spoken some harsh words one day, for Paran to bypass him and go to Bajitpur for treatment made one gasp at his sheer effrontery!

Kusum was cooking in the kitchen; she came out and laid out a stool. Shashi said, 'No, I won't sit.' Mokshada insisted, 'Be seated, son; do sit. Is it proper, once you've come to one's house, to leave without sitting awhile? I told Paran repeatedly, "If you're going to Bajitpur for work, all right, go. But mind you, as long as we've our Shashi, don't approach anyone else for treating your throat." Fancy comparing a government doctor with Shashi! Just think what my son said to that! The poor wretch keeps saying such outlandish things. He said, "Chhoto-babu is a busy man; he gets annoyed. What is the point of disturbing him, Ma?"'

On earlier occasions, Kusum used to give a knowing smile at such talk. Today her face showed no trace of a smile. She said, 'Chhoto-babu's medicine aggravated the sore, you know; that's why he went to Bajitpur.'

Mokshada intoned irritably, '*That's why he went to Bajitpur*! He told you that, didn't he, before leaving for Bajitpur? Will you keep making things up and saying whatever comes to your mind? Why don't you go to the kitchen, dear?'

Shashi was indeed waiting anxiously to see Kusum's smile; she smiled at last. Before leaving she said, 'Why should I make it up, Ma? Your son himself said this to me. I only said what I heard.'

Shashi returned home with some uneasiness in his mind. What did Paran think? The medicine he had last given him might normally aggravate the sore a bit to start with; was that why Paran panicked, losing faith in Shashi?

Days and nights went by, and Shashi's mind was in turmoil. He suspected Paran to have throat cancer; unable to know whether the prognosis was correct or not, he had no peace of mind. Perhaps not; perhaps it was just an ordinary sore that had worsened through Paran's neglect. Paran did not come; for Shashi to go on his own to ask him what the government doctor of Bajitpur had said hurt his ego. If only Kusum would suddenly arrive on some pretext one day! Why did she not? Because Shashi did not go to Kusum's? As a matter of course, there were often gaps of weeks or months in going to their house; yet, there had never been a dearth of chance encounters with her. One day, very early at dawn, as soon as he came out on to the path in front of his house, he noticed that Kusum was standing on the path in front of hers. It was evident that Kusum too had noticed Shashi. Did she beckon him? No. Did she approach him? No. Shashi stood there for some time. The lonely Kayetpara path that lost itself into the open fields even today lay as a royal road in Shashi's life: whosoever had stirred him, howsoever little, had left their footprints on this road. Of them, the only one still left was Kusum; now she alone walked along this road.

Slowly Shashi drew near Kusum.

'I had stopped on seeing you, Bou. I thought you would come closer.'

'You would keep standing and I would go near?'

'Is there anything wrong in that?' Shashi said smiling. 'How come you no longer call me to meet at the palm grove to ask anything of me, Bou?'

'What is there to ask about any more? Is anything new happening in the village?'

'Of course there is! A big hospital like that came up; you could at least ask how it is doing, what is the number of patients, and things like that. Your curiosity about me seems to be waning, Bou.'

Kusum now smiled sweetly. 'My goodness! Is that so? Maybe. If one thing wanes, another waxes; that's the way of the world, isn't it? The cloud of the sky decreases; the water of the river increases. Would the world move otherwise, Chhoto-babu?'

There was no quarrel; there could be no quarrels between them. Still, a fear had entered Shashi's mind that Kusum's conduct was getting sterner. Shashi did not know what there was to fear in that; only, he had felt a pang. Now happy, Shashi said, 'Well, what increased when your curiosity grew less?'

'Goodness knows what, but definitely something increased.'

These were the words that Shashi, who had come to ask about Paran, ended up exchanging with Kusum. It was as if this was the more urgent matter. Then, as he was coming away, he wanted to know about Paran. The sore in Paran's throat had abated.

Abated? Good. So it was the Bajitpur doctor's medicine that cured the sore? And Shashi's medicine had worsened it? Shashi could not imagine such unfair conduct on Paran's part. After allowing him to aggravate it, he denied Shashi an opportunity to ameliorate it; that Shashi's medicine had worsened the condition remained as the abiding truth! Paran might as well not have come to him to apply his lotion for a day?

The sore in Paran's throat had healed; but his health had not recovered. He had such a big build that he looked gaunt. He could do with a tonic. With a small dose of strychnine Shashi could make him a tonic that would restore his health in a matter of one month: with his frail body Paran worked so hard; strychnine was very useful for *muscular fatigue*. But Shashi could not bring himself to tell this to Paran. What if, complaining that after taking a dose of Shashi's tonic his health had deteriorated, Paran once again rushed to the government doctor of Bajitpur?

'Do take care of your health, Paran,' was all Shashi said.

'Originally I was no farmer, you know, Chhoto-babu; the work of a farmer doesn't suit me,' said Paran; and then with a wan smile he added, 'Even so, most of the land is mortgaged to my father-in-law.'

Shashi said, 'I hear that your father-in-law has no son, only three daughters. Everything he has he will gift to his sons-in-law. The mortgage is only on paper.'

Paran gave a huge yawn and said, 'My father-in-law desires that selling off our house and land here we go and stay with him.'

'Why don't you go?'

'How can that be, Chhoto-babu? Leaving my village, my home and homestead can I keep staying at my father-in-law's place!'

It sounded like an echo, as if someone was uttering someone else's words. Paran was not used to expressing such a forceful and well-thought decision in any matter! Shashi seemed to hear Kusum's father Ananta saying, 'Let's go Kusi, dear; disposing of whatever you have here, come over to my place,' and Kusum saying in reply, 'How can that be, Baba? Leaving my village, my home and homestead, can I keep staying at your place!'

Before the winter set in, this time Jamini Kabiraj's cough stopped for good; the poor fellow died after two days of fever. The cauldron for boiling herbal decoctions looked forlorn; in the cupboard lay all the phials, bottles and tin boxes full of medicines; leaning against the wall stood his hookah—the old Jamini's heartbeats and the clang of his pestle and mortar silenced for ever. When informed, Sen-didi's elder brother Kripanath arrived; he too was a kabiraj. He came along with his family, smoked tobacco from Jamini's hookah, and opening the cupboard surveyed Jamini's stock of medicines. It seemed as if in Jamini's cauldron the decoctions would once again start boiling; and the sound of Jamini's pestle and mortar would again issue forth. Only there was no question of Sen-didi wearing the insignia of a married woman again in this life.

But then it was heard that Sen-didi was in the family way.

When one heard it one of course did not want to believe it; but there was no scope to disbelieve it. This was after all not a rumour heard, but a fact witnessed. After being robbed of her singular beauty and becoming one-eyed, what divine mercy was it that eventually she was blessed with a child? Ah, let her be blessed. How could one do without this small compensation in one's life! How long could Sen-didi possibly go on picking up in the morning the doll forgotten by the grocer Srinath's daughter in the bakul grove in the evening! When Shashi heard, he grew pale; he turned completely ashen and morose. He went about with his head lowered in sullen silence.

Why, what happened to Shashi, the famous doctor of Gaodiya, the rising young leader? Sen-didi used to love him like her son; there was no irrefutable proof either that she no longer did. If today she had a son of her own to love, why was Shashi so disturbed by it?

Gopal asked him in some alarm, 'Well, Shashi, you're not ill, I suppose, are you?'

'No,' said Shashi.

'That's good; do be cautious at this time of the year, my son.'

Imagine Gopal telling Doctor Shashi to be cautious! He said this humbly, as a supplicant. Perhaps that was not what Gopal intended to say. Maybe the sight of Shashi's pale, downcast face made his heart pound; maybe that thumping is all he wished to communicate to Shashi's ears. Gopal after all had no other son, only Shashi.

Goodness knows what suddenly urgent business Shashi had at Bajitpur; leaving many tasks of the village unfinished, he went there. He spent an entire day quietly at senior lawyer Ramtaran's house and then he went to the government doctor's house. Shashi had of late developed great intimacy with this doctor. Now that he happened to be a guest, he came to be acquainted with the gentleman's thin and particularly harassed wife struggling to manage her household of a husband and two sons. In times of mental crises, wonderful comfort can be found unexpectedly from insignificant persons: inept at work, and equally so at conversation, timid and innocent, this woman seemed to win over Shashi within a very short time. Going to serve tea, she spilt some; trying to clutch her son, she was oblivious to her sari-end slipping off her shoulder; attempting to gather it up, she could not prevent her hair tumbling down over her back, and in her haste to go out of the room she even stumbled over the door-sill!

She kept muttering at intervals: 'Can't carry on anymore, good Lord!'

Indeed she could not. Still, she managed everything somehow or the other all by herself. She sought no cover for this either; all her slips and lapses were open for everyone to see. It scarcely took her an hour to expose her true nature; perhaps that is why her husband liked her, and so did Shashi!

Her name was Sushila. Introducing herself to Shashi, she said, 'My maternal uncle's house is at Teishgachha, about six miles from our village. Do you know him—Harishchandra Niyogi? I had been to my uncle's place once in my remote childhood and thereafter only once this time now after I came over here. My father was a munsiff, you know; I used to go places with him.'

'Now you do so with your husband.'

'Exactly. Look, it's just been six months since we came here and now he says he'll be transferred!'

Next morning, Shashi came and stood at the river ghat to return to his village. He was waiting to hire a boat when he came across Kusum's father Ananta.

Ananta said, 'Doctor-babu, what brings you here?'

'I had some work to do; waiting for a boat to return home.'

'Didn't you bring your own boat? I'm also going to Gaodiya; why don't you come along in my boat? Please then get into the boat and wait a bit; let me quickly go and buy a pair of saris from the market for my daughter. Hey, Hanif, bring the boat to shore for Doctor-babu to board.' Within a short time Ananta came back with a pair of saris bought for Kusum. Getting into the boat and sitting at some distance from Shashi, stretching his limbs, he said, 'My daughter has written, asking me to go, Doctor-babu. She wrote to me to bring a big boat right away, stay there for a couple of days and then we'll return together. What a good turn you've done me, Doctor-babu, I'm really at a loss for words to thank you.'

Shashi was surprised. 'What good turn did I do you?'

'Do you think my daughter hasn't written to me? As per your advice, she has decided to come and stay with me—what an eccentric girl she is really! That she listened to your counsel is itself a wonder. Do you know for how long I've been telling her this? You remember the year my daughter's father-in-law died an unnatural death? Since then I've been coaxing my daughter and son-in-law, "What's the point in continuing to stay there even as you suffer? Better come over to me for good." I didn't worry about my son-in-law's opinion; he is easy to convince; if my daughter was willing, he too would fall in. My daughter was the one who kept opposing. She would say, "There's my mother-in-law, my sister-in-law; why should they be willing to go and stay at my father's house?" Well, she had a point. So I kept silent until her sister-in-law was married. Then the only one left to worry about was her mother-in-law. She too was not unwilling. So then I said, why don't you come now? Not even now; citing a host of excuses, she held fast to the soil of this place. They lack in everything; goodness knows what happiness she found living there.'

True enough; what happiness did Kusum have in Gaodiya? Ananta was a well-to-do householder. The satin coat he wore and the scarf wrapped round his waist displayed that. Kusum could live most happily with her father. Now then at last, good sense had dawned on her. There would not have been much harm if it had dawned with due communication to Shashi. What motive could she possibly have had in writing to her father that Shashi's counsel had brought about her change of heart?

Divesting himself of his coat and scarf Ananta sat comfortably and said, 'In the month of Shravan[122] last year, when I came for the first time to take her back—you remember? I came along with you up to Bajitpur—that time too she had consented. But on the way she again changed her mind.'

'Indeed Paraner Bou is too childish,' said Shashi.

Ananta said, 'She is the youngest; after her two elder sisters were married off, she was the one to give me company; she was brought up with too much indulgence and so she became a bit whimsical by nature. I married her off to the best family and best groom; and hers was the lot to come to grief. In this world man proposes, and God disposes; this is what I've seen all my life, Doctor-babu. We are but puppets; an Invisible One is pulling the strings.'

Shashi smiled and said, 'If I could ever catch hold of him, I'd have a showdown with him.'

'If you want to intently enough, of course you can catch him. He is but a servant of his devotees.'

The boat left the river to take the route of the canal. After some desultory talk, Shashi asked, rather out of context, 'So Paran is going to sell off everything? House and homestead, land and landed property?'

'If they decide to live permanently at my place, what purpose would be served by leaving the house and property here? There's no hurry about it; they can dispose of it all taking their time. If you know of anyone willing to buy—'

'If I come to know, I will tell you.'

So Kusum was indeed going away, leaving Gaodiya forever? What was the need for such hurry? Shashi would go away too—to a far more distant place than Kusum, into the midst of strangers. Couldn't Kusum have stayed back in the village until Shashi left? Perhaps because Paran's health had broken down Kusum wanted to depart as early as possible to a place where Paran would find rest and he would not have to worry about his meal and rush to the field at five in the morning with his weakened body. Indeed Kusum was proceeding like a very intelligent woman. Even so, could she not have told Shashi about it? To hear about the affair of Moti and Kumud so early one morning Kusum had called him over to the palm grove; armed with an even greater purpose could she not re-enact the scene? On the pretext of giving him the information could she not come to Shashi's room even at an inopportune time—anticipating a situation where Gopal on rising from his nap would sit in the veranda, and she would necessarily have to keep sitting beside Shashi for a long time after closing the door? Was Kusum angry?

He had scarcely set foot in the house when Gopal said, 'Where had you been, Shashi? The Magistrate-sahib has been camping in the village since day before yesterday; his orderly came several times to call you; Shital-babu has been sending men mornings and evenings. Where you went, when you'll return, you did not inform me either. Run along right now. Go meet the sahib; make sure you put on your best clothes.'

Shashi said, 'It's late in the day and I've just returned home. Instead of having my bath and meal, am I to run along to meet the sahib now? What you say makes little sense.'

Gopal's enthusiasm was extinguished. 'Whenever I speak, you get angry, Shashi,' he grumbled.

'Why should I get angry? I haven't eaten anything since morning. Does a man not feel hungry and thirsty?'

'Not eaten? Not eaten anything since morning?' Gopal grew anxious. 'Go then and have your bath quickly. Hey, Kunda, where have all of you gone? Shashi hasn't taken any food since morning—I will drive out the whole lot of you now!'

In the afternoon Shashi paid a visit to the Magistrate. Shital-babu had shown him round Saatgaon School, Gaodiya Hospital, and other institutions. He made Shashi sit and they talked for long about the hospital. He listened to the story of Jadab's death with attention. In this one matter he showed great curiosity. Had Shashi witnessed the entire proceedings himself? Could he explain the matter in some detail then? Shashi was not in the right frame of mind today. Besides, he was morally constrained not to divulge the facts of Jadab and Pagal-Didi's deaths; that was to be preserved forever only in his memory. Finally, after arranging to have tea served to him and promising a contribution of a hundred rupees to the hospital fund the Magistrate gave Shashi leave to go. From there Shashi went to Shital-babu's house. He chided Shashi rather severely for disappearing without any information. Then he too offered him a cup of tea and let him go. Evening had set in. Shital-babu offered to give him a lantern for light on the way home; Shashi refused, saying he had a torch in his pocket.

Throughout the entire stretch he did not once light his torch, walking along in darkness. Going to his chamber in the hospital he sat down. The twenty-rupees-a-month compounder of the hospital probably had not expected Shashi's appearance at this hour today; he had gone somewhere. He returned nearly two hours later. But Shashi did not tell him anything. There were six beds at the hospital, of which only two were occupied by as many patients. After visiting them and leaving suitable instructions with the compounder, Shashi returned home. How his mood had soured today! Basudeb Banerjee's house was dark; in front of it was that big blackberry tree, snapping a branch of which a boy of the family had fallen to his death. What close relation Shashi had with death; still he could not forget that boy till today. Had he been wrong in his treatment? Did the boy sustain an internal injury that had eluded his detection? It was no longer any use today trying to reason about that. Still Shashi pondered. So many things like this about the village were imprinted in his mind. He was worried about this too. When after leaving his village he went off to faraway places, what if these innumerable such impressions were never to be erased from his memory? What if his thoughts were to be reduced to revisiting these disjointed snapshots and dissecting these incidents over and again? Shashi paused for a while at Srinath's shop. 'What news, Srinath? Daughter's fever? Take her to the hospital tomorrow; I'll give medicine.' As he walked along, he thought that to him people spoke only about their illness and asked for medicine. The paved platform under the bakul tree was strewn with fallen flowers; why were there so many flowers? No longer perhaps did Sen-didi sweep the paved base of the tree deemed holy in front of her house? Before entering his house Shashi noticed that the window of Paran's big room was lit up. Kusum had perhaps filled and lighted her big hanging lantern because her father had come.

Shashi felt a wrench. Perhaps tomorrow, perhaps the day after, Kusum would leave the village, never to return.

13

Shashi was not accustomed to doing anything on an impulse. He always tried to hold his suddenly-aroused desires in check. Even so, there are some spontaneous urges in people which are so extraordinarily strong that no one has the power to curb them. Rising in the morning seemingly without a thought, not choosing to ponder or judge a thing, going straight to Paran's house, standing before the kitchen door, Shashi said, 'Will you come to the palm grove, Bou?'

Kusum was surprised. 'To the palm grove! Why, why to the palm grove so early in the morning?'

'Come. I've something to tell you.'

'Tell me? I don't know, Chhoto-babu, whether to laugh or to cry. Today for the first time in my life you've come on your own to talk to me, that too in the palm grove! Please go ahead; I'm coming.'

Shashi sat on that fallen palm tree where one such morning Kusum had called him over and sat listening to the story of Moti. A little later, Kusum came, softly clanking the keys tied to her sari-end playfully. Why was she so cheerful—one who was to depart tomorrow forever? Let her face look a little gloomy, her eyes betray signs of secret weeping. Shashi could not utter a word. Looking gloomy himself he studied Kusum's feelings.

'Shall I laugh?' Kusum asked.

'Why, why will you laugh?'

Kusum smiled as she said, 'You once said that seeing me laugh soothed your soul; that's why I asked.'

'It's not for fun that I've called you here, Bou,' said Shashi.

'Oh! I didn't know that. You have forever acted frivolously, so if ever you do call me, I think it is only for frivolity you have perhaps done so. Let me sit down then and hear why you have called me.'

'What makes you say that I have forever acted frivolously with you, Bou?'

'Do you mean it was not frivolity? Then were you being jocular?'

Shashi said with some irritation, 'I can't understand what has happened to you, Bou.'

Kusum would still not give up talking in a light vein and be serious. She said, 'How can you understand? So many things happen to women; not everything can be understood. You may be a doctor, so what? This is no cold or fever.'

Shashi was stung. It was surprising that he could not understand Kusum whose tantrums he had indulged for seven years with some affectionate indifference. Shashi felt an inexplicable torment. What had been only a solid bulwark forming the boundary of his life suddenly revealed a hidden door which opened up a wide vista of possibilities and wonders. Why did Kusum's eyes not brim with tears? Once before when it came to going to her father's house she had enacted a fall injuring her hip; even though she did go finally, she came back within fifteen days. Here, in this setting, this was perhaps their last meeting; perhaps, never again in this life would they come so close to each other. And yet, Kusum did not sob even slightly, not say a single passionate word in a thick, tear-filled voice? Shashi's eyes grew intensely eager to see anguish appear on Kusum's face; he was intent on listening to her half-suppressed sob. Whoever knew that Shashi was so fond of the many signs, the many submissions in which her everyday speech and demeanour were mingled; that he loved intensely the low-key, desultory and never-ending appeal of her manners and ways? Kusum was set to depart for ever; and yet today in this palm grove sitting so near him she merely clanged her keys in play. How unfair of Kusum, how bizarre her madness!

A small weed disturbed with the toe scattered copious drops of dew. Shashi wished he would give Kusum a good shake so the fought-back tears would shed in this way and he would stand feasting his eyes on the sight.

Kusum asked, 'Having called me for conversation, why are you silent, Chhoto-babu?'

Shashi said, 'I hear that you are leaving the village forever, so I came to ask.'

'We will leave the day after tomorrow,' said Kusum without hesitation.

'But you didn't tell me anything?'

'When could I tell you? Do you come?'

'What even if I don't?' Shashi said irritably. 'Don't you know how busy I am with my work? Faking a fracture you could come all the way braving the rain to show me your hand; could you not come to give such important news?'

What an exquisite gesture of anger Kusum made at these words! Pushing back with her hands the loose strands of hair on either side of her face, she stared at Shashi so intensely as though he were an unruly boy whom she would at once give a slap or a smack. She had never been like this! When was it that Shashi had not insulted her; that he had showed any consideration for her injured vanity; that he had refrained from telling her anything which might leave her smarting from anger? She had never been angry with him, never given him a withering stare. Today at this small insult she reacted with the fierceness of a tigress!

But then, she did not say anything stern; she restrained herself. Seeing that the very manner in which she had expressed her anger had put off Shashi completely, she even retrieved by some strange skill her perpetual enigmatic tone of speaking. She said, 'Good heavens! What a child you are! To fake seeking treatment for a fractured hand I can go a hundred times let alone one, braving rain, storm or quake; why should I go to say that I was going away?'

'But you could have sent word through Paran?'

Kusum said, 'Why should I do that either? Why do I need to give my news to one who does not care to look me up? I myself forbade him to go.'

'I couldn't come for pressure of work; so you have completely distanced me from yourself, haven't you, Bou?'

Kusum smiled. 'Who said I had distanced you? Do I talk with an outsider sitting in a palm grove? I'm not quite that cheap.'

What was it that Kusum said? So explicit, full of explanation, and history-laden? Suddenly Shashi remembered that one day Kusum had quite unwarrantedly and unnecessarily insulted him alluding to his father. Such an awful thing had never happened before, so Shashi had not been able to forget it. He could not understand the reason for her ire either. It seemed Kusum had now explained her conduct that day after such a long time. *Not cheap*! What rustic, vulgar words! But then what else could have explained what Kusum wanted to say so vividly? Shashi could not decide what to do or what to say. Also it was incomprehensible to him what the necessity was of telling him this suddenly today. If she had said it from a feeling of wounded sentiment or if it had been a piteous complaint as was her wont, Shashi could have understood everything; but it was neither. It was an insolent remark of Kusum's, the language of arrogance. Wasn't it a flagrant misdemeanour on her part to give a piece of her mind to someone she was going to part from for ever in a day or two!

After considerable reflection Shashi said, 'Because you are going away you are speaking so aggressively, aren't you, Bou? You must be thinking when the ties have snapped, why don't I inflict all the harsh words I can?'

'What have I said to you, pray?'

'What you said will haunt me forever. That's why the other day I tried to clarify certain matters—the day you'd been to my place to get medicine for the pain in your hand. But you wouldn't hear me out, you understood nothing, you came away in a huff. Women are like this.'

Widening her eyes Kusum said, 'Where did you gather so much knowledge about womenfolk, Chhoto-babu? Women are this sort, women are that sort, in fact all sorts; only they aren't after one's heart—you know so much!'

'You're talking in an ugly manner today, Bou.'

'I am not, Chhoto-babu; let me speak. Let me say now whatever comes to my mind. Did I want to talk? Who asked you to find out that I'm leaving the village and going away? Who asked you to call me here? You know there's something the matter with my head, you know that I'm eccentric. Yet, two days before departure I need to be called and I need to be bothered with such nonsense! Aren't you content even after all the dalliance of ten years? We are foolish, rustic women unable to get at the meaning of all these pranks, Chhoto-babu; we die of anguish.'

There was no protesting this complaint, so Shashi could not utter a word. Taking his feet out of his shoes, and rubbing them on the dew on the grass he sat mutely with his head lowered.

By now tears had come to Kusum's eyes. Never before had she acknowledged her feelings to Shashi so frankly in tears. But then, she was a very tough girl; by drawing in two long breaths and wiping her tears twice with her sari-end, she managed to bring her emotions under control.

'I didn't think, Chhoto-babu, that it would come to this. If I could, I would have left the village much earlier.'

If Kusum were to weep a little longer, Shashi would no doubt have embraced her wildly without uttering a word; but her murmurs of discontent held him at bay. He could not forget that in all fairness that was not the way after so many years to answer all her grievances.

Shashi looked a bit wan. What could he tell Kusum? What could he do for her now? Whoever knew that in just two days' notice Kusum would land him in such a predicament; that she would bring such an upheaval in his organised mind? Shashi could not have perceived that if he kept sitting beside Kusum, the agony at the prospect of her leaving for ever would surge every moment ceaselessly like waves in his mind forming a turmoil within him. Ever since he heard the news yesterday, various strange thoughts had been milling around in his mind; this morning it seemed they had all been reduced to a bitter distress.

Kusum's body that seemed to be ethereally beautiful today Shashi could not hold in his embrace. What he did instead was to suddenly clasp one of her hands in a swift move. She was a bit surprised. They had been standing a little apart; perhaps because of her hand being pulled, Kusum was even drawn a bit closer; but what she had to say was something that she had never uttered nor thought of. 'Several times have I come to you on my own; is it proper today, Chhoto-babu, after calling me here, that you should so much as indulge in hand-holding and what else? I could very well react angrily, don't you think? My temper is quite unpredictable.'

Shashi was already crestfallen; now the blood seemed drained from his face. Who could have known that he also feared Kusum so much? Even so, he did not let go of her hand. He said, 'Be angry, but listen to my words first. Will you go away with me?'

'Go away? Where?'

'Anywhere. Anywhere wherever, let's go away tonight.'

Kusum replied forthwith, 'No.'

Shashi pleaded, 'Why? Why won't you go?'

Kusum said simply, 'Why will I go?'

Shashi said foolishly like a child, 'Why will you go? What do you mean, Kusum, why will you go?'

'Today you addressed me by name!' And with this, like a small girl nodding her head watching Shashi's devastated look with glowing eyes, Kusum said, 'I wonder how you could bring yourself to ask why I would go. Did you think that you would call me just when it suited you and that I would run away with you tamely? Does anybody do that?'

Shashi said, 'But there was a time when you would have.'

Kusum said, 'Yes, indeed I would have, Chhoto-babu. Let alone a clear call, even if you just threw a hint, I would go running to you. But do the days stay the same always? Is man made of iron that he would remain the same forever and never change? When I'm set on speaking, let me say this quite firmly: today even if you pull me by the hand, I won't go.'

Shashi let go of her hand and said, 'I never knew that you would be so fiercely angry, Bou. You uttered many lofty words. Well, why don't you realise a simple thing: can man always understand what goes on in his mind? Can he always know? Because I often caused you distress with my neglect, today you are out to avenge yourself. Is it not possible that any distress I gave you I did so unwittingly; that I was not aware of the degree of my attachment to you; and that now that I've come to know you're leaving, I've sensed it at long last? Besides, let me take a cue from what you said: man changes—all right, supposing I have been merely playing with you for so long; today I can change, can't I, Bou?'

How frantic, how eagerly imploring were Shashi's pathetic words! Who knew that he would have to appeal to Kusum so desperately one day? As she listened, her amazement knew no bounds. That Shashi was not all right physically was evident from his very looks; maybe Kusum felt that was the reason for this infirmity and distress. She said in a mild voice, 'What is this you're saying, Chhoto-babu? You'll pine for me?'

Shashi said candidly, 'My heart will break, Bou. I can never be happy in life then.'

Kusum said anxiously, 'How can that ever be? How insignificant I am to you! You say you can never be happy in life because of me? It'll only be a couple of days before you forget me altogether.'

Shashi said, 'You've entwined me in bonds over all these years and you think that I'll forget you in just a couple of days?'

Kusum said, 'What power do I have, Chhoto-babu, to bind you to me like that?'

Shashi said petulantly, 'Forget about all that humility of yours. I've no patience for talking nonsense. I don't even bother about what may or may not happen to me. Just tell me clearly, Bou: you were always mad about leaving home for me; what suddenly makes you change your mind today?'

'Such talk leads to quarrel, Chhoto-babu. Is it good to quarrel before taking leave?'

'I promise I won't quarrel, tell me.'

Kusum said with a pale face, 'What can I tell you, Chhoto-babu? You can understand so much yourself. Even a red-hot iron left to itself cools off steadily, does it not? I have nothing more left to desire or rejoice in. I want no happiness for myself. I have decided to spend the rest of my life doing my chores and serving the people of my family. I have no other expectation, no other wish. All my feelings and emotions have been blunted, Chhoto-babu. I used to hear people speak of heartbreak—now at last I know what it means. Whom are you calling, Chhoto-babu? Who will go with you? Is Kusum alive? She is dead.'

Kusum was dead: that fickle, mysterious, half-girl, half-woman, vivacious, indomitable, persevering Kusum. The reason why Shashi said no more is hard to comprehend; perhaps to take his time to ponder. Kusum was to stay here today and tomorrow. Whether he really had or had not anything to say was to be cogitated in the first place.

After she had kept standing silently for a minute or so, when she turned to go, Kusum only said, 'You are godlike, Chhoto-babu.'

After returning home Shashi could realise that there are some levels of imagination which man cannot attain except on very special occasions. Each single incident unlocks a different door of the mind, a door even the existence of which one was not aware of. So many big dreams, so many lofty and far-reaching desires cherished by him all seemed to have been rendered disconnected and redundant in one day—just as the impossible dreams of childhood do in youth. Shashi had wept bitterly as a child wanting to ride a perambulator fitted with rubber tyres and upholstered cushion; the desire to drive a motor car in Calcutta today seemed similarly trivial. Where would

Shashi go leaving his village? What was there outside the village that could steal Shashi's heart? A vast material world with a vast multitude of unknown people was all there was. What would Shashi find there?

The underlying meaning of Kusum's words became gradually clear to Shashi. Not just for a day or two but for a great many long years, Kusum had been crazy about him. Then, little by little, day by day, that frenzied love of hers had wilted, perhaps even withered away. Who could tell? However disastrous this might seem to Shashi today, this was but the only natural consequence. Kusum was a country girl, a housewife: how irresistible the longing of her heart must have grown so that day after day she had held herself out to Shashi like an offering. Only now Shashi could begin to realise: the fact that this fierce, starved love of Kusum had survived so vibrantly all these years was in itself miraculous. The love that had sprouted spontaneously had also died naturally in the normal course. Now Kusum's days would keep rolling in spite of her not seeing Shashi; her life would keep flowing even without Shashi.

Shashi was therefore not astonished at Kusum's change. If a house catches fire, the fire is eventually extinguished—both the fire outside and the trauma within. Why should the fire of Kusum's mind keep burning forever? His own desperation left Shashi amazed. Whenever it occurred to him that there was nothing he could do anymore, that whatever impossible thing he might make possible, he could never again make Kusum love him, Shashi felt restless in agony. Kusum[123] had bloomed and withered away; Kusum was dead—in front of his own eyes, in the margins of his inattentive mind. What trivialities had he been engrossed in to have allowed such an event to take place?

The trivialities were very much present. Shashi went to the hospital, examined patients and wrote out prescriptions, and opened boils too. He also had to go and visit a patient at Saatgaon. He had been doing these tasks for a long time: could he not do them mechanically like a machine for one day? Had anybody forbidden him to feel the pulse of his patients while contemplating Kusum absentmindedly? Why was Shashi so cross? Why did he have to scold a dying patient like that? What repentance, what self-reproach there was in his mind today! It was beyond anybody's comprehension. In a way, things have turned out well, haven't they, Shashi? A housewife has remained in her own home inviolate and pure; morality and ethics have been preserved. Seen from this angle, Shashi should indeed have taken some comfort. He of course had these age-old beliefs about good and bad. Still, not even once did it occur to him that the very things he had gone one day so pompously to point out to Kusum, had, in a different way, happened today. The advice to practise self-restraint after judging in a cool mind every aspect of the matter that he had once given her she could now follow easily even without comprehending or realising anything.

Next day Kusum came to his house to take leave of the women of the family. Somebody else might have ended up suspecting that this was a pretext to meet Shashi, but Shashi did not think so. Presumptions which were favourable to himself Shashi used to look upon as suspect. Still, instead of standing outside, he went to his room and completely ignoring what others might think called out: 'Paraner Bou, do come here for a while.'

Kusum came to the room and said, 'I've come to take your leave. Will you remember all the faults I committed?'

Shashi said, 'Won't I? Virtue and vice, good and bad, every small detail, even the most trifling thing about you I'll never be able to forget, Bou.'

Compared to yesterday, Shashi's expression of love today was far more explicit. If Shashi bore Kusum in mind the way he promised he would, how deeply he must indeed love her!

So Kusum was on the verge of tears when she said, 'To speak like this is to make me vain, Chhoto-babu.'

'When I speak the truth, I speak in plain language, Bou—clear and direct. I'm not used to throwing hints or making smokescreens.'

'You land me in trouble at the time of leaving.'

'Suppose you didn't?'

Shashi was trying even today to hold back Kusum in the village. Here was a Shashi who seemed to be difficult to recognise. Where did he pick up such abject behaviour? Where did he learn such mendicancy? He knew that Kusum would not stay; even if she stayed, she would not love; still Shashi waited anxiously for a reply. What proof was there that there was no resurrection? Didn't a winter rain ever give rise to a tidal bore in a dried-up river? Kusum could perhaps not understand herself; perhaps what she had said in the palm grove yesterday was a lie.

Kusum said with some apprehension, 'What will I do if I stay here, Chhoto-babu? That will be painful both to you and to me. Can I bear pain any more at my age? Maybe I'll end up hanging myself.'

Shashi might be unable, but Kusum was quite adept at speaking her mind by means of hints and gestures; she had acquired skill in the art by conveying her mind to Shashi in that way for so long. Shashi's face seemed to drain of colour. He said in alarm, 'No, Bou, no; don't you do any of that. One should not indulge in those theatricalities. Had you said this at the outset, I wouldn't have thought of asking you to stay. If your mind has soured to this degree, better go and stay in your father's house. Have I not told you from the beginning that you should exercise restraint and should carefully consider all angles before doing anything?'

'Had I not done so, I'd have hanged myself long ago, Chhoto-babu. May I go now?'

Shashi could not find any reason whatever for her seeking this permission that day.

After so much fuss, Kusum went to her father's place. Such was her nature, she had all along been inclined to dramatise life.

Not only the plan to quit the village, but many of Shashi's fancies had begun to flag as well; yet he found no reason for remaining in the village either. An atmosphere of order and discipline had been established in the hospital work; he could take leave now after appointing a doctor. If he were to disclose his plan to go, there would be a furore both inside and outside the house; and he would be harassed to death giving explanations and listening to counsels. There was no averting this. He was after all no Kusum that whenever he wished to pack up and depart there would be only a single soul in this big village to be perturbed.

This apprehension of possible uproar seemed to leave him inert. As for his mind, he was never in the right mood; neither was he keeping good health. There was a marked fall in his verve and vitality.

Nearly two months passed. One day, beginning in the morning, the inevitable peril of Sen-didi finally struck at about midnight.

The danger was real. Sen-didi seemed to be close to death.

To have the first child at an advanced age may be regarded as sudden good fortune, but it is risky too. Perhaps Gopal had this apprehension; around this time, he did not go anywhere leaving the village even for a day or two; he always enquired about her. He used to visit Jamini Kabiraj's sitting room frequently; when Jamini was alive, towards the end Gopal never made a call. Sen-didi's elder brother Kripanath had pledged complete loyalty to Gopal. Here was a man who had studied medicine well, but did not know the application; neither had he a good practice. Between intervals of quoting slokas from Charaka and Sushruta, whether he did or did not also recite hymns to Gopal is anybody's guess, but Gopal used to show him special favour. Had it not been so, Kripanath's good fortune of being allowed to stay along with his family in Jamini Kabiraj's house would not have lasted long; Gopal would soon have urged Sen-didi, 'Now, throw them out.' And Sen-didi would have told them, 'Now, make your way home.' In connection with a serious court case today Gopal had gone to Bajitpur. On the days he had any business in court, he did not return to the village; today he returned at about ten at night.

The news of Sen-didi came when Gopal had just sat down to his meal along with Shashi; the news was brought by Kripanath himself.

'It's an emergency, Dada; you have to come.'

His face pale, Gopal said piteously, 'What's the use of my going?'

'You have to, by giving some counsel—'

Counsel? There was nothing wrong in offering counsel in an emergency. Gopal hurried through his meal and got up. He tried to remain calm and composed, but could not suppress his restlessness. The women of the family looked at one another. A silent Shashi with lowered head went on with his meal.

Once there, what advice Gopal gave Kripanath he alone knew, but scarcely had Shashi gone into his room after his meal when Kripanath turned up again. 'You have to come, Shashi,' he said.

'Please do not address me in that way.'[124]

'Eh?' Expressing his surprise Kripanath paused to ponder this, his lean face looking even longer. Then he said, 'I'm your father's friend.'

Shashi said, 'You may go, sir; I am tired and sleepy.' Kripanath was silent, needing some time to overcome his discomfiture. Then, with tears in his eyes he began recounting the predicament as fluently as if he were reciting Sanskrit slokas. Unless Shashi visited, Sen-didi would not survive; goodness knows whether she would even if Shashi visited. Still, as long as there is life there is hope, they say; and hence Shashi-babu's presence was required. There was no other doctor in the village. Kripanath, though a doctor himself, did not understand such complicated matters; had it been cough and cold, he would cure it in a trice with pills and mixtures; but this was different. Other than Shashi, Sen-didi now had no one else to fall back upon. As he listened, Shashi was reminded of how Sen-didi had been stricken by smallpox. The germ of an unseasonal pox patient of Saatgaon after traversing fields and houses over two miles had settled in Sen-didi's body; Jamini's disciple had been the physician of the Saatgaon patient. At that time, Gopal in this house and Jamini in that one had not let Shashi treat Sen-didi. It took him so much argument, insult and blustering to save her—virtually overriding others with physical force. Today again, Sen-didi was on the point of death, from a different cause. Today there was no obstacle for him to treat her; Gopal himself had sent for him. But why had he called him? Who had given him the right, just because Shashi was his son, to send for him in this way? What did Shashi care whether Sen-didi died or survived? So many other patients had died at Shashi's hands; today Sen-didi was no patient of his either. Even if he should forget all other considerations, even if he only remembered that he was a doctor, and that a kin of the dying patient had come to call him, still he was within his rights not to go. His body was weak and ailing;

working all day he was exhausted: any call at this moment he could refuse rightfully indeed. Did he not need rest?

Kripanath went away, dejected. Dimming the light Shashi sat on his bed and lit a thick cheroot: of late he had taken to smoking cheroot instead of biri.

Kunda came to say, 'Shall I make your bed now, Shashi-dada?'

'Do it.'

As she fixed the corners of the mosquito net, Kunda said, 'Won't you go to see Sen-didi?'

Shashi flew into a rage, 'Are you joking with me, Kunda?'

Put out of countenance, Kunda burst into tears and said, 'Because you're giving me food and shelter, you flare up whenever I speak. What have I done to you? Rather than this, better to throw me out, Shashi-dada; let me go away wherever I can.'

Shashi softened and said, 'You keep talking stuff and nonsense, so I get angry.'

Kunda wouldn't stop sobbing; even as she wept she said, 'When did I talk nonsense? When did I joke? Once you saved her with your treatment; that's why I asked whether you would go to see her. Was that a fault too?'

Softening even more Shashi said, 'I'm not feeling well, Kunda; my limbs are aching. Don't weep; finish the work in hand quickly; I'll lie down.'

At around twelve in the night, pushing the door, Gopal called in a low voice, 'Have you gone to sleep, Shashi?'

Unwell that Shashi was, the drowsiness was by now drifting into sleep. Woken up by the call, when he responded, Gopal asked him to open the door. Shashi got up and did that. Gopal was carrying a lamp which he put down on the floor, and then he sat on the bed. Gopal looked dazed, depressed and grave; it seemed he would make no move at all to speak; in a gesture of silent appeal, he would keep sitting in his son's room in the dead of night without uttering a word.

At the end of his patience, it was left to Shashi to finally say, 'I am sleepy, Baba.'

'Sleepy? Yes, of course you would be; it's late now. Besides you're not well either. The poor woman is dying, or I wouldn't have woken you.'

Shashi kept silent. Gopal said eagerly, 'Won't you go? Not only is she dying, Shashi, she's in great pain!'

'Why didn't they call in the doctor from Bajitpur? Someone sent in the afternoon would have by now brought back the doctor.'

'That idea didn't enter anybody's mind. Besides, when you're present in the village, why would they send somebody to Bajitpur to call the doctor? It's not that they know any more than you do. That you would not go when called was beyond their imagination. Now Kripanath has fallen at my feet crying, my son. You drove him away insultingly, so he dares not approach you again.'

Shashi felt distressed; he said mildly, 'I too have my own sense of prestige and insult, Baba.'

'Shashi, he didn't insult you. Even if he may have said something unwittingly—' Gopal left it unfinished. Then both of them fell silent. Gopal kept fidgeting and looking miserably at Shashi. He unfastened his waistcoat and bared his chest; he had not found time after his meal to take his paan; now perhaps from habit or from mental agitation, he worked his jaw a couple of times in the vacuity of his mouth as if chewing his paan. Gopal looked particularly unsightly.

Shashi could not conceive the possibility of Gopal himself coming to request him. Was Sen-didi's life so valuable to Gopal? Why then had he tried one day to prevent him from treating her? Shashi had been mortified with sorrow and shame, yet he was amazed. When the scourge of pox had obliterated Sen-didi's beauty, pity arose in Gopal, such deep, unreasoning affection!

Shashi said, 'You go to bed. I'll go to that house after putting on my shirt.'

Gopal got up to go without saying another word. He was bereft of the power to force out anything more from his mouth. Shashi had inflicted much pain on him; the pain that he gave him today had no parallel. If Shashi had gone to visit Sen-didi when Kripanath came to call him, Gopal might have been spared this embarrassment.

When he was thus obliged ultimately to go, Shashi did try to save Sen-didi with very special effort indeed. He managed to upset this already distressed family late in the night. He snubbed and ordered people about sending everyone into a tizzy. There was much hurry and scurry; jars of hot water were fetched; a messenger was sent to the hospital to bring back medicines and instruments along with the compounder: anyone who saw him couldn't imagine that even a short while ago an indifferent Shashi was prepared to let Sen-didi die. Again, he was seized with the same doggedness with which he had once saved her. That day he had fought against external impediments; what had he to fight with today? Was it the impediments of his own heart?

Was the apathy of his mind not to be dispelled even after he had seen the dying Sen-didi? Everything was in his hand—life and death of these two. What could Shashi not do? Not merely Sen-didi, but even the trace of this newly arrived vestige of Sen-didi he could remove forever from the earth. Nobody would even question why this had happened. Was it only saving a life that Shashi had learnt; had he not also learnt how to terminate it? He could accomplish it so very easily, in a manner as though he were making an absentminded mistake. Would Shashi regret it too deeply for the rest of his life?

Towards the end of the night a male baby was born to Sen-didi; and at dawn Sen-didi expired. Sen-didi had so little vitality, her heart had grown so weak that after examining her for the first time, Shashi could not believe it; never had a look at her suggested that the real *engine* of her bodily systems had been reduced to such a state. Yet not even Shashi could imagine that she would not survive this time. A doctor himself, even he could not clearly understand why after recovering from her unconscious state, when she should have fallen asleep peacefully, her hands and feet suddenly went cold.

Shashi knew that such things do happen; something keeps developing in the human body which is beyond the knowledge and ingenuity of even the best brains of medical science today. This is no man-made machine after all. Still Shashi's blood-shot eyes due to keeping late hours grew even redder and his fatigue unendurable. There was nothing else he could do; going back home, he had his bath, had a cup of strong tea and lay down. Even as he was coming away, he had seen Gopal outside that house.

Just as Shashi had witnessed a couple of deaths in his familiar circle, he had also witnessed births in their families: some will die; some others will be born; that is the way of the world. Still, deaths such as this used to very much perturb Shashi who was habituated to death. Those who died were known to Shashi; with them he had a long-standing relation of love-hate, while those who were born were completely unknown. Shashi pondered: would Sen-didi have survived if he had tried a different line of approach, administered different medicines? Towards the end, he had given one or two injections rather hurriedly: had they proved too strong for the patient? Even if they had, what was his fault? He had deliberated long before he persuaded himself to administer the injections; other than that, there was nothing else he could do then. What he considered proper in his judgement and knowledge he did; what more could he have done? He had so far saved a large number of lives: should that not be reckoned too?

Gopal was overcome with grief. Such a change came over him that Shashi was ashamed to see that it had come to everyone's notice. Gopal had always been a gourmand; now he no longer had any fondness for food. He was known for his bad temper; now he no longer spoke harsh words to anyone. With a solemn, morose face, he sat on a mat in the outer room smoking tobacco and handling important or unimportant papers and documents, which had so long been as dear to him as dramas and novels. Probably he could not concentrate; yet he tried to spend his time by engaging himself in this habitual work. Shashi was surprised. All this seemed to him to be so utterly random. Whatever unexpected had happened in Shashi's life, this incongrous trait of Gopal seemed to him the most astonishing.

Gopal scarcely spoke with Shashi. Their worlds seemed to have now completely diverged. One day all of a sudden Gopal asked him, 'What did your Sen-didi die of, Shashi?'

'Her heart was damaged.'

'Maybe you couldn't detect it at the first stage?'

'At the very first stage I did.'

'Still she died?'

Shashi was suddenly angered by this. 'Even if the disease is detected at the first stage people may die,' he retorted.

'Perhaps because you hadn't given the two injections earlier—'

Leaving it unfinished, Gopal waited anxiously, expecting a reply. What truth was he trying to ascertain? Goodness knows. Shashi was totally confounded. Maybe Gopal had meticulously gathered all the information concerning his treatment. What did he possibly think? What unspeakable thought about his doctor son had occurred to him? Shashi went red in the face. He couldn't rely on himself to say anything.

'Kripanath was saying if she had been given one or two grains of musk in time—'

Now Shashi got up and went out silently. He was vexed and felt pity too. Here was a worldly-wise, elderly, family man: what childishness of his was this? Kunda asked, 'What's happened to Uncle, Shashi-dada?' And she asked this with some affectionate concern. Kunda's son had been seriously ill; with much effort, Shashi had restored him to health. A room in the brick-built house had also been allocated to Kunda; some work of the household had been allotted to her as well. A shrewish Kunda had changed altogether. There are women who have such small desires, failing to obtain which they grow violent and peevish. These days Shashi felt that Kunda's nature was not so bad after all; overall, she was a good girl. Under constant pressure of his work, Shashi scarcely found any time to take care of those around him; but he felt happy that Kunda took good care of Sindhu. In reply to her question, he said, 'I do not know, Kunda.'

Kunda said, 'You won't marry, Uncle was lamenting to me yesterday.'

Shashi said, 'Was it Baba lamenting to you or were you lamenting to him?'

Kunda smiled and said, 'Both of us were.'

Shashi looked at Kunda in surprise. Where did she pick up such apt conversation from? Suddenly it occurred to him that Kunda seemed to be very happy; her life was full of joy. Kunda was a bit sentimental, a bit envious too; her greed for saris and ornaments was rather intense as well. As for her husband, he had blended well with Gopal's clerks; yet Kunda was so happy that in her fancy she created one or two artificial sorrows and revelled in them; the same was the case with her grievances too. To Shashi, Kunda's existence had so far been as purposeless as that of an inert object. Today when he found the presence of such happiness in her meaningless life, he seemed to be somewhat puzzled. Kusum had turned Shashi into something he knew not what. Whenever he encountered someone, he would scan their faces with avid eyes trying to discover something. If there was a flash of a smile on the face and a sparkle of joy in the eyes, Shashi would be exhilarated. If anyone stood before him with tears in their eyes and affliction on their face, Shashi felt inclined to thrash them. He felt a sudden surge of liking for Kunda. 'What do you want, tell me Kunda?' He asked her affectionately. 'A very fine sari? A Benarasi?'[125]

Surprised, Kunda said, 'Why all of a sudden this talk of a sari, Dada?'

Shashi said, looking serious, 'Yes, I'll give you a sari, without any particular reason, Kunda. Just like that.'

Just like that Shashi had bought Kunda a sari. Meanwhile, Gopal's guru appeared on the scene. He was famously known as Bhola Brahmachari.[126] He had a healthy, hirsute body; his head, beard, moustache and eyebrows were shaven. He carried a jet black staff in his hand and wore a saffron-coloured robe and saffron-coloured rubber-soled canvas shoes. For nearly five years Gopal had virtually forgotten him; suddenly he remembered him so avidly that if he did this to the good Lord, even He would perhaps have descended. Gopal made him obeisance by prostrating himself respectfully and washed his feet with his own hands. A room in the inner quarters was got ready after scrubbing and washing it clean; there the brahmachari was put up. Shashi respected him; even though he was not too pleased at his sudden appearance at such a time, he still made his reverential obeisance.

The brahmachari stayed for seven days or so. Not for a moment in all those seven days did Gopal stay away from him. So many questions he had; so sincere was his submission! For his negligence a suit at Bajitpur court fell through. Let it be; a detachment had come over him, all those suits, litigation and worldly pursuits were inconsequential to him now. Not just for Sen-didi, Gopal had for long been asking himself: what was all this for? For whom was he amassing money and wealth with so much effort? He had a daughter, Sindhu; when she was married off sooner rather than later, she would go away to make another's home; who would be left then for Gopal to call his own? Shashi? About Shashi, he entertained no hope or confidence at all. What expectation could a father have from a son who hated him? In a way, it was he who had broken Gopal's heart.

It was very surprising that as in the case of Kusum, it was Shashi who had shattered Gopal's heart. So great was Shashi's fault in not being able to be the light of the lives of these two persons! With her broken heart Kusum had gone away; Gopal had not given up yet. Having submitted his anguish to the brahmachari, Gopal went aside; the guru called Shashi.

'Shashi, my son, you're learned and intelligent; it's needless to tell you that duty is far superior to whims.'

'Yes, sir.'

'What greater duty is there for a son than to show devotion and respect to his father?'

This was just the way the brahmachari used to give his teachings—in such firm language, without any preliminary talk; it was therefore very forceful. With a feeling of hurt Shashi said, 'That is a son's primary duty to his father, indeed. It is the natural creed of a son's mind, Baba, not something to instil with argument and logic. If the father's nature is bad, the son when he grows up may perhaps criticise him; but no matter what the father's nature may be, the uncritical devotion of the son's mind is not something to be erased by any means.'

Shashi was no ordinary youth. He set out to teach the guru like a guru. Seven or eight years ago, Gopal had got Shashi initiated to Bhola Brahmachari; and he had said his prayers for some days as well, modifying the guru's mantras to utter *namah* for *Om*,[127] being a non-Brahman. So much change had since come over Shashi.

Many were the erudite words that the brahmachari then spoke in a clear and concise manner, on listening reverently to which Shashi too gave learned replies; he could sense that his level of knowledge had gone much above that of his guru, but he was careful not to show it. The brahmachari came to like Shashi very much. Forgetting the complaints Gopal had made against his son and relegating the stockpile of banal homilies to the background, he engaged in discussing many matters with Shashi. Gradually it seemed that the master–disciple relationship that had been established between them several years ago stood repealed today. Not a word on religion, nothing akin to catechism on virtue and vice or worldly and otherworldly affairs; now they only talked sitting face to face, like two friends of unequal ages. It had hardly been two days since the brahmachari had arrived, before a mask of his, as it were, fell off for Shashi, and he allowed his disciple to be acquainted with his true self. He was an absentminded, ever-content man, somewhat like Jadab; he was a celibate under circumstances, not by choice; thereafter it grew into a habit. By and by, he told Shashi one or two anecdotes and possibilities of his life: the story of his ascetic life at the advent of youth, a nomad's vocation in quest of what the home could not provide. Such stories of journeys in search of the uncertain were what had always fascinated Shashi. He too had a long-cherished desire to go out into the world.

In his effort, at Gopal's request, to redirect Shashi's mind homewards, the brahmachari ended up stirring up the latter's predilection for leaving his home.

Having kept the guru's company for nearly a week Gopal seemed to have overcome his inertia. He must have reached some sort of understanding with himself, for it was noticed that his discharge of duties as well as his conduct with Shashi had become easy and natural.

'How many patients come to the hospital, Shashi?' he asked.

'Their number is increasing by ones and twos,' replied Shashi.

Gopal regretted, 'You're working yourself to death merely as an unpaid labourer. Why don't you at least take something for your salary? Your labour has a value after all. If someone had been employed, would he not have to be paid?'

'Does the hospital make enough money that I could take something, Baba? This is a hospital with a small turnover; if even I keep extracting my dues to the last paisa, how can it possibly run?'

Anyway, let Shashi not take anything for his salary; it was at any rate no longer Gopal's main concern—he had had a bit of conversation with his son, that's all. Such a deceptive, at times almost womanish, sort of behaviour was Gopal's wont these days that it sometimes left Shashi quite astonished and overwhelmed. What Shashi had told Bhola Brahmachari about Gopal was no casual remark: an unreasoning awe for Gopal was alive in him even today, he had said, and would probably remain forever. During the formative years of his life Gopal had built all the foundations of his mind: who could demolish them?

While making his way along the Kayetpara path, on some days Shashi could hear the cries of a child from Jamini Kabiraj's house, the cry of an infant. It sounded like a very small child to Shashi; he wondered if Bipin had such a tiny child. The persistent cries continued to ring in Shashi's ears long after he had gone far ahead. He did not like his own sentimentality. A baby that is born would of course cry at intervals; what is there to be so moved about? He heard enough of such baby's cries in his own house as well.

One day, some three months after Sen-didi's death, Shashi returned home quite late in the day when Kunda, clutching just such a crying baby to her breast came and stood before him. 'It's Sen-didi's son, Shashi-dada,' she said.

In the heat of the sun, unwashed and unfed, Shashi's face looked shriveled and seemed to turn a shade paler as he asked, 'Whose son did you say it is? Sen-didi's?'

Kunda said, 'Yes. As soon as he was delivered, he brought death to his mother. *Kipanath*[128] Kobrej's sister-in-law has a suckling baby; he was being breast-fed by her. She went away today, so Uncle brought him to me. I'll suckle him along with my Khuki. Hope he won't kill me too, like he did his mother!'

Kunda grinned from ear to ear; with Sen-didi's son swathed in a rug held out before Shashi, she said, 'I've been promised a gold chain for nursing him, Shashi-dada. Uncle has been very open-handed these days.'

'Who brought him?'

'Uncle himself did. He held him close to his chest like this, wrapping him in a rug, would not let the children of the house go near him. I couldn't stop laughing to see the way Uncle took another's son in his lap. Do you know what he told me?—"I took the child, Kunda; can you raise him? I'll make you a ten-*bhori*[129] gold chain for the neck." I said, "Give him to me, Mama. He will grow up along with my own children; no problem at all."'

Shashi said harshly, 'Why did you have to take this responsibility? You're so greedy for gold!'

'Is it out of greed for gold? That tiny motherless baby: if someone were not to breastfeed him, how would he survive? None of his aunts has an infant child. Apart from that, if Uncle ever asks me, I can't very well say I can't.'

Kunda looked on suspiciously; she understood in part, did not understand the rest. After some delay, all at once Shashi started changing. 'Why did you get so angry, Shashi-dada?' Kunda asked.

'No, I didn't.'

Sen-didi's son had stopped crying. Kunda gave him a kiss affectionately and proudly. Goodness knows what mischief she was spinning in her mind. Then once again holding the child towards Shashi, she said, 'How beautiful the boy is, just have a look, Shashi-dada! He'll resemble Sen-didi, I tell you. Just looking at his face is to feel drawn to him, isn't it?'

A tired Shashi said, 'Leave me alone, Kunda. I've just come and I'm quite exhausted in this heat; let me get some rest.'

Whom would Shashi get angry with? Whom could he tell? There was no doubt that Sen-didi's son was beautiful; indeed astonishingly so. The ravishing beauty of Sen-didi, which small pox had robbed her of, was recompensed together with interest in the son. Such a tiny child, with a complexion like pure gold! If the sight of his face had aroused compassion in Gopal, and if taking pity he had picked him up, hugged him to his heart and brought him home, who could have anything to say? This was a noble, praiseworthy deed. Indeed, Shashi ought not to feel such resentment and sorrow at this.

Did Shashi not feel the least bit of tenderness looking at the pretty-as-a-flower child of Sen-didi? Had Kusum left his natural instinct for tender feelings so impaired? His face glum and grave, Shashi went to have his bath. Later, with Kunda sitting nearby, Sen-didi's son in her lap, Shashi could not even eat properly. Little by little, his health had improved somewhat; what a hearty appetite he had today!

All through the early afternoon, Shashi remained in a stupor. Now he would have to do something; there was no keeping silent any more. No more discrepancy would do. As a languid Shashi lay in the stillness, a host of random thoughts started surprisingly falling into place; delicate sensibilities dropped off like detached flowers. Shashi felt that, like a lush object drying up in the heat of fire, he was growing into a rugged and rude man. Utterly reckless, heartless, and inconsiderate! Shashi's heart would long for Kusum. His heart would pine in acute desperation. By dealing rude blows to the self-esteem of such a mature, suitable son, what had Gopal reduced that heart to so the yearning now seemed risible? How could Gopal persuade himself to bring Sen-didi's son so blithely into the very house where Shashi lived? Had Gopal forgotten that even knowing that Sen-didi was practically on her deathbed, Shashi had been unwilling to go and treat her? Was Shashi's sense of pique so insignificant to Gopal and did Gopal nonchalantly ignore what Shashi might think or not think? Did he not need to feel even a bit diffident in Shashi's presence? Gopal's perception about his son was that even if, after bringing Sen-didi's son home, he kept nurturing him like his son, Shashi would keep silent and not bother at all. Who knows, maybe Gopal himself did not care whether Shashi kept silent or created a disturbance.

Next day Shashi sent urgent letters to the members of the hospital committee. At Shital-babu's house the committee sat for an emergency meeting in the evening. Shashi submitted his resignation letter, put up the draft advertisement copy for a doctor and proposed that the entire responsibility of the hospital pass on to the committee's able president Shital-babu.

The stunned members asked, 'But why, why, Shashi?'

'I'm leaving the village.'

This time there would be no more dithering, no more half measures. The preparations for his going away continued to proceed at an unstoppable speed. To Shital-babu, he explained the hospital-related matters in detail, submitted complete statements of accounts, and wrote out some instructions as well on the future course of action to be followed. In response to the newspaper ad for a doctor, quite a number of applications came in. After consulting the committee members, Shashi wrote out interview letters to some of the applicants.

Everyone murmured discontent; some even indulged in lamentation. Where was Shashi going, why was he going, what would fall to the villagers' lot if he went away? If ever a qualified doctor was needed, would they have to rush to Bajitpur as they had had to do before? Everyone demanded explanations from him and even tried to strike up arguments. Shashi neither gave any explanation nor indulged in any argument. With a mild smile welcoming their friendliness, he ignored their queries.

However, when the news got around, such a hullabaloo was raised everywhere that Shashi began to feel perturbed. Indeed, people had given him a place in their hearts, not just as a doctor in their interest but for his humanitarian qualities as well. If he was present in matters concerning the public, it instilled inspiration in them; they all felt reassured in relying on him. This was certainly not something to happen without any reason: how fortunate Shashi was to have been showered with this unsolicited love of the people! This was by no means a mere reward for good work. What great deed had he done after all? He had not picked up the spade for road reconstruction, sprayed kerosene in ponds and ditches for eradication of malaria, opened night schools, or set up village councils or student organisations. He had done nothing of the sort.

Yet, perhaps no one else in several villages far and near wielded greater influence than Shashi. If the people didn't love him, why would this happen?

Did Shashi not love those who loved Shashi? He had often felt intense disgust with the village and village life; in fact, for many years he had found no interest here. Yet, like the smarting of a wound, a lingering pain had persisted with Shashi; he felt a wrench in his heart at the thought of leaving the village. This was where he was born; this was where he grew up; with this village was his life entwined. Kusum was an immigrant; the day she wished she left, quite unperturbed; how could Shashi do that? At the time of departure, even tears would appear in the corners of his eyes. Surely they would.

Kunda wept. 'Why, Shashi-dada? Why are you going away leaving us behind?'

Having taken on the responsibility of Sen-didi's son, Kunda's workload had increased; still she rendered more service to Shashi. When he was in the house, on some pretext or another Kunda came time and again, and looked with tearful eyes at him; so many things she would have liked to say; not all she dared to utter.

'What's it, Kunda, what's happened to you?'

'Is it good to go away leaving all the near and dear ones, Shashi-dada?'

'Does nobody go like that, Kunda? Does everybody keep staying in his village or country forever?'

'Those who go do so to earn a living; what is your need to go?'

Whose affection did Shashi lack, yearning for which his heart wailed so bitterly that just this little bit of affection shown by Kunda was enough to arouse his attachment: he wished Kunda would show him even more affection, feel a bit more distressed.

The one who was distressed was Gopal; the poor fellow seemed to be left almost half-dead. In his own house he lived like a thief, watching from a distance Shashi's movements and conduct with scared, piteous eyes and collecting from others news about Shashi's plans and programmes. He lacked the courage even to speak directly to him. There was no knowing what his self-willed, disobedient son would end up saying in the course of conversation! Nobody could give Gopal specific information on where Shashi wanted to go or what he wanted to do. However, by all appearances they assumed that this was no ordinary trip for a short stay; Shashi's going would be a going away in the true sense.

Then one day, in response to Shashi's call for an interview, one of the applicants arrived at the village. His name was Amulya; he had passed out in the same year as Shashi. Shashi had forgotten his name; now it turned out that he was known to Shashi. Shashi had pleasure talking to him. That apart, how could he refuse his friend who had come as a candidate for this small job? No selection was anymore necessary; those who had been called to appear on later dates were now advised to treat their calls as cancelled.

Shashi allotted a separate room to Amulya in his own house. He told him, 'The few more days I'm here you'll have to make the rounds with me, Amulya. You must get acquainted with the patients and be conversant with how things run. From now on, the entire responsibility is yours. Most of those from the village who will call you are very poor; try to ignore the fee. They'll pay you of their own accord according to their capacities; village people do not dare to cheat doctors and Kobrejes.'

He took Amulya along to the hospital and placed a chair for him beside his. A bit corpulent, Amulya was calm and gentle by nature, but he did not lack enthusiasm. With rapt attention, he observed Shashi's work, went around seeing the equipment and wards of the hospital and asked questions about the rules and regulations. It seemed as if right from now, he was feeling a great responsibility. After he had heard that Shashi would go away never to return, he seemed to have earned the right to light his own lamp in the darkness of the entire newness of this place. Amulya offered a bit of criticism too: would this rule not be better framed, say, in this form, Shashi? Or this provision instead of that? These were good signs; an indication that he would perform well enough. Yet, inwardly, Shashi began to feel a resentment without any apparent reason. It seemed as if someone had come to dispossess him of a kingdom all his own: what care, what effort it had taken Shashi to build up this hospital of his—people knew it as Shashi Doctor's hospital! He knew precisely even how many surgical knives there were. Though he had always known he would one day go away from the village, he had never tired of making great plans to gradually turn it into a big hospital. Once he was gone, Amulya would be the one in command; perhaps there would be improvement, perhaps things would deteriorate, none of which Shashi would come to witness.

By thinking continuously about leaving the village, Shashi had reached such a state of mind as if he had forgotten that no one had ever asked him to go; that he was going by choice; that even now if he cancelled his plan, no one would come to say anything. It was as if he could not do without going, as if he was compelled to go, as if he was being driven out of the village; by no means could he stay back.

Well, what was his grievance about going anyway? Had he not in so many ways for so many years nurtured a desire to leave? What had happened to his vow of not wavering, of not being lax when the time came to prepare for leaving? Was he upset just because he visualised his successor in Amulya? One who used to spend his days dreaming of the vast and all-pervading expanse of life was not supposed to want to be bound by a fascination for this small hospital in this nondescript village called Gaodiya!

Having seen Amulya and heard why he had come, Gopal was even more confused. He could not keep silent anymore. At night when Shashi sat down to eat, Gopal, coming from nowhere, silently fetching a mat and laying it out himself sat by his side. Shashi's aunt came running with a glass of water and after putting it down was going to sit nearby; Gopal said, 'You go, Khanta; go and sit in the kitchen.'

When Aunt was gone, Gopal said, 'Where will you go, Shashi?'

'At present I'll go to Calcutta to start with.'

'Then after touring for some days in north India, you'll return home, I suppose? A matter of a month or so, is it?'

'From Calcutta, I'll go to England.'

'England?' Gopal had just taken a morsel into his mouth; going to swallow it, he almost choked. 'Why England?'

'To learn more,' said Shashi.

'That'll take quite a long time, Shashi, won't it?' Gopal sounded helpless. 'Not less than two or three years! I'll be left alone in the village for so long?'

Shashi was surprised. 'Left alone?'

No, not alone; Gopal would have a house teeming with relatives and dependants, a village swarming with friends and enemies. Even so, if Shashi were not there, Gopal knew not how to bring home to such a grown-up son today how devastatingly lonely he would become. Who else was there in the world occupying the heart of Gopal all by himself? Gopal did not know what norm of its own his heart had followed: he could not bring himself to love a single soul in the world, not even his own daughters; only for Shashi and for Shashi alone did his fanatical parental affection pervade his heart even today. All his solemnity and calm fell off; in a voice thick with emotion he said, 'Why must you go, my son? Is it out of anger towards me? But I didn't do you any harm, did I?'

Shashi said in a low voice, 'I am going in search of progress in life; what's there to be angry about?'

After pondering awhile Gopal said, 'When you return after three or four years, maybe you won't see me anymore.'

Shashi did not say anything about not returning even after three or four years. He continued silently with his meal.

'I'm old. If suddenly I die and you're not around either, who will look after all this, Shashi? Whatever I've earned by toiling all my life will go entirely to ruin.'

'You can give it away to anyone you like.'

'That's childish talk, Shashi, words spoken in rage!' Saying this, Gopal looked on eagerly. A hope belied. Shashi said nothing in protest. Gopal felt a burning sensation inside; how oddly perverse that child was whose mind was inaccessible! Why didn't Shashi say what was wrong with him, express clearly what he wished to do? Gopal was willing to forgo many a prerogative to assent to his son's wishes today; he would relegate his own reluctance out of sight. A capable man was disobeying his father: what could Gopal possibly do except bear everything quietly? He told Shashi something in this vein. His words had the ring of a strange entreaty. Realising what fury, awful fright and profound grief Gopal suppressed in his mind while talking to him, Shashi felt himself imperilled; yet he remained elusive. There was no one in the house who did not understand what matter father and son had started to discuss today; in every room, crowding behind doors and windows people were snooping, waiting to listen to their hearts' content if and when the two began to talk loudly. An unnatural hush was palpable. It was uncertain when the storm would break.

A storm did begin, but from a completely different direction. All of a sudden, appearing from nowhere Kunda stood clutching Sen-didi's son to her breast. She said, 'After finishing your meal, please see this child, Shashi-dada; perhaps he's running a temperature.'

Shashi neither lifted his face nor spoke a word. Gopal, stretching out his left hand said in an anxious voice, 'Does he have a fever? Let me see. Shashi, touch him, will you? I think it is fever.'

Shashi rose and went away quietly, leaving his meal unfinished.

It was just a request to place a hand on a tiny infant to ascertain fever. If in response he went away like that, the implication of his behaviour was simple enough even for Gopal to understand. With a surprised Kunda looking askance at him, Gopal, mortified with shame, had gooseflesh, perhaps for the first time in his life. Then with utmost effort he restrained himself. In his accustomed voice, he roared at Kunda, 'Off with you, remove yourself from my sight, off with you, you wretch!'

Kunda could not bear such shouting for no fault of hers; she stood petrified for a while and then went away weeping to her room. Soon enough, the curious female members of the family arrived there. For some days now everyone had been bewildered by the way things had been turning out in this family. The intrepid Kunda was the one who had of late won some favour with the men in the household. At her plight today, everyone was more or less delighted and surprised too.

'Why, Kunda, why did he scold you, eh?'

Was Kunda one to divulge things so easily? Hissing with suppressed anger she asked them all to go away. 'Why do you disturb me?' After much cajoling she relented a bit and then came out with the reason for Gopal's anger. 'It's all my miserable lot,' she lamented. 'Uncle forbade me several times to take Sen-didi's son into the presence of Shashi-dada, but I completely forgot. I'm a simple girl; can I remember these accursed complexities?'

They said, 'O, Kunda! Is it after this child was brought here that Shashi has been so cross? So he doesn't speak with his father, threatens to renounce domestic ties and leave home for good?'

'If not, what else?'

Kunda smiled slightly. Goodness, whoever knew that at bottom, our outspoken Kunda had such a twisted mind? She said, 'What would you know about what's brewing between father and son over this child? I can sense it. I went there taking the child precisely to watch what turns out when the two sat down to eat together. But then, I had not guessed that I would be abused so severely, Chhoto-mami.[130] And we've seen nothing yet. Just wait and watch what trouble breaks out over him. He is not after all the son of an ordinary mother.'

'On top of that, he's feeding from your breast, isn't he, Kunda? So if he's not the right one to set fire to the house,[131] then who is?'

Perhaps the boy had a slight fever; his pink complexion had grown ruddy. One could scarcely believe that such a violent storm was brewing centring round this exquisitely beautiful child whom one could hardly look away from. The women gathered round Kunda envied the unfortunate boy, although from maternal affection they were solicitous as well. 'Imagine one refusing to live in the same house with this infant! What a stony-hearted person Shashi is, devoid of the slightest trace of affection!'

That night a sleepless Gopal pondered long over he alone knew what; but next morning he sent Kunda packing to her uncle-in-law's house at Rajatala. With her went her husband and son besides Sen-didi's child.

After he had accomplished the work, Gopal seemed to be a great deal relieved. The cause of anger was removed; naturally, Shashi's rage would abate too? The fact that Sen-didi's son had come into the world had not infuriated Shashi; that the child had been brought into this house was the reason why he was fleeing home. This was an unfair demand of Shashi's, quite unreasonable behaviour; even so, when Gopal had ultimately redressed his grievance in all humility, could Shashi anymore think of leaving home!

In case the news did not reach Shashi's ears properly by word of mouth, Gopal himself, disregarding the consequences, went and told him, 'I've sent off Kunda to her in-laws' house today, Shashi.'

Shashi said, 'To Rajatala?'

'Yes, with Jamini's son too.' Whenever there was a reference to Jamini's son, Shashi spoke not a word. Gopal added, 'That's where Kunda will be staying from now on. I told them that they don't need to come here.'

Scaling down his voice to a conspiratorial tone as though he had acted in collusion with Shashi, Gopal said, 'In fact, my son, I've killed two birds with one stone. I've removed Kunda on the one hand; on the other, escaped from the responsibility of bringing up another's son. Let them now do whatever they like; I don't care. If she does write crying for money, I'll send her some; that's all, there ends the relationship.'

If that had been Gopal's wish, why had he taken over from Bipin the responsibility of Sen-didi's son? It was a let-off for Gopal that Shashi did not ask him anything more about this, for Gopal wouldn't have been able to answer. For Gopal, bearing Shashi's separation was not possible; to cast aside Sen-didi's son was not possible either: after much deliberation, therefore to save all sides, the clever trick he had played like a mature politician naturally demanded one or two such contrived, plausible words in its support. All this he had said not to establish a solid justification by arguing with his son, but to convey that he had admitted defeat. O my stony son-deity, give up your firm resolve now.

Not only because Sen-didi's son had been removed, if Shashi had found Gopal so eager to hold him back, he might perhaps have changed his decision; perhaps once again his plan to leave the village would have been cancelled. But it was too late now; long since, his mind had flown to the faraway land in quest of a new life; all that was left to do now was to arrive there bag and baggage: that too was only a matter of days.

Gopal's carefree, cheerful mood all through the day disturbed Shashi. He realised that Gopal had taken it for granted that all the discord between them had been resolved, and that henceforth the days would pass by as smoothly as they had. For Gopal to believe that such a complicated matter would so easily reach such an agreeable ending was no less surprising to Shashi. What exactly did Gopal expect from him? Why did he want so ardently to hold him back? Never would they agree in their opinions; there would be disputes over trifles everyday; love, affection, respect and devotion—all finer sentiments would be buried under *Himalayan* discord. Despite that, was Shashi to vegetate in the village living a narrow life riven with self-contradictions? With so vast a world lying out there, must their two conflicting personalities keep to this constricted corner of their domestic environment held under the spell of the inane and impractical emotion called filial affection?

No matter how grievous a blow Shashi may have received from Sen-didi's son being brought to their house, this as a reason for leaving home had become utterly insignificant today. The pretext of mental aversion was not adequate to compensate for the deep sorrow that the thought of leaving the village had given rise to in Shashi's mind; it needed to be countered by a far bigger allure, a bigger attraction. Yet it was impossible for Gopal even to conceive of that. If Shashi were to depart, that single factor is what Gopal would know forever as the sole reason for his departure: bringing Sen-didi's baby son home.

Shital-babu had sent for him. Taking Amulya along, Shashi went to his house in the evening. After treating Amulya to light refreshment Shital-babu let him go. As for Shashi, he was detained till after dinner quite late at night. Shital-babu turned out to be another bugbear for Shashi. He would call him morning and evening; and once there, Shashi would be driven almost mad with Shital-babu's ceaseless talk. On returning home, Shashi noticed that two mats had been laid out side by side at the eating place; and Gopal, who used to take his night meal at eight, was waiting for him today, not having eaten till eleven.

'Why are you so late, Shashi? Now have a quick wash and come, let's sit down.'

'You sit down, Baba; I've had dinner. Shital-babu would not let me come away.'

Saddened, Gopal said, 'Today I ordered a special menu, son. I thought an outsider has been staying in my house; he would go away in a day or two. Let me give him a special treatment for once. But you've come after eating elsewhere; how could I know that?'

'Who's the outsider?

'I'm talking of Amulya-babu. Poor chap, after calling him in, if we tell him to go, it'll hurt him greatly, poor boy.'

'Why will Amulya go away? He's the one who has been entrusted with the work at the hospital.'

'When you're present, what will he stay here for, pray?' Gopal sounded apprehensive.

'I think I'll start day after tomorrow.'

'Day after tomorrow?' Gopal could not utter another word. When Shashi had gone to his room, Gopal went straight to the outer veranda where he kept sitting on a wooden bench in the dark. A labourer was making arrangements for lying down; he made Gopal a chillum of tobacco and then, inhibited about lying down in front of the master, sitting on his haunches exhaled a sigh of exhaustion. Once again today, Gopal remembered the brahmachari. The deep sadness and detachment that had enveloped his mind following Sen-didi's death was dispelled in a strange way by listening to the dry spiritual discourses from the brahmachari's mouth. Today he felt utterly devoid of energy. His long and eventful life studded with extraordinary happenings seemed to him today to have had no meaning: it had come to absolutely no use. Right from the day Shashi was born, focusing his eyes on him alone, Gopal had dreamed his covey of dreams that soared into the sky and bloomed as *akash-kusum*.[132] After acquiring education, what dubious principles had Shashi learnt? Garden, house, land, wealth, kith and kin—Gopal had accumulated so much: were all these for his own sake? How many more days were left to him? If, rejecting all this, Shashi were to go away, would not Gopal's entire life be rendered futile?

At that late hour he went into Amulya's room. Waking him up, he said, 'Let me ask you one thing, son. Why did you not tell me that Shashi would be going away day after tomorrow?'

That Gopal should go to the extent of rousing a sleeping man in the dead of night for an explanation left Amulya flummoxed. He pleaded, 'I didn't know; Shashi didn't tell me when he would go.'

With displeasure in his voice Gopal said, 'He said everything else, only he didn't tell you this? You had something up your sleeve, my son, so you kept it dark.'

Looking abashed, Amulya said, 'Not at all, sir. What a thing to say!'

'*What a thing to say*! My son will exile himself from the country forever and you will occupy his place securely: admirable scheme of yours I must say! Now, come on, get up from the comfortable bed, will you? Pack up your things quietly and then come along; let's go.'

Gopal looked like a *dakath*; even his words sounded like those of a dacoit with murderous intent. Nothing of the strange dramatic conversation going on in Amulya's room stirred the consciousness of Shashi who was exhausted. He who was so keenly aware of life now lay bereft of sensibility like a puppet. And he was the one for whom Gopal out of parental affection created the bizarre scene at midnight and uttered the strange words from which Shashi would have acquired experience if only he were to see and hear them. After raving and ranting at Amulya in a muffled voice for quite some time, Gopal's hot head probably cooled a little; he retired to his room.

At dawn he woke Shashi up. Shashi saw Gopal was ready to set out on a journey, his trunk and bedding placed on the head of the labourer.

Gopal said simply, 'Tomorrow you're not going, Shashi. Today I'm going to the Baba in Kashi; I will stay at his ashram for seven or eight days. Without someone to keep watch over this house it won't do. After I come back, you can do whatever you like.'

'Why will you suddenly go to Kashi?'

Gopal asked a counter question, 'Well, Shashi, I've been harassed all my life managing the household. Now you're all grown-up; if my mind becomes restless can't I get a respite for just seven days? Can I not expect even this much from you?'

Shashi said in a mild voice, 'I didn't mean that. There's been no indication; that's why I asked. You didn't tell me anything yesterday?'

With a deep touch of resentment, Gopal said, 'If you can't stay, tell me; I'll cancel the plan. Who can ever reverse his own fate?'

Shashi said, 'All right, please go ahead. Even if I leave a few days later there's no harm.' Shashi offered Gopal his pronam. Seeing the faces of the two in the clear light of morning, it didn't seem that there had ever been any difference of opinion between father and son even in any trifling matter; that their lives flowed in two opposite directions.

That was to be the final departure for Gopal; he never came back. He was a householder wedded to the world. Lands yielding fruits and flowers and grains, chests full of gold and silver, with some people bound by family relation and some others by social, duties and responsibilities, compulsions and obligations—whatever he had earned throughout his life he gave to Shashi just as he would have given at death. Kunda came back after a couple of days. On his way, making a stopover at Rajatala, Gopal had picked up and taken along Sen-didi's son. He had given Kunda two hundred rupees as well so she could buy a gold chain; perhaps that was Gopal's last pledge to be redeemed.

What could Shashi do? This was a responsibility that could not be forsaken. Looking deeply despondent he cancelled the arrangements for departure one by one. Amulya went back home with two months' salary in his pocket. If Shashi were to keep staying in the village, how could he possibly do without having to put a finger on the pulse of each and every patient in the hospital? Work and responsibility were what constituted his life, and with these was his life occupied again. Can man's life-stream flow like a river along the course charted by its own free will? It proceeds along a canal of man's own making at the inexorable signal of an unknown force, which, like gravitation, is eternal and immutable.

Shashi would go to Bajitpur in connection with litigation. On his way back, lifting his eyes he saw by the canal a lightning-struck banyan tree spreading its withered branches and roots. Gobardhan beached the boat at the Gaodiya ghat. Nandalal's jute-stacking shed, now empty, was almost broken down. This brought to Shashi's mind the thought that Bindu's body laden with Nandalal's sin perhaps had broken down in the same way by now. Shashi did not move briskly these days; walking with a slow tread he entered the village. Shashi's eyes searched not for the complete and perfect image of the village formed by the landscape of trees and plants, ponds and ditches, but for human beings—those who lived in the village and those who had lived, in front of Srinath's shop, on the paved platform under the bakul tree, and on the Kayetpara path. Even today, one could hear the clang of the mortar and pestle in the outer room of Jamini Kabiraj's house; in this house, the vacancy created by people had been filled by people. Only Jadab's house was being swallowed up by the encroaching forest. Paran's house too was devoid of life. Beyond that was the palm grove which Shashi did not visit again. Never again in this life would Shashi take a fancy to climbing the earthen mound to watch the sunset.

Glossary & Notes

[1]**god of the sky**: Indra, king of the gods in Hindu myth, reigning deity of thunder and rain.

[2]**Kabiraj**: a physician (often also his surname) practising *Ayurveda*, a traditional Indian system of medicine, and also a treatise on the art of healing and prolonging life, sometimes regarded as the fifth Veda.

[3]**Kartik and Aghran**: months in the Bengali calendar, Kartik is mid-October to mid-November; Aghran (colloq., Agrahayan) is mid-November to mid-December.

[4]**shalik**: common myna or Indian myna.

[5]**shyaora** (or **sheora**): a medium-sized tree of the mulberry and fig family, it has medicinal use; sometimes linked to ghosts in popular or folk literature.

[6]**Chhoto-babu**: [literally, 'little master'] an address for, or reference to, the younger son of a respectable family.

[7]**ghat**: steps or a passageway, usually paved, leading down to a river or water-body for private or public use; a jetty or landing place where boats moor, people gather for bathing, drawing water or performing religious rites like *puja*s and cremations; a meeting ground for village women to discuss local politics and scandals.

[8]**biri**: tobacco flakes rolled in *shaal* leaf and tied with string, costing little; usually serve as poor people's cigarette.

[9]**paan**: betel leaf wrapped with a mixture of areca chips, catechu powder, lime paste, and optionally, some addictive and aromatic preparations; the juice aids digestion.

[10]**Goalapara**: locality of milkmen.

[11]**Hari bol**: shouting or a call for shouting the name of Hari, another name for Lord Vishnu, in a Hindu funeral procession.

[12]**Phalgun-Chaitra**: Bengali month, mid-February to mid-April.

[13]**majhi**: boatman; in rural Bengal, men are often addressed by their professional names.

[14]**mashay** (or moshai): an equivalent of mister.

[15]**rice diet**: taken during convalescence.

[16]**'jawle dnariye ki michha katha koichhi?'**: [literally, 'am I telling lies standing in water?'] a mainly rustic oath supposed to fortify one's statement incontrovertibly.

[17]**baap**: father; used reciprocally to address father or son.

[18]**Bagdi**: a so-called 'low-caste' Hindu, usually doing menial jobs for other castes.

[19]**Kayetpara**: *Kayet* is a short form of Kayastha, a Hindu caste next to Brahman in hierarchy; *para* is a quarter or locality. Likewise, **Bamunpara** is a locality where *Bamuns* or Brahmans live.

[20]**Baishakh**: first month of the Bengali calendar, mid-April to mid-May.

[21]**nayeb**: secretary to a zamindar.

[22]**Burrabazar**: [literally, 'big market'] a business district of Calcutta, then and now.

[23]**Barishal**: a city in present-day Bangladesh.

[24]**Bou**: [literally, 'wife' or 'bride'] address for a son's wife; one's own wife; may also be used by outsiders.

[25]**Ma**: mother; here, mother-in-law.

[26]**taalpukur**: a large, deep pond, with palm trees on its banks.

[27]**Paraner Ma**: Paran's mother.

[28]**Paraner Bou**: Paran's wife.

[29]**jatra**: an extended dramatic work performed in the open air by itinerant troupes enacting historical, mythological or epic themes.

[30]**Bnarujje**: variant of Banerjee; also Bandyopadhyay.

[31]**barbela**: part of the day traditionally regarded as inauspicious for beginning any important work or journey.

[32]**Bhutho**: a male name, an affectionate adaptation of *bhut* or *bhoot* meaning ghost.

[33]**Chhinath**: rustic corruption of Srinath.

[34]**muri and murki**: puffed rice, and sweetened fried paddy, respectively.

[35]**Pandit**: appellation for one with some mastery of Sanskrit; here, also such a person's surname.

[36]**Pagal-didi**: mad elder sister, a name mixing affection with scorn.

[37]**debata**: deity; here used for a living person as a mark of unreasoning, irrational reverence and faith.

[38]**Charaka** (1st-2nd centuries AD) **and Sushruta** (c. 4th century AD): sages versed in herbal medicine; basic textbooks of Indian medicine are attributed to them.

[39]**'...I'd been waiting for you..., dear!'**: a semi-ribald joke of a sort customary with elderly people, especially in a rural set-up in the past.

[40]**gamchha**: a piece of ordinary coarse linen cloth used as bath towel.

[41]**haat**: a village market; as distinct from the normal market place, it sits once or twice a week, thronged by traders and customers from distant places.

[42]**bhaddarlok**: tongue-in-cheek adaptation of *bhadralok* or a respectable man, a gentleman.

[43]**Baba**: father; also used as an affectionate address for someone much younger.

[44]**chyavanprash**: ayurvedic medicine for bronchial troubles.

[45]**makaradhwaja**: a medicinal sublimate of mercury, gold and sulphur.

[46]**Kobrej**: colloquial form of *kabiraj*.

[47]**Yama**: in Hindu belief, god of death, a fierce person.

[48]**Thakurda**: paternal grandfather; here, a considerably senior unrelated male.

[49]**Sita**: wife of Rama in the epic Ramayana.

[50]**'Pox in autumn too!'**: There was a belief that pox, known as '*basanta*', was associated with spring, also known as *basanta*.

[51]**Shashe**: a scornful distortion of Shashi.

[52]**Shetala** (colloq., Shitala): the presiding deity of all scourges, especially pox and pustules, with simple people regarding the scourge, particularly pox, as a blessing or mercy of the goddess.

[53]**shakchunni**: female ghost believed in by children and simple folk, an apparition of a Hindu married woman with conch-shell bangles on her wrists.

[54]**puja**: prayer or worship, whether austere (with just an offer of flowers anytime one likes to one's deity) or ceremonial (with elaborate ritual and offering on a particular day to a particular god or goddess); in Bengal, it is almost exclusively the goddesses who are worshipped except for the family deity Narayana. Unless specified, *puja* [plural, *pujas*] refers to Durgapuja (generally in October, according to the Hindu almanac), with wide connotation beyond just worship; for instance, *puja* spirit, *puja* holidays, *puja* market.

[55]**thetar**: scornful distortion of 'theatre', which used to be looked down upon as vulgar by puritanical Bengalis.

[56]**Prabir, Lakshman, Chandraketu**: mythological/epic characters.

[57]**Khuki**: nickname for a small girl.

[58]**you**: in their very first meeting, Kumud uses '*tumi*' for Kusum, 'you' in its more intimate sense in Bengali, offending her. The pronoun 'you' in English is used in conversation, irrespective of age, number, social status or relative social position of the speaker and the person spoken to; not so in Bengali where three distinct forms corresponding to 'you' exist in the singular: *tui, tumi, aapni*; *tui* is the address for juniors in the family and friends of any age, and the pejorative address for 'low'-caste/class people; *tumi* is the reciprocal address of familiarity among family members irrespective of age, among friends and lovers, and used by people addressing their unrelated juniors; *aapni* is used to address teachers and other social seniors/'superiors'.

[59]**Santras**: belonging to a family with the surname Santra.

[60]**Babu**: used as such, without mentioning one's name, by, say, a servant to/about his/her master; also suffixed with first names or surnames, but never with both, as a formal address, e.g., Kailashbabu or Kailash Babu; a term of respectful address like Mr or Sir; scribe, clerk; the word once meant an indigenous equivalent of a British Indian title like Ray Bahadur and referred to wealthy, fashionable, ostentatious gentry, now used ironically for one given to prodigality, foppishness and triviality.

[61]**sakhi**: a female friend or confidante; may particularly refer, as here, to the milkmaid playmates (*gopis*) of Lord Krishna.

[62]**Jana**: wife of King Niladhwaja and mother of Prabir in the epic Mahabharata.

[63]**Agnidev**: fire god in Hindu belief.

[64]**Arjuna**: one of the five Pandavas and a great warrior of the Mahabharata war, and Lord Krishna's friend.

[65]**bigha**: a measure of land, equal to 14,400 square feet.

[66]**Ravana**: demon king of Lanka in the Ramayana, who was killed by Rama.

[67]**Lakshman(a)**: Rama's younger brother in the Ramayana.

[68]**Urmila**: Lakshmana's wife.

[69]**Dada**: elder brother.

[70]**...Haru Ghosh's daughter into their midst**: here, some Ghoshs belong to the milkmen or Goala community, and hence deemed 'low-born'.

[71]**'...sister-in-law from the clutches of Ravana'**: an allusion to the Ramayana, where Lakshmana's elder brother Rama's wife Sita was abducted by the demon king Ravana.

[72]**Boudi**: elder brother's wife; also respectful address for a friend's wife.

[73]**Kashi**: Benaras or Varanasi, one of the world's oldest cities, and important site of pilgrimage for Hindus.

[74]**Gurudeb**: a spiritual mentor; religious head of a family.

[75]**ekadashi**: eleventh lunar day of each fortnight when certain rituals are performed, especially fasting by Hindu widows.

[76]**Paush**: mid-December to mid-January.

[77]**Magh**: mid-January to mid-February.

[78]**koi, magur and sholmachh**: climbing perch, walking catfish, and snakehead murrel, respectively.

[79]**Jamai-babu**: the son-in-law of a family, referred to as such mainly by the younger members; by village custom, he is everyone's Jamai-babu.

[80]**bhai-phnota**: Brother's Day, formally *bhratri-dwitiya*, a festival where sisters put sandalwood paste marks (*tilak*) on their brothers' foreheads, wishing them a long prosperous life, with exchange of gifts and sweetmeats, held on the second day of the bright lunar fortnight following Kali puja.

[81]**jarda**: scented tobacco flakes.

[82]**Paush festival**: held on the last day of the month of Paush when rice puddings and other preparations are made and shared with friends and relations.

[83]**rabi**: crop harvested at the end of winter, as compared to *kharif* harvested at the beginning of winter.

[84]**shaimana**: a corruption of '*shamiana*', a cloth awning or canopy used for gatherings, parties or functions and often made of colourful or striped calico.

[85]**Kaka**: younger paternal uncle; father's younger brother; polite/affectionate address for someone similarly placed.

[86]**Kalighat**: place in Calcutta famous for its shrine of Goddess Kali, one of the 51 'Shakti Peethas'—the holiest of holies in terms of Hindu Shakta [related to worship of Kali] pilgrimage centres.

[87]**Sealdah**: one of the two major terminal railway stations in eastern India, the other being Howrah, both serving Calcutta.

[88]**Radha**: consort of Krishna, united in love.

[89]**'He plays on the tabla and I sing.'**: a reference to the occupation of Calcutta's courtesans at one time.

[90]**Gita Govinda**: 'Songs of Govinda', a work by the 12th-century poet Jayadeva, a series of dramatic lyrics intended for singing, describes the love of Krishna for Radha and the *gopis*.

[91]**bish**: poison.

[92]**mejdi**: sister next to the eldest.

[93]**Chitpur**: a region in north Calcutta where most jatra companies' offices are located.

[94]**Khoka**: nickname for a small boy.

[95]**lakhpothi**: loosely, a millionaire.

[96]**siddha-purush**: one who has attained *siddhi*, a high degree of spiritual enlightenment and perfection.

[97]**pronaam**: an expression of respect for elders/'superiors', uttered as such with a gesture of joined palms and bent head, or performed by touching the feet, or more piously, wiping the dust off the feet (of the venerable person) and placing it on one's (the devotee's) head.

[98]**upobeeth** (or **poithey**): sacred thread worn diagonally across the chest by Brahman men.

[99]**mudi**: grocer.

[100]**Rath**: chariot festival of Lord Jagannatha. Literally, 'Lord of the World', Jagannatha is an idol of Narayana worshipped especially in Puri and throughout Odisha and Bengal, in the month of *Asharh*, the idol being wheeled through the town on a large chariot, and fairs centring this event being held with great enthusiasm and merriment.

[101]**Pandit-mashay**: respectful address for a learned man or pandit.

[102]**Puri**: a town in Odisha, on the Bay of Bengal, a popular seaside resort and among the holiest places for Hindus.

[103]**samadhi**: trance.

[104]**Kushi**: diminutive of Kusum.

[105]**munsiff**: a judge of the lowest civil court; a law officer.

[106]**Lokkhi**: Lakshmi, the goddess of wealth.

[107]**frock**: then worn by girls till their early teens in Bengal.

[108]**Jaya addressed Kumud by name**: that is, contrary to traditional Bengali/Indian practice.

[109]**panjabi**: kurta.

[110]**mongol ghawt**: auspicious pot.

[111]**ulu(s)**: a ritual of Hindu women where they keep uttering the sound/word 'ulu' by rapidly moving the tongue until they run out of breath, producing an 'auspicious' drone; done three times in a single spell, and an indispensable part of weddings and other rituals.

[112]**Urboshi**: a celestial beauty in myth.

[113]**'Sajano bagan shukiye gyalo'**: part of an iconic line in Girish Ghosh's famous play, *Prafulla*.

[114]**knachpoka**: species of bright green insect of which the hard wing is used by women to adorn their foreheads.

[115]**Binde**: affectionate adaptation of Brinda, companion of Radha.

[116]**Rai**: another name of Radha, lady love of Lord Krishna.

[117]**Shyam**: another name of Lord Krishna.

[118]**kadam**: *kadamba*, a spherical mildly fragrant flower of the rainy season with bright yellow-orange hairy growth, a favourite of children.

[119]**bioscope**: cinema.

[120]**Chait**: Chaitra or spring, when the cool southern breeze is believed to inspire romantic feelings in lovers.

[121]**bnoti**: large kitchen knife.

[122]**Shravan**: mid-July to mid-August.

[123]**kusum**: literally, flower.

[124]**'Please do not address me in that way.'**: Shashi is addressed as *tumi*, which he objects to.

[125]**Benarasi**: sari of Benaras, made of rich silk fabric woven with raised design, often in gold or silver thread (*zari*), once specialised in by weavers of Varanasi (Benaras), the traditional sari for Bengali brides, then and now.

[126]**brahmachari**: one abstaining from carnal pleasures and practising religious austerities.

[127]**namah for Om**: *Om* and *namah* are Sanskrit words uttered during Hindu prayers, denoting obeisance to a deity, the former being used exclusively by male Brahmans; 'Om', signifying Brahma, the supreme godhead, is spoken at the beginning of almost all mantras. Shashi, the son of Gopal Das, being a Kayastha, uses 'namah' as a lesser substitute.

[128]**Kipanath**: corruption of Kripanath.

[129]**bhori**: a unit of measuring gold and silver, still in vogue; equivalent to 13.6 gram, approximately.

[130]**Chhoto-mami**: wife of one's youngest maternal uncle.

[131]**'...set fire to the house'**: a Bengali colloquialism meaning 'bring discord to'.

[132]**akash-kusum**: literally sky-flower; an impossible thing; idle reverie.